P9-CLF-453

"Shirley Jump's stories sparkle with warmth and wit and glow with strong, heartfelt emotions. This is real romance."
—Jayne Ann Krentz, *New York Times* bestselling author

"A fun, heartwarming, small-town romance that you'll fall in love with . . . Shirley Jump is a true talent."
—Jill Shalvis, *New York Times* bestselling author

"Shirley Jump packs lots of sweet and plenty of heat in this heartwarming first book of her promising new series."
—Virginia Kantra, *New York Times* bestselling author of *Carolina Girl*

Praise for the novels of Shirley Jump

"Fast-paced and filled with emotion and larger-than-life characters, this is a beautifully written, heartwarming story."
—*RT Book Reviews*

"Shirley Jump weaves a story that hypnotizes from the first page . . . I love it, absolutely love it."
—*Coffee Time Romance*

"Lots of sizzle, wit, love, and romance."
—*A Romance Review*

"A hilarious and passionate contemporary romance that I found impossible to put down."
—*Romance Junkies*

The Sweetheart Bargain

SHIRLEY JUMP

BERKLEY SENSATION, NEW YORK

THE BERKLEY PUBLISHING GROUP
Published by the Penguin Group
Penguin Group (USA)
375 Hudson Street, New York, New York 10014, USA

USA | Canada | UK | Ireland | Australia | New Zealand | India | South Africa | China

Penguin Books Ltd., Registered Offices: 80 Strand, London WC2R 0RL, England
For more information about the Penguin Group, visit penguin.com.

THE SWEETHEART BARGAIN

A Berkley Sensation Book / published by arrangement with the author

Berkley Sensation Books are published by The Berkley Publishing Group.
BERKLEY SENSATION® is a registered trademark of Penguin Group (USA).
The "B" design is a trademark of Penguin Group (USA).

For information, address: The Berkley Publishing Group,
a division of Penguin Group (USA).
375 Hudson Street, New York, New York 10014.

ISBN: 978-0-425-26450-8

PUBLISHING HISTORY
Berkley Sensation mass-market edition / September 2013

PRINTED IN THE UNITED STATES OF AMERICA

10 9 8 7 6 5 4 3 2 1

Cover photos copyright © Shutterstock/Thinkstock.
Cover design by MN Studios.
Interior text design by Laura K. Corless.

ALWAYS LEARNING   PEARSON

Acknowledgments

Sincere thanks to the people who shared their knowledge that helped make this book possible. Their generous spirit gave me the information I needed to bring the characters in *The Sweetheart Bargain* to life, and I am eternally grateful to so many people for their time.

A special thank-you to USCG Lieutenant Commander Adam Merrill, who was a fabulous source of information about Coast Guard life, the Kodiak station, and a day in the life of a pilot. These are the guys who put their lives on the line every day, and for that they deserve a big round of applause and gratitude.

Luke's eye injury was a complicated medical situation; thanks to Dr. Daniel Krach and Dr. Paul Bodendorfer, two of the most knowledgeable ophthalmologists I've ever talked to. Hopefully I was able to create a realistic depiction of Luke's retinal detachment and the ensuing complications. Their assistants, Janice Richards and Paula Schomburg, were also super helpful and stepped in when I needed a doctor-speak translation.

Kay Anderson, founder and director of Pets Assisting Well-Being & Success (PAWS) Placement Services in Fort Wayne, Indiana, shared wonderful, heartwarming stories about the miracles that a furry friend can help bring about in a handicapped person's life. Her dog Carl touched a lot of lives before he passed, and his devotion to others served as a model for my fictional Miss Sadie.

A big thanks to my critique group: Janet Dean, Julie Sellers, Karen Morris, and Jeremy Asher, who read umpteen drafts of the first chapter before it became the book it is today. Thanks for your support, your input, and your patience! Thank you to my agent, Pamela Harty, for her support and belief in me, and to the Shirley Jump Reader Posse, whose enthusiasm and support are immeasurable. And a special thank-you to Kate Seaver at Berkley, who believed in *The Sweetheart Bargain* and brought Greta and the girls to life on the printed page.

My husband, who took over the housework and meals when I was on deadline, and who created the most memorable celebration ever for the sale of this book, deserves a shout-out and a mega thank-you. He's always there with a cupcake or a hug (or both!) when I need them most.

A final thank-you to my readers. You all make my job so rewarding! I love your letters and e-mails!

Any mistakes in this book are my own, and a direct result of long writing days with too little coffee and chocolate!

One

⸙

Olivia Linscott made the most insane decision of her life in less time than it took to microwave a burrito. Before she could think twice, or worse, hesitate, she'd packed what remained of her belongings into her car, loaded up on gas and 5-Hour Energy drinks, then ditched her life in Massachusetts and headed south.

All because a lawyer had shown up on her doorstep with a mysterious will, a crinkled photograph, and a butterfly necklace. Olivia's heritage, reduced to a nine-by-twelve manila envelope.

Now, forty-eight hours later, she was in sunshine instead of snow, catching the scent of ocean instead of exhaust. Outside the Toyota's window, the Florida coastline curved like a lazy snake, an undulating ribbon of blue-green punctuated by soaring seagulls and cresting whitecaps. It was a million miles away—and a good burst of salty, fresh air— from the choked, congested streets of Boston, where cars played Frogger with each other and dodged potholes the size of small elephants. Down here, Olivia could breathe, really breathe, in more ways than one.

She pressed the speed-dial button on her cell and waited for the call to connect. When her mother answered with her familiar chirpy hello, a wave of homesickness crashed over Olivia, and for a second she had the urge to turn around, to head back to everything familiar.

"Olivia! I've been waiting for you to call," her mother said. "How far are you now?"

"Only another mile or so to go." Olivia nestled the cell against her ear. "I've been ready to crawl out of my skin for the last five miles, just dying to get there already. Maybe I should pull a Boston and put the pedal to the metal the rest of the way."

"Olivia Jean, if you do, I'll fly down there and take away your car keys," her mother said, with the same tone she'd used when Olivia had been little and trying to raid the cookie jar before dinner. "Even if you are over thirty."

Olivia laughed. "Okay, okay. I'll keep it to twenty miles over the speed limit, like any respectable Massachusetts driver." On her left, a half-dozen bright, happy shops lined a wide boardwalk, across the street from the beach. A white-and-pink awning fronted the Rescue Bay Ice Cream Stand, a quaint little place with umbrella-covered tables and a giant plastic cow sporting a bright pink bow. An elderly couple enjoying swirled cones—one chocolate, one vanilla—raised a hand in greeting as Olivia drove past. She returned an awkward wave, just as a man walking his dog raised his hand in greeting and a shopkeeper sweeping the walk did the same. The instant welcoming atmosphere gave Olivia pause. It wasn't that Bostonians were frigid, exactly, but rather less overt in being neighborly.

There was something . . . warm about this town, something Olivia had liked the second she arrived. "Ma, you should see this place. It's like another planet."

"Well, we're still stuck on planet Arctic here. It's too darn cold to even look out the window, never mind go anywhere." Anna Linscott was no doubt bundled up by the fireplace in her Back Bay townhome. Olivia could see her now, sitting in the threadbare rose-patterned armchair Anna had owned since the day she got married, the blue-and-green afghan Nana Linscott had crocheted draped across her lap. "There was a ring around the moon last night. A storm is coming. I'm thinking three inches, maybe four."

"It's January and you're in New England. There's always a snowstorm coming."

Anna laughed. "True. But if I see a ladybug—"

"And she lands on your hand, spring is on its way." Olivia grinned at her mother's superstitious weather predicting. Half the time, Anna was more accurate than the guys at Channel 7, so maybe there was something to her folklore. Olivia glanced out the window again, drawing in another deep breath of balmy air. "This is bliss. Palm trees and beaches and—"

"Alligators and geckos."

"They won't bother you if you don't bother them." Olivia fingered the picture taped to her dash. A perfect Florida bungalow, painted in sherbet colors of pale yellow and soft salmon, trimmed in white, nestled in the middle of a neat yard, flanked by rows of blooming annuals and fruit-laden citrus trees. "Mom, do you think I'm doing the right thing?"

"I think you have to do this." Anna sighed, a mixture of support and worry. "Then maybe you'll finally have the answers you need, and deserve."

Olivia's finger danced across the picture again. Would she? All her life, Olivia had felt like a lock without the right key, a puzzle missing a piece. Now, maybe here, she'd find what she was searching for.

Herself.

And if not, she'd at least get one hell of a tan.

"Darn," her mother said. "Your dad's beeping in. I sent him to the grocery store. By himself."

Olivia laughed. "Say no more. I'll hold." She glanced again at the photo on the dash, then up at the GPS. *Distance remaining: 0.9 miles.* Butterflies danced in her stomach.

When the lawyer had rung her doorbell last week, Olivia insisted he must have had the wrong address, the wrong Olivia Linscott, and the wrong will in his hands. Did she have any relatives in Florida, he'd asked, and she'd said no. Everyone in her little family lived in Boston, and always had. They'd practically come over on the Mayflower, as Aunt Bessie said. No one moved away, except crazy cousin George, who went to Alaska to marry an Inuit woman he'd met at a Trekkie convention. Olivia had seen the pictures of their *Enterprise*-themed wedding. Quite inventive, considering they'd held it outdoors. In February.

Then the lawyer had asked if she knew the identity of her biological mother, and Olivia's world flipped upside down. Her mother. The woman who had given birth, then walked out of Brigham and Women's Hospital, leaving her newborn daughter behind.

Her birth mother.

A woman she'd never met.

A woman who'd never contacted her, never done so much as send a Christmas card.

A woman who had left her property in Florida, a porcelain necklace, and not much else. There'd been no letter, no explanations. No idea of who Bridget Tuttle had been.

Or why she'd abandoned her baby.

All her life, Olivia had wanted to know why. She'd toyed with searching for her biological mother on the Internet, then drawn back at the last minute, afraid the answers might not be ones she wanted to hear. And now, that door to a personal connection, a face-to-face, was closed. Forever.

She swallowed hard and pressed a finger to the photo again. Her only link to Bridget Tuttle remained in this piece of property and the town of Rescue Bay. Someone here had to have known her mother and would be able to fill in the blanks that now gaped like black holes.

Maybe this desperate need to know stemmed from all the changes over the last year. Maybe it was finally having a tangible reminder of someone who had been, up till now, a mythical figure. A ghost, really.

Olivia had prodded the lawyer for more information, but he'd said he was merely the messenger, a Boston attorney hired by the Florida probate, and knew less than she did.

He handed her the deed, along with the picture of the house and an envelope with the necklace, then wished her good luck.

She'd stood there for a long time, staring at that picture, before making the most impulsive decision of her life. Just . . . *go*.

Within days, Olivia had quit her job, loaded her car, packed up Miss Sadie, and headed south. And now here she was, hitting the reboot button on her life after a disastrous end to her marriage and too many years working a retail job that had been as fulfilling as cotton candy for breakfast.

In Rescue Bay, she wouldn't know anyone. She wouldn't turn a corner and expect to see the man who had promised to love her forever—which turned out to be one year and three months. She wouldn't face well-meaning friends determined to drag her to a bar, as if a few drinks and sex with a stranger solved anything. She wouldn't look around her half-empty Back Bay town house and think of dreams that had died a slow, reluctant death.

In Rescue Bay, she could start over. The sight of the sun and beach made her feel renewed, refreshed, reenergized. Maybe later today, after she'd settled in, she'd grab her suit and head for the beach. It was margarita weather, and Olivia wanted to soak up the warmth. To . . . thaw.

Yes, that was it. Thaw her bones, warm her heart again.

"I'm back," Anna said, her voice bright with laughter. "I love that man, but I swear, some days I could clobber him."

"Don't tell me. He was stuck in the bread aisle."

"He didn't even make it that far this time. He got sidetracked in produce. Apparently putting *apples* on the list had him flustered about Galas versus Fujis. And don't even get me started on the *bag of salad mix*."

Olivia bit back a chuckle. "Dad means well." She reached out to the passenger side and ran a hand down the whisper-soft white fur of Miss Sadie, her bichon frise and fellow adventurer—who had slept in her doggie car seat from Baltimore to Rescue Bay, Florida. *Lazy little puppy*, Olivia thought, smiling at the snoozing dog.

"Since your father retired," Anna said, "he's trying to help out more. He says it's his way of learning how to survive without me, should I suddenly be abducted by aliens."

"Mars would have a force to reckon with if that happened, Ma." Blood relation or not, Olivia had always been close to her mother. She'd treasured the story of how Anna, an OB nurse, had seen the abandoned baby girl in the hospital and moved heaven and earth—and her cautious husband, Dan—to adopt Olivia and bring her home. Anna had nursed her adopted daughter through colic and chicken pox, puberty woes and acne battles, lost puppies and first dates.

"Me? I'm sweet. Mild-mannered. And don't you dare laugh, missy. You were the one who outcried every baby in that nursery."

That homesickness wave rose again in Olivia, but she pushed it back. Mom and Dad were coming down to Florida in March, and Olivia had already made plans for a return visit for July fourth. "Loud and insistent, right from the beginning, right?" Olivia said.

"I prefer to call it . . . determined. You're a strong person, kiddo, and you always have been. Your father and I thank God every day for bringing you into our lives."

"I'm grateful to have both of you, too." Still, a ribbon of guilt flickered in Olivia's chest. With parents like hers, why did she still want more? Why did she want a connection with the one woman who had never wanted her?

Palm trees spread their wide leaves over Olivia's car as she turned off the coastal road and headed toward the center of Rescue Bay. The GPS came on again, still sounding about as excited as an MBTA conductor calling "Ashland" for the thousandth time, and announced the last quarter mile to her destination. "I'm almost to the house," Olivia said.

"Oh, good. Tell me everything you see, the second you see it. Goodness, I'm excited and I'm not even there."

The GPS announced one last left turn, then a second later said, "You have arrived at your destination."

Olivia scanned the street for the pretty little bungalow

in the pictures. This was it, the moment she'd been waiting for. She craned forward, looking left, right, north, south. "I can't find it. Maybe I got the address wrong—"

Then she saw the house. Or rather, what was left of it. Not one part of the building before her matched the picture the lawyer had given her. Maybe the structure had once been that happy, cheery landscaped home, but if so, that had been a long, long, *long* time ago.

Holy. Crap.

Her elation deflated with a whoosh. The perfect little bungalow turned out to be a run-down building on a dead-end street, with an overgrown, sprawling backyard and a decaying wraparound front porch. A swing hung from the front, creaking back and forth in the slight breeze. Time and sunshine had faded the sunny yellow paint to pale butter, darkened the bright white trim to dingy gray, and worn down the salmon shutters to anemic pink. One shutter hung askew, another was missing altogether, and the window boxes that had once held blooming annuals now held nothing but dirt and desiccated stalks.

She checked the address. Twice. Right place, wrong decade in the photo.

This was her inheritance? It looked like one more rejection, only from the grave. The woman who had abandoned her in the hospital twenty-nine years ago had abandoned this place, too.

"So . . . what do you think?" Anna asked. "Is it as pretty as the picture?"

Olivia scanned the lot, searching for something, anything, to redeem this . . . legacy. Anchoring the yard was the Rescue Bay Dog Rescue, or so the sign said. The low-slung white building sprouted chain-link kennels on either side like tentacles. Chunks of grayed wood siding displayed worn, naked wooden faces underneath peeling white paint. The eastern corner of the kennels had rotted away, leaving a gaping hole to the inside. The roof sagged in the middle in a deep concave bow. One strong gust of wind, and what was left of this place—of Olivia's inheritance and her future plans—would crumble. She bit back a laugh before it became a sob.

"Olivia? Are you still there? Did you find the house?"

"Uh . . . yeah. It's . . . a whole lot more than I expected." She forced brightness to her voice. "Turns out there's an animal shelter on the property, too. It's . . . it's closed down now."

"Animal shelter? Why, that's right up your alley. Sounds like the perfect place for you."

"Yup. Exactly what I imagined."

Why was she surprised? Her biological mother had left her crying in a bassinet, alone, unwanted. Now Bridget Tuttle had saddled her daughter with a disaster that looked just as abandoned as Olivia had felt all these years. The letdown hung heavy on her shoulders, ached in her gut. She fought the urge to cry.

She drew in a deep breath, straightened her spine. She refused to let this set her back. She was here for a new start, and by God, she was going to get one, even if it meant calling in the entire crew from *This Old House* to help her.

"I better let you go now, Ma, so I can get moved in and settled before dark."

"Okay. Take care of yourself."

"I will. You do the same." She gripped the phone, her last connection to the life she'd impulsively left behind, and wished she could send a hug through the cell. "I love you, Ma."

"I love you, too, honey." A hitch sounded in Anna's voice. "Call soon, okay?"

"I will." Olivia tucked the phone into her purse, then parked in the cracked driveway. Weeds sprang up here and there, determined green stalks asserting themselves in the broken concrete. She unbuckled the dog from her doggie car seat, then put up a palm in command. "Stay here, Miss Sadie, while I check things out. Okay?"

Miss Sadie barked, bounced a couple of times, then settled in the passenger seat. Olivia climbed out of the

Toyota and took a moment to stretch her legs, her back. Maybe if she got a little closer, she'd see that the house wasn't as bad as she thought.

Nope. It was worse. Like opening a candy bar and finding brussels sprouts underneath the wrapper.

"Damn." Olivia shook her head and had started to turn back toward the car when her gaze landed on a long, golden body beside the shelter.

Beneath the tattered remains of a red-and-white awning lay an emaciated golden retriever. Hurt? Dead? Sleeping? Olivia bent down, put out a hand, and kept her voice high, friendly. Nonthreatening. "Hey, puppy," she said to the too-thin, too-quiet dog. "Come here."

The dog didn't move. Didn't twitch so much as a floppy ear or raise its dark snout. Olivia inched forward. The golden retriever remained still. Olivia's gut churned, and she held her breath, waiting for any sign, any movement, anything.

Olivia took another step, then another, moving slow, cautious. All the while saying a silent prayer that the dog was alive.

And then, a slight flick of a tail, and Olivia's heart leapt. "Okay, puppy. Okay. That's good." She smiled and put out her hand again. A strong breeze whistled through and the building's roof swayed, creaked, then let out an ominous crackle. "Come on out from there, okay? Before you get hurt."

The dog didn't budge.

"Are you hungry? Hmm?" Olivia looked back at her sedan, loaded to the gills with boxes and clothes. Miss Sadie's tiny white butterball body popped up and down, her excited yips carrying through the lowered window and into the yard. When Miss Sadie was working in a therapy environment, she was calm, even-tempered, obedient. When she wasn't, the nearly four-year-old dog was all puppy. Now wasn't a time for puppy energy.

Olivia turned back to the golden retriever and as she did, her gaze roamed the depressing scene before her: over the missing and cracked siding, the ivy weaving its way into the casements, the still, silent air conditioner covered with Spanish moss. The lawyer had lied. This wasn't a gift—this was a catastrophe. A catastrophe Olivia had almost no budget to repair.

Had she made an incredible mistake? Thrown away her life in Boston, on a whim?

But what kind of life had she had, really? One where everywhere she went, everyone she saw, reminded her of her biggest mistake. Where living in a town house meant for two, then inhabited by one, festered like an open wound. She fingered her left hand, empty for the past two years—two years filled with changes and new directions—and knew she'd made the right choice.

She wasn't going back. She would make this work. What choice did she have? Olivia was tired of being a failure. Failing at her marriage. Failing at her previous job. Failing at taking risks. She had changed careers, finally pursuing her degree in physical therapy, and the day had come to put all this education in practice. She had a new job, a new start. This time, she was going to plow forward and not let anything get in her way. Even this . . . mess. She couldn't do anything about the house right this second, but she could start with the dog.

"Come on, honey." She patted her thigh. "Let's get you out of there." Olivia kept up an endless soft stream of soothing words as she moved an inch at a time, slow, easy. She kept her hand splayed and her tone low, cheery. "You hungry, puppy? Thirsty?"

The dog's gaze darted from her to the dense, overgrown shrubbery on the right, then back again. Olivia closed the gap to five feet. The dog tensed, the fur on its back rising in a Mohawk of caution. The dark chocolate eyes grew rounder, filling with fear. "It's okay, sweetie," Olivia said. "It's okay. I want to help."

Wary eyes flickered, and distrust gave way to hope. An ear twitched. The tail raised, lowered, then swished slow against the ground.

"Let's get you something to eat. Would you like that? I bet you would."

The dog shifted, rising on its haunches, then dropping again to its belly with a high-pitched whimper. Dark crimson blood, dried, crusted over, smeared against the animal's side. All that beautiful golden hair matted in painful bunches. The dog had moved so fast, Olivia couldn't tell if the injury was new or old, or the extent of the damage. Whatever had happened, this poor thing needed a human, even if she didn't know it.

Olivia had to get this dog to a vet, but if she got too much closer, the wounded animal might panic and run. Or worse, bite her. The dog could be feral, scared. Either of which could make it react with its teeth.

In the car, Olivia had dog treats. Maybe if she got a couple of those, the dog would let Olivia get close and evaluate its injuries. She pivoted back to the Toyota and unlatched the rear passenger door, careful not to let Miss Sadie out. Just as Olivia snaked a hand into the bag that held the treats, Sadie bounded over the seats, pounced on the bag, and knocked it to the floor. Olivia opened the door a few inches more, scrambling for the spilled dog biscuits.

A flash of white zipped past. Oh damn. "Miss Sadie!"

Too late. The bichon darted into the yard, barking hellos. The golden started, hips raised, ready to run. Damn, damn, damn. "Sadie! Quiet! Stay!"

The bichon heard the command in Olivia's voice and stopped running. She turned back, noted the displeasure in her mistress's face, and dropped to her haunches. Too late.

A glimpse of yellow fur, disappearing under the picket fence dividing her property from the house next door. A flick of a tail—

The dog was gone.

Olivia called the bichon back to the driveway and ordered her to sit. "Stay. I'll go look for him."

Miss Sadie sat, her pixie face filled with disappointment at missing the great adventure.

"I know you want to help, but you need to stay. *Stay.*" Olivia grabbed a handful of treats out of the car and headed for the hole in the wooden fence.

Hole was a generous description. Two boards were missing, a third broken in half. Olivia bent down and stepped one leg through—straight into a thick, green shrub. She pulled her other leg through and shoved past the jumble of green leaves and spiky branches that tangled in her hair, grabbed at her clothes, scratched at her face and arms. Finally, she emerged on the other side, a little worse for wear.

She straightened—and almost collided with a six-foot-tall wall of a man.

"What the hell are you doing?" he said.

Her mouth opened, closed. Not a single word came out. Her gaze roamed over him, and she had to remind herself to breathe. Damn. Hot, handsome, sexy. She swallowed hard and tried not to stare.

Too much.

Blue jeans hugged his thighs, and a black T-shirt sporting a Harley-Davidson logo outlined a defined, hard chest, muscled biceps. The man had short-cropped, deep brown hair, a chiseled jaw shadowed with rough stubble. Dark sunglasses hid his eyes, despite the setting sun behind him. On one side of his face, a jagged scar peeked out from under the sunglasses, which only added to the air of mystery. He looked—

Dangerous.

Not in the hack-you-into-tiny-pieces-and-bury-you-in-a-landfill kind of way, but in a mysterious, sensual way that said tangling with him would be unforgettable. That he was the kind of guy who could kiss her and leave her . . . reeling. Breathless. The kind her friends called a Mindless Man because one night with him would make a girl lose her mind—in a very, very good way.

Olivia brushed off the worst of the shrub debris from her hair and face. Chided herself for worrying about her appearance. Her priority was the golden, not some stranger with sex appeal and an attitude. "I'm looking for the dog."

"What dog?"

"The golden retriever that ran into your yard." Olivia peered around the man. She didn't see the dog anywhere. Then she spied the end of a pale yellow tail sticking out underneath the man's porch.

"Is it running away from home? Or from you?"

"Yes—no. I . . . I don't know." Damn, why did this man fluster her? "It ran over here because it's scared. I think the dog is hurt and needs to see a vet."

He leaned down, and she caught the scent of soap and sweat. A man's scent, tempting, dark. His sunglasses reflected back her own face, and nothing more. She couldn't see his eyes, but she could feel his assessing gaze. "Let me guess," he said, his voice low, teasing. "You hit the dog with your car and now you've had a sudden attack of guilt."

"Of course not!"

"Uh-huh." A slight grin played on his lips. "So you're just another Debby Do-Gooder, out to save the world?"

"I'm trying to save a dog, not the whole world. That's all." She thought of the house. Her complicated, disastrous new start. "I've got enough on my plate."

"You and me both, lady. You and me both." He let out a long breath and turned away.

In the distance, someone started a lawn mower. The low drone of the engine overpowered the chirping of the birds and sent the pungent smell of gasoline into the air. Crickets chirped in the deep grass, hidden under the carpet of green. A soft breeze tickled a path down the yard.

"Well, if you find what you're looking for," he said, "let me know."

"I already did." She bent down and splayed her palm to show the treats to the furry body under the porch. "Here, baby. Want some cookies?" The tail swished, but the dog didn't come forward.

"Sorry, lady, but I'm full. Though if you have chocolate chip, I'll reconsider."

"I'm happy to share, if you like liver-flavored biscuits."

"They make those?" He grimaced. "That sounds inhumane."

"That's because they're for the dog, silly." Olivia gestured toward the porch. "See him? Right there?"

The man turned. Scanned the space. "I don't see anything."

"What are you, blind?" She marched a few steps forward, and pointed again. "Right there. Now if you'll just help me—"

The tail disappeared. An instant later, the dog darted out of the yard and into a thick copse of firs and palmetto palms across the street. Olivia sighed. "Great. Now he's gone. Thanks a lot."

"You're blaming me?" He arched a brow, and the earlier friendliness on his face had been replaced by hard lines. "I'm not the one trespassing. And possibly stealing someone's dog."

He had a point. She hated that, but he did. "Okay, maybe I was trespassing. But it was for a good cause."

He smirked. "That's what all criminals say."

"I am not a criminal. I'm a good person with good intentions." Her chin jutted up. "Unlike you. You . . ."

"Ogre?" he supplied.

Unbidden, her gaze trailed past the lean definition of his face, along those broad shoulders, down his strong arms. A dark heat brewed inside her, a heat she hadn't felt in a long, long time. What would it be like to have one night of hot, crazy sex with a man like him? He had this . . . edge to him, that whispered *dangerous heartbreaker*, yet at the same time, he carried an air of animal confidence that said a night with him would be amazing. Unforgettable. Curl-your-toes-and-smack-yo-momma amazing.

Clearly, she had gone way too long without sex.

She cleared her throat. Tried not to picture him in bed. Or naked. Or both. "I . . . I wouldn't call you an ogre."

"Oh, really?" He arched a brow, and something like a smile flickered on his face. A delicious quiver slid through her veins. "And what would you call me?"

"I don't know, but it sure as hell wouldn't be Mr. Rogers."

He laughed. "On that, I would agree."

The moment of détente extended between them. An olive branch, thin, but a start. She put out her hand. "We got off on the wrong foot. I'm Olivia Linscott. Your new neighbor."

He ignored her handshake. "Well, Olivia Linscott, do me a favor from here on out. Stay on your side of the fence. Us ogres don't like to be bothered." Then he turned on his heel and headed inside.

If this guy was indicative of the typical Rescue Bay resident, then she was tempted to get back in the car and drive home to Boston. At least there the crusty New England attitude came with the zip code.

Instead, Olivia headed out to the sidewalk. She cupped her hand to block the sun in her eyes and searched the dark wooded thicket across the street for any sign of the dog. Nothing.

"It's okay, puppy. I'll wait. I'm here for . . ." She glanced again at the decaying buildings she had inherited, now complicated by an injured dog off somewhere licking his wounds and a run-in with a surly neighbor. She had a mountain to climb ahead of her, but the sense of purpose surged in her chest. She could do this. She *would* do this. "A long while."

She dropped a treat form her hand onto the ground. There would be time to work with the dog, to earn his trust. Time to change the dog's life.

Olivia headed back to her property. She paused in front of the dilapidated renovation project that had become her inheritance and her home and called Miss Sadie to her side. Olivia had spent the year since her divorce trying to regroup, refocus, figure out who she was and what she wanted. Here in Rescue Bay, she had a chance to do all of that, while also finding her roots and discovering the truth about Bridget Tuttle. It was an opportunity, she told herself. The one she'd wanted for so long.

Miss Sadie propped her paws on Olivia's knee. She bent down and gave the bichon an ear scratching. "We've got our work cut out for us, don't we, Miss Sadie?" Then she glanced again at the house, and the reality of the disaster in front of her washed over Olivia. The place needed a new porch, a new roof, new siding—and that was just the *outside*.

"I don't even know where to start. Or heck, how to hammer a nail." What had she gotten herself into? Her resolve wavered and she glanced at the dog, trying to convince herself more than Miss Sadie. "We can do it. Right?"

The dog barked, and the bravado that had held Olivia together for fourteen hundred miles crumpled. Burning tears rushed to the surface and spilled down her cheeks. She dropped to the ground and gathered the only friend she had in Rescue Bay into her arms.

Two

⚮

Greta Winslow celebrated her eighty-third birthday the way she celebrated most everything: with a heaping plate of windmill cookies and a double shot of Maker's Mark. Her father had been a Jim Beam man. He'd line up his empty liters along the top of the kitchen cabinets, and as the collection grew, they created a prism when the morning light first hit. When Greta was a little girl, she'd sit at the scarred kitchen table, the one with the black divot in the center from one of Uncle Abe's forgotten cigarettes, and watch the dance of colors. By the time her father died at the ripe old age of ninety-seven, the bottle row was two, some places three deep, but the rainbow still came every morning. Greta missed that rainbow. Missed her daddy something fierce, too. So she started her day the way her father always had. With a few nips of the hard stuff.

Esther Gerke frowned at the shimmering contraband amber liquid in Greta's glass. "Does Doc Harper know you're drinking that? At this time of day?"

"Doc Harper is still drying the ink on his degree. I like that boy, but he's got a lot to learn about getting old." Just to spite Esther, Greta took a long sip of the bourbon. It slid down her throat in one warm, practiced move. "Besides, what he doesn't know won't hurt me."

Esther's lips knitted into a knot. "It's scandalous. Drinking that"—she waved a hand at the glass—"devil's brew. And in here, no less." The last she added in a whisper, with a worried glance at the staff across the room.

Greta had been sneaking drinks into the morning room from day one. A couple bottles of Jim for the staff at major holidays and they all turned a blind eye to her morning "coffee." "Esther Gerke, I have seen you imbibe a time or two. Why that time at the Casino Night, you had three—"

"It was after five." She sat back in her chair as if that settled the issue. Beside her, a wedding ring quilt formed a lumpy blue-and-white cloud that poufed up and across the long table. Every Thursday morning for as long as anyone could remember—which at their age, wasn't much beyond breakfast—the Ladies' Quilting Club had met in the big room in the back of the Daily Grind across the street. Then the coffee shop had shut down, no word, no notice, and they'd had to move their quilting to the morning room at the Golden Years Retirement Village—a fancy name for an assisted-living facility that charged a small fortune to provide the comforts of home while a nursing staff hovered and fretted. Greta would have been just fine staying in her own house, at her own kitchen table, but her son had insisted on forking over the cash to keep her "safe." More like under constant observation like a captured escapee in Alcatraz. Greta didn't get into trouble, exactly; more like trouble found her.

So she got distracted sometimes. She forgot to shut off the stove, left the front door open, and occasionally forgot to pay at the Sav-A-Lot. Edward worried too much, and overreacted too often, acting more like a mother hen than a child.

Greta now lived at Golden Years and sat in the bright yellow-and-white morning room with all the other little old ladies—of which she was the smallest and the youngest—

purportedly quilting while they sat in high-backed oak chairs with wide cushioned seats and watched other residents drift in and out of the room. Greta had been bringing the same set of squares for the last six months. She didn't quilt—she groused. And that suited her just fine.

"What'd I miss?" Pauline Lewis breezed into the morning room in a burst of Estée Lauder. A waterfall of personal possessions tumbled out of her hands and into an empty chair—tote bag, purse, wool coat, knitted hat. Pauline dressed like an Eskimo heading to the Antarctic for the twenty-yard walk from her villa to the main building.

"Esther has been questioning my choice of morning beverage," Greta said. "Again."

Pauline leaned over and gave the Maker's Mark a sniff. "Nothing wrong with a little bourbon. Especially on your birthday."

Esther's lips knitted up tight.

"Anyway, I'm glad you two are here," Pauline said. She dug in her purse and pulled out a stack of envelopes. "Because I have an idea."

Greta groaned. "The last idea you had nearly got me killed."

Pauline waved that off, sending another Estée Lauder draft into the space. "You had fun on the kayak trip. And getting in the water is good for your skin. Besides, you're the one who keeps complaining a quilting club is boring."

"It is. It's what old women do."

Esther arched a darkly penciled brow. The woman of many facial expressions. And many floral dresses. Today's was a bright pink peony pattern that hurt Greta's eyes. "I happen to love quilting."

"I'd rather stick this needle in my eye." Greta held up the silver object of her pain and brandished it near her eye.

"Don't go doing that." Pauline dumped an envelope into each of their laps. "Guess who died?"

"Harold Twohig. Please say Harold Twohig."

"Greta, you are a horrible person. That man is your neighbor."

"No. He's the devil incarnate who happens to live next door." Greta sent a scowl at the easterly wall, and hoped Harold felt it in his bones.

Esther made the sign of the cross on her chest and whispered up a silent prayer. Probably asking God to smite Greta for her unneighborly thoughts. God didn't do any smiting. Not so much as a rumble of thunder. The Man Upstairs knew Harold well.

"Common Sense Carla," Pauline said.

"Who?"

"The advice columnist for the *Rescue Bay Daily*. Remember that woman who told Mitchell Walker that cleaning in the buff was perfectly fine?"

"Poor man ended up at the minute clinic for hours." Esther shook her head. "Who knew rust remover could do so much damage?"

"Clearly, she shouldn't have named herself Common Sense anything," Greta added.

Pauline shuddered, then leaned forward. "Anyway, as soon as I heard about Carla's demise, I . . . well, I took advantage of the opportunity."

"Took advantage?" Greta hadn't known Pauline to take advantage of anything other than the front of the line on Thursday buffet nights. "How?"

"I signed up as the new Carla." Pauline beamed.

"You?" Greta scoffed. "I'm sorry, Pauline, but you don't give the best advice. And you aren't exactly overflowing with common sense."

"I am too." Pauline pouted.

Esther leaned forward. "Has anyone seen the yellow thread? I need to tack my corners."

"Pauline, face it. Your advice is . . ." Greta searched for a polite word. Didn't find one. "Terrible."

Pauline pouted until her lower lip looked like that of an overdone Hollywood actress. "It is not."

"You advised Jerry Beakins to work out his issues with his neighbor over a cup of coffee. You know the result of that? Second. Degree. *Burns*."

"I never told him to *throw* the coffee," Pauline said. "He was supposed to use his words. Not his coffee."

"Where is that yellow thread?" Esther patted the space in front of Greta, then bent down to search under the table. "Are you sitting on it, Greta?"

"And you also told Betty Croucher that bee stings would help with her gout. Silly woman damned near had to buy an Epi-Pen factory." Greta wagged a finger at Pauline. "That is why this is a bad idea. We need an advice columnist who can actually give advice. Not inspire lawsuits." Though to be honest, the local paper had a circulation of, at most, a few thousand, so it wasn't like Pauline could wreak world-wide destruction or anything.

Pauline pouted. "I already told the paper I'd be the new Carla. My first column is due tomorrow." She dropped a pile of papers onto the table. "And now I have all these letters to go through, to pick the best one for my debut column."

"Maybe I can use white instead." Esther got back to searching the table. "Has anyone seen the white thread?"

The door to the morning room opened and in a whoosh of sunshine, Olivia Linscott entered the room. Olivia had come to work at Golden Years a few days ago, and Greta had liked her instantly. A major miracle, because Greta didn't like most people, and with good reason.

Olivia was a beautiful young woman—the kind people called willowy—with long blond hair, an easy smile, and wide green eyes. She almost always wore a dress, something the traditionalist in Greta liked, and only had a kind word for others. She entered the room and instantly seemed to make it . . . well, happier.

A snowy-white bichon frise marched beside Olivia, wearing a red vest emblazoned with THERAPY DIVA in glittering rhinestones, and MISS SADIE scrawled beneath that in stitched white cursive letters. Olivia, an animal trainer or some such thing, and the . . . what was that term she used? It took Greta a second, a second she blamed on the bourbon, and then she remembered. Olivia was an animal-assisted therapist. She and Miss Sadie worked with the folks at

Golden Years, encouraging those who were antisocial to open up and those who complained about physical therapy to smile, and in general, just brightened the place.

Truth be told, Olivia's enthusiasm reminded Greta of herself at that age. Back when Greta had seen everything in the world as half full. Now she watched the sand in her personal hourglass empty more each day. What she wouldn't give to be in Olivia's shoes, embarking on a new life, one where love and adventure lurked around every corner. Course, if it were Greta's life, she'd be doing it without the silly diva dog. A girl traveled fastest alone—and in sensible shoes.

"Oh, look, it's Olivia!" Esther got to her feet and did a paradeworthy wave. "Toodles, Olivia!"

Olivia and her little dog crossed to the quilting table, Olivia's high heels clicking on the tile floor. Miss Sadie plopped to the floor, her tongue lolling. "Why, good morning, ladies. Are you quilting today?"

"We would if we had some thread." Esther pouted. "I know I put it on the table. Why, I had three whole spools with me and now they've disappeared."

"Isn't that the strangest thing? Your thread is always disappearing on quilting day." Olivia shot a glance in Greta's direction. "Greta, have you seen Esther's thread?"

"Why, no. Not at all," Greta said.

"Maybe it rolled off the table," Olivia said. "Did you check the floor? I think it might be *under a chair* or something."

Esther bent down again, fussing around beneath the table. Greta nudged her purse farther under her seat and dodged Olivia's knowing glance. "I don't see it," Esther said.

"What a shame. Since it interrupts your quilting time and all, and I know how much you *all* look forward to that." Olivia grinned and winked at Greta.

"Yup. Damn shame," Greta said. Esther hushed her.

"How's the new job going?" Pauline asked.

"Good, but challenging." Olivia's gaze went over her shoulder to the people assembled for her morning group.

Most sat, eager for Miss Sadie to come over and interact with them. The dog's appearance had become a fun ritual for pretty much everyone at Golden Years. Only one woman sat to the side, slumped in her chair, staring out the window. "What do you guys know about Millicent Pierce?"

Esther's face turned down, and she tried not to stare at Millie, whose loneliness and despair carried through the room like cheap perfume. "Poor Millie. Lost her husband, then she got that cancer diagnosis. She's lived here three months and I don't think she's said more than two words in all that time."

Pauline nodded. "Her and her husband used to do everything together. Poor thing, I think she just misses him something fierce."

Olivia sighed. "Well, Miss Sadie and I aren't going to give up easily, are we?" The little dog swished her tail in response.

"Any big plans for the weekend, Olivia?" Pauline asked. "There's a barbecue here at the center if you want to come."

Olivia smiled. It was the kind of smile that warmed even Greta's heart—wide, welcoming, genuine. "I'll try, but I've got a lot on my to-do list for the weekend. I moved into a house that requires a lot of work. It pretty much defines *fixer-upper*."

"Bless your heart," Esther said. "It's always so encouraging to see young people take on challenges."

"This house is that and more," Olivia said. "The woman who owned it before me didn't exactly take care of the place." She toed at the floor, an uncharacteristically shy move. "Maybe you ladies knew her? Bridget Tuttle?"

Pauline's brows knitted together. "Wait, isn't that the one who was always rescuing dogs? I don't think we knew her, personally. One of those keep-to-herself types."

Esther nodded agreement. "She loved those dogs, though. She was always putting up signs, trying to get them adopted. Why I almost took in a poodle myself, but poor Gerald was allergic."

"Bridget was so colorful, wasn't she? Who could miss

her? With those bright orange skirts she wore and that terrible yellow hat." Pauline shook her head. "Wasn't much for fashion sense."

Greta saw Olivia bite her lip, then work a trembling smile to her face. Poor thing probably didn't like to hear such negative-Nellie comments about the previous owner.

"I know the house. It's next door to my grandson's little place." Greta leaned forward to change the subject. Goodness, why were they talking about dead people? Seems all the people around her ever did was talk about death, like it was another resident. "Have you met my grandson? He's available." Ever since Olivia had mentioned she was divorced, the quilting ladies had been conspiring to fix her up.

"Oh, I met him," Olivia said. "And it . . . well, let's just say it wasn't exactly a Welcome Wagon moment."

Greta waved that off. "Luke's been going through a hard time. He's not himself lately."

"Me either. Anyway, the last thing I have time for is a man." She brightened and let out a laugh. "Unless he's a handyman and willing to work for peanuts. Then you're free to give him my number."

"There's always time for love." Esther pressed a hand to her heart and sighed. "I just love a good romance."

"Don't we all," Olivia said, but her voice was quiet, soft.

Greta shot a glance at the young woman. Sounded like she was a little down on love, something Greta couldn't understand. Olivia had every quality any man in his right mind would look for—what fool had let her go?

They'd known the animal therapist for only a few days and hadn't had many personal conversations, which most days, suited Greta just fine. She was very much a live-and-let-live person—or drink-and-let-drink, in the case of the bourbon breakfast.

But something about the way Olivia had reacted to the information about Bridget Tuttle had intrigued Greta. She wanted to press the issue but decided first to do a little snooping and see what she could find out about the house, the Tuttle woman, and Olivia.

Olivia shifted to pet the dog, and Greta noticed the porcelain butterfly necklace that often hung from her neck. It looked old, the kind of thing someone handed down, and Greta would bet her grandmother's silver tea set there was a story behind that butterfly. It triggered a memory in Greta, but either the bourbon or her age whisked the memory away before it could manifest fully.

"Oh, I almost lost track of time. I have a therapy appointment to get to in a few minutes." Olivia gave the bichon's leash a tug. "Time for me and Miss Sadie to get to work. I'll see you later." Olivia leaned down to Greta's ear. "Oh, and Greta, I'll be sure to stop at the Java Hut before I come in tomorrow and bring you one of those giant chocolate chip cookies. If you don't tell Doc Harper, I won't."

Greta crossed her heart. "What he doesn't know can't hurt me."

Olivia laughed, then turned back to the group of seniors sitting by the television. The little bichon trotted over to each one and gave them a friendly greeting with her pert black nose. Millie ignored the dog and barely even looked up when Olivia greeted her. The others got involved in a game of hiding the treat for Miss Sadie—six pairs of hands outstretched, but only one held a little snack. Laughter and smiles came from that corner of the room, from all but poor Millie.

Greta wondered about Olivia a little while longer, then took a sip of her Maker's Mark and got back to the subject at hand. Pauline's newest crazy idea.

She started to push the letters back toward Pauline. The woman was messier than a pig in a cheese factory. Then a pale-pink sheet of paper on the bottom of the pile caught her eye, and she snatched that letter back. She fished out her reading glasses from her purse and then shut the clasp again real fast—before Esther's thread spools could fall out. One quick hand swipe when Esther wasn't looking, and the world was safe from her needle. Greta was in no mood for quilting today, and especially not now, when they had bigger fish to fry.

"Dear Common Sense Carla," Greta read, "I've recently moved to town to make a new start in life. I've changed my career, changed my address, and changed my attitude, but I have yet to find true love." She skimmed to the end. "Do you have any advice on how I can find Mr. Right? Signed, Forlorn in Florida."

"That one sounds like all the others," Pauline said. "I want a challenge for my first letter. Give me a good love triangle or a secret baby mix-up."

"Lord almighty, Pauline, you have got to stop watching reruns of *Days of Our Lives*." Greta fingered the letter, then cast a glance at Olivia, who was chatting with the group across the way, her pretty face bright and animated. "Hmm. New in town. Changed career. Looking for love. Who does that sound like?"

"I swear, it's like somebody absconded with every spool of thread in the building." Esther threw up her hands. "How are we ever supposed to get any quilting done?"

"That sounds like someone who's lonely," Pauline said, then grabbed a pad of paper and pen. She clicked the pen and hovered over the lined sheets. "I know. I'll advise that she join a quilting club and make some friends."

"Why don't you just make her a sign that says 'Lonely Old Maid' and mail it to her?" Greta leaned across the table. "If you're going to do this column, you need to do it right."

"What do you mean?"

The idea spun and shaped itself in Greta's mind. Brilliant. Why hadn't she thought of it sooner? "To do this right, you need a team for this, Pauline," Greta said. "A team of people who have wisdom. Experience. Heart."

"Where would I find that?"

"Right here, of course. What else do we have to do with our day?"

"We could quilt," Esther said, then let out a gust of frustration. "If we had some thread."

Greta nudged her purse farther under her chair. Across the room, Olivia caught the movement. She shook her head and mouthed a *tsk-tsk*.

"All of us?" Pauline squeaked. "Become Common Sense Carla?"

"It's perfect. We can meet here every Thursday and go over the letters and help you draft a reply."

"But Thursday is our quilting day. When will I quilt?" Esther asked.

"There are six other days in the week, Esther. Pick one." Greta glanced across the room again at Olivia. She was such a pretty young thing, with a nice smile, and though Greta thought the whole idea of working with dogs and cats was crazy, she had to admit Olivia had good intentions. She was just the kind of girl Greta wished her grandson would marry.

Just the kind of girl . . .

A lightbulb flickered to life in Greta's head. It was a crazy idea, but the perfect one to get this sleepy little town—and her drab existence—back to life again. And maybe, just maybe, help bring Luke back . . . not back anywhere special, just *back*. She hated seeing her grandson so broken. He was a good boy—man, really—but one who had suffered more than anyone she knew.

Yes. It could work.

"We'll give advice," Greta said, the idea coming together as brilliantly as the light shining through her father's bottle shelf, "and help it come true. Give people a . . . a nudge in the right direction."

"You mean . . . meddle?"

Greta sat back, clasping her glass of Maker's Mark in her palms. "Why of course." She smiled. "We're old ladies. It's what we do best."

Three

The shades drawn. The door locked. The air conditioner silent.

Luke Winslow sat in a hot, dark, silent prison, doing a damned good job of being pissed at the world. In a closet hung uniforms he would never wear again. Medals he never wanted in the first place. And a career that had been destroyed in a single moment. People lost, lives gone, all because he'd screwed up. He wanted nothing more than to be left alone with his regrets.

The doorbell rang.

He ignored it the first time. The second. Probably one of the neighbors. Again. Over the last few weeks, they'd been by more times than he could count. With casseroles. Flowers. Good wishes.

He'd ignored them all. Mighty hard to do when Lois and Doug next door kept an eye out for any potential movement on Luke's side of the fence, just so they could send a hearty wave and a loud "Howdy, neighbor" his way. Next they'd be inviting him to a barbecue or that neighborhood block party they insisted on hosting twice a year. All he wanted, especially today, was to be left the hell alone.

After the appointment he'd gone to this morning, he wanted to pass one day after the other, with no change, no drama, nothing. He didn't want to find a new job or start a new life or, God forbid, put on his happy face. He just wanted the world to go away.

The third ring came with an insistent knocking, and a chirpy "Luke? Are you in there? I brought dessert!"

His grandmother Greta. Who was as relentless as a pit bull. The reason he loved her, and the reason he'd better answer the door—before she took it off the hinges. He opened the door and tried to work a smile to his face, but it failed halfway through. "I'm not hungry, Grandma."

Next door, Lois popped to her feet. Knowing her, she would also be waving something bright and pink; Lois was almost always armed with neon gardening tools from her arsenal. "Howdy, Luke! Nice day we're having," she called.

He gave her a painful nod in return. Greta sent the neighbor a wave. "Grandma, for God's sake, get inside, before Lois decides to pay a social call." He led his grandmother into the house and shut the door.

Greta handed Luke a white paper box. The scents of chocolate and peanut butter wafted up to greet him. Cookies, or brownies, or some other treat from the Tasty Tidbits Bakery on the boardwalk. Grandma had brought him six such boxes in the last month. No doubt an excuse to eat the sugar her doctor had outlawed. "I'm not hungry," he repeated.

"Of course you're hungry. And so am I." She barreled her tiny frame past him and into the house. "Do you have any coffee?"

"Grandma—"

"Lord, it's dark in here. You are not a bat, living in a cave." She went around the room, flicking on lights and lifting the shades. As the sun hit the space, Grandma's petite body became a sharp silhouette against a yellow background. "Are you trying to roast yourself alive? My goodness, Luke, no one likes a sweaty pig." She spun the dial on the thermostat down to arctic. Outside the house, the air conditioner kicked on with a surprised jolt.

"I'm fine."

"And I'm Oprah Winfrey." She stepped up to him and though he could only see her outline, he knew the stance she had taken. A fist propped on her hip—replaced last year after a nasty fall down her front steps—and her chin raised to give him "the look." Grandma Greta stood a good foot and a half shorter than Luke, but when she gave him that I-don't-believe-you look, she seemed ten feet tall. She paused and put a hand on his arm. "What's the matter?"

He started to say *Nothing* but knew his grandmother would see right through the lie. After all, he was, like she said, living like a sweaty pig in the dark. "I saw Dr. Ebersol today."

"What'd he say?"

"That the results of the first surgery weren't what they hoped." Luke shook his head. "I like how they put that. Not what they hoped. Code for *it didn't work and I'm as bad off as I was before.*"

"No improvement?"

He shook his head and cursed the opaque blurs that had become his line of sight. "Nothing measurable. But with time, he said, or a second surgery, or hell, a visit from the vision fairy—" He cut off the words before he let his frustration boil over onto his grandmother.

He'd known before he'd even seen Doc Ebersol that the news wasn't going to be good. Luke had spent too much time in the water, then too much time in the twisted wreckage, then too much time in transit, then too much time waiting for the specialist to get to Anchorage. The scar tissue had taken hold, and that, along with the severity of the retinal detachments and the orbital fracture in his left eye, had done its damage. Permanent damage.

Still, he'd hoped like hell after the surgery, then during that monthlong wait before he was cleared to travel back to Florida, that it would all improve. Patience, the doctors had said. Patience. He'd had two months of patience and dashed hopes and it hadn't gotten him anywhere except half blind, with one eye ten times worse than the other, creating a confusion of shitty vision.

A tender hand on his arm, and his temper eased. "I'm sorry," Grandma said. "But you know, it's still awfully soon. Your body needs time to heal . . . It'll get better."

All things the doctor had said, too, but Luke had pretty much stopped listening by then. Nobody could give him a definitive answer about whether he would get better or worse or stay the same. Luke Winslow, who was used to taking charge, taking the wheel, and being the first one into the fray, was stuck in a gray blurry world, waiting for a miracle that might never come.

Doc Ebersol had reminded him today that retinal detachment recoveries varied from patient to patient. His retina could detach again, or he could improve. Or he could stay the same, locked in this in-between world of dark shadows and blurred vision, a common result of a "macula off" retinal detachment like Luke's. The road to recovery depended on a million factors—the scar tissue's impact, the success of the reattachments, the health of his eyes. It wasn't just Luke's vision that was iffy—it was his future, too.

"Maybe things will get better," he said.

"They will. And in the meantime, you need to find something to keep you busy and your mind off things. A hobby."

He snorted. "A hobby? What, quilting?"

"Lord, no. Something fun."

"Like being It in a game of blindman's bluff?"

"That is not funny." A laugh bubbled out of her. "Okay, maybe it is. A little." She turned back to his living room and, in a flurry of movement and sound, grabbed the paper plates and empty soda cans scattered all over his coffee table and end tables. It was her way of showing she cared without actually having to say the words. No one would describe Grandma Greta as warm and fuzzy. Still, she loved him, in her own way.

Luke took the trash from her and nodded toward the sofa.

If he didn't step in now, Grandma would be scrubbing the floors. She'd taken care of him almost all his life, from the day Luke's mother died in a car accident when he was three. Edward, Luke's father, had poured his grief into work, spending sixty, seventy, sometimes a hundred hours a week at the office, avoiding his son's daily questions of *why*. But Greta, she had been there, with hugs and peanut butter sandwiches and bedtime stories. He loved her with a fierceness that bordered on a lion's, and hated to see her taking care of him when, at her age, the only one she should be taking care of was herself.

"I'll do that," he said. "You sit. I'll make coffee."

"Your coffee is terrible, worse than the coffee at the retirement prison. But if you insist . . ."

"I do."

She followed him to the kitchen, snagging a few more dishes on the way. She laid them on the counter, then sat in one of the walnut chairs ringing his kitchen table. A slight breeze whispered in and out of the one open window. Late-morning sunlight spread in an arc over the kitchen table but had yet to reach the shadowed counters.

Rather than chiding or hovering or doing the housework for him, his grandmother just sat and waited for the coffee. He was grateful for that. One thing Greta was right about—having something to do kept his mind off things. Even if it was just doing the dishes.

In the weeks since his accident, he'd learned ways to cope, to manage the simplest of chores. For the most part, he kept the house tidy, organized, every chair and plate returned to its designated space. But on the dark days, as he called them, the easiest of jobs became ten times harder. Still, he didn't want to worry his grandmother, so he feigned sight he didn't have.

Luke wrangled the stopper into the sink, turned on the water, and loaded the dirty dishes, keeping one hand in the sink to watch the level. When it was deep enough, he turned it off and squirted some soap over the whole thing.

He turned and tugged the carafe out of the holder, filled

it with water from the sink, then poured the water into the dispenser. The carafe and the pot blurred into unrecognizable dark blobs in front of him, drifting in and out of his line of vision. He cursed, blinked several times, and started pouring again. A few scoops of grounds in the basket, and then he fumbled his hand over the pot and depressed the on button. As he turned away, water dripped in a steady stream onto his bare feet. He let out a curse and grabbed a towel, but his quick wiping only served to whoosh the puddle over the counter and onto the floor. "Coffee will take a minute more."

His grandmother rose and pressed a gentle hand to his back. "Let me help."

"I can do it!" Then he hung his head. "I'm sorry. I'm . . . frustrated."

"And I don't blame you one bit. I've been on that road a time or two myself. When I broke my hip, I had to ask for help for everything from opening a can to using the can, and you know how I hate to be needy. But relying on others got me better faster and back to my old tricks. You know what my daddy always said. Asking for help doesn't make you a fool. Falling on your ass because you were too stupid to speak up does."

He chuckled. "True."

"My daddy was direct, but wise." She grabbed a second towel, then pressed it into his hands. While he cleaned up the spill, Grandma refilled the carafe and added the water to the coffeepot. A few seconds later, the pot began to percolate and the scent of freshly brewed coffee filled the kitchen. "There. Now we can visit."

He dropped into the opposite chair and took a cookie he didn't want. *Be social, be nice.* "So . . . what's new with you, Grandma?"

"I'm old. Which means everything new has passed its warranty." She leaned forward. "Your father sends his regards."

Luke snorted. "Does he?"

"Well, not in so many words. But I'm sure he worries about you."

"I haven't seen my father in six months," Luke said. "Trust me, it's better that way."

Greta didn't say anything to that. Luke didn't have to be able to see clearly to know she was sitting there with her lips pursed, biting back a few choice words for her son. The conversation would undoubtedly boomerang right back to the same place. Edward Winslow didn't approve of his son's choices and made his disappointment clear on a regular basis. Joining the Coast Guard instead of the Navy, becoming a pilot instead of a SEAL, living alone instead of creating a legacy of namesakes.

And the biggest disappointment of all? Getting injured and becoming what his father considered a "drag on society."

Luke changed conversational direction. "So, what kind of trouble are you ladies getting into at the retirement home?"

"Trouble? Lord, I wish there were trouble. It'd give me something to do besides wait for my next colonoscopy."

He chuckled. "Give it time. I'm sure Harold Twohig will do something to stir things up."

"Stop it. You know the mention of that man's name gives me indigestion." She let out a gust. "I swear, he was put on this earth to test me."

Luke bit back a smile. Greta's long-standing feud with Harold Twohig never ceased to amuse Luke. For twenty-five years, they'd lived on the same cul-de-sac in Rescue Bay and argued over everything from the posted speed limit to Harold's penchant for mowing the lawn at first light on Saturday mornings—and always wearing his short-shorts and no shirt. Grandma had gone to the town council to complain that Harold's beer gut was an offense against humanity and causing her permanent nausea. When Harold moved into Golden Years and once again became Grandma's neighbor, the feud began to boil all over again. "And are you passing the good neighbor test, Grandma?"

"I do believe God still loves a sinner who gets a C." She

leaned forward and crossed her hands on the table. "Anyway, I'm not just here to bring you cookies."

"More like bring *you* cookies. And avoid the doctor's prying eyes."

She waved that off. "That man and his nutritional guidelines. I'm old enough to eat sugar all day, by God."

Luke chuckled. "You are indeed, Grandma."

"In case you didn't know, I came by to tell you that"—Grandma's voice rose into a happy range—"you have a new neighbor."

He leaned back in his chair. The sunlight illuminated his grandmother's face, turned the outline into features. The blurriness eased a bit. For now. "How do you know?"

"Just because I live in that prison your father put me in doesn't mean I'm not tuned in to the pulse of this community."

"Pulse of this community?" Luke laughed. "More like nosing around everywhere you go. I swear, you were a bloodhound in a former life, Grandma."

She raised her chin. "That is how the best information is obtained. Like the information that your new neighbor, who works at Golden Years, by the way, is pretty. And single."

Single? He thought of the sassy blonde who'd marched into his yard the other day. She had gumption, he'd give her that. She'd been by several times since, calling for the dog, but he'd stayed inside rather than tangling with her again.

Still, the thought of tangling with her—in any shape, way, or manner—had put a lot of dark, sensual images in his head late at night. He'd tossed and turned, imagining the lithe figure of his new neighbor riding on top of him, her hair loose and tempting around her shoulders, her hands hard on his chest, her body hot and slick with sweat and desire. Calling out his name, begging him for more . . .

Damn. It had been a hell of a long time since Luke had been with a woman.

Over the past few days, he'd found himself wondering about Olivia. Thinking about her when he knew damned well he shouldn't. Luke knew the reality of his future, and a woman like that sure as hell didn't figure into that dark timeline. Nor did a woman like her want a man who had made the mistakes he had.

No woman would. And for that reason alone, he'd be smart to keep his distance.

For a while, he'd thought maybe she was a renter. In one month, gone the next. In Florida, plenty of people came for a temporary stay, a break from winter's cold. But there'd been a delivery truck from a local hardware store, and a pile of boxes on her curb on trash day, clear signs she was no temporary visitor. Couple that with her determination to rescue that stray, and she'd piqued his curiosity.

Luke got to his feet, crossing to the percolating coffeepot. "Don't try to fix me up, Grandma."

"Why? You're single. She's single. As well as beautiful. Employed. You should ask her on a date."

He whirled around so fast, he brushed one of the mugs on the counter and sent it spinning. He'd never even seen the mug there.

The world had narrowed on him, like curtains closing. He had always been a man of action, but now, he'd become someone who couldn't make a cup of coffee without bringing in help. He took a breath, clenched his fists, released them. Wallowing in self-pity only made the mud deeper and thicker.

"I'm not in any condition to date anyone. What woman is going to want this?" His hand went to his face, and he cursed himself for letting that self-pity creep in again.

The air in the kitchen stilled. The coffeepot perked away, one *glub* at a time. Outside, the faint sound of sirens rose and fell. Greta crossed to Luke and put a hand on his left cheek. Her soft fingers inched up, pausing by the scar that zigzagged down from his hairline. Such a small injury, but such big implications. "Oh, Luke, this doesn't have to stop you from having a life, you know."

He turned away from her touch. "What kind of life do I have now?"

"What happened changed the life you *had*, Luke. Not the one that's ahead of you."

"I'm a pilot, Grandma. A pilot who can never fly a plane again. I'm half blind and all I can look forward to right now is more . . . nothing. Oh, I can collect my disability pay and maybe stand on the corner with a cup of pencils, but the life I had is gone." He let out a low curse, then shook his head. So much for not wallowing.

"You don't have to be a pilot. You can—"

"All I've ever wanted to do is fly. You know that." His lifelong dream, jerked from him in a split second, one bad decision. "I'm done."

Greta sighed. "Life is about change, Luke. And part of that is what makes every day an adventure. And when life hands you lemons, you make limoncello."

He smiled. "Another bit of wisdom from your daddy?"

"Of course. And a useful tip. How do you think I survived that move to the retirement home?"

His gaze went to the open window, to a yard that no longer held crisp green grass and bright yellow flowers but had blurred into dark spheres and pyramids like a twisted geometry problem from God. His entire world cast in shadow.

Some days, his vision cooperated and he could see the world through a gauzy film. Those were the good days, the ones when he thought maybe this wouldn't be so bad. He'd find a way around it, maybe a way back to the Coast Guard. Other days—the dark days—his eyes refused to show him anything beyond shades of gray. At first, the bright days had filled him with hope for recovery, and then he'd begun to curse them as a cruel, temporary gift.

His grandmother's hand was on his shoulder again, but he barely felt it. Didn't hear her words. His mind saw another darkness, one teeming and churning like an angry machine, the sea reaching up in whitecapped waves, a growling beast below him. The helo pitching and rolling in the storm, the flight controls shaking in his grip, and the white faces of the crew.

Lowering the rescue litter, hearing Joe shouting through the headset that they were burning through fuel too fast. *Hurry the hell up, it's getting bad out there—*

Then watching the cable whip in a wild arc, then catch in the mast, and like a rebounding yo-yo, jerk back up. Luke tried to shift the helo away, but the cable was faster, snarling in the transmission hub and the rotor blades, rendering the flight controls useless. After that, nothing but black. A void in his memory. A blessing and a curse.

"I'm sorry," Luke said softly, to the breeze dancing over his skin, wishing the words could carry far enough to reach those he had left behind.

And the one he would never see again.

"I know you are," Grandma said. "I know you are."

The coffeepot beeped the end of the brewing cycle. Luke started toward it, but Greta stopped him. "I'll get it. You sit. Have some cookies."

Luke turned toward the table, crossing the kitchen in a memorized number of steps. On a good day, he could see the checkerboard pattern in the tile. On a bad day, the checkerboard became a runny puddle of color.

Outside, a bark sounded, then something scratched the back door. Luke peeled back the curtain, and for a second, the bright sun blinded him. He blinked, drew farther into the shadows of the house, then glanced down, concentrating until the blur became a shape, a form, an animal.

The dog. Back again.

"What's that?" Grandma asked.

"A dog. I bet a hundred bucks it's that stray the new neighbor's been looking for." As soon as he said the words, he knew what his grandmother was going to suggest. Damn.

"Well, then here's your perfect opportunity to do a good deed. You know what my daddy always said. Favors done for the neighbor fine—"

"Are best accompanied by a bottle of wine." Luke shook

his head and let out a chuckle. Leave it to his grandmother's quirky sense of humor to bring a little lightness to his day. It made him glad—some—that he had opened the door to her and her cookies. "Does most of Grandpa's advice come attached to a bottle of liquor?"

Greta thought for a second. "Yup. You know your grandpa. He looked at the world through whiskey-colored glasses."

Luke released the curtain and it swung into place over the window. The dog scratched again. Insistent. Needy. For a second, compassion swept over Luke.

He had no business caring for a dog. Hell, he could barely take care of himself. He stepped back. "Well, if she wants her dog, she can get it herself."

Grandma swatted his arm. "I raised you better than that, Luke Winslow. Now go be a good person and help poor Olivia out." Before he could stop her, his grandmother undid the lock on the door and tugged it open.

He started to argue, but the damned dog had already wriggled past his legs, into the house, and then dropped to the kitchen floor. Luke opened his mouth to order it out, then stopped.

The dog's breath was coming in fast, shallow pants of distress. Its tail thumped a weak patter against the tile. Friendly. Grateful.

The dog needed help. Poor thing. That damned compassion returned in a stronger wave. Luke bent down and reached out a hand. The dog didn't growl—heck, it barely moved. Then, a quick, friendly flick of the tongue against Luke's thumb. *Help me, help me*.

Luke's hand hovered over the furry body, then descended in a tentative pat. The dog leaned closer, panted faster. "Grandma, I think you better go get the neighbor. Dog's sick or something."

"Oh, goodness, where does the time go? I'm supposed to be at bingo. I'm calling the B-4 . . . and after." Greta pressed a kiss to his cheek, then spun on her heel, moving insanely fast for a woman with a hip replacement. "I'll see you soon, Luke."

And just like that, she walked out the door, leaving him with the dog, and a problem he didn't want. A problem that was going to require the very thing Luke avoided.

Involvement.

Four

∞

The drill screeched in disagreement, then sent the stripped and now useless screw spiraling away, pinging off the step-ladder and rolling onto the floor. It spun off into a dark corner, then *plink-plink*ed through the floorboards.

"Okay, okay," Olivia said to the stupid yellow hand tool. "You win. I'm *not* smarter than a ceiling fan."

Miss Sadie watched from her perch on the worn blue-and-white-striped sofa, little nose twitching. Above Olivia, multicolored wires dangled from the ceiling fan motor. The metal cylinder hung askew and swung back and forth, se-cured by the single screw she'd managed to install. Another screw had also gone AWOL, joining the first two deserters she'd lost earlier. In the wall across from her sat a saw that had lodged itself into the framing. And beneath it all, a pile of building supplies she'd bought with good intentions and no instructions.

Olivia sighed. "Good thing I'm not working as a carpen-ter or I'd be broke." A break was in order. Maybe a drink, too, or two, regardless of the hour. She'd been at this most of the morning and hadn't made any kind of dent. The house looked, if possible, even worse now than when she'd walked in that first day.

Not to mention, she'd scoured the ramshackle bungalow top to bottom and found nothing besides a collection of dog curios, a lot of clothes in a size eight, financial records for the shelter, and a business card for a lawyer. No notes, no cards, no journals, nothing that told her who her mother had been. Maybe she'd missed something. Behind the peeling wallpaper or loose floorboards there could be a secret stash, but Olivia doubted it.

For the past few days, Olivia had tried a dozen times to get up the courage to ask about her mother. But every time she tried to broach the subject at Golden Years or any other place she went in Rescue Bay, the questions lodged in her throat. What if the answer hurt more?

Her mother had, after all, left her a house, an object as inanimate as a shrub. No notes. No letters. She'd never come looking for Olivia, never tried to explain. Instead, she'd dumped a money pit in her daughter's lap, and like she had at the hospital more than thirty years ago, Bridget had left.

Tears brimmed in Olivia's eyes. Miss Sadie hopped down, then came over and nosed at Olivia's leg. She chuckled, then came down from the ladder and patted her intuitive dog. "You're right. Self-pity doesn't help anything, does it?" And self-pity wasn't part of the kind of person Olivia was. Even if the last year or so had felt like being tossed into a hurricane, then hung out to dry, then tossed back again. She acted, she didn't dwell. "Okay," she said with a determined sigh, "let's try this again, Sadie."

Olivia started to reach for the drill when the soft creaking above gave way to a louder screech. She scooted back, just as the screw unraveled itself from the hole and the fan's motor came down, bounced off the top of the stepladder, then dropped like a stone onto the wood floor. On impact, the motor split in two and regurgitated wire guts.

Damn.

"Great. Now what?" Olivia put a hand on her hip. Miss

Sadie scrambled off the couch and danced around the motor, barking at it for scaring her and nearly taking out her mistress's toes.

Olivia sighed. "What I need is help, Miss Sadie."

The dog didn't put up a paw.

"Or maybe something to help relieve this . . . stress." Olivia stretched right, left, but it didn't ease the tension in her shoulders, her neck. The move, the new job, the search for answers, coupled with the long days and late nights spent on the renovation had left every muscle in Olivia's body achy and tired. "You know what my friends would say? I need a fling. One good, no-strings-attached night with a good-looking man."

Miss Sadie barked, wagged her tail.

"Oh, you think that's a good idea, do you? Well, I'm not going to disagree. But if I have a fling, it's going to be with a man who knows how to use a hammer."

A sharp banging sounded on her front door. "Hey, maybe that's him. You think, Miss Sadie?" The dog barked. Olivia laughed, then crossed to pull open the door. Or rather, yank open the door, which had stuck like an elephant in a cow chute.

She'd expected another delivery from the hardware store, or the mailman, or a new care package from her mother. Instead, she got her neighbor. Mr. Ray-Bans.

Every time she saw the man, she had to suck in a breath and remind her heart to keep beating. A couple days' worth of stubble dusted his chin, while those damnable sunglasses kept his eyes hidden from her view. Coupled with thigh-hugging jeans and a worn pale-blue T-shirt featuring a logo for a beer company, the whole effect was . . .

Devastating. In that sexy guy-next-door kind of way.

And she was not interested. At all. The last thing she needed to complicate an already complicated life was a man. But a part of her wouldn't mind spending a few hours finding inventive ways to forget the growing list of DIY projects.

Oh yeah. That would relieve her stress. And then some.

Her face heated and she hoped like hell he hadn't overheard her conversation with the dog and couldn't see the crimson burning up her cheeks.

"Your dog is over at my house," he said, before she uttered a word.

"My dog?" Olivia glanced down at her feet. Miss Sadie had plopped her tiny butt on the entry rug, tail swishing back and forth, an invitation for the guest to come in and play. "She's right here."

He arched a brow. "That? That's not a dog. That's a hairball."

"Hey—"

"Sorry, hairball," he said to Miss Sadie with a tender tone, then lifted his gaze to Olivia's. "I meant that other dog. The one you keep tearing up my yard to find."

He'd found the golden? Relief surged in Olivia's chest. For a while there, she'd worried the dog might have died. Olivia put a hand to her heart. "Oh, thank God. I've been putting food out and calling him every day."

"I know. I hear you."

"Sorry." She gave him a teasing grin. "Am I disturbing your beauty sleep?"

"That's a lost cause for me." He shifted his weight from foot to foot, then grimaced and extended his hand. "Anyway, if I don't at least introduce myself, I'll catch hell from my grandmother. Luke Winslow."

"Olivia Linscott, in . . . in case you forgot."

"I didn't forget your name, Olivia."

The four syllables of her name rolled off his tongue like a song. Very, very nicely. Her face heated, and she cleared her throat before she shook his hand. He had a warm, firm grip. "Greta's grandson, right?"

"Guilt by DNA." Something that could almost be a smile—but wasn't—flickered on his face. "She says she knows you."

Olivia nodded. "I work over at Golden Years, me and Miss Sadie. I love your grandmother. She's a hoot. And a half."

"A barrel of trouble is what she is." He let out a snort of amusement that contradicted his words, then thumbed toward his house. "Anyway, I think you're right about that dog being hurt. I don't know anything about dogs or taking care of one, so you need to come get it."

"Okay, let me grab my keys."

Luke started down the front steps, moving slow, cautious. The second tread creaked a warning before cracking under his weight, but the step held. He turned back. "You should get that thing fixed before someone gets hurt. In fact, this whole porch sounds like it's about to fall off."

"It'd save me some demo work if it did." She grabbed her keys off the table by the door. "I would fix that step if I knew how to use a power drill. Or a receptacle saw. Or—"

"Receptacle saw?" Confusion arched his brow, and then he chuckled. "Do you mean a *reciprocating* saw?"

"Whatever it's called, it sure isn't reciprocating with cutting when I use it."

"Maybe it doesn't like you."

"Or maybe it's just stubborn. Like most men." She blew her bangs out of her face as she stepped onto the porch. Miss Sadie barked disagreement about being left behind, but Olivia wasn't going to chance spooking the golden again. Geckos scattered across the walkway, and in the distance, birds called to each other. "If I had the money, I'd hire someone to do all this. I thought it would be easier. I thought—"

As Olivia tugged the door shut behind her, the handle popped off in her hands, slipped out of her fingers, and dropped to the porch. Hardware followed in a clatter of metal on wood.

The last straw fell in an almost imperceptible whisper.

Tears blurred her vision. Tears of frustration and regret and worry and a million other emotions. It was hot, she was tired, and there was a ceiling fan in pieces on her living room floor. Her bank account was bordering on anorexic, and the list of things the house still needed ballooned more every second. Before she could stop them, the tears spilled over in a noisy snuffle.

"What the hell are you doing?" Luke said.

She sniffled and swiped at her face. Oh damn. The last thing she wanted to do in front of a near-stranger was break down. "Crying. I'm sorry. It's been a really bad day and this house, this move . . . it's not going how I expected." Though she made a valiant effort to suck it up and quit crying, the tears refused to stop.

"Cut it out, will you?"

She didn't. She couldn't. The dam had broken, and there was no plugging it again. She tried to apologize again—the man barely knew her and here she was, a blubbering mess— but it came out as a choked sob.

"Oh, hell." He hesitated, then took a step forward and placed a hand on her arm. The touch lasted a second, no more. A second of heat, of connection. "Do you have any duct tape?"

"Wh . . . what?" She blinked, fat teardrops blurring her vision. "Did you say *duct* tape?"

"Slap some duct tape on, and your problem's solved. It works for everything. Electrical, plumbing, structural."

"I . . . I don't have any duct tape." Apparently she hadn't bought *everything* in Home Depot.

"I'll make you a deal. Get that dog out of my kitchen and I'll give you some. I've got an extra roll . . . or ten."

"Because you're a guy, right?"

"Of course. It comes with the testosterone. In fact, they hand it out at puberty."

She laughed, and finally the tears stopped. They started walking down the sidewalk, in the kind of odd comfortable stroll between two people who didn't know each other but had something in common, even if it wasn't much more than a zip code.

Luke intrigued her. This handsome, mysterious, wounded man with an attitude the size of Toledo, tempered by a soft spot for dogs and damsels in distress. There was something very, very appealing about that. Either that or her hormones had kicked into overdrive when he showed up.

"So you work at the retirement home with Miss Sadie?" he said. "Is she a therapist too?"

"Sort of. She's my bichon frise, aka 'the hairball,' as you dubbed her. She and I are a registered team, doing animal-assisted therapy."

"So she's a useful hairball, huh?" He paused when he crossed from the concrete sidewalk to the crushed-shell driveway. "What's animal-assisted therapy? Is the dog doing all the heavy lifting?"

"Not exactly. Sometimes, patients living in retirement homes, nursing homes, rehabs, have trouble getting excited about therapy. They're in pain, or they're depressed, or just plain unengaged. Animals can bridge that divide, and not just get people smiling, but encourage them to interact. There's something about handing Miss Sadie a dog biscuit that's so much more fun and rewarding than handing a therapist a toothbrush."

He considered that, then nodded. "And sometimes, people who don't want to talk will talk to a dog instead of a person."

"Exactly. A lot of these patients had to give up their pets when they moved into Golden Years, and just seeing Miss Sadie can change their attitudes. Studies have shown that spending time with a dog can lower blood pressure, reduce anxiety, and just increase overall well-being. It's amazing how much a little ten-pound dog can do."

"Too bad she can't use duct tape."

Olivia grinned. "For a guy who doesn't say much, you really know how to deliver a punch line."

He headed down the driveway, pulverizing shells along the way. "That's me. A man of few words, and even fewer witty comments."

"Put that in a personals ad and you'll attract every woman in the tri-county area."

"And don't forget my amazing skill with duct tape. There's a real bonus for the ladies." A smile curved across his face, and it hit her hard, sending a shiver down her spine and a hot rush of desire through all the other parts.

What was that about a fling with a sexy stranger?

"I'll, uh, have to put that to use," she said, then coughed to cover the fact that she was thinking about putting something other than his duct tape to use. "If you're offering, that is."

Before he responded, an older dark-haired woman next door hopped to her feet and started waving. "Yoo-hoo, Luke!"

"Oh, great. Lois Blanchard. Don't talk to her," Luke muttered. "You'll only encourage her."

"But she's your neighbor. You have to be friendly."

"If I start being nice," he said, leaning over and lowering his voice, his breath a quick, hot caress along her neck, sending thoughts of one-night stands and hot nights in his bed careening through her mind, "it'll ruin my reputation as an ogre."

Oh. My. God.

She wasn't having a single ogre thought about him right now. Oh no, her thoughts ran more down the rip-his-clothes-off-and-use-him-for-his-body road. Then she jerked herself back to the present moment, and the woman heading toward them.

Lois darted across their lawns, wearing a floral capri set that matched the pansies sitting on her lawn. A tall, wiry woman, she wore a bright yellow visor and color-coordinated garden clogs. "You're the new neighbor, aren't you?" she said to Olivia.

"Yes, I am. Been here only a few weeks." She recognized Lois now. It was the bright clothes that gave her away. "I've seen you walking the neighborhood in the mornings."

"Yup, that's me and the Constitutional Crew. My sister and brother-in-law. You're welcome to join us, you know."

"Oh, thank you, but I'm usually heading out to work about that time." Not to mention, the Constitutional Crew usually sported matching neon-colored sweatsuits.

"Too bad." Lois turned to Luke. "You're welcome too, Luke. I'm sure Ben would love to have another guy to temper us ladies and our talk about bingo and knitting."

"An offer I could hardly refuse," Luke said, his tone dry as the Sahara, "but my mornings are . . . busy."

Lois made a little face, then flashed Olivia a bright smile. "I'm so sorry Doug—that's my husband—and I haven't come over to say howdy yet. You'd think we'd have more time as retirees, but good golly, we're busy as bees." She gave Luke a light tap. "Why didn't you introduce me earlier?"

"With your keen Welcome Wagon skills, Mrs. Blanchard, I figured you had already met the newest addition to the block."

She waved a hand. "Oh, I've been so busy working in that garden, trying to get my azaleas to cooperate with my pansies. The soil here, it can be tricky. Luke, you should grow something. Your yard is starting to look . . . well . . ." She made a sour face. "I'm sure you've got a gardening plan all set for this season."

"Oh, you know it. Posted it right next to my brand-new gardening spade."

"Wonderful! If you need some tips—"

"I know where you live." Luke gestured toward his house. "We'll have to catch up later, Mrs. Blanchard. Olivia and I have something to take care of."

"Oh. *Oh* . . . okay." She smiled, then patted Olivia on the arm. "Nice to meet you. And let me tell you, this man here is a bona fide hero, so you're smart to latch onto him."

Before Olivia could protest that she wasn't doing latching of any kind with Luke Winslow, Lois had returned to her pansies. Luke started off down the driveway again, and Olivia hurried to catch up with his long strides. "Lois seems nice."

"She's actually a serial killer," Luke teased. "Why do you think she does all that gardening?" Across the way, Lois had returned to rooting in the soil. She noticed them looking and sent over another wave. "A word to the wise—don't let your dog dig in her tomato patch."

Olivia bit back a chuckle. "You're terrible. I think the people in Rescue Bay are wonderful. I love that coffee shop downtown. You know, the Java Hut? Everyone there is so friendly."

"We're a tourist destination. Being friendly is a town law."

She glanced over at him. "So what was that about you being a hero?"

"Nothing." He scowled, and a shade dropped over his features. "Nothing at all."

They had reached the front walk, but Luke kept going, heading for the back door. He lived in a typical Florida bungalow, low, squat, painted a soft gray with white trim. A few shrubs ringed the front and offset a lawn that had long since turned brown. Citrus trees lined the eastern property line, their branches laden with bright orange and yellow fruit. Ripe oranges and lemons peppered the ground.

Luke stepped onto the back porch, shaded by a simple aluminum awning, then opened the door and held it for her. She stepped into the darkened space. Before she processed the room, her gaze swept the kitchen. Over the checkered tile, under the maple table, past the oak cabinets. "Where's the dog?"

"I left it here and unless it can open the back door, it's got to be around somewhere." Luke came in behind her, and she stepped to the side to make room for him.

He was a tall man, broad in the shoulders, and even though the kitchen was spacious, with Luke standing beside her the space seemed small, tight. She shifted closer to the sink. Dirty dishes sat in soapy water, waiting to be washed. A tower of pizza boxes propped up a stack of white take-out boxes and empty soda and beer cans. Budweiser paired with Coke, in a long straight line of white-and-red aluminum.

Despite the mess on the counter, the chairs and table sat square against each other, and no knickknacks cluttered the shelves or counters. A tidy and at the same time almost neglected space. There was an air of emptiness about the house that she couldn't put a finger on. Then she thought of the disaster she lived in and decided the pot had no business calling the kettle anything at all.

"You didn't lure me over here with the ruse of a dog, did

you?" she asked, the words a tease, meant to break the tension between them. Instead, Luke turned to her, his thoughts unreadable, hidden behind those sunglasses.

"If I were going to lure you, Olivia," he said, the syllables sliding off his tongue like a long, slow caress, "I'd use something a little more inventive than a stray dog."

The darkened space wrapped around them. Cozy, intimate. Tempting. For a second, she entertained a few non-neighborly thoughts about Luke Winslow. The same thoughts of him in her house, in her bed, in her . . . Yeah, *those* thoughts that had spiced her last several nights. "I'll . . . uh, keep that in mind."

Things had shifted from a tentative détente to sexy innuendo. Her nerve endings stood on alert, hyperaware of Luke's presence. Of the deep timbre of his voice, the dark notes of his words. Of the careless sexiness of his unshaven face, his wayward hair. And of all he had hidden behind those sunglasses.

Yeah, she needed to get involved with him like she needed to start a home improvement business. Then why had she looked for him every time she'd been in her yard? Why had she wondered about him at least a dozen times in the days since that first disastrous meeting?

Rescue the dog, get out of here, and get back to work. And stop fantasizing about the neighbor.

"Why don't we uh, look in another room?" she said.

He cleared his throat, as if he shared the same awkward thoughts she'd been having. "Good idea."

She waited for him to lead the way. He didn't move. "Uh . . . which room?"

He waved down the darkened hall. "Pick one. Don't touch anything."

Olivia headed down the hall. No dog. She turned right— dining room. She flicked on the wall switch, flooding the room with light.

A long pale maple table centered the space, flanked by a half-dozen matching chairs. A dying fern struggled for light in the corner, beside a Cannondale bike leaning against the wall. The china cabinet held a few dishes, the buffet nothing more than a silver bowl. Except for a slight layer of dust, the room was as tight and organized as library shelves. Neat stacks of papers sat on one end of the table, anchored by a trio of small white boxes, like the kind used for jewelry.

Olivia bent down, looked under the table, and didn't see the dog. She was about to turn and leave when those boxes aroused her curiosity. She reached out, drew her hand back, then reached again. What was Luke doing with so many boxes of jewelry?

She told herself she wasn't going to look inside. That she didn't care what Luke Winslow had on his dining room table or why he maintained his distance. Was it just because they were still essentially strangers? Or did he have something more to hide, like Lois and her garden?

Before she could think twice, she had pried the lid off the top box on the pile, then flipped open the blue velvet box inside.

Nestled on a soft cotton bed sat a hefty and impressive gold medal, hanging from a thick red-white-and-blue-striped ribbon. Two anchors flanked either side of a circular emblem.

United States Coast Guard.

Coast Guard? Him?

That man's a bona fide hero.

"I told you not to touch anything."

She wheeled around at the sharp tones. As she did, the box slipped from her grasp and landed on the tile floor with a clatter. She scrambled to pick it up, flipped the lid closed, then wrangled the white top back in place. "I'm sorry. I just . . ." What excuse did she have? "I saw the medal, and I was curious. What's it for?"

She held out the box to him. Instead of taking it, he cursed, then turned on his heel. "Just get the damned dog and get out."

She stood there for several long seconds, the medal box heavy in her hands. What had caused the sudden shift in mood? Was it something to do with the medal? But that didn't make sense. Weren't medals given for doing good things? Why would he be angry about that?

Whatever the reason, she refused to pry. Prying meant getting involved, and she had enough on her plate right now. A plate that sure as heck didn't have room for a relationship or the messy task of straightening out someone else's baggage. Hell, she barely had time to fix her own. So she put the medal back on the table and left the room to do what Luke had asked—get the dog and get out.

She went the opposite direction from where Luke had gone and headed into the living room. This room, like the others, was neat and tidy, but the lights were off, shades drawn. The air conditioner pumped a steady stream of cool air into the space. She flicked on a small table lamp. Her gaze swept the room and then, finally, in the corner under an end table, lay the golden.

"Hey, there you are," Olivia said. She bent down, keeping one hand splayed, and inched her way toward the dog. The golden watched her, wary, tense, and then as Olivia closed the gap, the dog scrambled back, deeper into the shadows. Olivia retreated. Tried again. Same result. The dog's eyes remained wide, its tail still, its breath coming in fast bursts. "Oh, puppy, I won't hurt you. Come on out."

More scrambling back and panting hard. Scared. Olivia couldn't blame him. Poor thing had surely been through a lot.

"Let me try."

She turned toward Luke's voice. He was leaning against the doorjamb, watching her, still wearing those damned sunglasses even though the room was dim. Had he been there the whole time? "Sure. He's a little skittish. You'll probably have better luck with him. After all, he came to your house. Obviously, he trusts you."

"I can't imagine why."

"Maybe because he can relate to _you_." The words were out before she could stop them.

He scoffed. "Or maybe he's just like you."

"Me?"

He took a step forward, those sunglasses locked on her features. Why did he wear them still? In the dimly lit house? Did it have something to do with the scar? The medal?

Still, she got the sense that even if he couldn't see well in the low light, he could see everything about her, while keeping everything about himself hidden. She wanted to look away, wanted to do anything but connect with this man, but every time he came within five feet of her, that intoxicating thread began to knit a little tighter.

"You're the one who came marching into my yard"—he took another step closer to her, his voice low, dark— "demanding that I help you find that dog."

She raised her chin. "I didn't demand. I . . . asked." Then she shot him a smile and eased her tone. "Nicely."

"I think we're using different dictionaries." The darkness in his voice yielded to a slight uptick. "My definition of *demand* is flanked by a picture of you."

She laughed, and, as if joining in on the moment, the dog's tail thumped. Luke turned toward the sound, and when he did, the light caught his features and she saw the rest of what the sunglasses had been hiding. She sucked in a quick gasp.

The wide arm of the sunglasses striped a black band across the scar running down one side of his face, spidering away from his left eye in thick red lines. An angry indent punctured the space above his brow.

"What . . . ?" The sentence trailed off, caught in the awkward tug-of-war between curiosity and propriety.

He swung back to face her. "You're staring at me. I can feel it. I'm not a goddamn freak of nature."

"What . . . happened?"

"You want to see? You want to know?" He cursed, then ripped off the sunglasses. A dark wash deepened the blue in his left eye, and though his right eventually zeroed in on her, the left didn't. The pieces filtered into place. Luke's inability to see the dog. The way he measured his steps. The dusty but tidy, organized house. The sunglasses. The attitude.

She reached out a hand, curious, concerned. "Are you okay? I mean, is this . . . is it . . ."

He jerked away. "You're not here for me. You're here for the dog."

She sensed the angry growl of a wounded animal trying to keep others away. How she knew that feeling. In the days after her divorce, she'd called in sick, curled up on the couch, and avoided the world. The dishes had piled up, the dust had multiplied. She hadn't answered the phone or the door or done a damned thing for days. Then her mother arrived, and wouldn't take no for an answer, dragging Olivia out for a terrible lunch at a loud, busy restaurant with waiters who sang off-key. And made her laugh for the first time in forever.

After that, her days had brightened, one after another, and she'd once again found herself and her spirit. Maybe Luke needed to do the same.

"I'm sorry. I didn't mean to pry."

"Then don't." He let out a gust and surveyed the living room. "Where's the dog?"

"He's right there. Can't you—" She cut off the sentence. "Sorry."

"What do you keep apologizing for?"

"Nothing." It didn't take a rocket scientist—or an idiot therapist—to realize that the pain from the scar had penetrated far deeper than the surface of his skin.

"Then stop doing it and just tell me where the dog is."

"In the corner, under the end table. The one closest to the hall."

He moved forward, with short, tentative steps. He skirted the coffee table, almost nicking it with his shin, before coming to a stop in front of the end table. He bent down. "Hey, you. If you don't get out of there, someone's going to put a coaster on you."

The dog's tail thumped again. But he didn't move.

"Come on," Luke said, his voice softer this time, a low, bass song. "You don't want to stay there."

The tail thumped some more. The dog inched forward,

long nails scratching against the wood floor. But still he didn't emerge.

"If you stay there, you'll have to live with me. And I'm not nearly as much fun, or as nice, as that one." Luke thumbed behind him. "She's got dog food and treats and a friend for you. Everyone needs a friend, right?"

The dog's tail rat-a-tatted.

"So do me a favor, and come on out. The dark is no place to live. Trust me."

Olivia watched from the sidelines, her breath caught in her throat. *Sometimes, people who don't want to talk will talk to a dog instead of a person.* Her heart broke for the injured man, trying so hard to connect with the injured dog. And for the dog, so scared to trust.

After a moment, the golden crawled forward, then rose on all fours, and pressed his nose to Luke's leg. His tail wagged, slapping against the end table. Luke put a hand on the golden's thick neck, and the dog jerked his nose to Luke's wrist.

"Can you keep him there?" Olivia whispered. "I want to check out the injury."

Luke nodded and began to scratch behind the dog's ear. The golden leaned into his palm and let out a contented groan. "Just a few minutes more," he said in a quiet, almost singsong voice, "while the mean lady from next door checks you out."

"Hey!" she whispered. "I'm not mean."

Luke shot her a grin, then went back to scratching the dog. "Just do what you gotta do."

"By the way, it's definitely a he," she said.

"Well, whoever this dog is, he took a chance coming to my door for help. Good thing you're next door."

"Yeah, good thing." He was far too thin for an average male golden. Olivia leaned in closer and looked at the dog's belly. The cut ran along his side, a long, nasty gash that looked a few days old, maybe longer. The blood had crusted and dried. The wound didn't seem infected, but she wasn't sure. Even without touching the dog she could tell the poor thing was malnourished. The dog's thick coat hung limp from his skin, and his ribs rippled under the golden fur. Who had done this to this beautiful animal? And why? Olivia resisted the urge to hug the dog to her chest and protect him from ever being hurt again.

She sighed and rocked back on her heels. "He looks better than the first day I saw him, but he's not out of the woods. I can do basic care, but he needs a vet. I don't know one in town yet. Finding a good local doc is on my to-do list."

The dog lay down and rested his head on his paws. Luke gave him a final pat, then rose. "I know a vet."

"Good." Olivia got to her feet too, as the dog closed its eyes and seemed to go to sleep. For whatever reason, the golden was comfortable here with Luke. Then why wasn't Olivia? Why was every cell in her body hyperaware of his every move?

"Thank you, Luke," she said.

He shrugged. "I didn't do anything."

"You did a lot. You calmed him down. Made him feel at home." Olivia looked down at the dog, who had moved his snout in the direction of Luke's feet. "Made a friend, too. Not bad for an ogre."

He laughed. "I'm back to that, am I?"

He had a nice laugh, the kind that came from somewhere deep inside him. Luke Winslow surprised her. A man who could shut the door on himself so fast it could knock a person over, then switch gears with a smile, a laugh.

"You keep rescuing dogs and people are going to confuse you with a nice guy."

"Trust me, that's never going to happen." He moved closer to her. His scent wrapped around her, drawing her in, closer. Her heart hammered in her chest, and she wondered what secrets lurked in the storm-tossed hue of his eyes. "Why are you here?"

"For the dog. Remember?" But was she? Because right now, it seemed she had passed concern for the golden and edged into concern for the man. She wondered what would happen if she dragged him to a restaurant where the waiters harmonized. Would they find common ground over a greasy pizza and a tinny rendition of "Moon River"?

"No, I mean, here, in Rescue Bay. Next door to me."

"I"—she paused—"I'm looking for something."

He reached up and captured her jaw with his hand. His hand was warm, big, the kind of touch that begged her to come closer, to trust, to open herself to him. She resisted for one long second, her breath caught in the mesmerizing mix of this mysterious, complicated man. Then she leaned into his touch, wanting . . . wanting more than she could say.

"What happens if you find it?" he said.

"I haven't planned that far. This is all so"—she released a breath—"so complicated."

His thumb traced along her jaw, her lower lip. Her pulse thundered in her head, and she inhaled deeply the sweet, spicy scent that surrounded him. "Too complicated."

She nodded, whatever words she might have been thinking lost. Her gaze locked on Luke's blue eyes, on the mystery of that scar, on the dark storm warring in his features.

"Don't think I'll be your knight in shining armor," he said, his voice low and dark, and in that sound, she heard an echo of pain. "I don't do rescue. Not anymore."

She shook her head. "I won't."

What did he want? What was in that touch? The heat between them? Her heart raced, even as she told herself this man wanted nothing to do with her. That she wanted nothing to do with him. But oh, right now, for this moment, she wanted that touch, wanted . . .

Complicated.

"If you know what's good for you, you'll leave, Olivia," he said, her name a melody on his tongue, his mouth so close to hers that the heat of his words danced across her lips. "Because I just want to be left alone."

"Me too." The words escaped in a rush. She wanted to run. Wanted to stay. Wanted to know what he was going to say or do next.

"I'm no good for you," he said, each word softening more than the one before, his gaze locked on hers, mesmerizing, powerful, undeniable. "For anyone." The last escaped in a growl, and then he closed the gap between them and lowered his lips to hers. "Damn it, Olivia." Her name now a harsh whisper on his lips, sending a rush through her.

The kiss erupted between them, a hot, fast, furious tangle of mouths. Her hands wove into his hair, drawing him closer, wanting more of that . . . anger, that passion. Desire ignited inside her, leaping from nerve to nerve like an electrical spark. Heat flooded her veins, rushed over her in a tidal wave. She surged toward him, seeking, yearning, needing. Images teemed in her mind, of his hands, his mouth, his body. The two of them coming together, separating, hungry for something to fill the void, to find the one thing that would fill the empty nights. This wasn't just desire, it was a want that rushed over her like a tsunami, demanding and strong.

Damn.

An instant later, he broke away from her, and disappointment flooded her veins. His jaw hardened and he shook his head. "That shouldn't have happened. I'm sorry."

"It's okay, it's—"

"We, uh, should call the vet." He turned and took a step to the right. She told herself she was glad. Relieved even.

Yet a part of her wanted him to kiss her again. To take her to those dizzying heights one more time, then take it further. If he had, would she have found herself in bed with the neighbor, enjoying a little afternoon delight?

That would be a mistake, because she knew, as sure as she knew her own name, that getting involved with Luke Winslow would shatter her world in new ways. He had an edge about him, about his touch, his kiss, his words, that tempted and scared her, all at the same time.

Right now, she didn't need complicated. Didn't need to fall for a self-proclaimed ogre. Even if he was sexy as hell and could kiss like . . .

Like no man she'd ever met.

He fished a cell phone out of his pocket, flipped it open, pressed a couple keys, then cursed. "Damn type is so small."

"Let me." She put out her hand. "Please?"

"Fine." He plopped the phone into her hand. "It should be under Tuttle. Diana Tuttle."

Olivia's hand stilled, her finger poised over the keypad. "Did you say Tuttle?"

"Yeah." He glanced at Olivia. "Maybe you know her? She's the daughter of the woman who owned that house you live in."

Her gaze dropped to the screen. Luke had already typed the first three letters. Olivia hit search, and in a second, the name returned. She traced over the letters. Diana Tuttle.

Her sister.

Five

❧

"Greta," Esther whispered, "this is crazy."

"No, it's not. It's a good idea," she said, shushing Esther with her free hand while she waved at Pauline to angle the car farther into the parking lot. After she'd left Luke's house earlier, she'd dug her cell phone out of the suitcase she called a purse, then called the girls for some necessary backup. By the time Pauline got her teeth in and her hair poufed, Greta about had a conniption fit. It took a good fifteen minutes for Pauline's giant white Cadillac to prowl down the street, at Pauline's usual speed of *turtle*.

"What are we doing here anyway?" Esther asked. "I'm missing my shows, you know. I hate to miss my shows."

"We're here to make sure we . . . give the right advice." That was what Greta had told the girls they were doing—offering their wisdom to Olivia. She didn't mention the meddling she intended to do, which would hopefully result in pushing Olivia and Luke together.

"If you ask me," Pauline said, "the best advice comes from the heart and—"

"Oh, for Pete's sake, Pauline, it does not. It comes from

making the decisions for people and shoving them to-ward those choices. If you ask me, most people don't know what the hell to do with themselves."

"We aren't making decisions. We might even be breaking the law." Esther put up her hands, as if that would shield her in the car from such bad choices. Maybe she should have done the same with the bright orange dress she had on today. The thing could be used to direct airplanes on the runway. "Isn't this trespassing?"

"We are observing. That's not illegal," Greta said. Lord, there were days when these women drove her to drink. Where was their sense of adventure? Their penchant for a little trouble? "Were you all nuns as teenagers or something?"

"I went to a Catholic girls' school," Esther said.

"That explains a lot." Greta muttered the words. Pauline bit her lip to keep from laughing, and Esther's face scrunched.

Across from them, Olivia's car had pulled into the vet-erinarian's parking lot. Greta waited, sure the passenger-side door would open and her grandson would emerge. But no, only the driver got out. Olivia. She went to the back door and carefully drew out the golden, balancing the big dog in her arms and shutting the car door with her knee.

No Luke.

Hmmmph. Greta sat in Pauline's Cadillac and turned that over in her mind. Somehow, she needed to get Olivia and Luke to talk, maybe go on a date. She'd expected that they would take the dog to the vet together. She'd been so sure when she left that Luke's love for animals would win over his need to be alone.

Clearly, his pain ran deeper than she'd thought. She sighed, her heart breaking for her wounded grandson.

She needed to get him to enjoy life again. Luke used to be one of those hard-charging, go-after-whatever-he-wanted kind of young men. All energetic optimism and reckless abandon. Even when he'd been a little boy, Luke had been the first one into the surf, the first one to climb a tree, the first one to ask out a girl. Greta hadn't been surprised one bit when he'd signed up for the Coast Guard, opting for a military career that would allow him to save people right here in the United States. He'd been courageous and ambitious, which had gotten him advanced quickly. But ever since the accident, that spark had dimmed in Luke, and though Greta had done everything she could to help him find it again, he'd kept the doors shut. Literally.

If she could just get Luke to see that life hadn't ended, just changed . . .

"Here's the plan," Greta said. "We go over there and ask Olivia to go to lunch with us over at the Shoebox Café after she's done with the dog thing. Meanwhile, I'll call Luke and ask him to walk down and meet me for lunch. As soon as he arrives, we conveniently ditch Luke and Olivia and go somewhere else."

Esther's jaw dropped. "What do you mean, ditch them? We're not getting lunch?"

"We're not here to fill our bellies, Esther."

"But I'm hungry. They had eggs this morning for breakfast. You know I don't like eggs. I need a starch in the morning."

"Then we'll stop and get you a muffin," Greta said. *Lord, grant me patience and keep me from slapping Esther Gerke. Thank you. I'll drop an extra couple bucks in the collection plate on Sunday. I swear.* "Are you in?"

Pauline shrugged. "Sure. I don't have anything to do today. And maybe we can add some of the details of our adventure to the column—"

"Absolutely not. This entire mission is top secret."

Across from them, Esther's lips pursed again. But she didn't protest. Probably afraid they'd skip the promised muffin.

Olivia cradled the dog in her arms and headed for the vet's office. She held the dog with no more effort than a sack of potatoes; the poor thing was so sickly it didn't seem to weigh much despite its size. Greta motioned to Pauline and Esther to follow her. She ambled forward, her purse dangling from her forearm, as if she spent every afternoon strolling downtown Rescue Bay.

"Why, hello, Olivia," Greta called. "What are you doing here?"

Olivia stopped when she saw the trio of women and shot them a grin. She shifted the dog's weight in her arms. "I'm beginning to think you ladies are following me," she said with a laugh.

"Not at all. We just had errands to run downtown today, and this is all a coincidence, right, ladies?"

"Oh, yes, coincidence," Pauline said.

Esther didn't say anything. Pauline nudged her. Hard. "Yup. Nothing illegal about that."

Greta drew in a deep, fortifying breath. And people questioned why she needed a little Maker's Mark in the morning? Goodness gracious. Greta put on a smile and nodded toward the dog. "Is that the pooch that was on my grandson's doorstep earlier today?"

"Yes. He's hurt and malnourished," Olivia said, "so I'm bringing him to the vet to get looked at."

"Poor baby," Pauline said, reaching out to give the golden a gentle pat on the head.

"You know, all these errands have kept us so busy we forgot to eat. We're famished," Greta said. "How would you like to join some old ladies for a little lunch after you're done?" She leaned toward Olivia, because she could already see her readying an objection. "You need to eat, right? And there's the best little diner just around the corner."

Olivia hedged. "Oh, I don't know—"

"Please do," Pauline said. "It'll be nice to dine with someone other than ourselves."

"Thanks for the offer, ladies, but I have to get the dog into the vet. I'm not sure how long that's going to take. Besides, I'm not hungry."

"I am," Esther said.

Greta shot her a glare.

"Thanks again anyway, Mrs. Winslow, ladies, but I'll have to take a rain check." Then Olivia turned on her heel and headed toward the building. The automatic glass door opened with a whoosh and Olivia disappeared inside.

Greta sighed. So much for Operation Happiness. Her first attempt at matchmaking had fizzled before it even got a chance to work. "Well," she said to Pauline and Esther. "We're going to have to work harder if we want to get those two together."

"Don't you think love should come about naturally? Without any nudging?" Esther said.

"Of course not. Where's the fun in that?" Greta watched the retreating figure of the woman she was positive was her grandson's perfect match and wondered whether it was possible to recruit a dog to join their team.

Either that, or they needed a miracle, and as favors from God went, Greta didn't think she had too many credits left in the Big Guy's ledger.

"We're going to make this romance happen," Greta said, "because Luke needs that woman. He's just too stubborn to realize it."

"Stubborn? Gee, wonder where he got that trait?" Pauline put the Caddy in gear, then shot Greta a grin. "And I mean that in the nicest way, Greta."

Esther's stomach growled and she pressed a hand to her gut. "Ladies, before we change the world, can we stop for muffins?"

Greta sighed, cast her gaze heavenward, and prayed for patience. God's response sounded a lot like laughter.

Six

Olivia sat in one of the hard plastic chairs of the waiting room and drew in a deep breath. The air-conditioned cool air filled her lungs, expanded her chest, but didn't slow her stuttering heart. She kept a hand on her knee to keep her leg from tapping her nerves against the tile floor.

Her sister. She was about to meet her sister.

Of course, Diana Tuttle, DVM, didn't know that. Probably didn't even know Olivia existed. Or if she had known, and she hadn't looked her up, maybe she didn't want anything to do with a long-lost sister.

Maybe if Olivia had pushed harder for information, she would have learned about her sister by now. But every time Olivia started to ask about Bridget, the questions lodged in her throat. After the disappointment of the house and the lack of any kind of note or letter or explanation, Olivia hadn't had the heart to dig for more information.

It didn't take a Mensa applicant to figure out why Olivia wasn't asking questions. She was merely doing what she did best—avoiding hurt and disappointment. She'd had enough of that to last a long time.

Now she sat in the waiting room, nervous energy bubbling inside her, and envied a woman she had never met the relationship she'd had with a woman who was already gone.

Olivia glanced around the room, taking in the bright yellow and orange plastic chairs, the butter-yellow tiled floor, the parade of animals painted above the wainscoting. The waiting area of Diana Tuttle, DVM, was cheery, happy, pretty. The staff who had greeted Olivia had been friendly, warm, all boding for a good experience at the vet.

A couple sat across from Olivia, taking turns trying to calm a yowling cat inside a carrier, while a heavyset man in the corner kept a tight hold on the leash of a curious chihuahua nosing around the chairs and end tables. Olivia glanced at the six-panel oak door that led to the exam rooms, then again at the clock, then back again at the door. The nerves tightened her throat, and in her arms, the golden lifted his head, brown eyes wary. Olivia exhaled and forced herself to relax. "Sorry, buddy." She stroked one long golden ear, and the dog settled with a sigh.

The door opened again and a short blond vet tech in animal-print scrubs held up a folder. "Chance?"

It took a second for Olivia to recognize the name she'd impulsively given to the stray dog when she'd checked in. She got to her feet, holding the too-thin golden close to her chest. All this time, the dog hadn't complained, hadn't done much more than just lie in Olivia's arms, trusting the human.

"That's us," Olivia said, then headed through the door, following the bubbly tech to a floor scale. Olivia laid the dog on the rubber mat, then stepped back. The digital numbers flickered, then stayed at a very low forty-two pounds.

A healthy golden would weigh at least twenty or thirty pounds more than that.

Olivia wanted to just drop a bag of Purina at Chance's feet, but she knew too much food too fast could be as deadly as too little. She'd given Chance a scoop of dog food before bringing him in today, but she was willing to bet the dog was still hungry. The tech tut-tutted as she wrote down the weight, then led the way to room number two. The young blonde chatted the whole way: small talk about the weather, the goofy St. Bernard due in at one, and the litter of kittens born last night.

Olivia barely heard. All she could think about was the sister she was about to meet. The only biological family Olivia had. Was she ready for this?

Ready to meet the sole tie to Bridget? To Olivia's heritage?

"In here," the tech said. "Do you need some help with him?"

"No, I've got it. He doesn't weigh much." Olivia laid the golden on the stainless steel exam table. He let out a sigh and dropped his head to his front paws. In a few minutes, Olivia had gone through the preliminary information with the tech, who took a few notes and readied a couple of syringes on the counter. "That's it. The doctor will be in soon and we'll get this big guy fixed right up," the tech said, giving Chance a quick, gentle pat before stepping out the back door of the room.

Olivia shifted from foot to foot. Chance lifted his head and glanced at her, as if telling her to calm down, that he was the one who should be nervous. "You're right, boy," she said to the dog, giving him a tender rub behind the ears. "Okay, let's just worry about you for now."

The door to the room opened again and a tall, thin blonde in a white lab coat entered the room. She could have been Olivia's twin, with the same frame, same hair color, but most of all, the same wide, forest-green eyes. Was that what their mother had looked like too? There'd been no pictures at the house, and the Google searches Olivia had done had turned up a few grainy black-and-white newspaper images of a tall woman in a floppy hat, usually holding a rescued dog.

"Hi, I'm Diana Tuttle," Diana said, putting out her hand. Her voice was peppy, friendly. Her eyes soft and warm, her features animated. "And who do we have here?"

DIANA TUTTLE, DVM was embroidered on one side of her lab coat and would have made her look official, maybe even clinical, except for the bright pink T-shirt she wore underneath. On the shirt, a cartoon drawing of a dog and cat in wedding attire was emblazoned above the words SHAKESPEARE'S LOST MANUSCRIPT: WOOFEO AND MEOWIET.

Olivia liked her on the spot.

"I'm Olivia. And this is Chance." Olivia shook hands with Diana—the words *my sister* rocketing inside her. Her only sibling, well, that she knew of. But more, the only living tie to Bridget Tuttle and the answers Olivia had searched for all her life. Except that wasn't exactly the kind of thing one blurted out, especially with the dog between them.

On the way over, Olivia had debated whether to tell Diana the truth, but now that the moment was here, she faltered. What if Diana didn't know about Bridget's other daughter? What if she didn't want to know? What if she kicked Olivia out, the interloper who had inherited Bridget's house? So instead, Olivia shook hands, noting Diana's firm, warm grip, then released her sister's hand and waved toward the dog. *Take care of him first*, she reminded herself. The rest could wait. It had waited this long, after all. "I found Chance in my backyard a few days ago, but it took some time to entice him to come close enough to catch him. He's definitely hurt, and underweight."

"Poor baby," Diana cooed, leaning down to examine the dog with a gentle, practiced touch. "Let's see what we have here. Okay, honey? Don't worry, Chance. It'll all be fine. I promise."

Her sister had the same light blond hair that Olivia had, but styled in a shoulder-length, no-nonsense blunt cut. She was about the same height, and a similar build, but a little younger. Olivia guessed her to be twenty-nine, maybe thirty. She had a wide smile that reached her green eyes, and a tendency to tuck her hair behind her right ear, something Olivia did, too. An inherited trait? Or just a habit?

Or was Olivia looking for a connection that wasn't really there? After all, they'd grown up half a country apart, with different parents. There was no reason to think they had anything in common besides some DNA.

And one wounded dog. Not exactly enough to build a family reunion on. Olivia worked a smile to her face and told herself it didn't matter. But deep down inside, it did.

A lot.

For all practical purposes, the dog before Diana should have been dead. Underweight, malnourished, dehydrated, and cut from shoulder to belly with a deep, infected laceration that had crusted over and healed poorly. Chance looked up at her from the exam table with wary eyes that quivered with hope.

Save me, he seemed to say. *Please*.

Diana worked fast, inserting an IV into a vein in the dog's foreleg, taking his pulse and temp, drawing blood for a heartworm test. The laceration would need to be opened up, cleaned, then stitched, but overall, Chance had lived up to his name. Thank God he'd been brought in before things got much worse.

"He's had a bad time of it," Diana said, running a hand down the dog's fur. He barely stirred, save for a couple of friendly flicks of his tail against the table. Poor puppy. "I'm not sure what happened here, but it looks like he got caught under a fence or something that tore open his belly and it didn't heal well, so now it's infected. I'm going to shave it down, clean it up, and stitch it up again. He'll need a round of antibiotics, for sure. But most of all, he needs rest, food, and water, and a lot of TLC from Mother Nature."

Olivia let out a sigh. Relief showed in her eyes, in the way her shoulders eased. "You're sure?"

"Yup." Diana picked up the white plastic test package she'd set on the counter a few minutes earlier. "And he's lucky. The heartworm is negative. Though I'd recommend getting him on some preventatives today. Since we don't know where he's been, we should also test for parasites at the next visit and get his shots up to date."

"Will do. Thank you."

Diana smiled. "Just doing my job." She leaned back

against the counter, and picked up the dog's chart. "If you don't want to take on all this by yourself, I can help you rehome him. Though he's on the mend, he's far from out of the woods, and he's going to need a lot of care in the coming weeks. Unfortunately, our local animal shelter closed down a"—the words still caught in her throat, the grief hitting her anew—"while ago, but I can give you the addresses of a couple in nearby towns."

"No, I'm good. I think I'll adopt him." Olivia smiled and gave the dog's muzzle a gentle touch. "Do you, uh, know why the shelter closed down?"

"The owner got sick." Four words, not nearly enough words to encompass the slow, painful decline of Bridget Tuttle. For the first time in her life, Diana had found herself wishing she'd gone into people medicine instead of animal medicine, because she'd sat by Bridget's bedside, doing nothing but feeling helpless and trying to ease the pain of her mother's decline and her losing battle against pancreatic cancer.

But in the end, her mother had cut Diana out of the will, leaving what few possessions Bridget had to a stranger up in Boston, some woman by the last name of MacDonald or something. That after-death slap had stung. Still did. Diana, a veterinarian, should have inherited the shelter. She'd tried, a hundred times, to talk her mother into resurrecting it, promising to help get it running again, maybe even moving her practice over there. But Bridget had always refused, saying she had other plans for the property.

Plans that didn't include her daughter. Her child. Why would her mother do that?

Diana had thought she and her mother had no secrets. Turned out she'd been naïve about that, too.

Diana fiddled with the pen and wondered when it would get easier to accept what her mother had done. How she had, in the very end of her life, turned her back on her child. Diana cleared her throat. "The, uh, shelter was shut down a few months ago and no one has reopened it yet."

"I'm sorry," Olivia said.

I'm sorry? An odd response. Diana studied the woman across from her, then the notes on the chart. Olivia Linscott. A new transplant to Florida, she'd said, who had found the dog in her backyard. Something about Olivia looked familiar, though, but Diana couldn't put her finger on the connection.

Diana refocused on the chart, the dog before her. "I'll need to keep Chance here for a couple of days, but then he should be good to go home."

"Okay." Olivia made no move to leave.

"You can pay at the counter on your way out. Linda will have your bill."

"Okay, thanks." Olivia shifted her feet but still didn't turn away.

"He'll be fine." Diana gave the dog a gentle pat. "We'll take good care of him, and I'll call you if anything changes."

Olivia nodded. Stayed where she was.

Okay. Clearly, another owner reluctant to say good-bye, to trust her furry baby to strangers. Diana bent over to scoop up the dog. She turned toward the door that led to the surgery behind the exam rooms and reached for the handle.

"Diana?"

She pivoted back at the sound of Olivia's voice. Weird for a customer to call her by her first name. "Did you have a question, Miss Linscott?"

Olivia swallowed. She had taken a hold of the exam table, and her knuckles whitened with her grip. Was she that worried about the dog?

"Can I ask you something?" Olivia said, her gaze on the exam table.

"Uh, sure." Maybe Olivia had gotten really attached to this stray. Diana did a little mental prep of her usual speech about the dogs in her care, and how Chance would be fine in the kennels for a couple of days while he recuperated.

"Did you . . ." Olivia paused, took in a breath, released it, then raised her gaze to Diana's. "Did you know Bridget Tuttle?"

The question hit Diana like a left hook. She backed up a

step, until the doorknob poked her in the hip. "She's my mother. Well, she was my mother. She . . . passed away."

"I know."

Diana looked at Olivia—really looked at her, seeing her for the first time as more than the owner of a patient, and in that instant, Diana made the connection. It was in Olivia's green eyes, a green like her own, like her mother's, a dark, forest green unique to the Tuttle girls.

Before Olivia opened her mouth, Diana knew what Olivia was going to say. Knew why the name had rung a bell. For a second, Diana wanted to tell her to stop, not to speak the words out loud, not to turn Diana's life upside down.

But Olivia didn't hear that mental plea. She gave Diana a tentative smile, then exhaled a deep breath and said, "I'm your sister."

Seven

∞

Three days.

Luke stayed in his house, staying away from the windows, telling himself he didn't need to get involved. He'd done his good deed for the week by bringing Olivia to the dog. She'd taken it to the vet, and probably gotten it medicated and bandaged.

The dog was fine, just fine. Then why did he keep on waiting for the familiar scratching at his door? Why did he worry about an animal that wasn't even his?

And why did he keep thinking about a woman who had brought nothing but trouble to his life? Yet think about her he did. All the time. When he rolled out of bed, he wondered if she was next door, brewing coffee. When she came home at night, he wondered if she ate alone like he did, in a chair in front of a TV playing something inane. And when he went to bed, he wondered whether she was doing the same—and what exactly she was wearing, or not wearing, when she climbed between the sheets.

"Ridiculous," he muttered to himself, and headed down

the hall, away from the kitchen, where it was all too easy to walk outside and show he cared.

As he did, he passed the dining room. His step faltered. His hand automatically went to the wall for the light switch. He flicked it on, then off almost as fast. The brightness was too much, too . . . bright. He preferred the dim light filtering past the blinds, just enough to outline the shapes in the room.

His gaze caught on the bright white squares a few feet away. The medals, still packed in their cardboard boxes. Medals he never wanted, never earned or deserved. Medals he would give back in a second if it would change anything.

"Damn you. Just . . . damn you." He backhanded the stack of boxes and sent them clattering to the floor. He heaved a breath, but it didn't ease the tight, sharp pain in his chest.

Against the wall he could make out the slim frame of his bike. For an instant, he could feel the wind riffling down his back, hear the *swish-swish* of the tires against the road, feel the rush of exhilaration as he raced down a long, sloping hill . . .

His hand skimmed over the hard rubber wheel. The tire spun with soft, almost silent clicks, spinning easily beneath his touch, whispering a tempting song in the quiet. *Feel the wind against your skin, the pavement beneath your seat. Get outside, enjoy the world again. Ride . . .*

Luke jerked the wheel to a stop. He wouldn't be riding this or any bike, not now, maybe not ever. Or jogging again, or doing anything that required vision. He missed the adrenaline rush of a good workout, the mindless pounding of his body, the sweaty exhilaration at the end. He missed doing something that forced his lungs to expand, his body to work harder, faster. He wasn't the kind of man who sat around all day—

And yet that was what he had done for months.

The urge, no, need to do *something* gnawed at him like a rat. It was Saturday morning, and for ten years, he'd spent his Saturdays running or biking, something that got him outside, worked up a sweat, pounded out the week's stresses, and got him as close to flying as he could be on the ground.

He closed his eyes, and in his head, he was out there again, hitting the pavement, while birds dipped into the glistening waters of the ocean and the soft caress of a spring breeze rippled down his skin. He inhaled the sweet tang of the ocean, mingled with the crisp scent of fresh-cut—

Those days had passed. He needed to quit thinking about what used to be. But as he turned away, he misjudged the turn and elbowed the bike, sending the Cannondale crashing to the floor. Luke cursed and bent to pick the bike up again.

He jerked the carbon frame back into place. As he did, his knee collided with the footlocker beside the bike. Pain shot up his leg. A fast string of cursing didn't ease the pain but sure made him feel better.

He started to turn away, to limp back to the sofa. To re-treat, as he had done so many times before. As his hand left the bike's frame, a sudden fierce yearning for the life he used to have, the man he used to be, rose in his chest. He paused in the dim light, the dust tickling his nostrils.

"Goddammit," he said again, but the curse had become a sob, a tear in his throat. He dropped to his knees beside the footlocker, his hands reaching along the sharp, hard corners, the smooth metal hinges, then back to the hasp at the center. The open lock sat heavy in his palm.

In his mind, he could see what wasn't much more than a shadowed rectangle in the dim light. He knew every inch of the black footlocker, its sturdy body, its brass hardware, the silver lock on the front. A gift from his grandmother on the day he signed up for the Coast Guard. *So you have somewhere to put all those medals they're going to give you*, she'd said.

If she only knew.

He turned, shifted onto the floor, and lifted the lid. His hand snaked beneath the folded uniforms, the leather shoe-polishing kit, the pristine white T-shirts. He stopped when he brushed against a thick folded paper, then the glossy surface of a photograph.

Joe.

Like an electric spark, the memory slammed into Luke, vivid, real, as if he were back there, two months ago, taking the helo up. The SAR alarm blaring in the station, the booming of the ops watchstander's voice. Fishing vessel taking on water, five souls on board. Weather is a bitch, snow mixed with rain, wind gusting up to forty knots, swells up to twenty feet in frigid waters off Alaska's coast.

"Jesus Christ, Ace. My mother could do a better job with that takeoff," Joe said, as he settled his helmet on his head, his smile bright in the darkened interior of the helo.

"You going to be a backseat driver again?" It was a familiar argument, one that had been raging since flight school. Every mission, the two of them debated who had the better helo skills. Neither wanted to concede or admit to a draw. Instead, they teased each other like brothers every time they were in the air.

"Hey, if you get all tuckered out, I'll be glad to take over the stick," Joe said, his voice a slightly muffled staccato in Luke's helmet. "You might need your energy for tonight when we hit the bar and score some pretty ladies to take home. That is, if you ever find a woman who meets your high dating standards."

"Hey, I'm just waiting for your little sister to come on the market again."

"My sister has taste, dude. She'd never go for a slacker like you."

"If she has taste, then why is she related to you?"

Joe grinned and flattened a hand against his chest. "Because I'm irresistible."

That last smile hung in Luke's memory. Heartbreaking. Bittersweet. One quick smile, and in the next moment, the shit hit the fan and Joe had never smiled again.

Luke stumbled to his feet, clutching the paper and the photograph. The last photo he had of Joe, taken in some seedy bar near AIRSTA Kodiak, the two of them celebrating after a mission. One dark hair, one blond, raising beers to the camera, arms around each other's shoulders, goofy grins on their faces. Mike had taken the picture, taken it a month before—

Before Luke's mistakes had killed his best friend.

His fingers skimmed over the paper, thick bond paper, folded three times, then in half again, creased from being in Joe's locker ever since they'd landed at Kodiak and realized the danger they'd be facing.

The letter. The one almost every guy in the military wrote and hoped like hell would never get sent. Then came that day—

The helo pitched and rolled in the violent Alaska storm, as if Mother Nature were getting revenge on the humans who had soiled her beautiful land. The rescue swimmer's cable whipped up and down in the powerful wind, making the thick steel seem as light as dental floss. Joe turned in the co-pilot's seat, the ending already written on his face. "Promise me, Luke. If anything happens to me—"

"Don't say that shit." Luke held his death grip on the controls and issued a silent prayer. "Let's get this mission done, get back to town, and get drunk like we always do."

But Joe had known. Damn it, he had known. Joe cursed a prayer as the winds tossed the helo like a stuffed animal in a dryer, and the cable jerked, and the bottom fell out of Luke's stomach.

Joe's eyes gleamed bright in the darkness and his voice rose above the whine of the engine. "Promise me, Luke. Please."

He'd held Joe's gaze for one long second while time stood still and a glimmer of hope remained in Luke's chest. "I promise."

Sharp, agonizing pain shot through Luke's heart, cut off his airway. Hot tears rushed to his eyes, and this time he didn't stop them. He let them fall, until the tears became sobs that threatened to tear him in two. He collapsed to the dining room floor and rocked like a child, clutching the photograph, and hating himself.

Promise me.

Joe had asked one thing of him, one simple thing, and Luke had sat here in the dark and let Joe down. Again.

Luke sucked in a deep breath, then shoved off from the footlocker and got to his feet. No more of this shit. He'd been living in the dark too damned long. It was time to face what lurked in the shadows he'd been avoiding.

He retrieved an envelope and a stamp from the hutch drawer, scrawled an address he knew by heart onto the front, and slid the letter into the envelope. He added a second piece of paper, writing *Joe wanted you to have this*, then sealed the envelope. Before he could think twice, he crossed to the front door. He snagged his sunglasses, then stepped out into the bright Florida sunshine.

Three feet down the walkway, he stopped, the envelope a heavy brick in his hand. Everything in him wanted to turn back, to shove all of this crap deep into the footlocker again.

To take the coward's way out.

He heard a rustling, then spied a familiar golden body heading his way. The dog sauntered over to him from Olivia's yard, its movements slow, its tail glinting gold in the sunlight as it wagged back and forth at a furious pace. The golden sidled up to Luke and pressed his cold nose against Luke's bare leg. As if the dog knew, understood.

A friend, when Luke needed one most. Luke hesitated only a second, then reached down and buried his hand in the dog's soft fur. "Hey, buddy. Glad to see you up and about."

Luke's hand traveled down the golden's body, shifting his touch to a gentle one when he hit the shaved area along one flank. The bare skin startled him, and his hand followed it to the hard edges of a bandage and tape. "Been through a lot, haven't you?"

The dog's tail just kept on thumping against the back of Luke's leg. Silent assent.

"You and me both." In his other hand, Luke fingered the envelope. He thought of the bandages and wounds he had. Wounds he wasn't sure would ever heal. All the while, the dog pressed against him, friendly, happy, as if he hadn't been found half-starved and injured a few days earlier. Even now, ready to start over, to trust again, to open his heart to humans.

"All right," Luke said, to the dog, to himself, to the envelope. "All right." Then he made the journey down the driveway to the mailbox. The dog kept pace beside Luke, so close his tail tickled the skin of Luke's calves. The dog dropped to his haunches, waiting while Luke opened the plastic door, slid the envelope in, and propped up the red flag.

"All right," Luke said again, then lowered himself beside the dog and buried his face in the golden's fur.

Greta loved her son, she really did, but there were days when she could see a viable case for throttling him. "How did I raise such a stubborn child?" she asked Edward.

He sat across from her in a corner booth at Suzy's Family Dining. The breakfast crowd of snowbirds filled the cozy country-themed restaurant, strategically located a block away from Golden Years. Suzy herself often played hostess and pitched in to clear tables or carry orders. The scent of bacon and coffee filled the air, and the low hum of conversation rose and fell in waves.

Edward arched a brow. "You, of all people, are wondering where I got my stubborn gene from?"

Goodness, what was with people calling her stubborn lately? Didn't they see she was just trying to do what was right for her grandson? That made her loving, not mulish. Well, maybe a little mulish. But for a good cause, so it didn't count.

She and Edward visited this topic at least once a week, during their morning breakfasts. She always asked if he'd seen Luke lately, and Edward always had a reason why he hadn't visited his only child. Too busy, too much travel . . . whatever. She'd gotten tired of the standoff game these two played and the wall between them that neither seemed interested in breaking down.

"I might be stubborn, but I'm also reasonable," she said. "You aren't being reasonable."

Edward scowled. It was an expression Greta knew well because she often saw it on the other stubborn Winslow male—Luke. "I have tried to talk to my son, Mother, and he is not interested in talking with me. Besides, I've been traveling—"

"Excuses. Again." Greta reached for the syrup, ignored Mr. Bossy Pants's pointed disapproval, and sent her pancakes swimming in a maple pond. If it were up to Edward, Greta would be eating nothing but vegetables and salmon all day, and taking enough vitamins to choke a horse. She'd gotten to eighty-three without his help and by God, she was going to get to eighty-four the same way. Just to watch the constipated look on Edward's face, Greta added a pat of butter to her pancakes, too. "Luke needs his family right now, more than ever."

The waitress came by just then, saving Edward from answering. Greta sat back while the girl refilled their coffee mugs. The girl's name flitted away from Greta's brain, though Greta remembered the waitress was Merle Parker's granddaughter, a little spit of a thing, barely out of high school, but fast on the refills and good with the order details. "Thank you," Greta said.

"No problem, Mrs. Winslow." She slid a piece of paper between the salt and pepper. "There's your check, whenever you're ready."

Edward was already reaching for his wallet. Greta put up a hand to stop him. "Is your ass on fire?" she asked. "Because we've only been here ten minutes and you're already getting ready to leave."

"I have court in thirty minutes, Mother. I don't have time—"

"You don't want to talk about it, is what you're really saying." Greta shook her head. "I swear, if I hadn't seen your birth, I'd question whether you had any of my DNA. Whether you see it or not, you're a lot like your father, God rest his soul."

Edward snorted. "Dad never had a serious conversation in his life."

Her late husband, Edward senior, had been the only person who could always make her laugh but had also never been one for long talks or big arguments. He'd lived in a bubble that revolved around his law firm and his family and had left the heavy lifting to Greta. He was a good man but never really plugged into the family. Maybe that was where Edward got this distance from, because it sure hadn't come from Greta. "In the end, your father always did what was right. And took care of his family."

That scowl returned to Edward's face. "I have taken care of my family, Mother. I've done nothing *but* do that since Lisa died. I worked seventy hours a week to keep a roof over our heads and food in our bellies and the tuition paid at Luke's school. I was there for him."

"You were there for him financially, yes, but he needed a father who gave him love, acceptance, support. Then and now." Ever since the day her daughter-in-law had died in a car accident, leaving Edward a widowed, clueless single father, Greta had stepped in as surrogate mother to Luke. She'd hoped in time Edward would come around and do the job himself. Instead he'd worked. And worked. And worked. And his son had grown up without him hardly noticing. Now they were two adults who shared little more than the same blood type, and it hurt Greta's heart to see it.

Edward shook his head, then slid a twenty in with the bill. "That's where you're wrong. He's never needed any of those things from me."

Greta watched him walk away. She pushed the pancakes to the side, her appetite gone. How she wanted her boys to bury the hatchet, before it was too late and she was gone. As much as she liked to think she was going to be around a long time, just to torture Harold Twohig, Greta could hear the ticking of Mother Nature's clock. Every year, that witch seemed to speed up the second hand. Which meant Greta needed to take some drastic measures to get these two stubborn men to stop butting heads and instead start *thinking* with their heads.

Eight

❧

Three days.

Olivia had dropped that little DNA connection bombshell in her sister's lap, and then, after an awkward couple minutes of small talk, grabbed her purse and left. Diana's office had called regularly with updates on Chance's progress, but Diana herself hadn't called. And when Olivia had gone in to pick up Chance yesterday, Diana hadn't been there.

The dog had a ways to go in his recovery, but he had put on a few pounds in the days he'd been at the vet's. His eyes seemed brighter, his coat shinier. He was up and moving around within an hour of Olivia bringing him home, all signs she took as good portents for the future.

For three days, Olivia went to work, came home, worked on the house, and called it therapy. She ripped down wallpaper, tore up carpet, and demolished walls, until she collapsed into bed at the end of the day, exhausted and sweaty. At night, Chance curled up on the floor by her bed, while Miss Sadie took the foot of the queen-sized bed, her little head hanging over the edge, watching the newcomer with wary interest.

Today was Saturday, which gave Olivia a full day of working on the house. More like destroying it, given how much trash she'd carted outside. Earlier this morning, Chance had wandered next door when Olivia let him out, something he'd done the day before, too. As far as Olivia could tell, Chance spent his time outside hanging out either under the shelter's roof or in Luke's yard. The dog really seemed to have taken a shine to Luke, whether Luke liked it or not. The thought made her smile. Miss Sadie stayed glued to Olivia's heels, a bouncing bundle of energy, glad to have her mistress's undivided attention.

With a huff, Olivia stuffed one more bag into the trash barrel, then tipped the brown plastic container on its wheels and hauled it down the driveway. The wheels groaned under the burden. Just as she set the barrel beside the boxes she'd hauled to the sidewalk earlier, Olivia saw Greta marching down the sidewalk, carrying a white plastic bag. Her bright blue sweater and pale gray pants offset the white curls on her head and the white sneakers she wore. She had on oversized sunglasses that nearly dwarfed her features.

She started waving the second she saw Olivia. "Olivia! Just the person I wanted to see!"

Olivia laughed. "You just did see me. Yesterday. At Golden Years. And I'll be back there Monday." She brushed the bangs off her forehead with the back of her hand. "But it'll be nice to have some company. I've started having political debates with the dogs. Definitely a sign I've been working on this house too long and spending too much time by myself."

Solitude had been the one by-product of moving to Rescue Bay that Olivia had underestimated. She was used to having friends nearby, relatives a quick T ride away. She talked to her mom almost every day, but outside her job at Golden Years, her social life was almost nonexistent. She missed the impromptu visits of friends and the last-minute nights on the town or trips to the mall and girls' day at the beauty salon. Soon as she had the bulk of the repairs done on this house, she vowed to work on making some friends in Rescue Bay.

Then she thought of the ten-page to-do list she'd created, and realized she might be collecting social security before that happened.

"I bet you haven't eaten a single healthy thing today," Greta said, leaning in and giving Olivia an inquisitive eye, looking a lot like Olivia's own grandmother when she did that. "Probably wolfed down one of those cardboard granola bars for breakfast and worked straight through lunch."

Olivia chuckled. Greta knew her well. "Is that dietary criticism from the woman who throws out everything green on her plate?" Olivia wagged a finger at Greta. "Don't think the kitchen staff at Golden Years hasn't noticed you stuffing the broccoli into your napkin."

Greta raised her chin. "I am old enough and wise enough to say no to vegetables. At my age, I should be allowed to eat cake all day."

"I agree. Though I don't think Doc Harper would."

Greta waved off the mention of the internist. "That man thinks brussels sprouts are delicious. If you ask me, he isn't right in the head." She hoisted the bag in her hand. "That's why I brought us some world-famous Rescue Bay deli turkey sandwiches. *If* your world is composed of downtown Rescue Bay, that is." Greta rolled her eyes. "That Randy has illusions of grandeur. He always did like to exaggerate—just ask his ex-girlfriends."

"Greta!"

"Hey, it's a small town. People tell you way more than you want to know." Greta made another face, her nose wrinkling. "And believe me, there are some things I know about people that would give a clown nightmares."

What else do you know about Bridget Tuttle?

That question had lingered on Olivia's tongue for days, ever since she'd told the women in the quilting club that she owned the house. But every time she got close to asking them for more information, Olivia changed her mind. The craving to know was quickly overpowered by her fear of what she'd find out. Would the answers be worse than the questions?

After all, her sister didn't want anything to do with Olivia, and her biological mother had left Olivia nothing more than a huge headache of a renovation project. As far as Olivia could tell, Bridget hadn't been very social or interested in anything other than the rescue shelter. Olivia had come all the way to Florida with a dream of a mother who had loved her, had left her some kind of letter or journal, or some kind of answers, and instead there'd been nothing. The connection she'd always craved turned out to be as whisper-thin as the clouds in the sky.

Greta pressed the bag of sandwiches into Olivia's hands. "Here. Have lunch with an old lady. Then we can both tell Doc Harper we did one healthy thing today. The man will probably keel over with joy."

Olivia readied an excuse, thinking of the work still left to do before the sun set today, but Greta was right. She had barely had time to do much more than gulp a cup of coffee and gnaw on a day-old bagel for breakfast. She accepted the bag with a grateful thanks and peeked inside. "There are three sandwiches in here."

"Oh, did I forget to mention I brought one for my grandson, too?" Greta pressed a hand to her chest and shook her head. "I tell you, when you get old, your mind just becomes a sieve."

Just the mention of Luke Winslow sent a rush of heat through Olivia. That man . . . oh my, could that man kiss. She could only imagine how good he would be at everything else in bed. He was also a distraction she didn't need. She'd thought when she met Luke that maybe he'd make a great back-on-her-feet fling. Instead, the more she got to know him, the more she uncovered a complicated, layered man who was anything but a fling.

She needed to steer clear of that. She'd already screwed up one marriage and had no intentions of adding to her personal relationship detritus. Even with a man like him, who tempted her in ways in which she hadn't been tempted in a long, long time.

"I'll, uh, let you get over to Luke's," Olivia said, taking one of the paper-wrapped sandwiches before handing the bag back to Greta. "Thanks again for lunch."

"You're welcome, dear." Greta took a step forward. Stopped. Winced. Let out a sharp gasp. "Goodness gracious. There are days when this hip just likes to bite me back." She rubbed at the outside of her leg and grimaced. "Lord knows what I was thinking, walking all the way here from Golden Years. Sometimes I forget I'm not twenty anymore." Her face scrunched and she took a couple of slow, painful steps down the sidewalk. "See you later, Olivia. Oooh, ouch."

"Wait. Let me help you." Olivia put out an arm and waited for Greta to slip hers into the crook. Olivia took the bulk of Greta's weight, and then the two of them made their way the few hundred yards from her house to Luke's driveway, then down the walkway to the front door. Along the route, Greta winced a couple more times. Olivia resisted the urge to chide her for walking so far and instead vowed to go easy on Greta at her next therapy appointment. Stubborn and determined, Greta had probably overdone it.

"You doing okay?" Olivia asked.

"Yes, yes. Almost there."

They climbed the three porch steps, slowly, with Greta putting one foot on a step, then the other, before exhaling and taking the next step in the same manner. When they reached the door, Greta let out a sigh of relief and leaned on the jamb to push the bell. "Thank you, dear. I appreciate you helping me over here. Now if you could just stay a bit and help me to a chair, I'll call a cab for the trip back. I'd ask Luke, but he's . . . well, he has his own challenges."

That meant seeing Luke. But Olivia couldn't just leave Greta standing on the porch. "Of course, of course."

The door opened and Chance squeezed out between Luke and the door, his tail thwapping a happy beat against the wall. Olivia gave the dog a tender pat. "So this is where you got off to again, you silly dog."

"He's always over here. Like he thinks he lives here or something."

Olivia tousled the dog's ears, then raised her gaze to Luke. For once, he didn't have his sunglasses on, which made the full force of his blue eyes hit her hard and fast, like lightning. The scar had healed more, no longer an angry red, but now faded to a dark pink. He'd shaved, and the smoothness of his cheeks and jaw made her think of that kiss. Lord help her, she wanted another one like that. Right now. Damn.

She redirected her attention to the dog. "I'm sorry about the dog. Chance comes over here every chance he gets."

"Chance?" Luke asked.

She shrugged. "That's what I named him. When I went to the vet's they needed a name for the chart, and Chance sounded good to me. He's gotten a second chance at life, and I think all of us deserve that, don't you think so?"

"Yeah, I do." His voice was low, quiet.

"I think he's attached to you," Olivia said, giving the dog a tender pat.

"Clearly, he didn't get the memo about me being an ogre." Luke's gaze lingered on her features for a long, hot second before his attention went to his grandmother, still clutching Olivia's arm. "Grandma, are you okay?"

"Just that darn hip. I'm fine. I brought you lunch." She gestured toward Olivia, who held up the bag from the deli. "Lord knows you'd die of malnourishment if you were left to your own devices."

"Pizza contains all four food groups, you know." His features softened, and he gave Greta a grateful nod. "But thank you. I appreciate you thinking of me."

Whenever Luke interacted with his grandmother, Olivia saw another side of him, a side that cared, worried, tended. She suspected that was the real Luke underneath all the anger, but she still didn't understand where the bitter side came from. What had happened to bring out this other Luke, a man who lived in the dark and growled like a dog backed into a corner?

Luke's attention swiveled toward Olivia again. Like a spotlight. A smirk flitted across his lips. "And thank you too."

"Oh, I didn't—"

"We better get these sandwiches out of the wrappers before they get soggy," Greta interrupted, taking the bag from Olivia and thrusting it into Luke's hands. "Aren't you going to invite us in to eat with you? Be a good host, Lucas, and don't leave us ladies to swelter on the porch."

For the first time since she'd met him, Olivia saw Luke get flustered. He sputtered, then stopped, frustration in his brows and his stony expression. She could tell he wanted to refuse but would clearly never deny his beloved grandmother anything. "Of course, Grandma. You know how much I *love* to entertain," he said.

Greta shrugged at the dry sarcasm and patted her grandson's cheek. "It does a body good to socialize. Keeps you from talking to yourself."

Luke sighed but opened the door wider and stepped aside. Greta headed in first, followed by Chance, then Olivia.

"And no snide remarks about the Early Bachelor décor," Luke said as she passed him.

Olivia grinned and glanced up at him. "I had no idea that pizza boxes and beer cans were de rigueur for accent pieces."

"Don't forget the boxers on the floor," he said against her ear. "They add the perfect touch of I-don't-care-what-the-designer-thinks to the space."

Her face heated and a ribbon of desire unfurled in her gut. A boxers man. Oh. My. Now her mind was picturing his muscular body in a pair of plaid cotton shorts. Showing off a lot more than just his delicious legs. "Those, uh, those might be hard to ignore."

And hard to keep on, should she ever find herself in a bedroom with him. A part of her wanted to journey to that destination. Very, very much.

A grin curved up one side of his face. "I'll keep that in mind."

Greta was already in the kitchen, bustling around,

grabbing plates and napkins. "Come on, you two. Sit, sit," she said as they came into the kitchen, with Chance taking a space by the back door. The golden let out a contented sigh and slid to the ground, watching the humans.

"Did I ever tell you my grandmother is bossy?" Luke said to Olivia. But he placed a kiss on Greta's cheek and did as she asked.

"Someone has to tell you what to do and take care of you, you big lug. At least until you get yourself a wife." She wagged a finger at him.

His face paled two shades. "Grandma, I'm not—"

"Oh my goodness!" Greta popped to her feet. "Will you look at the time? I'm meeting the girls for lunch. I darn near forgot. Luke, you can have my sandwich. I'll see you both tomorrow."

Then she was gone, whirling out of the kitchen so fast, Chance let out a bark of surprise. The front door shut with a decisive click. And Olivia and Luke were alone.

"What the heck was that?" Olivia asked.

"That was us getting snookered by a woman more than twice our age." He chuckled and shook his head.

Olivia had fallen for the entire hurting hip act, hook, line, and sinker. She'd never imagined Greta would try to fix her up with Luke. But then again, hadn't Greta talked about Luke almost every time Olivia saw her? Olivia glanced at the table and realized this had been Greta's plan from the first *ouch*. "Well, that explains why she only laid out two plates."

"My grandmother is smart as a fox but as obvious as a billboard. Anyway, if you want to go, I'll understand. She kind of roped you into this."

"If it's okay, I'd like to stay. I've . . ." She swallowed, then met those blue eyes, those hypnotic, tempting eyes. The loneliness that had bubbled inside her earlier disappeared, replaced by something else, something far more dangerous. Yet she didn't move, didn't change course. "I've been alone a lot lately and I'm tired of my own company. It'd be nice to talk to someone who isn't covered in fur. I mean, if you don't mind me staying."

"I don't mind, Olivia." He slid one of the sandwiches over to her, and a grin lit his face. He leaned in closer, close enough for her to catch the dark, woodsy scent of his cologne, get a glimpse of his hard, muscular chest beneath the faded gray tee that he wore, and close enough to want him to move closer still. "But I can't guarantee I won't growl. Or bite."

"That's okay, Luke," she said, her voice dropping into the same deep, dark range as his. She held his gaze for one long, hot moment. "Because sometimes I bite, too."

Nine

∞

Diana hated being on this side of the desk. She fought the urge to pace, to tap her foot, to sigh, to do anything that would betray her nerves. God, she really was a total introvert, wasn't she? No wonder she spent her day with furry creatures.

Her gaze landed on her son. He had a brown mop of hair, with laughing blue eyes and an infectious smile that she saw far too rarely nowadays. He'd worn his favorite jeans, shredded at the hem, frayed at the knees, and reluctantly put a blue button-down shirt over his favorite BRING ME THE HORIZON T-shirt. She'd tried to nix the jeans, then given up the fight. Sometimes, she'd learned, it was easier to say yes to one thing and no to another.

Jackson slumped in the chair, doing his best impression of a sullen teenager. Most days, Jackson earned an Oscar in that category. She worried that he had gotten a little too thin, his skin a little too pale. The boy, no, not a boy anymore, a teenager edging toward young man, could put back more food than anyone she knew, but it seemed like none of the calories stuck.

For the thousandth time, she wondered if she could have done things differently and had a different outcome for her son. Chosen a better man to be Jackson's father, or worked less often, or gone to the playground more when Jackson was little. If she had, would her son be less angry now? He seemed to have developed a perpetual chip on his shoulder, and she worried that it was more than normal teenage "the world sucks" attitude.

The only person who'd connected easily with Jackson had been Bridget. Jackson and his grandmother had had a special bond, and when she died, his attitude toward Diana had shifted to outraged defiance, as if he blamed her for their loss. Diana wished she could find a way back to the little boy who'd asked her for one more reading of *Ferdinand the Bull*, the same boy who would snuggle up on the couch at the end of the day and snack on peanut butter and Ritz crackers.

Beside her, Jackson let out a dramatic, impatient sigh. "How long do we have to be here?"

"It shouldn't take too long."

"Whatev." Jackson looked at his nails, then picked at an errant thread on his shirt. "This stupid school isn't going to want me. I don't know why we're wasting our time."

Diana bit back a sigh and prayed for patience.

Jackson got out of his chair, headed for the window, and blew a circle onto the glass. "I don't understand why I can't stay where I am."

Or at the place before that. Or the one before that. Jackson knew the reasons, and Diana didn't reiterate them.

Three schools in the past two years. All she wanted for her son was stability and had found far too little of that. She prayed this school, with its stomach-twisting price tag and stellar reputation, would be the right one for her son. Paying the tuition would mean some sacrifices, but in the end, if Jackson was happy, it would be worth every dollar.

"You'll enjoy it here, Jackson. They have a heck of a science program."

He didn't respond. Just stared out the window some more.

Jackson, her only child. Once, Diana had dreamed of having three, four, maybe even five kids. A whole houseful of noise to compensate for the silence of her childhood. Sean hadn't wanted kids at all, and she'd foolishly hoped when Jackson was born that Sean would fall in love with their incredible son and change his mind. He hadn't.

Now, ironically, Diana was the one with a sister. A *sister*. The very thing she'd prayed for as a child but wasn't so sure she wanted or needed at this late stage in life. She hadn't even realized that Olivia Linscott and Olivia MacDonald were the same person. Her married name, Olivia had told Diana. She was divorced now, and ready to make a new start in Rescue Bay, and hoping to get to know Diana, and through Diana, their mother. Diana sighed. She'd deal with the whole Olivia thing after she figured out a direction for Jackson. Her son came first and always would.

The door opened and an older, trim man in a designer suit strode into the room. He had a shock of white hair and light blue eyes that seemed to zero in on and assess Diana, then soften when his gaze dropped to Jackson. "Hello, hello. Nice to meet you. I'm Ron Miller, principal here."

Diana rose, shook with the principal. "Nice to meet you."

Miller turned to Jackson. "And you, young man, you must be Jackson."

Diana sent her son a warning glare. They'd been over this a hundred times in the car. *Don't play angry teenager, not today.*

Jackson hesitated, then worked a polite smile to his face and put out his hand. "Nice to meet you . . . sir."

She let out the breath she'd been holding. Miller grinned, then waved Jackson back into the visitor's chair.

Miller came around his desk and took a seat. He laced his hands on the desk, then met Diana's gaze. "This is just a preliminary meeting. No pressure, just a general get-to-know-you, and so you can get to know us here at Prince. We want to make sure both sides feel a good fit before we get too far into the process. Okay?"

Diana nodded. Jackson raised one shoulder, then let it drop.

The tolerant smile stayed on Miller's lips. "Tell me, Miss Tuttle, why do you want your son to attend Prince?"

Diana shifted in her chair. "It offers the perfect education for him. Jackson's got a real interest in science, and I want to do everything I can to help him pursue that."

Miller nodded, then turned to Jackson. "And you? Why do you want to go here, young man?"

"My mother said it'll be good for me."

Not the answer Diana wanted to hear, but not the worst answer he could have given. She worked up a smile of agreement.

Miller chuckled. "Well, at least you're honest, Jackson. And you're smart. Your test scores were"—he paused to flip through a few papers on his desk—"quite good. Surprising, even."

"So he's in?" Diana had worked for months to get Jackson into Prince Academy. The school had a wait list as long as her arm, and just to secure this interview, she'd had to ask the owner of one of her patients for a favor. Sending Jackson here would mean a longer commute in the morning, along with the belt-tightening, but Prince Academy offered the kind of education that could ensure Jackson's future, and that meant more to her than anything.

"Well, let's cover a few more issues first." Miller leaned across the desk. "Does Jackson's father agree with sending him to this school?"

She bristled. Even without mentioning his name, just the thought of her ex sharpened Diana's spine. "Jackson's father isn't involved in any decisions." She didn't add that she had kicked Sean out for good a year and a half ago. He'd been no kind of father to their son, and the chaos Sean had brought to their household had lingered, even after she'd gotten Jackson into counseling. Sean had been a sporadic father at best, a horrible influence at worst. One of these days, she'd have to honestly answer Jackson's questions. Hopefully that day was a long way off.

"We'd like to welcome Jackson to our school," Miller said, and then the tolerant smile became a pained look, "but . . ."

She heard the word, and the nerves in her stomach turned to a heavy, thick stone. "But?"

"But there's a problem." The principal steepled his fingers and looked at Jackson as he spoke. "You have gone to three different schools in two years, which concerns us greatly. Your grades were good, but you had many discipline issues at those previous schools."

She tried a smile. "Jackson is simply . . . an energetic boy who really needs to be challenged. I think he was bored in the other schools."

But it was more than that, and both Diana and the principal knew it. Jackson had been through so much in his short life, and losing his grandmother after his father's sudden disappearance from his life had multiplied those issues. She thought of her son, so angry, so scared, and so worried about the sand shifting under his feet. He was acting out, the psychologist said, trying to get attention, to feed that constant worry that he'd be alone. *Give it time*, the counselor said. *Time and patience. He'll find his way.*

Right now, all Diana wanted to find was a school that would provide stability and a challenge for Jackson. He was attending Rescue Bay Middle School, a good school, for sure, but one that had made it clear Jackson's days there were numbered. He'd spent more time in the principal's office than the classroom. At the last parent-teacher meeting, the principal had suggested she "explore other educational options."

"Mrs. . . . Miss Tuttle." Miller pressed his lips together, then met her eyes with a kind, work-with-me gaze. "We need to be realistic. Jackson may not find his best home at a school like this. We have quite a long list of expectations for our students."

Jackson let out a snort. She covered his hand with her own. He shifted away from her.

"I like you, Jackson," Miller said. "You're a very bright boy, and a very energetic one. You're also very astute about scientific principles and had above-average test scores in that area, not to mention an amazing science fair project last year. You won the state competition with that research about asthma and air quality. That was high-school-level work, which normally would make you the perfect fit for us." Miller turned his attention back to Diana. "But his discipline record gives me pause. Prince Academy takes only the best students, the ones who are most committed to their education."

Unspoken message: Spending a good part of the week in suspension didn't show educational commitment.

"Jackson really wants to go here and—"

Miller shook his head. "I'll reconsider his application in a couple of months, provided his disciplinary issues are resolved."

Meaning, get her kid straightened out and there might be a slim chance he'd be able to attend the school. It was a message she'd heard before and had expected, even as she'd hoped Jackson's academics would outshine his discipline record. She nodded, thanked the principal, then got to her feet and headed out the door, with Jackson following behind her.

The defeat hit her hard. When was all this going to get easier? When would she and Jackson find their way again? Diana felt like she'd been living in limbo for the past few weeks, and all she wanted was some forward motion.

Her life was a disaster, her son was a mess, and on top of that, she had a long-lost sister she'd never known about living here in town, in the house that Diana had hoped would be hers one day. Jackson might be the one in counseling, but right now, Diana could use some therapy of her own.

"Let's go get some ice cream," she said to her son. "Chocolate chunk. Sound good?"

Jackson sat in the car, a silent angry stone.

A double scoop, Diana decided. With extra whipped cream.

* * *

The sandwich could have been made of glue and cardboard for all Luke noticed and tasted. The second Olivia said, "Sometimes I bite, too," his libido had roared. She sat a foot away, but still he cursed the expanse of the kitchen table. He wanted to touch her, to taste her.

This close, he could see the outline of her breasts under the dark-blue T-shirt. Could catch the light floral fragrance of her perfume, mingled with the coconut in her shampoo. Thank God for the table, because otherwise his desire would be broadcast, loud and clear.

He shifted in his seat. *Focus on something other than her breasts, Romeo.* "You still channeling Bob Vila next door?"

"More like Murphy's law, but yeah." She got to her feet, and when she did, Luke noticed she was wearing dark shorts that emphasized her tight butt, her shapely peach legs. He bit back a groan. Olivia crossed the kitchen, then loaded the plates into the sink.

Luke rose and followed with the empty glasses. Instead of returning to the table, he stood beside her, grabbing a towel to dry as she set about washing the few dishes in the sink. It was such a scene of domesticity, of normalcy, that for five seconds, Luke could believe he was an ordinary man in an ordinary kitchen leading an ordinary life with two-point-five kids and a dog in the yard.

It was . . . nice.

Olivia rinsed a plate and handed it to him. "Have you lived in Rescue Bay long?"

"I grew up here, just a few streets away. Spent most of my childhood with Greta, which was"—he chuckled—"an adventure."

"I bet." She slid the plate under the running rinse water, then handed it to him. "What about your parents? Brothers? Sisters?"

"My mother died when I was three. My dad wasn't good at being a single parent, so Greta stepped in."

"I'm sorry."

"Thanks." He didn't remember much about his mother, only that she had seemed like the polar opposite to his uptight, distant father. His mother had been the one to color pictures with him, to bake cookies in the middle of the day. When he thought of her, he heard her soprano voice singing, everything from pop tunes to lullabies. "As for siblings, I'm the only one."

"I grew up an only child, too."

He grinned. "Look at that. Something we have in common."

"According to your grandmother, that'd be enough to call the preacher."

The thought of that both terrified and warmed him. So he laughed it off as a joke. "My grandmother is a hopeless romantic, but don't tell her I told you so. She'd never admit that out loud."

"That's not such a bad thing to be. I think the world needs more hopeless romantics," Olivia said quietly, circling the next plate with a sponge.

"Are you saying you're a hopeless romantic, too?" he asked.

She snorted. "No. I've seen the reality of how that turns out. So no more getting wrapped up in hearts and flowers and love poems."

"Then I guess we could never be after all, because I'm one hell of a poet."

She laughed, then splashed a handful of soap bubbles at him. "Sure you are."

"I am." He took the glass, dried it, and held it to his mouth like a microphone. "Roses are red, violets are blue, I'm a terrible poet and you are too."

Merry laughter burst out of her. "Oh yeah, you're going to woo the ladies with that one."

"That's my diabolical plan." If not for the dim shadows crowding his line of sight, Luke could almost pretend he was his old self again. The joking and laughter felt odd, yet right at the same time, like slipping into a pair of shoes that had spent too long in the closet.

"So what about this house?" Olivia asked. "How long have you lived here? I was just wondering, because I moved into the place next door without knowing much about it or the shelter."

"I'm not much help there, sorry. I've only lived in this house for a few weeks. I bought it after I enlisted. I was making pretty decent money and wanted an investment. I rented it out while I was away, which paid the mortgage and left me a decent chunk of profit. Grandma was the one who talked me into real estate, but I think she did it because she secretly wanted me to move back here."

"And you did exactly that."

"Yeah, I did." He didn't want to think about the why. If the accident hadn't happened, Luke would still be climbing into the cockpit, still be plucking people out of the frigid waters of Alaska. Still be doing his job, living his dreams.

"Isn't that tough, though? Living on your own when you're . . ."

"Go ahead." He scowled. The reminder, always there, even as he tried to pretend it wasn't. "You can say it. Half blind."

"Can I ask you what happened?" she said.

"No, you can't." He shook his head and cursed himself for barking at her. "Sorry. I just don't like to talk about certain things."

She let out a gust. "You and me both."

"Then let's call a moratorium on talking about all the crappy things in our lives."

"Deal." She handed him a damp glass. "I still can't believe Greta pulled the wool over our eyes like that. Your grandma made it sound like feeding you today was a dire emergency. Maybe it was, considering you are a bachelor who will, I quote, die of malnourishment if left to your own devices."

He patted his belly. "I'm a long way from malnourishment."

"I agree."

"Hey!" he said, flicking the towel at her hip. "Aren't you supposed to stroke my fragile male ego?"

She laughed and dodged the towel the second time. "Truce! Truce! I mean that in a good way."

Just like that, she had eased the mood, tugging him out of the dark place with her light touch, her lyrical voice. He dried the glass and tucked it away. This felt good, better than anything he could remember in a hell of a long time.

"A good way, huh? Well, that definitely strokes my male ego." And more, but he didn't say that out loud. Just being around Olivia did a lot more than pump up his ego.

"Well, maybe I should change tactics. I wouldn't want you to get a swelled head," she said.

"Might be too late for that."

"Oh, I'm so sorry," she said, her teasing tone saying the exact opposite. "I'll try to behave."

The innuendos thickened the tension between them, raised the temperature in the small kitchen. He didn't want this moment to end. Didn't want her to leave.

"You know, I might not be very good at cooking lunch or dinner, but I can make a hell of a breakfast," he said. "If you're ever in the mood for an omelet, you know who to call."

"Oh, really?" She had finished the dishes and turned, putting her back to the draining sink. "Do you deliver?"

He shifted closer to her, his gaze dropping to those tempting lips, then her breasts, then back up to her eyes. God, he wanted her, and all the sass and fire that came in this enticing package of Olivia. "Oh, I do, but my delivery area is very, very limited."

"Well, that might be a problem." She raised her chin, her mouth so close to his that her words whispered across his skin. "Exactly *how* limited?"

"Just upstairs." He thumbed toward the ceiling, then took another step, enough to bring him within touching distance. "Though properly motivated, I can be swayed to deliver a plate next door."

"That's good to know, because sometimes I get cravings for omelets at the oddest times," she said. "And I assume you'd expect a tip?"

"Only if the service is outstanding."

"I suspect"—she took in a breath, her chest rising and falling, her gaze locked on his—"that it would be all that and more."

Desire rushed through him, igniting parts of Luke that had gone dead ever since the accident. He reached up to brush her hair away from her face, telling himself to keep his distance, not to complicate her life. Instead, he drew her closer, until their mouths met and he was tasting the sweetness of Olivia Linscott. She let out a soft sound, curved into him, and opened her mouth against his. Her tongue slipped into his mouth, sending a racing fire through his veins. His erection pressed against his jeans, a painful reminder of how long it had been since he'd been with a woman. God. Damn.

The urge to take her upstairs, to take her to his bedroom and make love to her for the rest of the day, the whole night, until they were both exhausted and spent, rose inside him, fierce, fast. Her pelvis pressed against his, a sweet, agonizing pressure that threatened to undo him.

Then she reached up, her hands coming up to cup his face. Her fingertips brushed his scar, and though it didn't hurt, it sent a shock wave through Luke. He jerked back. What was he doing? He was a man who destroyed things, who hurt the ones he cared about. Who let people down.

Who got them killed.

And a woman like her deserved so much more than Luke Winslow could ever give.

As if on cue, Chance scratched at the door. "Your . . . your dog needs to go out," he said, then cleared his throat and made himself say the next words. "And you should go."

The moment of silence told him the harsh words had hurt her. He refused to feel bad about that. He was doing her a favor. Maybe someday she'd see that and breathe a sigh of relief that she'd dodged a destructive bullet.

"Yeah, I agree," she said. The light warmth had faded from her voice. "It's past time for me to get back on my side of the fence."

He stayed where he was until he heard the door click. Then he turned to the wall, pulled back his fist, and let it fly. His fist exploded into the plaster, and for one brief second, he felt relief. Then the pain hit him all over again.

Like a familiar friend who had overstayed his welcome.

Ten

∞

Every time Olivia thought about Luke's hot-and-cold response, she told herself she didn't need a man like him in her life. Right now, she wanted uncomplicated. Easy. A man who would take her to bed, then leave in the morning, without any messy emotional connections or morning-after regrets. And Luke Winslow was anything but easy.

That didn't stop her from looking out her window every five minutes to see if he was crossing the divide between their properties. Or wondering if she had misread his signals.

Hadn't she learned her lesson when her marriage went south? Scott had been the kind of guy every mother would choose for her daughter. A respectable doctor, intelligent, handsome, soft-spoken. A good man, she'd heard dozens of times before she married.

The ring had barely lost its wedding-day luster before she realized that good man was also a womanizer who had married her because she completed his image, the perfect portrait of a respectable family doctor building his private practice. She'd been nothing more than one more achievement to hang on his wall. A trophy on his arm that he could trot out to patients and colleagues as part of his local-boy-makes-good picture.

If she ever got involved with someone else, she'd be the one calling the relationship shots. She wouldn't be so quick to trust, so blind to shortcomings, and definitely not so fast to open her heart.

Despite the long, hard day of working on the house, sleep refused to come that Saturday night. Olivia tossed and turned, alternately sweating, then freezing, covers off, covers on, and when she did doze off, her dreams were filled with images of Luke.

Sunday morning dawned, and by the time her second cup of coffee kicked in, Olivia had decided she would steer clear of Luke Winslow. She'd come here for answers, for closure, and getting busy with the neighbor didn't bring her either. Every time she was around him, he brought her dangerously close to the very precipice she'd vowed to avoid. The one where she leapt without thinking. She'd done that with the move here, and look how *that* had turned out. No more thoughts of Luke. She'd focus instead on the reason why she was in Rescue Bay—for answers about Bridget.

She sat at the kitchen table, fingering the butterfly necklace, and staring at Diana's business card. Below the office number, she'd listed an emergency contact number.

Her cell rang, dancing across the kitchen table with the vibrations. Olivia scrambled to pick it up, then balanced the phone between her shoulder and her ear as she grabbed another cup of coffee. After her sleepless night, she needed an IV drip of caffeine. "Hello?"

"Olivia?"

The unfamiliar voice jarred Olivia. She'd expected Anna's daily call. "This is her."

"It's Dr. . . . uh, Diana. Your sister? Uh, and vet." The words came out hesitant, unsure, with more questions than answers. The feeling echoed in Olivia's chest.

"Hi. I'm glad to hear from you." Olivia clutched the phone and tried not to let her eagerness explode across the cell connection.

A pause, a bit of silence, then, "I was just wondering how Chance was doing."

"Great. He's great."

"Good. Glad to hear it." The line hummed for a moment. "I was wondering if you could . . . well, the office closes at four tomorrow. Mondays are our early day, and, well, anyway, I was thinking"—Diana paused—"maybe you'd want to chat for a little while after work."

Olivia hadn't realized how much she'd hoped and prayed for Diana to say exactly that until she heard the words. Her sister—and the key to the mother Olivia had never known. "I would love to talk with you," she said. "My last appointment should finish by three, so that works out great. Do you want to meet somewhere? Have some dinner?"

"I don't think this is a conversation for a restaurant. We could meet at my office, but there's always an intern or someone around, checking on the animals," Diana said. "I think this should be . . ."

"Private," Olivia finished.

"Yes."

"We could meet here, if you wanted. That way you could see Chance, too."

Diana agreed, though she sounded reluctant, and Olivia wondered if she'd made the right move. After all, the inheritance of the house had to be a sore point for Diana. But it was too late—the offer had been made.

"I'll see you Monday, then," Diana said, and then she said good-bye and hung up the phone.

Olivia finished her coffee, then took a walk around the house, hoping maybe some elves had come in while she was sleeping to finish the myriad of projects. No such luck. So many things undone, so many things yet to do. With Diana coming over on Monday, Olivia wanted to pull off a renovation miracle, if only to show her sister that she was taking care of their mother's legacy. But her sore muscles and achy back threatened to stage a mutiny if she so much as picked up a hammer. "Miss Sadie, what we need is a few hours off. You up for a ride?"

Miss Sadie yipped, then raced to the door, sitting her butt down to wait, tail swishing against the floor. Chance lurched to his feet and Olivia gave him a sympathetic smile. "Oh, buddy, I don't think you'd like spending the day riding around in the car. I hate to leave you here alone."

Her gaze went to the window, to the gray bungalow next door. Maybe Luke would watch Chance for her. It might be good for the dog, who could use some socialization. Yeah, right. She wasn't attaching a leash to the dog and bringing him next door because she wanted to see Luke again for a little socialization of her own. Yeah, not that at all.

She climbed his porch and was about to knock when she heard the sound of the back door opening and the screen door slamming shut. Chance perked his ears up, then clambered down the steps and around the side of the house, with Olivia tagging behind. Luke stood in his backyard, his back to her.

He had on khaki shorts and a faded red T-shirt. Her gaze landed on his legs—strong, defined, muscular, with heart-shaped calves—and took its sweet time rising. She could almost feel his skin under her palm, the firmness of those thighs against hers . . .

Chance nosed Luke, and he turned around, then looked at her. She jerked her gaze to his face, with a little flicker of guilt at being caught checking him out.

"Hey," he said.

Not much of a greeting, but then again, they hadn't had much of a good-bye the last time they'd seen each other. She put on a face that she hoped said she didn't care that he'd shoved her out the door so fast, there were skid marks on his kitchen floor. "I hate to bother you, especially after yesterday, but I needed someone to watch Chance. I wouldn't ask if I had anyone else to take the dog. Believe me."

"I know you rightly think I'm a jerk, but trust me"—he took a few steps forward—"I was doing you a favor."

She arched a brow. "A favor? Really? Where I come from, that kind of thing is called rude."

"I was saving you from a bad relationship."

"Who said I wanted a relationship?" She parked her fists on her hips and tried to pretend being this close to Luke didn't affect her. Didn't make her want him to kiss her again. For God's sake, she was only here to drop off the dog.

He closed the gap between them and dropped his gaze to her mouth. "You have *relationship* written all over you. You're a settle-down, bake-a-pie-in-the-fall kind of girl."

She snorted. "Not anymore. That didn't get me anywhere but divorced."

He arched a brow. "Do I detect a jaded tone in your voice?"

"Honey, I'm so jaded, you could color me green."

His eyes, his thoughts, all remained hidden by the sunglasses. But a simmering heat seemed to fill the space between them when those dark frames locked onto her eyes. "Don't you know what it does to me when you call me *honey*?"

"It was just a—"

"You flip this little switch inside me," he went on, coming even closer to her, until she caught the scent of his cologne, could see the tick of his pulse in his neck, "that makes me forget all the reasons why I should stay away from you. This little switch that makes me want to scoop you up, carry you to my bed, rip those clothes off you, and taste every single, solitary inch of your body."

She gulped. "All that from one little *honey*?"

"All that." Another step. "And more."

"I'm sorry." Was she? She didn't feel sorry, not at all. In fact, a masochistic part of her wanted to call Luke *honey* again just to see if he would do what he promised. The images were already rolling through her mind in a delicious private reel.

"No, you're not sorry," he said, reading right through her. He raised her chin with his index finger, then traced her bottom lip with his thumb. "You are playing with fire, Olivia, and I'd hate to see you get burned."

She raised her chin away from his touch. "I'm a big girl, Luke. I know what I'm doing."

"Oh, really?" A grin quirked up one side of his mouth. "One of these days, I may ask you to prove that."

She swallowed hard. Damn. Was there an outrageous amount of pollen in the air or something? Because right now it was hard to breathe, and it seemed every single thing she said brought them circling right back to the subject of sex. She kept telling herself she wanted a one-night stand, yet when she was one *honey* away, she hesitated. Maybe Luke was right about her. Maybe she did want the fenced-in yard and the pie in the oven.

"Besides, a woman like you," Luke said, "will meet another Mr. Right."

She scoffed. "Well if you see any growing on trees around here, let me know."

He put a little distance between them. His tone shifted from that low bass that made her want to tear his clothes off to the more temperate sound of a neighbor passing the time of day. Was it the thought of another man being her Mr. Right? Or was it disappointment that she hadn't risked that fire by calling him *honey*?

"Around here, a small village could be hiding in the shrubs," Luke said. "My yard looks like the Congo."

That was an understatement. She could hardly tell he used to have a lawn, never mind flower beds. In Florida, the vegetation got a three-hundred-sixty-five-day growing cycle, and in Luke's yard, it looked like every plant and tree had made good use of the time. "Glad to see I'm not the only one with a project list."

"I've let mine sit for a long time. Too long." He turned and took in the weedy overgrowth. "Maybe it's time I tackle this . . . mess."

She got the feeling he was talking about something other than the yard. She wanted to probe but reminded herself of her no-relationship policy. Opening other people's closed doors would only entangle her further with a man who had No Trespassing painted all over him.

Chance nosed at Luke's leg. He reached down and gave

the dog a gentle ear rub. "You want to do some yard work? You any good with a rake?"

The dog wagged his tail and barked.

"Are you sure you want to keep him here with you? He's still recovering, and he needs to take it easy. But I don't like leaving him alone, and he's not really ready to be around a lot of people yet."

"That makes two of us," Luke said quietly. Then he straightened and nodded toward the garage. "Come on, Chance, let's see how those paws handle the shrub trimmers."

"You wouldn't."

He tossed her a grin. "Don't you trust me, Olivia?"

That comment sent a sizzle through her veins. Instead of answering, she said good-bye and headed back to grab Miss Sadie. But her thoughts remained on Luke, and her mind kept running images of him with his shirt off, working on the yard, skin glistening, muscles flexing—

If she kept it up, she was going to need a cold shower. Or a whole lot of chocolate. Maybe she needed to get a vibrator or an X-rated book or something while she was out. Find something else to occupy her nights than thoughts of her neighbor. But after the way he'd looked at her, and touched her, and put those images of tearing her clothes off into her mind—

Well, that was not going to be an easy task, *honey*.

She opted for the chocolate and pulled into the parking lot of the bright yellow-and-white Tasty Tidbits Bakery located right next door to the Java Hut on the boardwalk, and a block away from two churches. The scent of chocolate and peanut butter wafted out the door to greet her.

Olivia stood in the shop, debating whether to buy cookies for her meeting with Diana tomorrow. Did it scream of desperation or make her appear friendly? In the end, she called her mother, the font of everything wise. "You always told me to bring something to any important event," Olivia said. "But what am I supposed to bring for the first time I have a real conversation with my biological sister?"

Anna laughed. "That's easy. Chocolate. And don't worry about it so much, sweetie."

"I'm working on that." Olivia leaned over the glass case and ordered a dozen double chocolate chip cookies from the gray-haired woman behind the counter. "I'm trying not to get my hopes up too high, but . . ."

"They're up there all the same," Anna said. Her voice was soft, tender. "It'll go great, I'm sure. And besides, having a dog come to stay is a good sign for your future. It means you'll have faithful and sincere friends ahead, to help you overcome the obstacles in your life."

"I could use a few faithful friends who are handy with a hammer and nails."

Anna laughed. "If you want some money—"

"Thanks, Ma, but I want to do this on my own." Succeed or fail, it would be Olivia's achievement either way, and she wanted—needed—this one big change to be hers, and hers alone. Ever since the divorce, she'd had that FAILURE sticker on her head. The move, the house, the new job, were all steps to erase it and fill her with that sense of accomplishment that had been missing from her life over the last year or two.

"I'm proud of you," Anna said.

"Aw, thanks, Ma." Olivia watched the baker assemble the cookies into a box, nestling them carefully in parchment paper. "I'm still worried about seeing Diana. I wish—"

"If wishes were horses, beggars would ride," Anna said.

Olivia laughed. "You say that all the time. What on earth is that supposed to mean?"

"I have no idea," Anna admitted with a laugh of her own. "It's something my mother used to say to me when I was a little girl. I'd get upset or worried about something, and she'd say, 'If wishes were horses, beggars would ride. If turnips were watches, I would wear one by my side. And if *ifs* and *ands* were pots and pans, there'd be no work for tinkers!'"

Olivia paused a second, turning that over in her mind, then shook her head. "It doesn't make a bit of sense."

Anna laughed. "No, it doesn't, but it made you feel better, didn't it?"

"Okay, it did," Olivia admitted. "You're always right, Ma."

"Of course I am. And when you're a mom, you'll always get to be right too." Anna paused and her voice softened. "I miss you, honey."

"I miss you too, Ma. Say hi to Dad for me." The homesickness hit Olivia in a wave again, and though she knew it was snowy and cold in Massachusetts and balmy and warm here, she missed the state, the people she knew there, the world she used to inhabit. "I can't wait until you guys come down for a visit in March."

"Me too. Take care of you," Anna said. They said goodbye, and then Olivia tucked the phone back into her purse and fished out some bills to pay for the cookies. As she did, a trio of people came in—two women, one man, laughing and debating the cookie choices.

Lois Blanchard and her Constitutional Crew—her brother-in-law and her sister. Today's matching sweat suits were a pale blue, with bright pink sneakers on the women and lime green for Ben. A three-year-old towheaded boy ran circles around the women, tugging on Lois's sister's shirt. "G'ma, cookie. G'ma, cookie."

"Olivia!" Lois enfolded Olivia in a quick hug, like a long-lost cousin. "So nice to see you, neighbor." Then she drew back and waved to the people with her. "I'd like you to meet the Constitutional Crew. My brother-in-law Ben, my sister Emmaline. Our mother got all fancy with the last baby's name, you know. And Emmaline's grandson, Tucker."

Emmaline gave her older sister a dismissive wave. "You're just jealous because I have a prettier name than you do."

"I am not. Lois was our grandmother's name. It doesn't get any better than that."

They sounded like sisters, and a part of Olivia envied the two their connection. Would she banter with Diana like that someday? Or would they maintain this civil connection, like co-workers?

"How's the garden coming along?" Olivia asked Lois. "I meant to tell you that I really liked the pink flowers you added. They're a nice pop of color. You've got me all inspired to fix up my landscaping."

"Thank you, thank you." Lois beamed with pride. "It'll be so nice to see something blooming in your yard, too. Bridget—that's the previous owner—never turned a spade of dirt in all the years she lived there. She was always so busy with those dogs. It's a noble cause and all, but she could have at least found a minute to plant some shrubs or perennials." Lois waved her hand. "Jazz the place up."

"You knew Bridget?" Olivia said.

"Not well," Lois said. "We were more waving neighbors than anything else. You know, the kind where you wave as you're taking out the trash or bringing in the groceries. Like I said, she was always so busy with those animals."

"I keep hearing that," Olivia said. The picture of her biological mother painted someone with little time for the people in her life. Because she was selfish or because she was so busy with the shelter?

Olivia had moved here to find out what kind of person Bridget had been, who she was, what she'd been like, and thus far, she'd learned . . . zilch. Maybe Monday's meeting with Diana would fill in a few blanks.

"Here's your change." The brunette cashier leaned over and deposited some coins into Olivia's palm, then put out a hand. "I almost forgot to introduce myself. Carrie Parks. Owner of the Tasty Tidbits Bakery and a lifelong resident of Rescue Bay. I'm as much a fixture of this town as the lighthouse."

"Olivia Linscott. Massachusetts transplant."

The two exchanged small talk about the Boston weather, Carrie's cousins in Rhode Island, and the balmy days in Florida. Lois, Ben, and Emmaline debated the lowest-calorie menu item while Tucker buzzed the café tables like an airplane.

The entire scene brimmed with hospitality and neighborliness and should have helped ease the homesickness in

Olivia's chest. But if anything, it made her miss Boston more. She had yet to find where she fit into Rescue Bay—or if she fit here at all.

"Welcome to Rescue Bay, by the way," Carrie said, as if reading Olivia's thoughts. "It's so nice to see a new face around here. Our snowbirds are mostly retirees, so when we see someone under the age of fifty in the middle of winter, it's about as rare a sighting as snow."

"There was that year Merlin Brooks brought back that trophy wife from Vegas." Emmaline wagged a finger.

"She wasn't a trophy. She was an I Wish I Had Viagra." Ben arched a pale blond brow to emphasize the point.

"Your mama would swat you if she heard that, Ben." Lois shook her head. "Forgive my brother-in-law, Olivia. He's a little lacking in the manners department."

"G'ma, what's a Viagra?" the little boy asked, tugging on Emmaline's shirt again.

"Something your Grandma Emmaline thought was funny to put in Grandpa Ben's Christmas stocking," Ben muttered.

Emmaline just smiled, then grabbed her grandson and her husband and headed for the glass case to pick out their treats.

Lois turned to Olivia. "How's the work coming on the house? It looks like one of those TV shows over there, except without the hunky carpenter and the camera crew."

"I'm getting there. One nail at a time," Olivia said. "It's going to be a lot of work, but in the end, I'm sure it'll be worth it."

Though she wasn't sure if she was trying to convince the neighbors or herself. She'd put in hours of sweat and tears on the house, on her new job, and on trying to connect with her sister, and thus far, she felt like she was swimming upstream and not making any progress.

"You know, I see you at Luke's house a lot." Lois put up her hands and shook her head. "I don't want to know why or what you're doing over there, and I'm not saying anything bad about my neighbor, but I do think you should steer clear, dear."

"Why?"

Lois leaned in and lowered her voice. "This is a town where people like to talk. And they're already talking about you. About how you're living in Bridget's house instead of her daughter, how you're coming in with all these fancy ideas about animals and elderly at Golden Years, and about how you're taking up with that"—Lois bit her lip and put on one of those fake smiles that always preceded a back-handed slap—"well, let's just say that Luke didn't leave the military under the best of circumstances."

"I know he got injured, so I assumed there was an accident or something."

"Oh, there was an accident. A tragedy, really. I heard all about it from Susan Mandel, who heard the details from her sister-in-law, whose brother is in the Coast Guard, too. I hear . . ." Lois looked around the room. Her family was busy at the counter, still debating chocolate chunk versus macadamia nut. She cupped a hand around her mouth and leaned in to whisper. "I hear he killed someone."

The word sounded harsh in the small space. "Killed, as in accidentally? Or as in on purpose?"

Lois shook her head and her eyes widened. "No one knows."

"Well, thanks for telling me," Olivia said, though she wasn't quite sure if that was the right response. How did one react to a neighbor saying that kind of thing? Either way, the Luke she knew couldn't be a killer, so whatever happened had to have been an accident.

If so, it would explain his hermit existence and the way he lashed out at people who got close. If he felt guilty for hurting or killing someone else, that might make him react with anger, sort of like a hurting animal.

Her heart broke for Luke a little more. The part of her that spent her days helping people recover their lives, their spirit, wanted to go to him with a hug, some words of understanding. But she also knew that sometimes, people had to claw their own way out of the darkness.

Lois had started toward the glass case, then turned back

at the last second and put a hand on Olivia's arm. "One other thing I heard, that I think you should know, is about your house. I don't know if you know, but Bridget had a daughter who lives here in town. She's our local vet, so I'm sure you'll meet her someday. Diana Tuttle?"

"I've heard of her," Olivia said, not revealing anything. If she told Lois the whole story, she had no doubt it would be all over Rescue Bay before the sun set.

"Well, Diana's not too happy that her mother didn't leave the house to her," Lois said. "Bridget probably ordered it sold to pay for that shelter of hers." Lois frowned. "You poor dear. I'm sure you didn't know any of this when you bought it."

"I knew pretty much nothing," Olivia said.

"I heard from my cousin the lawyer that Diana has been looking into probate court. I think she feels like the house should be hers. Though why she waited so long to do anything, I'll never know. I mean, you're already there, tearing up things and building new things."

The information hit Olivia with a cold punch. "She's fighting for the house in probate?"

"I'm so sorry, dear." Lois patted her arm again. "You've been such a lovely neighbor. I'd hate to see you have to move."

Carrie came around from the other side of the counter and thrust a white cardboard box at Olivia. A jaunty red bow tied out of string held the lid in place. "Don't forget your cookies. People say my desserts are the best way to make friends."

"Then maybe I should have gotten two dozen," Olivia said. She walked out of the shop and climbed into her car, greeted by a flurry of puppy kisses from Miss Sadie. It wasn't until Olivia pulled into the driveway of the house that was supposed to be the beginning of her new life, one that would hold the keys to everything she had wondered about since the day she was born, that she faced the ugly truth.

She might not be wanted here any more than she had been that first day in Brigham and Women's Hospital.

"Don't get rid of your winter coat, Miss Sadie," she said to the dog, "because I'm not so sure we're here to stay after all."

Eleven

Four hours of hard, sweaty, backbreaking work, and the forest that had been Luke's backyard began to resemble something civilized and green again. He'd trimmed and raked, bagged and weeded. Or at least as best he could. The shrubs were probably cockeyed, and he'd undoubtedly pulled half perennials and half weeds. He couldn't tell the damn things apart even when his vision had been 20/20. But the yard looked better, and with a good mowing, it'd be something to enjoy.

Chance stayed with Luke the entire time, mostly lying in the shade and watching the human's progress. Luke talked to the dog, mostly because it was better than talking to himself, but also because it seemed like the dog listened. Understood.

Crazy thoughts. He'd been alone too damned long, that was for sure.

A little after three, Olivia returned. Chance got to his feet and met her at the end of the driveway, tail wagging, head butting up against her palm for a little affection. She indulged the dog, talking in sweet low tones about nonsense, just cooing praise and affection. Chance lapped it up, pressing his long golden body against her thigh, his tail moving at hurricane speed.

Envy curdled in Luke's gut. Insane. He was a man, not a dog, and he didn't need somebody babbling at him. He wasn't three years old, for God's sake, and rushing to greet his father at the end of the day, still hopeful back then that there'd be a day when he got more than an absentminded hello and a *Get the paper*.

Yet envy the dog he did.

Olivia lifted her head and though his vision wasn't much for details, he could see her dazzling smile. The envy shifted into something that could have been joy, except he wasn't so sure he could recognize that emotion anymore. "Hey, Luke," she said. "You've been busy."

He cleared his throat and closed the distance between them. "Keeps me busy. This yard was so overgrown, I figured it wouldn't be long before some of these shrubs swallowed the house."

"You did a great job." She propped her fists on her hips and looked around. "And you did a hell of a lot of work in such a short period of time."

"It was good for me. Kept my mind occupied." Instead of focusing on her, and picturing her in his bed. Lately, that particular thought occupied most of the space in his brain. Especially after that innuendo-laced conversation earlier today.

Not to mention Olivia had changed into a pale-blue sundress and some kind of heeled sandal that boosted her height a couple inches. Her breasts perked under the heart-shaped bodice of the dress. Tempting.

"You didn't happen to see anyone over at my place while you were out here, did you?" she asked.

He didn't remind her that he could hardly see his own yard, never mind hers. "Nope. Didn't hear anything either. Why?"

"It's probably nothing, but when I pulled in the driveway, I noticed the door to the shelter was open. It's happened a couple times before and I don't know why it worries me. That place is falling down. The door latches are probably loose." She shrugged. "Maybe it was the wind."

There hadn't been much of a breeze today, though, just the steady heat of Florida's sunshine. The open door bothered him, but he passed off the feeling. Olivia was right, the place was in disrepair, and undoubtedly the doors were loose. "Or maybe Chance went over there when I wasn't looking. Since you found him there the first time, maybe he still sees that place as home."

"Yeah. Maybe." She was silent a minute more, then brightened. Still, her mood seemed off somehow, troubled. "Anyway, thanks again."

"Anytime." It was the kind of offhand comment people threw out all the time, but for the first time in a long time, Luke meant the word. He'd enjoyed Chance's company and the bonus of seeing Olivia twice in one day.

"I'll leave you to your landscaping. You're probably making Lois's day."

He snorted. "I'd need a lot more than a weed-whacker to do that. She keeps trying to talk me into a horticultural plan, whatever the hell that is."

"You are *definitely* not a horticultural-plan kind of guy." He wanted to ask her what kind of guy she thought he was, but before he could, she turned to go, Chance padding along beside her.

He clutched the rake. The wooden handle pressed hard against his aching hand, the new calluses building on his palm. The internal war between the need for solitude and the need for more of what he'd had over the last few days waged again, but this time, instead of turning back, caving to that need to retreat, he took a step forward. "Olivia, wait."

She turned back. "Yeah?"

"You know, it might be good exercise to take Chance down to the beach. The area around the old lighthouse has a nice sloping hill. And, while you're there, you can get a taste of the pirate lore of Rescue Bay." His grip on the rake tightened. "I could show you sometime, if you want."

What was he doing? Asking her on a date? Using those old legends of pirates and buried treasure? How many Rescue Bay teenagers had used the same line to persuade some girl to go parking? Really, this was the best he could come up with?

Interest sparked in her eyes. "Pirates? What pirates?"

He leaned on the rake with both hands. "This area is famous for shipwrecks and pirates hiding out when they were avoiding capture. The bay made the perfect place to hole up for a few days, but they had to be careful navigating past the rocks, which is where the lighthouse came into play. Legend has it that the lighthouse was good luck."

"Good luck?" She let out a breath. "I could use some of that."

So could he. Hell, all three of them, the dog included, could use a little turn of fortune.

Olivia turned right, then left, peering past the trees that lined Gull Lane. "So where is this famous lighthouse? I've never seen it."

He leaned the rake against the wheelbarrow and walked over to Olivia. He put a hand on her shoulder and gently turned her west. His fingers itched to trail down her arms, glide along her spine, over that sweet ass, and—

He cleared his throat. "You, uh, can only see the very top of it from here. It's located on the inward curve for the bay side, so sometimes you don't notice it when you're driving down the gulf side, but it's there. Look past the trees, and a little to the east. Do you see it?"

She shook her head. "I'm not as tall as you."

"Let me remedy that." He bent over and scooped her into his arms. She laughed, then wrapped her arms tight around his shoulders and leaned into his chest. A perfect, warm fit. He inhaled the floral scent of her perfume, as light and beautiful as she was.

"What are you doing?" she asked.

I don't know. "Helping you see."

She arched upward, and his gaze traveled down her neck, past the enticing scoop of her dress, lingering on the swell of her breasts. He wanted to drop his mouth to her peachy skin, to taste her there, and everywhere. She arched some more, and his cock hardened, and then she flashed a bright happy smile at him. "I see it. Just the top, like you said."

"It's beautiful, isn't it?" he said, still cradling her against his chest, his gaze locked on her lips.

"Well, all I saw was the top, so I can't really judge that."

"Trust me. It is." He watched her lips part as she inhaled, then again with the exhale. He didn't want to talk about beaches or lighthouses or raking. He wanted to lose himself inside her deep green eyes, for an afternoon, an evening, a month.

Her lips formed a little O. "I, uh, should get down before I hurt you."

"You couldn't hurt me."

"Oh, I can, Luke. You underestimate me." She scrambled out of his arms and back to the safety of the ground. She brushed at her dress, even though there was nothing to whisk away. More, he suspected, to break eye contact.

He turned away and began to load more debris onto the wheelbarrow. The work eased the desire brewing inside him. Some.

"Maybe someday I'll get over there to see the lighthouse," Olivia said.

He noticed the word *I*, not *we*. A slip of the tongue? Or a *Keep Away* message?

"Assuming, that is, that I can ever make enough of a dent in that house to take some time off," she went on. "Speaking of which, I better get back over there. I have a to-do list as long as my arm and I'm running out of daylight. Thanks again for watching the dog." She pivoted and started toward the drive.

"Olivia?"

She turned back. "Yeah?"

"You know, if you want to bring Chance back tomorrow, say around dinnertime . . ."

"Oh, uh, I can't. I have plans."

He scowled. Plans. Right. He didn't need a sledgehammer

to the side of the head to get the hint she'd been giving him today. "Yeah, no problem." He turned back to the clippings and started raking. Twigs and leaves jumped up under the forceful moves, spattering against his bare shins.

Then a touch on his shoulder. He jumped, then settled when he caught the scent of that floral, dark perfume. "Luke? Can I take a rain check?" Olivia said.

"Yeah, that'd be great." That odd emotion from earlier surged again in his chest and bloomed into a smile on his face. A damned smile, as if he were seventeen again and the girl of his dreams had just agreed to go to the prom with him.

The feeling lasted a minute, maybe two, and then Luke remembered that dating Olivia meant opening up to her. Telling her about what he'd done. The mistakes he had made.

Dating Olivia meant letting her get close, letting her rely on him, trust him. Luke raised a hand to the scar that cut a crescent into the side of his face, and the smile disappeared. He tossed the rake into the wheelbarrow and headed back inside, where the dark welcomed him with open arms.

Twelve

⧜

The last time Diana Tuttle had been this nervous, she'd been a sophomore, lying in the backseat of a Buick with Sean Baxter on the night of his senior prom, her dress shoved up around her waist. Sean was smiling that charming grin of his and telling her he had protection.

Fifteen years later, she had a son and Sean was long gone. That was what she got for trusting men. No wonder she worked with animals all day. Animals never broke your heart. Never let you down. Never ran out when you needed them most.

Or showed up when you wanted them the least. Like Olivia had.

Diana stepped onto the porch of the house that she had grown up in, the house she knew as well as she knew her own, her hand automatically going to the knob, before remembering that someone else owned this house now.

Her sister.

A sister her mother had never mentioned. A sister she didn't want or need. Diana wished Olivia would just go back to Boston and stop trying to force a relationship where there'd never been one before. Diana wasn't here for a connection, for God's sake. She was too old for that whispers-in-the-dark and giggles-over-dinner sisterly bond.

She intended to tell Olivia that, straight off, before the other woman got any ideas about the two of them becoming buddy-buddy.

Before Diana could raise her hand to knock, the door opened, and Olivia stood on the other side, her face filled with hopeful nervousness. Diana wondered if right now, the two of them mirrored each other. "Hi. I'm sorry I'm late. We had someone bring in a dog that had been hit by a car and . . ." She shrugged.

"No problem. I understand. Do you, uh, want to come in?"

No, she didn't. She didn't want to enter her mother's house and see the marks of another woman in the furniture, the décor, the dishes in the sink. She didn't want to build a relationship with someone who had, right or wrong, stolen what should have been Diana's. Diana grew up in this house. Diana had dusted that furniture, raked those leaves. Not Olivia. But she bit her tongue and nodded instead.

Olivia opened the door wider and stepped to the side. "Forgive the mess. I've been doing some renovations."

Renovations? It looked like a hurricane had made landfall inside the tiny bungalow that Diana had lived in for half her life. Plaster and lath lay in a dusty pile to one side of the living room. Two thirds of the walls had been stripped back to the studs, and the threadbare mauve carpet that had once been acreage for a Barbie and Ken village was now gone, exposing stained, dusty oak floorboards.

"Let's go in the kitchen," Olivia said. "I made some coffee."

Diana followed behind Olivia, walking in this surreal world that was familiar, yet not. Hers, and yet not.

Olivia had the same trim figure as their mother, the same blond hair, and the same smile. But it was her eyes, those deep green eyes, that Diana knew. Bridget's eyes.

There was no doubting the family connection. The question was why Bridget had never told Diana that she had a sister. She had spent hours with her mother, especially toward the end, when Diana had closed her practice down for two weeks and spent every day tending to Bridget. She couldn't find a moment to say, *Hey, you have a sister and I thought it'd be nice if she inherited the house*?

Diana stepped into the kitchen and stopped dead. Most of the cabinets were gone, the countertops ripped out, the flooring removed from one side of the room. A piece of plywood was set up over the two remaining base cabinets, serving as makeshift counter space. "Oh my God. It looks like a bomb went off in here."

Olivia laughed. "That might have been an easier approach than the one I took." Then she sobered and pressed her lips together. "I'm sorry. I bet you have a lot of memories in this kitchen. And I bet it's hard to see it like this. Maybe it wasn't such a good idea to meet here."

"You're right. It is incredibly hard to see it in your hands instead of mine." Oh, shit. She hadn't meant to say that out loud. "I'm sorry. I . . . I guess I was surprised that Mom left the house to you."

"Not as surprised as me." Olivia pressed her lips together again, as if trying to hold back a tide of words. "I, um ordered Chinese food. I figured you'd be hungry after work and maybe didn't have time to eat. I wasn't sure what you liked, so I ordered a variety. And I got some cookies from the bakery in town, too." A nervous hitch filled Olivia's voice. She crossed to the coffeepot, then back to the table, then back to the pot again. "Uh, coffee?"

"Thanks." It would at least give Diana's hands something to do. She fought the urge to run out the door. Olivia was clearly trying hard, and it wasn't her fault that Diana wanted to scream. The person Diana really wanted to yell at wasn't here, and never would be again.

Olivia brought two mugs over to them, then sat in the chair opposite. It was the same dented chrome-and-laminate table that Diana had sat at for as long as she could remember. She could remember coloring pictures at this table, eating chicken nuggets for dinner in that same seat, and fashioning a homemade Christmas card for her mother under the brass light that still hung from a slightly tarnished chain.

She could also remember sitting here alone, until the sun dropped behind the trees and the night birds began to call, waiting for her mother to come home. She'd fix herself a sandwich or a can of spaghetti, then tuck herself into bed, never able to fall asleep until she heard the click of the front door.

So many memories wrapped up in this house, both good and bad. Diana wasn't sure whether to cry or scream. Instead she sat there with that polite tolerant face every woman learned and watched the dark-brown coffee shimmer in her mother's mug.

Olivia broke the silence first. "I guess I should start at the beginning. I had no idea who my biological mother was until a lawyer showed up at my door a few weeks ago and told me she had left me this house. I was at a crossroads in my life, and I decided I really wanted to get those answers I'd never had, so I packed up my car and headed south."

"You just . . . moved? Like that?"

"It was crazy, and there are days when I still think about going back home to all the people and the things that I know." Olivia shrugged. "But I want answers more than I want that."

"And if you get the answers, are you leaving then?"

Olivia toyed with her mug. "I don't know. I've got a job I love here, and the weather can't be beat, but it's hard being away from all my friends and family. Lonely."

Empathy filled Diana. She knew that feeling, oh, she knew it well. Hadn't she felt that way a hundred times during her childhood? During her terrible relationship with Sean? How many times had he come home, pulled up a chair to the dinner table, and vowed this time things would be different, and they'd be a real family? Then he'd be gone before the dishes were cleared and her heart would break all over again. Before Jackson was born, Diana had struggled, alone, and knew that ache of wanting another person to talk to at the end of the day. Her hand splayed across the hard surface of the kitchen table, almost close enough to touch Olivia's palm. "Rescue Bay is a welcoming community. I'm sure that will change the longer you live here."

What was she doing? *Inviting* Olivia to stay? That wasn't the plan.

The trouble with her plan, though, was that Diana was starting to like Olivia. To relate to her. Connect.

Olivia dropped her gaze to her coffee cup. The Chinese food take-out boxes sat between them, filling the air with the sweet and spicy scents of pineapple, chili peppers, and soy sauce. But neither of them made a move to open the boxes or to take a bite. "What was she like?"

And there it was, the first of the hard questions. The reason why Diana had stalled and delayed and found a hundred reasons not to call Olivia for days. A part of Diana wanted to stamp her feet like a three-year-old and say, *She was* my *mother; you don't have a right to know about her.*

Diana bit her lip and searched for the right answer. "Complicated."

"How so?"

"My mother . . ." Diana caught herself and tried again with words that sounded foreign on her tongue. "Our mother was dedicated to her causes. Not so much to the people around her. I'd be sitting here, at this very table, waiting for her to come home. She'd forget about dinner and soccer games and everything else if there was an animal in trouble or a dog loose on the highway. And I'd . . . fend for myself."

"Did she ever get married?"

"No." Diana shrugged. "I don't think she could love a whole lot of people at one time. I don't mean that she was hateful or self-centered, it's just that so much of her energy went into this shelter that it was like there wasn't much left over."

The conversation between them was like a minefield, each of them trying to take a step forward without detonating the fragile peace. Olivia's nervous energy had calmed, but still she held tight to the coffee mug. "I wish I knew why she left all this to me."

"Yeah, me too." Diana got to her feet and put her cup in the sink, even though it was half full. She just couldn't sit there another second and pretend she wasn't hurt and confused by her mother's actions. That she didn't resent Olivia for doing nothing more than being the name on the will.

Diana flipped the handle on the faucet, a move she'd made a thousand times in her life, and watched the water fill the mug, then spill over into the stainless sink. Then the image blurred and it wasn't until Olivia came over and shut the water off that Diana realized she was crying.

"I'm sorry," Olivia said. "I didn't mean to upset you."

Diana wheeled around. "Well you did. You upset me just by being here. In this house. Changing everything. It's not yours. I don't care if she left it to you, it's not yours. And I want it back." Then she crossed the kitchen, snagged her purse off the chair, and rushed out of the house, getting into her car and driving until the tears blurred the road into a gray puddle.

Thirteen

As Monday drew to a close, Luke had spent an hour, maybe two, on his porch, as the sun went down, and darkness dropped its heavy blanket over Rescue Bay, and the mailbox disappeared into the ebony night. He stared at it anyway, as if he could recall the letter he'd sent by will alone.

No mail winged its way back to his head. Idiot. Why the hell had he sent that letter? He'd been morose and a bit drunk. Never the best time to make a decision. That he knew firsthand, after standing up for Mike when his friend had married someone he'd known for, oh, twenty minutes, one crazy weekend in Vegas.

The streetlights flickered to life, and all up and down Gull Lane, porch lights came on and mothers called their children home. Rescue Bay settled in for bed, and still Luke stayed on the porch.

Next door, he heard a jingle, then a door closing, then a series of patters. He got to his feet, coming to stand on the top step. The streetlights illuminated a familiar slender form, and two smaller shapes at her feet.

Olivia.

Something dark stirred deep inside him. Maybe it was the night covering them, the months he'd spent alone, or just the sassy fire she evoked, but desire rushed through him every time he saw her. He thought of nothing but kissing her. Touching her. Holding her in his arms, her tight body pressed against his.

His groin tightened, and he gripped the porch post until the rough wood scraped his palm. Damn that woman.

He didn't realize he'd said the words out loud until he heard the clatter of the leashes, and then Olivia's voice. "Luke? Is that you?"

Damn. "Yeah."

Then she was coming up the walkway, with the dogs pattering along beside her, and the desire was roaring inside him, oblivious to the mental war he was waging. He thought of her lips under his, her body against his, and he wanted her all over again. He wanted to take her into his house, take her upstairs to his bedroom, and lose himself inside her until nothing mattered but making her moan.

Damn the woman.

"What are you doing outside so late?" she asked.

"Thinking."

"It's a good night to do that. Or to walk the dogs." She raised the leashes, and the dogs' collars jingled again.

"You shouldn't be doing that, alone, at this time of night."

"This isn't the combat zone in Boston." She laughed. "It's Rescue Bay, for Pete's sake."

"You think nothing bad happens here?" He came down a step. Another. A third, until he was standing even with her, and the heat between them rivaled the lingering heat in the Florida air. "You can't trust everyone in this town."

She paused a beat. "Can I trust you?"

He had a sharp, sarcastic retort readied, but it died in his throat when he thought about trust and other people and the man he used to be. "No, Olivia, you can't." He turned to go, then froze when her hand touched his arm.

"I'm sorry. That wasn't . . . I didn't mean to ask . . ." She let out a gust. "I'm sorry."

It was the second time she said it that hit him in the gut. He hung his head, closed his eyes, and reminded himself that nothing he had done was Olivia Linscott's fault. She just happened to be the one he kept hitting with guilt shrapnel. "Forget what I said."

"Okay."

He heard the collars jingle again and realized she was going to leave and head off on her walk. "Why are you walking the dogs at this time of night anyway?"

"I have a lot on my mind. A lot to process." She sighed. "I can't sleep."

He let out a short laugh. "Join the club. I'm a charter member." His gaze went to the road he couldn't see, the streets that had once been friends but now were filled with hazards. "I used to run at night. I liked how quiet it was, how empty the world was. It was just me and the pavement. But now . . ." He shrugged.

"You're welcome to walk with me and the dogs."

"I don't think that's a good idea. I'll probably end up falling on my face."

"Yeah, you probably will." Then she leaned in closer. "But then you'll get back up and try again because you have to. Besides, you can't stay on the damned porch all night."

He damned well could, but that didn't mean he wanted to. Or he should. And the thought of the quiet, empty house and his quiet, empty bedroom just depressed the hell out of him.

"I'm not going that far or fast because Chance is still healing, so it's not like you're going to run a marathon tonight," she said. "I guess the better question is whether *you* trust *me*."

Her voice dropped when she said that and stirred the desire inside him back into a fast hurricane. Trust her? Hell, he didn't trust anyone. Especially not himself around her. Every time he tried to stick to his best intentions, that train derailed.

"Do you, Luke? Do you trust me?" Now her voice had

shifted into the higher ranges of teasing, and he could see a grin curving up the side of her face.

He liked that smile. A lot.

"Maybe not with my social security number, but to walk with me in the dark . . . yeah."

"I think the latter is far more dangerous. I'm not always the most coordinated woman in the world."

"That's okay. Neither am I."

That made her laugh. He liked the way she laughed, liked that his words could bring that out of Olivia. "Then we'll just stumble along together. And let the dogs lead the way."

He hesitated only a second, then fell into place beside her. They started down the walkway, toward the yellow pools of light that dotted the sidewalk. His vision skipped from pool to pool, and he thought how like a runway those circles of light looked.

His hands flexed, as if he were nestled in the pilot's seat of the MH-60's snug cockpit, reaching for the collective and the cyclic. Ready. The tower's commands echoed in his head while Joe shifted into the co-pilot's seat and the crew readied themselves behind him, olive-green helmets blending in the dark, their chins blocked by the thick black barrel of the mic. The rescue swimmer and the flight mechanic sat, tensed, silent, waiting while the medic chattered away his nerves. Luke could hear the whirr of the blades, the whine of the engines, the chatter on the radio. The familiar lift in his stomach as the helo rose, taking man from ground to air, a miracle every time that something that weighed close to ten tons could rise with so little effort.

The sounds in his head shifted then, to screeches and creaks and the shriek of the storm battering the helo. One minute he was up, wrestling the stick, trying to hold against Mother Nature's determined wrestling; the next he was down, the helo a plaything against the ocean's fury. The helo dropped, someone screamed, and the world went black.

"You okay?" A pause. "Hey, Luke. You okay?"

He jerked his attention back to the present day. He was

here. In Rescue Bay. On the hard concrete sidewalk. With Olivia. The dogs. The moon above, the streetlights before him. No ocean, no storm, no helo. "Uh, yeah. Sorry. Got lost in my thoughts."

"I do that all the time. Hey, watch the dip in the sidewalk." She touched his elbow, a moment of guidance, then went back to talking as if nothing had happened, but it touched Luke in a place he thought had gone dead a long time ago.

Push her away. Don't drag her into your mess.

"I'm one of those think-while-I-drive people," Olivia went on, oblivious to the storm stirring in Luke, "which probably isn't a good idea, because I'll forget where I'm supposed to turn or go right past the exit for the mall."

"I can honestly say that has never happened to me."

"Not much of a shopaholic?"

He snorted. "The last time I went to a mall, I was seventeen and picking out a tux for prom."

"Let me guess? Robin's-egg blue with a ruffled white shirt?"

"Nope. Pale gray with a fuchsia tie." He shook his head at the memory. What would it have been like if he had known Olivia in high school? If she'd been his date then? Would they have ended up together, driving a minivan and raising a bunch of kids? Or would he have broken her heart and driven her away? "The stupid things a horny teenager will do for prom night nookie."

"And did you get any?"

"Not so much as a kiss good night. My date broke up with me during the second-to-last song."

"Oh, that's harsh." She gave him a light jab in the shoulder. "And with you all sexy in your tux and everything."

He laughed. "I don't think any man looks sexy in pale gray and fuchsia."

"Some men make anything look sexy."

Her voice had dropped when she said that, which stirred that fire in his gut again. He thought of that kiss, and how damned good it had been. He'd gone a long time without a woman in his life or in his bed, and right now, in the dark intimacy of the quiet night sky, he wanted this one.

Not just because of the way she had awakened his desire, but because of that laugh, that half smile, the way she seemed to bring sunshine to his darkness.

Tell her the truth, his conscience urged. *Tell her now, before she gets tangled up any more.*

Chance spied something in the dark and lunged to the left, bringing his leash whipping against Olivia's legs. She stumbled, and Luke reached for her, and then she was in his arms, against his chest, and the switch in his brain turned to *on*. The dogs circled them, barking and playing, tangling the leashes around Olivia and Luke.

They had stopped outside the golden reach of the street-lights, at the end of a cul-de-sac, beside a wooded area punctuating the space between two dark houses. The world was asleep, unaware of the brewing tension at the end of Gull Lane.

Luke barely noticed. All he saw was Olivia's wide, shimmering eyes, the way her lips parted and her breath whispered against his skin. He caught the sweet floral fragrance of her perfume, offset by darker undertones of sandalwood or jasmine or some such thing. She drew in a breath, her chest rising, breasts just brushing his chest.

"I'm having a hell of a time resisting you." The words were almost a growl.

Her green eyes glistened and she raised her chin. "Then don't. Not tonight. Please, Luke."

Two words, two powerful words. *Please, Luke.*

He leaned down, tangled his fingers in her hair, and pulled her to him, until their mouths met in a frenzied kiss. Heat exploded inside him, stoking the desire that had been building for weeks. She opened her mouth against his, danced her tongue inside, and he deepened the kiss, at the same time stepping her back, until she bumped up against a tree and he pressed into her.

His erection strained against the fly of his jeans, throbbing, begging for release. Olivia tipped her pelvis up, pressing into him, sending his brain into a dizzying tailspin. He slid one hand down, snaking it under the soft hem of her T-shirt, then up the smooth expanse of her belly until he reached the lace edges of her bra. He skimmed two fingers over the peaked nipple and she let out a gasp, arching against him. He slid back the lacy cup, then covered her breast with his palm, running his thumb over the tip until Olivia was nearly crying with want. She reached down, closed her hand around his erection. Even through the hard denim, he could feel the outline of her fingers on his cock, and when she started to slide her hand up and down, he damned near exploded.

He dipped his head, at the same time he lifted the tee and covered her breast with his mouth. When his tongue flicked over her nipple, Olivia let out a sharp gasp and threaded her fingers through his hair, urging him on with her touch. She brought up one leg between his, rubbing against his cock, the harder pressure a sweet agony.

Something rubbed against his leg, no, scratched, over and over, up and down one leg. It took him a good thirty seconds to realize it was Olivia's dog. At the same time, Chance tugged on the leash, nearly toppling Olivia and Luke. The dogs barked, a light went on in a nearby house, and sanity returned.

Luke drew back, smoothed Olivia's bra back into place, then tugged down the T-shirt. "Uh, this might not be the best place to do this."

"I agree." She was breathing heavy, as was he, and for a long second, they just stared at each other in the dark, chests heaving, unspent desire charging the air. "We better get these walks dogged. Uh, dogs walked."

"And when the dogs are done?"

She glanced at him, and he couldn't tell in the dark if she was smiling. "We'll see where they lead us."

By the time they returned to Olivia's house, Chance was panting hard and whining to go inside and lie down. Olivia could identify. Her heart was still racing and she wanted to go inside and get to a bed, too, but for an entirely different reason. Olivia had told herself the whole way back that she would say good night to Luke and leave it at that. Keep things on a neighborly basis. No more.

But as they took the three steps up her porch and the front door loomed like a big question mark, she decided she didn't want to be cautious, take-it-slow Olivia again. Hadn't she vowed to leave that woman behind? To let this new life open new dimensions in herself?

And where had slow and easy gotten her, anyway? Divorced and alone. Sleeping in an empty bed every night. She'd gone for the walk to forget all the things going wrong in her new life. The house, her sister. Then along came Luke, a very welcome distraction. No, more than a distraction, but what more she didn't want to know, so she didn't ask herself that question.

She sure as hell didn't want a relationship—her life was complicated enough right now, thank-you-very-much—but that didn't mean she wanted to live in an empty black hole, either. Especially after that kiss.

Oh my God, that kiss. Amazing, incredible, toe-curling. And when he'd taken her breast in his mouth? Dear God, she almost climaxed right there in the cul-de-sac. She'd been reeling ever since. She turned to him, laid a hand on his arm. "Why don't you come in for a little while?"

"You sure?"

"Stop asking questions and just come in," she said. Because if she thought about it too much, she'd change her mind, and right now, she didn't want that.

She bent over long enough to unclip the dogs from their leashes, and when she turned back, Luke was there, reaching for her, pulling her toward him, kissing her. Fire rushed through her veins, and she clawed at his back, drawing him closer, until his chest was crushing hers and she could hardly breathe.

He kicked the door shut with his foot, then drew back long enough to capture her gaze. His blue eyes glinted in the dark, catching the hall light. "Bedroom?"

"Upstairs."

He bent down, scooped her into his arms, then started up the stairs. She clung to him, kissing him, touching him, aware of nothing but the heat between them and the urgent need to have more, more, more. His free hand slid between them, fumbling her shirt up and over her head. When the air hit her chest, her nipples puckered beneath the lace of her bra, and Luke let out a groan, then covered her lips with his, devouring, nipping, tasting.

He nudged the door open with his knee, then crossed to the bed in two quick strides. He leaned over and deposited her gently on the covers, before stepping back. She lay there, arms above her head, legs spread, breasts peeking over the lace of her bra, on display for him, feeling more wanton than she ever had before in her life.

"You are beautiful," he said.

Her face heated, and she turned away. "Thanks."

He sat on the edge of the bed, cupped her jaw, and turned her face until she was looking at him again. "You are beautiful, Olivia," he repeated.

She wanted to look away, to deflect the compliment, but Luke wouldn't let her. So she swallowed those doubts that said she wasn't a woman that men desired or a woman that made a man want to be faithful, and said, "Thank you," her voice soft, vulnerable.

Then he leaned down and kissed her, but took his sweet time doing it, letting the fire build between them again, a little at a time. When she arched against him, he shifted until his long length covered hers, his shoes tumbling to the floor with twin thuds.

He ran a finger along the lacy edge of her bra, teasing at the curve over her breast with the very tip of his finger. Ice and fire ran through her veins. "Luke, Luke. Please."

He grinned. "Please more or please stop?"

"Please stop teasing me and give me *more*."

He chuckled. "Your wish is my command, milady." Then he reached around her, fingering the clasp until it sprung free, and her breasts spilled over the fabric. Olivia began to wriggle out of it, but Luke stopped her.

"Let me." With agonizing slowness, he peeled down one strap, then the other, following the satin's path with his mouth, kissing her shoulders, then the little valley beneath her neck, then the swell of her breasts. His mouth closed over the right one and he sucked the nipple into his mouth. She gasped at the sharp fire of his tongue teasing the sensitive nub. His free hand slipped down to her waist, fumbling to undo the buttons and zipper of her jeans.

She rose up on one elbow, which made him suckle her nipple harder. "Oh, God, you don't make this easy. And I mean that in an oh . . . oh, good way." She fumbled with his fly, then yanked his jeans down and off. His boxers followed, and his hard cock throbbed against her belly.

She curled her hand around its length, loving the way he gasped and froze for a second, enjoying her touch. She stroked up and down, toying with the tip with her thumb, then sliding her hand down the full length and pausing to swipe her finger across his balls. She twisted her grip as she came up and Luke let out something that could have been a groan or a curse, but sent a clear message of *don't stop*.

His mouth covered hers again, hot, hard, insistent. Then he slid his fingers under her panties and into her warm, wet vagina. She sucked in a breath between her teeth and bucked up against his hand. He rubbed his thumb up and down her clit, and that fast, Olivia felt the pounding rush of an orgasm sweeping over her, bursting in her brain, obliterating thought for one hot, sweet second.

"That was fast," he said, a tease in his words.

"It's, uh, been a while for me."

"Me too." His eyes met hers in the moonlight. "So that means we can either take it slow, or very, very fast."

"How about very, very fast the first time? And then the second time, make it last."

A smile curved across his face. "Your wish is my command."

She laughed, then gave his cock one long, hard stroke. "Then don't make me wait."

He groaned. He pulled his hand out, then tugged at her panties, so fast, she was surprised they didn't tear. The panties joined the rest of their clothes somewhere on the floor, and then the two of them were naked, warm skin meeting warm skin, like heated silk along her nerve endings. He nudged her legs apart with his knee and settled between them, his cock poised at her entrance. "Protection?"

"I . . . I don't have anything." She didn't want to tell him that she hadn't bought a condom since her divorce. It wasn't the kind of thing one put on a grocery list.

"Neither do I." Reality popped up like a weed. What were they thinking? They weren't teenagers. They knew where unprotected sex could lead—to very bad decisions and mega consequences.

He shifted away from her and flopped onto the bed. He willed his body to stop insisting he go back to what he was doing. He should be grateful he'd stopped when he did, before they got too close. Before it got . . . complicated. "I'm sorry. I didn't exactly plan this."

"Neither did I," she said, echoing his words. "It just . . . happened."

He draped an arm over his head and didn't say anything for a long minute. Cold now, Olivia reached out and dragged the edge of the blanket over them. As the quilt settled onto Luke, he let out a gust and swung his legs over the side of the bed. He grabbed his boxers and jeans off the floor and tugged them on. "I can't do this," he said. "I can't be the man who does the dishes and comes home every night and takes the dog for a walk."

She sat up in the bed and clutched the sheet to her chest. "I didn't say I wanted any of that. Last I checked we were just kissing. Or, well, more than kissing."

"And that's the problem. More than kissing leads to . . . complicated. And I don't do complicated."

It was as if a winter wind had skated into the room and

settled its icy grip on Olivia's heart. She could tell he was gone, that he had left her, long before he got to his feet and said good-bye.

It wasn't until she heard the front door shut that Olivia allowed the tears to fall.

Fourteen

∞

The pounding woke Luke from a sound sleep. "Go away!"
He rolled over and stuffed a pillow over his head.

More pounding.

Luke opened one eye. Glanced at the bedside clock. Six
in the freakin' morning. Who the hell—

He let out a curse, swung his legs over the side of the
bed, and got to his feet. He dragged on yesterday's shorts
and T-shirt, then headed out of his bedroom and down the
hall. The knocking—more like punching—of his front door
continued. "I'm coming, I'm coming," he grumbled. What
the hell was with people? Didn't they realize what time it
was? Luke undid the locks, then pulled open the front door.

Leaning against the jamb was a six-foot-seven freak of
nature. Lieutenant Mike Stark had the body of a football
player, the height of an NBA center, and the brains of a
physicist. He'd been Luke's nemesis in boot camp, the man
who could outrun, outpower, and outanswer anyone else in
the unit. The two of them had been stationed at AIRSTA
Kodiak at the same time, which could have ended up as an
epic fail, with two hardheaded mustangs intent on proving

their worth as officers. Instead, he and Mike had become friends after a messy fight in a bar over a woman neither of them remembered.

"Took you long enough. What, are you sleeping in now?" Mike said. "Retirement got your lazy ass in bed half the day?"

"It's six in the morning. Early, by most people's standards. And I'm not retired. I'm out."

"Same difference. Why are you being such an ass? Did someone piss in your Wheaties this morning?" Without waiting for an invitation, Mike stepped past Luke and into the house. He turned back and pressed a bag into Luke's hands. "Here. I figured you wouldn't have anything decent to eat, so I stopped and got us some health food."

Luke peeled open the bag and inhaled. "Doughnuts? You call that health food?"

Mike reached past him, plucked out one of the sugary treats, and took a bite. "Yup. I'm rewriting the food pyramid."

"Turning it upside down is more like it."

Luke hadn't seen any of the guys since he'd left Alaska. They'd been a tight crew, bonded by experiences most people could never imagine. Mike being on his doorstep was like a visit from a brother. A welcome irritation.

"You know I was never one to play by the rules," Mike said. "Especially when it comes to food, alcohol, and women."

"Or mixing the three." Despite the early hour, Luke found a smile curving across his face. Damn, he'd missed Mike. He hadn't realized how much until now. "You want some coffee?"

"As long as you can make it strong enough to fry my hair, yeah." Mike followed Luke down the hall and into the kitchen.

Luke took his time making the coffee and got through the process without dumping a pot of water on his feet this time. He told himself not to wonder about Olivia and whether she was hating him right now. He'd done a shitty thing last night. A cowardly thing. Taken the easy way out, which wasn't like him. Or didn't used to be like him. The man he was and the man he'd become were like Jekyll and Hyde. He wasn't sure which version he disliked the most.

Luke dropped into the seat across from Mike.

"So how bad is it?" Mike asked.

Leave it to Stark to get right to the point. "The doctor says I should regain limited vision. But it'll never be perfect. And that means I'll never fly again."

"You could work ground or—"

"No!" The word exploded out of Luke and he got to his feet, crossing to the coffeepot and pouring two cups while he inhaled a few breaths and worked the beast out of his system. "I don't want to go back to half a career. All I ever wanted to do was fly."

Mike got up, took one look at the scar on Luke's face, and shrugged, nonplussed. "Well, you're not completely hideous. You could always get a job as a male stripper. How's your affinity for bow ties?"

Luke chuckled. "You're an ass, you know that?"

"Yeah, that's what my ex says."

"Ex? I thought you and Jasmine—"

"Are over. I got the final divorce papers last week. On my birthday, no less. Happy birthday to me." Mike raised an imaginary toast. "Quick tip. Never marry the first woman who sleeps with you after a long deployment. When your dick does the thinking, you make poor choices."

"Sorry."

Mike shrugged. "It is what it is. I miss the kids like crazy, though. I was heading to Georgia to see them, but then I got a text from Jasmine saying she left yesterday to see her family in Toledo. She made it clear I'd be an uninvited guest if I tried to tag along." He shook his head and cursed. "Anyway, the kids get back in about ten days, and since I'm temporarily between residences, I thought I'd come down here and bug you."

"When are you heading back to base?"

"Few weeks. I have a lot of leave saved up. Was saving

it to finally go on a honeymoon and all that, but now . . ." He shook his head, then got to his feet and crossed to the pot to refill his mug. He stayed by the window, his back against the sink, and drank the coffee. "Anyway, I figured it might be a good idea to come down here and live the beach life with you for a little while. Hot sun, hot girls in bikinis . . . Kodiak can wait."

"You got the wrong beach for that. You want to hit the other side of the state. Miami. Boca. Here, the average beachgoer is collecting social security."

"Well unless they changed retirement age, I'd say you have a few hotties here. One right next door." Mike arched a brow.

Luke got up and looked out the window. Olivia was out in her yard, bent over, doing what he didn't know. Gardening, he presumed. She had on short red shorts that stood out against the contrast of her long, peach legs. He didn't have to be able to see that well to know that she looked enticing, gorgeous, and sexy enough to turn any man's head and make him lose his mind.

Heat pooled in his gut. He could still see her, sprawled on the bed, the moonlight kissing her pale skin, that smile he liked so much playing on her lips. If they hadn't run into that little condom snag—

Well, it was a good thing they had. Because as much as he wanted Olivia—and Lord help him, he wanted her a hundred times more than he'd wanted anything in his life, even that Mustang he'd begged for back when he was sixteen—Luke knew he'd be no good for her. Olivia was a settle-down girl and he was a head-for-the-hills guy.

He cleared his throat. "She's just my neighbor."

"Well, you know, I always thought Mr. Rogers had the right idea." Mike grabbed the coffeepot and poured a fresh mug, then swiped the bag of doughnuts off the table.

"What are you doing?"

"The neighborly thing. Offering the neighbor some breakfast. And finding an excuse to meet her." Mike grinned. "Wouldn't Mr. Rogers be proud?"

A hot poker of jealousy lanced Luke's chest. How could that be? He barely knew Olivia. She irritated the hell out of him, with her do-gooder deeds, and her concern over a stray dog, and her always nosing around his house. Yeah, she was sexy as all hell, and had that little laugh that made him think of music, but she wasn't his girlfriend or anything. He had no ties to Olivia, no claim to her as solely his.

Mike was his friend. He shouldn't care if Mike dated Olivia or hell, married her.

But he did. A lot.

"Listen, she's just getting over a divorce." Luke wanted to kick himself for giving Mike the *she's single* information. "Probably not the best time to go over there."

Mike turned back. "Oh really? You got to know her already?"

Luke scowled. "She lives right next door. It's hard not to."

"Well, if you ask me, she looks hot. As in the working-in-the-sun-too-long kind of hot. And hot people need to eat. So come with me and be a gentleman."

"I don't—"

"Know how. I know. It sucks being the socially awkward one, doesn't it?" Mike laughed. "Just follow my lead. I have enough gentleman in me for both of us." Mike was still laughing as he pulled open the back door and led the way down the drive, and back up Olivia's, then around the house and into Olivia's yard.

When she saw them, she straightened and brushed her bangs off her forehead with the back of her hand. The rising sun caught her from behind and cast her hair in gold like a freaking halo. Damn. Every time he saw her, a chain reaction of fireworks combusted in his solar plexus. He glanced over at Mike and could practically see the other man drooling. "Hey, Luke. You're up early."

"He's turning lazy now that he's a civilian again," Mike said, stepping forward and proffering his free hand. "I'm Mike Stark. I used to serve with this doofus over here."

Olivia pulled off a gardening glove, and shook with Mike. Luke had to force himself not to rip Mike's arm out of the socket. "Nice to meet you. Sorry I'm such a mess. I don't have any appointments this morning, so I'm trying to get some outside work done before it gets too warm out."

"We thought you might like some breakfast." Mike handed her the coffee and the doughnut bag. "Not sure if you're a fan of doughnuts, but—"

"I am definitely in the doughnut fan club." She smiled, and the sun behind her brightened. "There's nothing a good glazed can't make better."

"I ate the glazed," Luke said, then wanted to kick himself for being such a moron. Since when did he clam up like a mute around Mike? Then utter one idiotic phrase? "Sorry."

"I can be swayed by a good jelly-filled, too," Olivia said, withdrawing the doughnut from the bag. She took a bite, sending a dusting of powdered sugar onto the curve of her chin and leaving one sweet dot of jelly on her upper lip. Beside him, Mike let out a low groan.

"Damn," Mike whispered.

"Be nice or I'll chain you to the fence," Luke muttered.

Mike chuckled. "I'd like to see you try, wimpy." He turned back to Olivia and affected a nonchalant stance. "So, Olivia, Luke was wondering if you'd like to come over for dinner sometime."

Luke would have punched Mike, but the other man had wisely moved away a few steps. "Mike . . ."

"Dinner?" Olivia raised a brow in Luke's direction. "I didn't know you cooked. I thought it was all pizza boxes and beer over there."

And boxers on the floor, Luke remembered telling her. Boxers that had been on her floor just last night.

"I cook," Mike offered. "Not a lot of things, but I can roast a chicken that will make you swoon."

"Who the hell says *swoon*?" Luke said.

"I do. After I catch the fainting ladies who eat my roast chicken. My supersecret barbecue recipe will make your taste buds cry."

"Somebody's going to cry," Luke muttered. Since when did Mike cook? Or have a secret recipe for anything?

"Considering I've only had time to grab a sandwich here and there, a little home-cooked food sounds amazing," Olivia said.

"So, is it a date?" Mike asked. "Tomorrow night? Say, seven?"

"A date? With the two of you?"

"No, not a date," Luke said, wishing again that Mike were close enough to slug. "Just . . . a meal. Everybody's got to eat, right?"

Make it clear he wasn't pursuing her. That this was just a friendly neighborhood get-together. Even if his every other thought was about her in that bed, ready, willing—

"Well, when you put it like that," she said, laughing, and he wondered if she was laughing at him or with him, or with Mike, "how can a girl refuse? Should I bring dessert?"

"You already are—"

This time Luke did slug him. Mike oomphed. "Dessert would be fine, thanks," Luke said. "We'll, uh, let you get back to your garden." Then he grabbed Mike by a fistful of T-shirt and hauled him back across the two yards. "What the hell were you thinking?"

"What are *you* thinking? You have Miss America living next door to you and you don't ask her out? What's wrong with you?"

"I'm just not in the mood for dating right now. I . . ." He shook his head and let out a curse. "Just leave me alone, will you? I don't need someone butting into my life."

Mike put up two hands and backed up a couple of steps. "Whoa, down there, Rover. I'm merely pointing out that the Luke I know would have never ignored a pretty woman."

"Well, I'm not that Luke. Not anymore." He stalked into his house, letting the screen door slam behind him. He grabbed a couple of beers, then settled in front of the television to watch a show he didn't give a damn about to try to forget a woman he did.

It was a good ten minutes before he heard the creak of the screen door and the sound of Mike's heavy footfalls crossing the kitchen, then clomping down the hall and finally stopping in the living room.

"What the hell is your problem?" Mike asked.

"Gee, your sympathy is overwhelming." Luke turned back to the TV.

"I'm not here to be your shoulder to cry on, Luke. I'm the one who's going to kick your ass and get you to leave the pity party."

Luke wanted to hate Mike. To tell him to get the hell out of his house. But instead, he shook his head and grinned. "For the record, you could never kick my ass. I'm faster and wilier than you."

"Wilier? That's a word, Einstein?"

"It is in my dictionary. Here. You might as well join my pity party. I'm serving Guinness today." Luke waved to the other chair. He slid the second beer in Mike's direction.

The two of them sat and drank for a few minutes while a car chase flashed across the TV screen and the bad guys got away before the commercial break. The air conditioner kept up its hum, and the clock ticked past the minutes. Mike didn't say a word, just let his friend wallow.

"You got a place to stay while you're on vacation?" Luke asked.

Mike shrugged. "I got a room at the Marriott over in Tampa."

"I have a spare room upstairs if you want it. Sheets are clean, but the bed squeaks when you roll over, so no overnight guests. I don't want some half-naked stripper in my kitchen when I come down to get my coffee."

"Is that your way of asking me to stay?"

"Hey, somebody needs to roast that chicken." Luke raised the beer in Mike's direction, and the two of them laughed the comfortable laugh of two friends who had been through hell and back.

Luke settled back in his chair, feeling a degree closer to good.

Fifteen

~~

The paper sheet chafed her ass, and Doc Harper chafed her nerves. Greta knew the young internist meant well, and he was just doing what that fancy medical school taught him to do, but seriously, the man needed to lighten up a little. He tut-tutted over this, tsk-tsked over that, and made that face she hated—the one that looked like a lemon had been shoved up his nose—when she admitted she hadn't eaten a salad in six months.

"I feel fine," Greta said, adjusting the slippery hem of the cotton exam gown. The material was some ungodly print with daisies on a pale blue background. It was enough to make anyone a little sick to their stomach. "I don't see why you want to waste money on tests."

"Just a precaution, Greta. Your heart is strong, but I'm concerned that you said you've been feeling so tired lately."

"I'm eighty-three. I'm supposed to be tired."

"Maybe so. But humor me, will you?" He glanced down at a small square thing he called a tablet and swiped his finger across the screen, then tapped a few things. He was a handsome man, the kind Greta herself would have liked when she was his age. Trim, tall, with short brown hair and dark blue eyes. He was one of those crazy athletic types who jogged every day, biked on the weekends, and thought the whole world should feel the burn. A little anal-retentive with his schedule and his ordered charts and lists, but overall, a decent enough young man. She wondered why no one had scooped him up and saddled him with a mortgage and a couple of kids.

Doc Harper tapped some more. "I'll schedule you for next week—"

"Next month. I have things to do this week. And there's nothing that says rush me to the hospital, or for that matter, rush me to the morgue, on that little chart of yours."

"No, there isn't." Doc Harper sighed and leaned a hip against the white laminate counter. "You are a stubborn woman, you know that?"

"Why does everyone keep saying that? I don't see it."

He laughed and returned his attention to the tablet thing. "Okay. Next month it is. But I don't want you overexerting yourself. And for Pete's sake, will you please try to sneak a vegetable or two into your diet?"

She scowled. "Some days, I swear you are trying to kill me."

He laid a hand on top of hers and gave her a smile. "Quite the opposite, Greta. Quite the opposite."

After he left, she got dressed, pausing a moment to catch her breath before heading out of the exam room. A half hour later, she was back in the morning room. Pauline and Esther were sitting at a table by the French doors, a pile of papers on the table before them, their two heads, one Clairol chestnut, the other God-given gray, pressed together as they talked. Esther had a pile of cards on her side, along with her little rubber stamps and her colored inks. The woman made a simple birthday card into a three-week art project.

"What diabolical plan are we concocting today?" Greta asked, as she slid into the third chair.

"How'd the doctor appointment go?"

Greta waved Pauline's concern off. "Fine. Same prescription

as always. Eat my vegetables, get my beauty sleep, and steer clear of Harold Twohig."

"Doc Harper didn't say that."

"No, but he did say to reduce my stress level, and steering clear of Harold Twohig is numero uno on that list."

Pauline shook her head. "I don't understand why you hate him so much. He's not a bad person. Why, he organized the toy drive this past Christmas. He gave dozens of children a merry Christmas."

"Probably scared them half to death is what he did, with that Grinch face of his."

Pauline laughed. "Okay, that might be so. But underneath the pointy nose is a decent human being."

"I'll believe it when he stops torturing me with that devil music he plays late at night. Someone needs to put the world out of its misery and ram that saxophone up his—"

"Greta!" Esther said. "Don't say it."

Greta threw up her hands. "What is the point of being old if I can't curse, and then blame it on dementia?"

Pauline just shook her head, apparently deciding that the Harold Twohig conversation was a lost cause. "Anyway, I'm glad you're here. I'm working on this week's column. We need to pick a letter to answer. And I'd like to give a status update on the first letter. People love that kind of thing."

"Oooh, is there news on the romance front for Luke and Olivia?" Esther said. "I just love a good happy ending."

"Nothing concrete yet," Greta said. Luke and Olivia were moving as slow as mules in mud. Greta needed to find a way to light a fire under their butts. "I'm planning a little fact-gathering mission for later in the week."

"Here's a good one," Esther said, tugging a letter out of the pile. "Dear Common Sense Carla, my first grandchild is due in a month and my son and his wife are planning on naming the child after the town where the baby was conceived. How do I tell them this is tacky and offensive? Signed, Worried Grandma-To-Be."

Pauline got her pad and pen ready and looked to the other two for input.

"Dear Worried Grandma-To-Be," Greta began. "It could be worse. They could be naming the child after the position they used for conception. Suck it up, and give the kid a cute nickname. Like Buddy."

"I can't write that," Pauline said. "What will people think?"

Olivia entered the morning room just then, heading for the assembled group seated by the entrance. They greeted her and Miss Sadie like long-lost friends, with happy smiles and excited chatter. Greta smiled. It was nice to see the way Miss Sadie and Olivia lifted the mood in this place. Why, it almost made it livable. The way the staff raved about Olivia, Greta was sure some place would want to snatch her up and pay her a better wage. This was why she had no time for Doc Harper's silly tests. Her grandson needed a wife, and Greta couldn't rest until she made sure he had one. This one.

Greta spun back to the other women. "Ladies, we need to step up our game where Olivia and Luke are concerned. Time to implement plan B."

"What's plan B?" Esther said.

Greta chewed on her bottom lip. She thought of Luke, and how his face had lit when she and Olivia had shown up with the sandwiches. How he'd watched Olivia's every move, hung on her every word. Luke was smitten, even if he didn't realize it. Maybe if the two of them got a little closer, spent some quality alone time, Luke would finally realize that Olivia was the one for him. "I don't know yet. But whatever it is, I think it better end up with the two of them doing the horizontal mambo. Because we all know most men think better with their—"

"Greta!" Esther shuddered and waved a hand.

"It's true. And if they get a little cozy under the covers, Luke will finally wake up to the fact that Olivia is his soul mate." Greta tapped the letter in Esther's hands. "And nine months later, they can name my first great-grandchild Sand in Your Britches."

Esther shook her head. Pauline laughed so hard, one of

the orderlies rushed over and asked her if she wanted oxygen. But Greta just smiled. She'd found the secret to healing her heart without one damned test from Doc Harper.

It lay in healing her grandson first.

The pancakes had been a mistake.

Diana had thought making chocolate chip pancakes, Jackson's favorite, would be a good way to start off a Wednesday. But Jackson gave them a nonplussed half glance. "What, am I five? I don't eat that crap anymore." He shook his head, then headed out the door, adding a slam for a punctuation mark.

Diana dumped the whole stack into the trash and sat down at the table, nursing a cup of coffee and wondering how on earth her happy-go-lucky toddler had turned into a disgruntled teenager.

"I love you," she said to the door, but Jackson was long gone, and the words fell on deaf ears.

She headed in to work, and once the stream of patients and owners started, Diana got lost in the usual Wednesday craziness, starting with rounds with the overnight patients and then the slate of surgeries she had every week. She'd just finished her second spaying of the morning when Linda poked her head in the door. "Call for you on line two."

"Can you take a message? I'm in the middle of suturing."

"It's the principal at Jackson's school."

Diana sighed. "Okay. I'll be there in a couple of minutes." She finished stitching up the incision, then handed off the terrier to the other tech working with her. "I might be a minute, so wait before bringing in the next patient."

She washed her hands, then ducked into her small office next door to the surgery. The scent of alcohol hung in the air, mingled with the scents of dogs and cats. Two dogs in the kennels in the back of the building warred for loudest bark, but the shut door kept the sound muted enough for a conversation. Diana picked up the phone and pushed the blinking red button. "This is Diana Tuttle."

"Mrs. Tuttle, this is Rescue Bay Middle School. I'm sorry to bother you, but Jackson didn't show up for school today, and since this is his fifth unexcused absence—"

"What do you mean, he didn't show up? I saw him leave this morning." Alarm pitched her voice higher. *Fifth* absence? When were the first four? How did she miss this?

"He didn't arrive at school today. I'm sorry. As I said, since this is his fifth unexcused absence, we'll have to have a meeting with you and him and the principal before he'll be allowed to return to classes. He'll need to sign an attendance contract before we let him return."

Diana mumbled agreement, thanked the school secretary, then hung up the phone. It took ten minutes to clear her schedule and get out the door, while calling and texting Jackson's phone at the same time. There'd be several frustrated owners today, but for Diana, nothing came before her son. Nothing.

They were all each other had, even if Jackson didn't realize that.

She drove home, slowly, gaze going left, right, looking for Jackson. By the time she entered her empty house, the alarm in her chest had bloomed into a near-panic. She got back in the car, checked her phone. Nothing. No response. She called him again, but her call went straight to voice mail.

"Where are you?" she said, but of course, Jackson didn't answer.

Diana put the car in gear again, then wound her way through the tangle of streets that made up her neighborhood. As she turned onto the main street, her phone rang. She grabbed it up and pressed the green button. "Hello?"

"Diana, it's Olivia."

"I'm sorry, but I don't have time to talk. I'm . . ." She didn't want to dump her personal life on a person who was still essentially a stranger and someone who had no business knowing about Diana's personal problems. "Busy."

"I know, and I apologize for interrupting your day, but I stopped at my house, well, at your mother's house and—"

"I don't really want to hear any renovation stories right now." The words came out of Diana, sharp and biting.

"I'm not calling about the house."

Diana peered around the corner of Shell Lane, then whipped her attention to the left, to the park behind the elementary school. "I'm really busy—"

"I think your son is here."

Diana sat up, slowed the car. "What did you say?"

"There's a boy here and he says he's not leaving because this is his grandmother's house. He wouldn't talk to me, and I, well, I assumed that he was your son, so I called you."

Diana exhaled, and nodded. Relief eased her shoulders and her grip on the steering wheel. Thank God, Jackson was okay. "Yes, he's my son. I'll be right there."

A few minutes later, Diana swung her car into the driveway of the house that was still, and maybe always would be, her mother's house to her. She parked, but instead of getting out of her Honda, she hesitated for a moment, half expecting to see her mother out in the yard, filling the dozens of bird feeders that still hung from the trees, or crossing the well-worn path from the house to the shelter, her arms filled with bags of dog food.

But then the image cleared and reality struck her hard. The house, falling apart at the seams and flanked by building supplies. The shelter, a tattered shell of a building empty of the animals that had once found refuge there. Now the sister Diana had never wanted lived there, putting her own stamp on every square inch.

Diana sighed, then strode forward. Olivia came out of the house and down the steps. As she headed down the walkway, Diana couldn't help but think again how much her older sister resembled their mother. It was like seeing the young pictures of Bridget, the one from Diana's childhood. Exuberant, energetic, happy.

"Where's Jackson?" Diana asked.

"Hanging out in the shelter. I tried to—"

"You let him stay in that decrepit building?" Diana marched forward, waving at the aging frame, the holey roof. "It could come down at any minute. Why would you let him stay there?"

Olivia swung in front of Diana and parked her fists on her hips. "First of all, I didn't *let* him do anything. I found him there. Someone, and I suspect it's Jackson, has been going in and out of the shelter for a couple weeks. And when you see him, you'll see why."

"What do you mean? What is he doing in there?"

"Follow me. You'll see." Olivia smiled, then started forward.

They ducked inside the animal shelter. Diana paused while her eyes adjusted to the dim interior. Dust motes floated in the sunshine streaming through the holes in the roof. The musty scent of disuse hung in the air like a sad cloak.

Diana heard the sounds first, familiar noises that told her what had drawn her child into the building. Soft barks and yips, coupled with the quiet, calming murmur of her son, came from around the corner, at the back of the shelter where the kennels were. "Hey, no, you can't do that," Jackson was saying. "Be nice to your brother. There. Enough for you and him."

Diana glanced at Olivia. "Puppies?"

Olivia nodded. "I don't think they're more than a few weeks old. Jackson has been here, I bet, pretty much every day, checking on Mom and her babies."

The two women turned the corner and went down the hall. Sunlight dappled the floor and washed circles of gold onto the concrete floors, and glinted off the kennel gates. At the far end, in the shadows of the shelter, was an open kennel door, held in place by a large rock. The tail end of a blue plaid blanket that Diana recognized as the one she kept in the guest bedroom peeked out from the corner of the kennel.

Inside, three gold and brown puppies scampered around a thin, exhausted-looking female lab mix. A half-empty bowl of dog food sat in the corner. In the center of it all was Jackson, far enough from Mom that he didn't seem a threat to her, but close enough for the puppies to climb all over him.

Here was the reason he had skipped school. The reason why he hadn't told her where he was going. The reason why she was missing a bag of dog food and a blanket.

Jackson glanced up, saw Olivia and his mother, and scowled. "Why did you call her?"

"She's your mother."

"You're supposed to be in school today," Diana said. "What are you doing here?"

"She's too weak to go out and get food," Jackson said, pointing to the mother dog. "Someone needed to take care of her."

"I could have done that if you had told me about the puppies."

Jackson's face set in that stone mask that said he didn't like being called out on a mistake. "I can take care of them. They're my dogs."

"Jackson—"

"I've been taking care of them, Mom. For weeks. You didn't even notice. And if I told you about them, you would have taken them somewhere. They might have ended up dead. At least here, I know they're okay. And I know they're going to live."

Diana bent down, scootching forward a little at a time, her hand out, nonthreatening, until the mother dog raised her snout and nuzzled the open palm. She kept her voice low, calm, though inside she wanted to both punish Jackson and hug him. "I would have never let that happen. Honey, I'm a vet. I love animals."

He looked up at her and his eyes glimmered in the dim light while the puppies tugged on the hem of his jeans and gnawed on his shoelaces. "Yeah, but not everyone does. And Grandma was the only one who wouldn't kill them."

Diana bit her lip. She wanted to tell her son that that was the reality of shelters, that sometimes they had to do the very thing they didn't want to do—put an animal to sleep—to be able to handle the continual influx of unwanted pets. That her mother had held a strict no-kill policy until the shelter got too overwhelming physically and financially and she'd had to shut her doors. That sometimes this was how life worked, and it sucked, and if she could change the world, she would.

But she didn't say one word of that because right now her son was looking at her with that same look he'd given her when he was seven and had come home crying from school because some fifth-grader told him Santa wasn't real. She couldn't dash his dreams then, or now.

"Well, they're going to need some shots," she said. "And Mom needs to be checked out. Why don't I come back later today with some supplies, and we can make sure these guys get the best start possible?"

Jackson's eyes filled with hope, and for a few seconds he was her little boy again, the one with tearstained cheeks and a trembling bottom lip, a little boy who desperately needed to believe in Santa and miracles. The angry, distant teenager had been left outside the kennel gate. "Really, Mom?"

"Yeah, if it's okay with Olivia." She glanced at her sister.

"Fine with me." Olivia gave Jackson a kind smile. "Plus I think I know the puppies' dad."

"The golden you brought in the other day?" Diana nodded. It all made sense.

"I found him out here, right in front of the shelter, in fact. I bet he was guarding his family-to-be."

Diana got to her feet and glanced at her son. One of the puppies had latched onto Jackson's jeans with his teeth and was pulling at the hard denim, while another puppy tried to snag his brother's tail. "They are cute."

"Can I keep them?" Jackson asked.

No was her immediate answer, but she bit her tongue again, unwilling to spoil the moment. "Let's get them through their first few weeks, and then we'll talk about it. Okay?"

He nodded, then buried his face in the third puppy's fur. "Okay." He nodded again. "Okay, Mom."

Her heart swelled, and she had to root her feet to the floor
so she wouldn't rush in there and topple Jackson with a hug.
Instead she stood to the side, and through the glimmer of
unshed tears, Diana watched a puppy steal her troubled son's
heart and fill him with joy for the first time in forever.

After a while, Olivia and Diana headed out of the shelter.
They hit the bright sunshine and paused in the yard. "He
can come by anytime he wants to feed them or play with
them. If you tell me what to do, I'll make sure they have
whatever food and things they need."

Diana sighed and glanced back at the ramshackle building. "It's not really safe for them in there. But I know Mom
won't be happy to be moved right away. If you can take care
of them for a couple days, then we'll see about bringing them
in to the office."

"Whatever it takes is fine. It's been kinda lonely around
here, so the puppies might be good company."

Diana toed at the ground. "I'll be back, as long as that's
all right with you."

In the distance, a car horn beeped and a bird called out.
A light breeze danced in the air, rustling the sturdy green
leaves of an orange tree.

"I'd like that," Olivia said.

Diana glanced again at the shelter. Her son was skipping
school, and there would be hell to pay for that down the
road, but right now, she wanted to hold on to this moment,
to that smile on his face. "Thanks."

"Anytime."

Diana exhaled and waited until a passing car turned off
the street and they were left with silence again. "I'm sorry
for being so . . . angry earlier. This whole thing is hard for
me." Still was, and Diana had no idea when it would get
easier. "I didn't expect . . . well, I didn't expect you."

"I didn't expect you either." Olivia gave her a smile that
was half sympathy, half hope. "We'll just play it by ear.
Okay?"

"Yeah." Diana had the strangest urge to hug Olivia. But
instead, she gave her a little wave and headed to her car.

Sixteen

❦

Olivia checked on the puppies once more, bringing Jackson a couple of grilled cheese sandwiches before she ran over to Golden Years for her afternoon appointments. She welcomed the break, to give her a moment where she wasn't wondering where she stood. With Luke. With Diana.

Her relationship with Diana, if one could even call it that, was still new and tenuous. Still, a part of Olivia reveled in the words *my sister*, words she'd never spoken or thought in her life until now. She wasn't quite sure how, or whether, they would get any further than cordial acquaintances. And whether she wanted that. After all, she'd gone all this time without a sister. Who said she needed one now? Especially one who didn't seem to need her?

Deep down inside, though, Olivia craved that connection. It was as if Diana held the other keys to Olivia, to figuring out why she was here in Florida, looking for a mother who hadn't ever looked for her.

Then there was Luke and the barbecue at his house tonight that she'd agreed to go to. That was a whole other kind of complicated relationship. She'd intended just to have a one-night stand with him, one hot, unforgettable night. Yeah, that plan had gone well. What kind of woman planned a one-night stand with the neighbor but didn't plan ahead for protection?

A clear sign that she was more of a multi-night kind of girl. And look how well *that* decision had turned out. She'd screwed up a marriage, she'd screwed up a fling. Maybe she should just enter a convent and give up on men altogether.

Inside the morning room, Greta, Pauline, and Esther were gathered around a stack of papers. As soon as Olivia approached, Pauline let out a squeal, gathered all the papers into one pile, then dropped her purse on top. Olivia grinned. "You ladies look suspicious today."

"Who? Us?" Greta gave Olivia a blank look. "We're just talking about the Sweetheart Dance next month. Pauline thought it might be a good idea to do a little mixer, you know, to get some of the singles to pair up."

Olivia considered that. "I think anything that gets people here to be more social is a good idea."

Greta fingered the sheets. "And maybe we could get some of our younger staff to participate. You know, lead the way for the rest of us."

Olivia could read the attempt at matchmaking from ten miles away. No way was she falling for that again. "Or maybe you and Harold Twohig could have a couple's peace treaty."

Greta scowled. "I would rather cover my face in fire ants."

"Oh, goodness, no, Greta." Esther blanched. "When they bite you, they sting. You'd get all swollen up and—"

"It's a figure of speech, Esther. I wouldn't really do that. Any more than I'd go out with Harold Twohig."

"I don't know," Olivia said with a smile. "Seems to me the lady doth protest too much. I think you secretly like Harold. He's not a bad-looking guy, you know."

"If you like men who resemble earwigs." Greta shuddered. "No, thank you."

Olivia laughed, then gave Miss Sadie's leash a gentle tug. "You ladies have a nice day. I'm off to my appointments."

The chair screeched as Greta got to her feet and started walking with Olivia, telling Pauline and Esther she'd be right back. "So, have you seen my grandson lately?"

Olivia's cheeks heated, but she cleared her throat and willed the blush away. She'd seen Luke all right—*all* of Luke—just before he ran out of her house. But that wasn't the kind of thing she'd mention to the man's grandmother. Or anyone else, for that matter. "Every once in a while," she said instead.

"I called him this morning. And he called me meddlesome. *Me*. Meddlesome." Greta shook her head. "I think he's just being grumpy."

"Well, Luke does have grumpy down to an art."

"It's because of all he's been through," Greta said quietly, her voice serious now. "He doesn't like to talk about it or let people know what he is going through. He suffers in silen e, I suppose you could say."

"I can understand that." Hadn't she done the same after her divorce? She'd retreated to her house and stayed there for days, as if solitude would make it better. It hadn't. "But his friend is there now, and they invited me to a barbecue tonight."

"Oh really? He didn't mention a friend at the house. Or a barbecue. With you." A smile spread across Greta's face, a smile that said she had a preacher and a church on speed dial. "That's *wonderful*."

"It's just chicken on the grill," Olivia said, "nothing more. So don't be getting any ideas, Mrs. Winslow."

"Who, me?"

Olivia chuckled. "Yes, you. Don't you remember talking me into walking you over to Luke's, then running out the door to leave us alone?"

Greta glanced at the ceiling. "Maybe. I'm not saying anything that might incriminate me."

"Listen, I appreciate the fact that you and the other ladies care about my happiness. It's nice. It's like having another family here, and that's made this whole move easier."

Greta took Olivia's hand in her own warm, soft one. "Sweetie, you *are* part of the family. I consider you the granddaughter I never had."

Emotion burned Olivia's eyes. She hadn't realized how much she missed having family around her until now. With Anna and Dan more than a thousand miles away, having Greta and the other ladies serve as her surrogate family washed Olivia with warmth. She gave Greta's hand a squeeze. "Thank you. It's been hard for me, not knowing"—she drew in a breath, then decided if she kept running from the questions, she'd never have the answers—"why my mother left me her house but never had anything to do with me."

Confusion filled Greta's light blue eyes, then sharpened as she put the pieces together. "That house on Gull Lane? The one that . . . Oh my. You're Bridget Tuttle's daughter? But I thought . . ."

"Diana is my sister."

"Oh." Greta's lips pursed. "Oh . . . my. Well, I thought I knew about everything in this town. But I didn't know this."

"No one did, as far as I can tell." Olivia glanced at her watch and shifted her bag of therapy supplies on her shoulder. She could spare one more minute. And maybe, finally, if she started talking about what Bridget had done, she'd gain some closure, and some answers. "That's what confuses me. Why would she leave me the house but not so much as a letter or a note? Why go all my life without contacting me? Why . . ." Olivia sucked in a breath, the last question lodged like a gumball in her throat.

"Why would she give you up and not want you?" Greta reached up and cupped Olivia's face, and in that simple touch, one that conveyed sympathy, understanding, and love with her soft, wrinkled palms, Olivia could have been Greta's granddaughter. "People do stupid things all the time, honey. Things they regret. And sometimes the way they try to make up for the mistakes they make is just as bumbled, because they don't know what else to do. Whatever your mother did or didn't do, I'm sure she did it with love."

Olivia turned away. "She never even knew me."

Greta gently brought her attention back. "Maybe she knew you better than you think. I didn't know Bridget well. I don't think most folks did. She kind of stuck to herself and poured everything she had into that shelter. Sometimes people do things like that to make up for pain that lies deep, deep inside." Greta's wrinkled, velvety palm served as a balm against Olivia's cheek. "And if you ask me, there's no deeper pain than losing your child. Whether it was your choice or not."

"Thank you."

"Don't thank me. Just find your peace with all this. You may never have the answers. But if you keep letting the emotions of the past rule your present, you'll never find your future, dear." She straightened and gave Olivia's arm a pat. "Now, you better get to your appointment. I know Millie needs you and Miss Sadie."

Millie. The one patient Olivia had yet to connect with. She dreaded the appointment.

"She doesn't show it," Olivia said. "She won't interact at all with me or the dog."

"Give it time." Greta's wise eyes softened. "She's in a dark place, and she's having trouble finding the light."

"I can relate to that. Thanks for all the advice, Greta. You're the best grandma anyone could ask for," Olivia said. She gave Greta a quick hug, then headed down the hall, with Miss Sadie trotting along, her little white tail wagging in anticipation. Miss Sadie seemed to sense the change in Olivia's demeanor, or the more purposeful stride, and shifted into work mode at the same time.

Before Olivia even reached the room, she knew they had their work cut out for them today. After several weeks of trying to engage Millie during the group appointments, Olivia and Millie's therapy team decided to try some one-on-one with Miss Sadie and Millie to try to encourage her to step out of her self-enclosed shell.

Thus far, most of the patients at Golden Years had responded well to Olivia and Miss Sadie. The days when someone who had suffered a stroke lifted her arm to toss a treat for Miss Sadie, or a heart patient opted to walk farther down the path just because he was enjoying the time with the dog, warmed Olivia's heart and told her she had made the right choice in giving up her retail job for this one.

But then she encountered patients like Millie, who didn't respond at all, whose walls stayed up, and who made Olivia wonder if a better therapist could do a better job. Those days she questioned her career choice and her skill.

Olivia drew in a deep breath, then gave a light knock on the door before entering the therapy room. "Hi, Millie! How are you today?"

No response. Millie sat in an armchair by the window, her hands in her lap, her long white hair brushed back from her face and hanging loose around her shoulders. She had on a pair of pajamas, even though it was the middle of the afternoon, and scuffed pale-pink slippers. Olivia knew, from talking to her therapy team, that Millie often refused to get dressed for the day or to do much more than basic care. Depression emanated from Millie in waves. Even Miss Sadie sensed it and slowed her happy dog pace as she neared Millie.

"Miss Sadie wanted to say hello," Olivia said, then gave the dog a signal with her finger. Miss Sadie plopped onto her butt and let out a little yip.

No response.

"Why don't we start with something simple today?" Olivia said. She fished in her pocket for a Cheerio, Miss Sadie's favorite snack. "Would you like to give Miss Sadie a snack?"

Millie shifted in her seat and shook her head. Olivia bit back a sigh.

"Are you sure? She'd really love it if you did."

Millie ignored her.

Miss Sadie glanced over her shoulder, with that *What do you want me to do now?* look. Olivia reached in her bag and pulled out a trio of colored cups. "Millie, I'm going to hide a treat for Miss Sadie. How about you point to which color cup you want me to hide it under?"

No response.

Olivia tried for another ten minutes, but Millie either ignored her or looked away whenever Olivia asked her a question or tried to engage her. Miss Sadie even tried sitting right in front of Millie, eager to interact, and except for a brief flicker of something that could have been a smile or could have been annoyance, there'd been no response. Finally, Olivia gave up, packed up her bag, and headed out of the room.

"How'd it go?" Kris, the occupational therapist on Millie's team, asked when Olivia came out to the nurses' station.

Olivia sighed. "I don't know what I'm doing wrong."

"Maybe nothing, hon," Kris said. The short brown-haired woman had worked at Golden Years for ten years now and almost always had some bit of wisdom to impart. The other therapists on the team looked to Kris for guidance and leadership on a daily basis. "Sometimes the patient needs to make the choice to be open to the therapeutic process. Millie has to decide she's going to leave all that emotional weight at the door, and just . . . do it. We can't force her. She has to decide on her own."

"I'll keep working with her." Miss Sadie let out a little yip. "And so will Miss Sadie."

"That's the spirit." Kris smiled. "You never know when the breakthroughs are going to come. You just have to be patient and open. And don't forget to leave your own emotions at the door, too. Sometimes patients sense your stress, and that just adds to the wall they have up."

"I know. I just feel like such a failure. All the other patients have responded so well."

"You can't change everyone's life in one day, O Super Handler." Kris grinned, then went back to work.

Olivia headed off to her group appointment and thought about what Kris had said. Had she let her own frustrations show today? Brought her worries and stresses about the house and her mother to work? Next appointment with

Millie, Olivia vowed to leave all that at the door, as Kris had said, and make the patient the priority.

By the time she had finished her appointments for the day, a mix of anxiety and anticipation swirled inside her. When she got into the driver's seat of her car, Miss Sadie hopped across the divide and cuddled into Olivia's lap. "Silly girl," she said softly, giving her bichon a loving pat. "Read my mind, huh?"

Miss Sadie let out a little yip and pranced a bit before settling down again.

"Maybe you should be the therapist and I'll be the assistant. Would you like that, puppy?" Olivia rubbed Miss Sadie's ears, then let the warm, slobbery love of a dog wash over her. The unconditional devotion eased the tension in Olivia's shoulders, and by the time she had Miss Sadie strapped into her seat and the car in motion, the anxiety had dissipated.

She swung into the driveway, parking to the left of Diana's car. Miss Sadie beelined for the dog door and headed inside the house, undoubtedly for an after-work nap. Olivia headed toward the shelter. As she traveled the well-worn path, she realized her mother had walked this same path. Her mother's shoes had been the ones that flattened the grass, scuffed up the dirt. And now, Olivia was following in those footsteps.

Diana stood in the doorway of the shelter. Olivia had never seen a picture of Bridget, but she suspected their mother looked much like her daughters. Was she seeing a younger version of her mother? Seeing the way she looked when she'd built this shelter and embarked on her mission to save homeless pets?

"What?" Diana said when Olivia approached. "You're staring at me."

"I'm sorry. I just . . . well, I've never seen a picture of our mother and I wondered if she looked like you."

In an instant, sympathy flooded Diana's green eyes and softened her features. "Actually, she looked more like you."

A rush of hot tears raced up Olivia's throat and to the back of her eyes. "She did?"

Diana nodded. She cast her eyes to the ground, and Olivia read an echoing pain in Diana's eyes. No wonder the two of them kept circling each other like wary dogs. They each came into this with their own hurt and betrayal. Olivia with Bridget's abandonment, and Diana with Bridget's secrets.

Diana reached into her back pocket and tugged out a cell phone. "Actually, I have a couple of her on my phone. They're from last summer, before she got sick again." Diana scrolled with her fingertip, then flipped the phone's screen toward Olivia. "This is Mom."

Mom.

Olivia stared at the image of a tall, thin woman with long blond hair and a wide smile. But it was her eyes—laughing, dancing green eyes that peeked out beneath a wide-brimmed straw hat—that grabbed Olivia. "She looks happy."

"She was. When she was here, at least. This place was her life."

Olivia detected a note of bitterness in her sister's words. Perhaps she wasn't the only one left behind. Olivia danced her finger down the image, skirting along the lines of Bridget's floral-print sundress, her neon-pink flip-flops. "What was she like?"

"Unpredictable. Spontaneous. Devoted to the dogs." Diana shrugged, then tucked the phone away. "I never saw her as much as I wanted to. She was always here."

"What happened?"

"Cancer." Diana let out a low curse and shook her head. "She wouldn't let anyone else run this place, even though I offered, and it fell apart. Did I add stubborn to the list? Because she was that, too."

"And your dad? I mean, is he . . . still around?"

Diana was shaking her head before Olivia finished the question. "I don't know who my father is. Or yours. Mom wasn't much for long-term relationships."

"Oh." The picture Diana painted of Bridget was filled

with contradictions. A woman devoted to her cause, but not to her children. Or her home. Had she poured everything she had into the shelter, with nothing left over for the people in her life?

"Listen, I better get back in there and make sure Jackson isn't spoiling those puppies too much."

"Can I help?"

"I've got it under control. Thanks." The words were friendly, but the message was clear. Diana wanted some time alone, some distance from the painful subject of their mother. She stepped away, then turned back. "If you could bring out a bowl of warm water and some rags, that'd be great. I bet these little guys could use a bath."

An olive branch. Olivia nodded, then headed inside. She fed Miss Sadie, let Chance out, then grabbed a bucket and a stack of old T-shirts. Miss Sadie clambered onto the sofa, tucked herself into a ball, and fell asleep under the warmth of the waning afternoon sun. Chance, however, came outside with her. "I bet you want to see your family, huh, buddy?"

Chance wagged his tail, his ears perked. He nosed the door of the shelter open and wriggled inside, then trotted down the hall and around the corner to the kennel. Diana greeted the dog, then bent down and peeked at his wound. Chance whined until she released him, then tiptoed into the kennel.

Jackson's face, annoyed and aggravated when his mother was around, exploded into a smile at the sight of Chance. "There you are." He wrapped his arms around the golden's neck, then gave him an affectionate ear rub. Then Jackson glanced up at Olivia. "Where did you find him?"

"Right here, a couple weeks ago. I took him into your mom's office, and she fixed him up."

"He's healing really well," Diana said to Olivia with a nod of appreciation, before returning her attention to her son. "He's going to be just fine."

"Yeah. Okay. Good." Jackson redirected his attention to the dogs. Angry teenager still filled his face. The cold war between parent and child was nearly palpable.

"I brought the water and rags," Olivia said, hoisting the bucket. "Do you want some help?"

Diana glanced at the rambunctious puppies, wrestling and tumbling all over each other. "Each of us take one?"

Jackson nodded. Olivia dropped to her knees, put the bucket between the three of them, and doled out the rags. They each grabbed a puppy, then took turns wiping their wriggling bodies. The female slid between Olivia's wet hands and scampered to the side before Olivia could scoop her up again. "They're so slippery."

Jackson's puppy pounced forward, knocking into the bucket and sending a spray of water over everyone, but especially Jackson. At first, his face pinched with frustration. "That's my favorite shirt. Cut that out." He corralled the puppy and dragged him back.

At the same time, Olivia's puppy twisted away again and head-butted the bucket, in Jackson's direction. This time, the water sprayed across Jackson's face, down his shirt, and onto the puppy, who shook his body and sent a rainstorm of soapy water onto everyone else.

Diana started laughing first. Then Olivia, then finally Jackson. Their laughter filled the empty building, echoed off the crumbling walls, bounced off the leaf-covered concrete floor. It lifted the room like helium as they finished the puppies and dried them off.

"God, those dogs were a pain in the butt," Jackson said, getting to his feet and wiping the worst of the soapy water off his jeans.

"So were you, when you were a baby. You used to hate baths. Half the time, I ended up soapier than you."

Jackson looked down at the puppies and grinned. "Guess that was what you call payback."

"Definitely." Diana reached out and ruffled her son's head. He blushed and made a little face but didn't move away. Diana's green eyes met Olivia's, and in their depths Olivia saw gratitude. Hope.

"Sounds like a water balloon fight in here."

They turned at the sound of the male voice. Mike stood

in the doorway, grinning at the three of them, but his gaze stayed on Diana. Luke stood just behind Mike, wearing those sunglasses, a barbecue fork in one hand.

"Didn't mean to interrupt," Luke said. "But you said you wanted me to check things out if I heard an intruder. Didn't know it was a dog-washing party."

"And you came to my rescue with a barbecue fork?" Olivia grinned. He'd come to check on her, to make sure she was okay. Maybe he wasn't as uninterested as he claimed.

"Don't forget the brawny men." Mike flexed a bicep.

"Men, plural?" Luke said, his tone dry. "I only see one brawny guy here."

"Hey, I try not to flex my muscles too often. It drives the women crazy."

"You mean it drives them away." Luke thumbed toward Mike. "Forgive my friend. He's still stuck in Cro-Magnon Man mode."

"Me? You're the one who got a visit from Miss Manners." Mike leaned toward Olivia. "That's a story for another day."

Luke scowled. "No, it's not."

"Just ask Luke about the time he spilled a gravy boat on the admiral's wife. Damned near got sent to the brig for that one." Mike gave Luke a playful jab. "Totally uncouth, this one. You can't take him anywhere."

"I'll remember that," Olivia said.

Mike thrust a hand in Diana's direction. "I'm Mike Stark, flight mechanic with the Coast Guard and temporary roommate of the Neanderthal."

"Diana Tuttle. Local vet and mother of a budding Neanderthal."

The men laughed at that, and Jackson shot his mother a look of annoyance—tempered with a half smile. At their feet, the puppies tumbled and wrestled, using the adults' feet as staging.

"Thanks for checking on me," Olivia said to Luke. "It turns out my intruder was Jackson. He's been checking on some puppies that were born in the shelter."

Mike's gaze took in the space. "Not the safest place to have puppies."

Diana nodded. "We're hoping to move them in a couple of days. We're letting Mom recuperate a bit, and then I'll take them to my office."

"Just keep an eye on that beam there," Mike said, pointing at the ceiling. "If you want, I can come by and check the place out later tonight. I was a contractor before I went into the Coast Guard."

"That'd be great," Olivia said. "I have no idea what I'm doing, and the problem is there's so much to do."

"I can see that."

Luke cleared his throat. "We better get back next door."

"Oh yeah. Chicken on the grill." Mike turned to Diana. "Hey, if you're not doing anything, why don't you come, too? You can bring your Neanderthal-in-training, too. Us guys can sit around and grunt while you ladies make up a list of our bad habits."

Diana laughed. "Now that's an offer I've never had before."

A grin quirked up one side of Mike's face, a grin that spelled interest in the pretty blond veterinarian. "Stick with me, and you'll get plenty of those."

"Oh, for the love of all that is holy, leave the women alone." Luke grabbed Mike's T-shirt and tugged him to the side. "Let me go hose him down."

Diana and Olivia laughed as the men left, then headed back across the lawns to Luke's house. When they were gone, Diana and Olivia gathered up the cleaning supplies and headed for the house.

"I didn't know you knew Luke Winslow," Diana said. "I haven't seen him for at least four years, maybe longer."

"You know Luke?"

"Rescue Bay is a really small town. He's a couple years older than me, but we went to the same high school. He was quite the athletic star back in those days. All-around best athlete, salutatorian, best smile, all those things. The girls were all gaga over him. Mr. Popularity, that was Luke."

"Really?" Olivia's gaze went in the direction Luke had gone. The glimpses she'd had of a different man, one who joked and teased, hinted at the one he had been before. Was that man still the true Luke? "The same guy?"

Diana tipped the bucket of soapy water onto the driveway, then bent to wring out the rags. "I heard he was in an accident when he was in the Coast Guard. I don't know what happened, but I heard it was bad."

"His vision was damaged," Olivia explained. "That's why he wears sunglasses pretty much all the time. To make it easier to see, and, I think, harder for others to stare."

"That I can understand. In a small town, gossip can be a contact sport." Diana fished in her pocket for her keys. "Anyway, I better go get Jackson before that mother dog adopts him as one of her pups."

"Wait, aren't you coming to dinner? Mike invited you."

Diana turned her keys over and over in her palm. "Oh, I don't want to intrude."

"You wouldn't be intruding. You'd be providing backup. I can't be the token girl with those two self-proclaimed Neanderthals." Olivia leaned toward Diana and thumbed in the direction of Luke's yard. "Besides, I think Mike is very interested in you."

"In me?" She pressed a hand to her hair. A flush filled her cheeks. "Well, maybe he's the one with vision problems, because I'm a mess and I smell like dog."

"He must like that." Olivia nodded toward the break in the fence. "Check it out."

Mike and Luke were standing by the grill. Mike had his back to the grill, and his attention on Olivia's house. When he saw Diana looking his way, he raised his beer and tossed her a grin.

The pink in Diana's cheeks deepened to crimson. "I'm not looking for a relationship right now. I have enough on my plate. But you, you should go for Luke. He's definitely interested in you."

Olivia laughed. Did her sister realize how parallel their

lives were, even though the two had grown up miles and years apart?

"What?" Diana asked.

"I said the exact same thing when I moved here and met Luke. And let's just say that despite my vow not to get involved, Luke and I haven't exactly kept things . . . platonic."

"Really?"

Now it was Olivia's turn to blush. "Really. There's strength in numbers, sis, so let's go over there and show those guys how very *uninterested* we are."

Diana glanced at Mike one more time. A smile curved across her face. "Sounds like a plan."

Luke didn't know whether to punch Mike or hug him for the barbecue idea. He figured he'd wait until the night was over, then decide.

Being around Olivia was pure torture. His body remembered being naked with her. Kissing her. Tasting her. Running his hands down her sweet, soft skin. How close, so, so damned close he'd come to being inside her.

Every time she laughed or moved or the breeze sent a tantalizing snippet of her perfume his way, he wanted her all over again. She had changed from shorts and a tee into a butter-yellow dress that skimmed over her curves and belled around her knees. She had on simple white flip-flops that kept it all simple, casual. As if she could kick off the shoes at any second and run through a meadow.

"For God's sake, I'm turning into a damned Hallmark commercial," Luke muttered to Mike. The two of them were tending to the chicken over a hot fire, like the he-men they'd purported to be. Really, Mike was cooking and Luke was staring at Olivia. "What is it with that woman?"

"Who? Olivia?"

"Of course, Olivia." Luke scowled. "Are you listening to a word I say?"

"Only the curse words."

That made Luke laugh. Damn, he was glad Mike was here. Mike had a way of making even the worst situation seem like a minor setback, and always had. Luke tipped his beer Mike's way, then headed over to the women. Olivia and Diana were busy setting up the picnic table on the patio—an old, wooden thing that had been here since he'd bought the house and that he had sat at maybe once since he'd moved in. They were draping a checked piece of cloth over the wooden surface, then laying out silverware and dishes he hadn't even realized he owned. Olivia's dogs sat on the grass and watched the entire process.

Luke followed Olivia into the house, where she started spooning store-bought potato salad into a serving bowl. A platter of her homemade brownies sat on the countertop. Mike and Luke hadn't actually made anything for their impromptu barbecue, letting Winn-Dixie do all the heavy lifting. Turned out Mike's supersecret barbecue sauce consisted of mixing two different flavors of Sweet Baby Ray's.

Now the women were turning the men's pathetic attempts at a meal from a bachelor mishmash into something almost . . . civil. "Where did you find all this stuff?"

"In your hutch," Olivia said.

"My . . . what?"

Olivia laughed. "The big glass-and-wood thing in the dining room. There was a tablecloth in one of the drawers, and these dishes in the cabinet."

"I didn't . . ." Luke chuckled and shook his head as he put the pieces together. When he'd been recuperating in Alaska, Greta had offered to put the house together for him. He'd sent her a check and she'd done the rest, picking up furniture and dishes and food. She'd even filled the salt and pepper shakers and made sure he had napkins tucked in a little holder on the counter. Taking care of him, just as she had when he'd been a little boy and his father had broken yet another promise to be home in time for dinner. Back then, Greta had eased Luke's disappointment and loneliness with macaroni and cheese. Today, she'd done it with tablecloths and dishes. "My grandma. Trying to make me domesticated."

"And how's that going?"

"Oh, I'm a regular Martha Stewart now," he said, his tone dry. "Stick around for the homemade ornaments and tree-decorating class later."

She tossed him a grin. "I'd pay good money to see you making Christmas ornaments."

"Does that mean you'll be here at Christmas?" he asked, then wanted to kick himself. What the hell? Why had he asked that? What was he doing? Making plans for ten months from now? Hell, he didn't even know what *he* would be doing by then.

He almost snorted. What he'd be doing? He'd be doing the same damned thing ten months from now, ten years from now. His vision would never be a hundred percent again and any man who held on to the thought that he could return to the life he'd had would be a fool.

"I'm not planning on going anywhere, Luke. You're stuck with me." She hefted the bowl into the crook of her arm, then grabbed the ketchup and relish in the other hand, with the mustard dangling between two fingers. "Can you get the door, please?"

"Here. Let me take that." He reached for the dish, but the dim light made it hard to judge the distance and just as he took the bowl from her, the patterned vessel slipped through his fingers and crashed to the floor, spraying stoneware chips and mayonnaise-coated chunks. Luke cursed and bent to pick up the worst of it, but the mess blurred in and out of his vision, melting into the tile's pattern.

Olivia grabbed his hand. "Wait. You'll cut yourself."

"Goddammit, I'm not an invalid! I can do it!"

She recoiled, and a wave of regret hit him hard. When did he become this person who barked at people? A man who let a broken bowl make him so angry he couldn't see straight? He rocked back on his heels and ran a hand through his hair. "I'm sorry."

But it was too late. The screen door slammed behind

Olivia. Luke sighed, then got the dustpan out of the closet and began scooping up what he could see, then tossing it into the nearby trash can. He heard the door open again and he turned, but instead of Olivia's lithe figure, he saw the hulking shadow of Mike standing in the doorway.

"Can't leave you alone for five minutes, can I?" Mike said.

Luke scowled. Because Mike had found him like this, weak and covered in potatoes, and because Mike wasn't Olivia. "I don't need your help. I'm cleaning up the mess."

"Are you? Because it seems to me, both messes are out of control. Outside I see a woman who looks ready to either cry or rip you a new one. And you're in here, on your hands and knees, with your kitchen covered in potato salad. Did you two have a food fight?"

"Very funny. No, we didn't have a food fight." Luke waved at the stoneware shards. "I dropped the fucking bowl."

Mike grabbed the roll of paper towels on the counter, then bent down beside Luke and began swiping up the potato salad.

"I said I don't need your help."

"No, you don't. But you're getting it anyway. You can growl at me all you want, butterfingers, and I'm not going anywhere. I'm tougher than that. Just remember, not everyone will take your crap and keep coming back for more." Mike laid a hand on Luke's shoulder. "So get that through your thick skull and quit biting the hands that help you."

Luke rested his arms on his bent knees. "You're right. I'm an idiot."

"Yup. You are."

"Hey!"

Mike shrugged. "You said it. I'm just agreeing. Now let's get this cleaned up. There's barbecue chicken, cold beers, and beautiful women waiting for us outside. The trifecta of perfection."

The two men worked together, and a few minutes later they had the mess cleared and the kitchen set to rights. Luke changed his clothes, then headed outside with Mike. Olivia and Diana were talking, joined now by the lanky figure of Diana's son, Jackson.

It looked like a Kodak shot of a family reunion, and for a man who had been doing a damned good impression of a hermit for the last few weeks, the crowd took a bit to get used to. Mike gave Luke a nudge. "Don't forget to wear your nice mask. Don't want to give people indigestion, you know."

"Then maybe you better stay out of sight."

Mike chuckled, then headed for the grill and began loading the meat onto a platter. Luke adjusted his sunglasses against the glare of the setting sun. Olivia watched him, her expression unreadable. Cold, almost. He couldn't blame her, especially after he'd transformed into King Kong back in the kitchen.

"Uh, dinner's done," Luke said. "Extra stuff is on the table, except for the potato salad, which met with an unfortunate accident earlier. There's beer in the cooler for everyone. Except those who are too young to shave."

"That's you, buddy," Diana said to her son.

"Yeah, I know, Mom. Quit treating me like a baby, will you?" Jackson dropped onto the bench of the picnic table, back into angry teenager mode. Miss Sadie got up, padded over to Jackson's feet, and laid her little body beside his black-and-white Converse sneakers.

Frustration pinched Diana's features. She started to say something, changed her mind, and instead crossed to the grill. "Can I help you?" she asked Mike.

"You bet." Mike broke into a grin and handed her the platter.

Luke sidled over to Olivia, reaching into the cooler behind her for a beer. He held it out to her. "Peace offering."

"Thanks." She popped off the top but didn't drink.

He slid a leg over the worn board that formed the bench of the picnic table and sat beside her. "I didn't mean to bite your head off earlier. I just get . . . sensitive when people try to help me. I'm not used to needing help."

"Asking for help doesn't make you weak, you know. It makes you smart."

Wise words. Words he knew he should take to heart. But for a man who'd spent most of his life being independent, doing for himself, and being the leader, hard words to accept.

"Yeah, well, I haven't been that very often either." He set his beer on the table and wrapped his hands around the icy amber bottle. "Anyway, I just wanted to say I was sorry."

She held his gaze for a moment, then nodded. "Apology accepted."

Two words, but they eased something in Luke, allowed the tension in his frame to uncoil. He took a deep sip of the beer, and it hit just right, cold, smooth, satisfying. For the first time all day, he felt like things would be okay. Olivia sat beside him, in the kind of comfortable silence that came with knowing someone a while. He liked that.

A lot.

A cold nose nudged Luke's elbow. He reached over and scratched Chance behind the ears. "I swear this dog is here more than he's at your house."

She grinned. "He likes you."

"Clearly a sign he's not the brightest dog in the world." The masochistic part of him wondered if the dog's owner liked him just as much. Granted, she'd been naked and in his arms just a couple of days ago, so it was probably a safe bet to think yes, she did like him.

He liked that, too.

A lot.

Olivia laughed. "I don't know about that. Dogs are good judges of character."

Luke kept on rubbing Chance's ears. Easier to do that than to discuss the kind of character the dog was judging. If Olivia knew the truth about Luke, about what kind of man he'd been when people needed him most, neither she nor Chance would come within ten feet of him. The golden groaned and leaned into the touch, unconditional love. The damned dog was growing on him. "I think he's just buttering me up for another walk."

"He loves those walks. Soon as he sees the leash, he gets all excited."

The two of them exchanged a heated look, the memory of their moonlit walk and where it almost led charging the air. Olivia blushed and glanced away.

"Tell me you're talking about leashing the dog, not Luke. There are certain things that are definitely TMI in my world." Mike laid the platter of chicken in the center of the table, then took a seat beside Luke. "From what I hear, that leashing thing is all the rage in literature these days."

Diana grinned and settled onto the bench beside Olivia. "Oh really? Is that where your reading tastes lie?"

A sexy grin slid across Mike's face. "Any time you want to see my library, I'd be glad to show it to you."

Diana shook her head. "Men. Always looking for sex."

"And what exactly is wrong with that?" Mike asked. "Sex is a healthy expression of one's body."

Luke snorted. "Now there's a pickup line that's sure to win over the ladies."

"Oh, are we talking winning over ladies?" Mike asked. He leaned across the table. "Because if so, I have a tale to tell."

"Don't."

Olivia glanced at Luke, then at Mike. "What tale?"

"Don't do it," Luke said.

"Don't worry, I'll stick to the PG version for the kids."

"I'm not a kid," Jackson said.

"No, you're not," Mike said, his voice lowering into common respect, "but there are ladies here, so a gentleman keeps the story clean."

Jackson shrugged, appeased. "I get that."

"Did Luke ever tell you the story about the time he rescued a cat in a tree?" Mike said to Olivia.

"Nope."

"I don't think—"

Mike waved off Luke's objection. "We're up in Kodiak, waiting around for the next call. Some days are so busy, you think you're going to turn into a human tornado; other days are so slow, you're watching soap operas in between playing cards."

"A closet *Days of Our Lives* fan?" Olivia asked Luke.

"Not me. Mike was the one who got weepy watching *Days.*"

"I plead the fifth." Mike put up his hands. "Anyway, while we're out on a regular patrol, this call comes in from this lady who docked her boat on one of the little islands off the coast. Doing some bird-watching or something like that. Anyway, her cat got loose, climbed a tree, and wouldn't come back. Weather's on its way, and the lady's sister, who was along for the ride, can't talk the woman into leaving until she's got the cat back."

"She brought her cat along when she went bird-watching?"

"Probably made the whole thing more interesting," Luke said.

"Luke and I decide what the hell, we're not doing anything, so we head on over there. It's not far from the base, and the weather's good. Visibility's four miles, low clouds in the sky, but the forecasters say there's a storm coming in fast from the east. Before we can get to the lady, the weather kicks into overdrive. Ops is on the radio, saying there's a boater in distress a few miles away, so we abort the cat mission and the patrol to head for the Mayday call. It's a sailboat, caught in some rough water out on the east side of Kalsin Island. Whitecaps everywhere, twenty-five-knot winds. The captain's inexperienced—"

"And a little drunk—"

"And trying to impress these two cute brunettes who are with him by pretending he knows what he's doing, but he's in over his head. One of the girls was smart enough to call the Coast Guard soon as the boat started taking on water. The wind is getting vicious, the ocean is snarling, and the danger quotient goes from one to a thousand in seconds.

Luke's the PIC—pilot in command, his first day in the chair—but he's cool as a cucumber, holding the helo steady. We lower down the swimmer and pluck all three people off the boat just before it went down. A few hairy moments at the end there because the boat started listing bad, but Luke kept calm, got us in and out fast."

"Quit making me sound like Superman and General Schwarzkopf all rolled into one."

"Just telling it like it happened." Mike grinned. "But I left out the best part. Once we got the helo on deck, the two girls wanted to thank the man who saved their lives. They climbed right over the crew and up into the cockpit to give Luke-boy here a Doublemint-twin hug."

"Damned near suffocated me. It was your job to keep them in the back."

Mike shrugged. "What can I say? I was blinded by beauty."

Luke scoffed.

"Oh, I forgot the best part. On the way back to base, we buzzed the island and scared the hell out of the woman's cat, which leapt out of the tree and right into her arms. You couldn't have written that ending if you'd been in Hollywood."

Olivia and Diana laughed. Jackson gave Luke a look of guarded respect.

"That's incredible," Olivia said. "Quite impressive, too. Saving multiple lives in one swoop."

"Just doing my job." Luke shrugged, pretending he didn't care that Olivia was impressed.

"But what really made Luke a legend was what happened the next day," Mike said.

"Mike—"

Mike ignored Luke's interruption. "The sailboat folks had a touch of hypothermia from being out in the wet and cold for so long. We took them to the hospital after we got them off that boat, and that night, the boat's owner had a heart attack. Because he was in the hospital when it happened, they were able to save him, get him into surgery and put in a stent. If he'd been out on the water, he wouldn't have been that lucky."

Luke shrugged it off. "Coincidence, nothing more."

"We started calling him Double after that. Not just for the Doublemint twins—"

Luke scowled, and shifted in his seat. He wished Mike would just shut the hell up, but both Olivia and Diana were hanging on his every word. Even the kid had his attention glued to Mike.

"But for the double save, too. Remember what Joe used to say? That Joe, had a saying for everything." Mike shook his head and smiled. "He said you—"

The mention of Joe's name was tinder to a simmering flame. Luke jerked to his feet. What had he been thinking, agreeing to this insane barbecue? He didn't need people around, reminding him of what used to be and how he had screwed that all up, not just for himself, but for Joe, too. A man who'd killed his best friend was no hero, and Luke wished Mike would understand that.

"Quit telling these bullshit stories," Luke said. "The man who did all that doesn't exist anymore. So let him go once and for all."

No one said a word for a good thirty seconds after Luke stalked into the house and slammed the door. Miss Sadie jumped up into Olivia's lap, as unnerved as the humans at the table.

"I thought maybe he was getting better," Mike said. "But I guess I was wrong."

Olivia had seen this same wall in patients. Their anger, frustration, from the hand that fate had dealt them, made them put up a stack of emotional bricks and lash out at those who loved them.

"I asked him about what happened, but he won't talk about it."

"He should," Mike said. "It's a story I think he *needs* to tell. He hasn't talked to anyone about that day, and I'm no psychiatrist, but I think just getting it out there will help him a hell of a lot."

In Mike's deep blue eyes, she could read concern for his friend, as well as an unbreakable bond of loyalty. Luke was lucky to have such friends. She glanced at the closed, dark house and wondered if he realized that, too.

The three of them cleaned up while Jackson tossed a tennis ball with Chance and Miss Sadie in the yard. Miss Sadie, who had little interest in fetch and more interest in catch, ran after the golden, who did all the hard work of retrieving the ball. Jackson kept the distances short, which allowed Chance to trot after the ball without too much effort.

Olivia came up to Diana, the two of them loaded with dishes and condiments. They were standing by the back door, watching the boy and the dogs. From time to time, Jackson's annoyed-with-the-world expression would flicker into a smile. "He's a good kid," Olivia said.

"He's a challenge, that's what he is." Then a smile, much like Jackson's, curved across Diana's face. "But yeah, at his heart, Jackson is a good kid."

"He loves animals. Does he work with you?"

Diana let out a laugh and turned to open the door, waving Olivia in first. "God, no. We'd probably kill each other. He's your typical teenage boy who is going through a very long I-hate-my-mother phase."

Olivia opened the fridge and stowed the ketchup and mustard inside. She found plastic wrap in one of the drawers and started stowing the leftovers. Mike headed down the hall to find Luke. Deep inside the house, Olivia could hear the low murmur of the television.

Diana and Olivia worked together well, dividing up the kitchen duty without a word, making something as simple as cleaning up from dinner a quick and easy task. It wouldn't seem like a big deal to most people, but to Olivia, who had never shared anything with a sibling, the event was a giant step forward.

"Once the renovations are done, I was thinking of getting the shelter back up and running," Olivia said. "Maybe

Jackson would like to help with that. It would give him something to do, and a sense of accomplishment. There's plenty he can help do until then, just clearing out the place and getting it ready to be fixed up."

Diana wrapped up the chicken and tucked it in the fridge. "I think he'd like that. And it would keep him out of trouble."

Olivia plucked a brownie from the platter and took a bite. She leaned against the counter while behind her, warm water filled the sink. "I went through a difficult phase when I was a teenager. My mom talked me into volunteering at an animal shelter, partly to keep me out of her hair and partly to teach me about caring for something other than myself. I worked there on weekends, walking the dogs, feeding the animals, all the way through high school and college, and even after I graduated and was working in a horrible retail job. I would go there, and whatever stress I was feeling from work or my marriage would disappear."

"Is that what led you to what you do now?"

"Yep. I met a woman who did animal-assisted therapy when she came in to adopt a rescue mutt one day and she told me about how rewarding it was, not just for the patients, but for the dog and the handler, too. Then someone dropped off Miss Sadie and the rest, they say, is history. I started going to night school to get my therapist's license, joined a group that did animal-assisted therapy so I could get licensed as a handler, and got the job here."

"I'd love to know more about what you do," Diana said. "Maybe someday you could come in and talk to me and my staff, and let us get to know Miss Sadie. See her in action."

Olivia met her sister's gaze and nodded. "I'd like that. A lot."

Diana ran a hand over the edge of the counter and let out a long breath. "I'm sorry that I've been so . . . standoffish and cold. This whole thing is really difficult for me. It's a lot to absorb all at once."

"I feel the same way." Olivia folded the dish towel, then

folded it again. "I've never had a sister, so I don't even know where to go, how to build this . . . relationship."

"Me neither." Diana bit her lip. "Please understand that I'm still grieving the loss of my mother, and you being here is a reminder of how much she kept from me and how little I knew her. I'm not blaming you, Olivia, but I'm saying I need time. A lot of it." Diana gathered her purse off the counter and fished out her keys. "I better get Jackson home. Thanks for the invite."

After Diana was gone, Olivia wiped down the counters, then pulled the drain plug. She watched the soapy water drain and wondered for the hundredth time why she had thought this process would be so easy. *Just pack up and go, and it'll all work out.* Yeah, so much for *that* plan.

"Looks like I came in at the right time because all the hard work is done," Mike said as he entered the kitchen. "Hey, where's Diana?"

"She had to get Jackson home. Speaking of hard work, do you mind taking out the trash for me?"

"Is that all? What, no shelves to hang or floors to sand?" He tugged the white plastic bag out of the trash can and tied the top. "Give me a real challenge."

"If you want a challenge, I've got one next door," Olivia said. "One that would make Bob Vila drool. It's not just the shelter that's about ready to fall down, it's the house too."

"Let me take this out, then we can head over there and I'll give you my two cents."

"I'd appreciate that. I'm pretty much flying blind over there. All I've got is a *Renovations for Dummies* book and a big balance on my Home Depot card." Olivia laughed. "I'm definitely in way over my head."

"Most folks are when they take on a project house. Give me a minute and I'll head over there with you."

"Sure. I was going to talk to Luke before I left." She thumbed toward the back of the house. "Unless you don't think that's a good idea."

"I think it's a great idea." Mike's face softened. "I know Luke can come off as a total jerk sometimes, but trust me, there's one hell of a guy under that gruff exterior." He hefted the trash, then headed out the back door.

Olivia dried her hands on a towel, folded it and hung it on the hook, then paused by the hall mirror to fix her hair, even as she told herself she didn't care what she looked like, that she wasn't interested in Luke. Except she was, in complicated ways that scared the hell out of her. She'd wanted him for just a one-night stand, a quick, hot tryst with the hot neighbor, but the more she got to know him, the more she cared—

And that created the tangled web she'd intended to avoid. Hadn't she learned her lesson with her divorce? Closed-off men offered nothing but hurt in the end, and she'd had enough of that for a lifetime. For two lifetimes.

Yet she was drawn to him all the same, to the man who appeared in flashes, like peeking behind the wizard's curtain and finding the real man hidden behind all the flash and roar. The problem? Luke had made it clear he had no intentions of letting that protective curtain fall.

She found Luke in the living room. The shades were drawn, the TV on low, the image flickering in the shadowed space. Luke sat on the sofa, elbows on his knees, fingers steepled over his face.

"You okay?" she asked.

"Yeah." He straightened up, but his shoulders remained hunched.

She sat on the edge of the coffee table and faced him. "Want to talk about it?"

"No." His sharp retort sliced the air like a razor.

She bit her lip. "Okay. Well, I'm going to go home. The food's put away and the kitchen is cleaned up. I just wanted to make sure you didn't need anything before I left." She got to her feet. Luke reached out a hand and caught hers.

"Thank you."

She shrugged. "It was nothing. Just a few dishes and—"

"I didn't mean for cleaning up the kitchen. I meant for . . ." He shook his head and let out a breath. "Listen, I know I've been a jerk lately. I'm trying to act like a human, and it's like I forgot how to do that."

"I think we all do, once in a while." She told herself not to care, not to get wrapped up in this man, but she could see the pain etched in every inch of him. She'd seen it enough in patients who had lost their ability to do the simplest of tasks, who were angry that fate had stolen their freedom.

The two dogs had followed her into the room. Chance had lain by Luke's feet, while Miss Sadie stayed close to Olivia. Chance raised his head and pressed his cheek against Luke's calf. Luke reached down and rubbed the dog's ears. A ghost of a smile appeared on his face.

She thought of all those angry patients whose mood lifted when Miss Sadie walked into the room. Who found something as simple as giving a dog a biscuit a rewarding experience. The dog loved them, just because, and they returned the emotion. Even in the few weeks she had been working at Golden Years, she had seen so many patients make remarkable progress, simply because they wanted to connect with the dog. Miss Sadie's presence, her willing and eager face, and her friendly acceptance of all, regardless of their abilities or age, encouraged people to walk a few steps farther, to toss the ball a few more times, to receive a furry hug or damp kiss in return. The dog worked miracles.

Maybe another dog, one who had a little experience with hurt and pain, could do the same for Luke.

"You know, I don't have time to take care of Chance properly," she said, keeping her tone casual. "Maybe I should bring him to Diana's practice. See if someone wants to adopt him."

Luke didn't say anything for a long moment. He scratched the dog's ear and Chance returned the favor by slapping the couch with his tail and pressing harder against Luke's leg. "I could watch him for a few days. Give you some time to find him a home or something."

"That would be great," Olivia said. "I can send some food and bowls back with Mike tonight."

On the television, some inane commercial with dancing French fries filled the screen. Tinny music blurted from the speakers. Luke hit mute, then turned to Olivia. "Send it back with Mike?"

"Yeah, he's coming over to my house for a little bit. Give me an opinion on the remodel. He really knows his stuff."

Luke scoffed. "He also knows a pretty woman when he sees one."

She cocked her head and studied him, but his expression betrayed nothing. Maybe Luke should have been a professional poker player. "Are you jealous? Because I assure you, there is nothing going on between Mike and me. And even if there were, it wouldn't be any of your business."

"Why wouldn't it be any of my business?"

"Because you have made it abundantly clear that there is nothing between you and me." And that, she realized, stung. She, the one who'd said she wanted a one-night stand, was, at her heart, exactly what he accused her of being—a picket-fence kind of gal. The only problem—building a picket fence and settling in the 'burbs had been her biggest failure. Her marriage had been over almost before it began.

"You don't want to get involved with me," Luke said, and his gaze shifted to somewhere far off, somewhere she couldn't see. "So do yourself a favor. And don't."

Seventeen

⁓

Mike walked every square inch of Olivia's property. Peeked in the attic, looked at the foundation, peeled back a loose section of wall. He borrowed some weird gadget with red and black wires from Luke, then tested the electrical panel. With a flashlight, he ducked under the sinks to inspect the plumbing. All the while, Olivia held her breath.

After an hour, Mike dusted off his shorts and handed back her flashlight. "Well, I have good news and bad news."

Surely the news couldn't be that bad, Olivia reasoned. She had hope that the house could be something wonderful. After all, she'd left behind everything and everyone she knew for this move. She'd taken a huge chance, changed her whole life, to take on this house. She drew in a deep breath. "Okay. What's the bad news?"

"The place is a total gut job. You might as well chalk it up to a lost cause. Sell it for the land and move."

She stared at him for a long while, digesting his words. Lost cause? Gut job? Nausea pitched and rolled in her stomach. "And what's the good news?"

He gave her a weak, sympathetic grin. "You did one hell of a good demo job."

The last little bit of hope Olivia had been holding on to fluttered to the floor. "Are you sure?"

Mike sighed. "Listen, the last thing I want to give you is false hope. Or put a bow on a mule. This place is in rough shape. A lot of years went by without doing basic maintenance, and that means things are in pretty bad condition. It's going to take a hell of a lot of work, not to mention a sizable investment, to get this place where you want it to be. The shelter, on the other hand, is in a better state. It's got some storm damage, but that can be fixed. I can shore up the weak areas, fix a few things for you, if you want. That'll buy you some time until you decide what you're doing with this . . ."

"Monstrosity."

"I was going to say *project*, but you put it much more eloquently." He grinned, then sobered. "Listen, why don't I call around, get you some quotes from some contractors. This is too big a job for one person. Heck, for two people."

"My budget is only big enough for one person." She dropped onto an overturned bucket and put her head in her hands. "I don't know what to do."

"My advice? Take your time. The work will be there tomorrow. If there's one thing you learn in construction, it's to take your time and measure twice. That goes for everything."

She sighed, then got to her feet. "Well, thanks anyway. I appreciate the advice."

"Anytime. I'm sorry, Olivia. I wish I could tell you it was all cosmetic, but it's not. You need new electrical, new plumbing, a new roof . . ." He threw up his hands.

"It's okay." Olivia retrieved Chance's bowls and the container of food she'd bought for him, then coiled a leash on top of the plastic tub of dog chow. "Can you bring this back to Luke? He's going to keep Chance for a while for me."

"Was that Luke's idea?"

"I let him think it was mine."

Mike raised a hand, and she high-fived him. "Good for you, getting him to rejoin the land of the living without even realizing he's doing it."

"It was an easy sell, really. He and the dog seem to have a bond and I thought"—she shrugged, and try as she might to keep the caring from her voice, it came through all the same—"it would be good for him."

Mike's blue eyes softened. "You're good for him, too."

She scoffed. "I doubt that. He just kicked me out and told me to forget him."

"I never said he was smart." Mike grinned. "Just that you're good for him. Trust me, Luke is a great guy. I'd lay down my life for him, without hesitation. And so would any of the guys he served with." Mike's gaze went to the small dark house next door. "He's gone through a lot, more than one man should have to handle."

"I wish he'd talk to me about it. Every time we get close, he shoves me away."

Mike's nod was filled with sympathy. "Don't give up on him. Okay?"

She glanced at the property next door. Luke's house had gone back to the way it was before—shuttered and dark, the blinds drawn. Then she looked back at her house—the monstrosity. She worked a smile to her face. "How could I do that? Apparently, I'm the champion of lost causes."

Greta brought the extra-large coffee cup to Thursday's Quilting Club, the one printed with MY DAILY SHOT KEEPS ME FROM KILLING PEOPLE on the front. Given the way things had been going, she was going to need the oversized cup of morning strength. She'd called Luke this morning and when she'd asked about Olivia, he'd told his grandmother to ask Olivia for answers. Then he changed the subject. "Ladies, no quilting today. We have to strategize."

Esther's eyes widened and her face paled. "No . . . no quilting?"

"Esther, it's not the end of the world."

"Maybe not in your world," Esther said, "because you don't have a grandchild waiting for a powder-blue-and-white quilt for his twin bed."

Greta shot Esther her death-ray eyes. It didn't work. Esther stayed upright and breathing. "If you help me, then I'll have great-grandchildren, and then I will *happily* quilt with you."

After she spouted that lie, Greta had to take not one, but two sips from the coffee cup. Thank God for Maker's Mark.

Pauline snorted. "I'd pay good money to see you happily quilting, Greta."

"Hush up, Pauline," Greta whispered. Then she forced a work-with-me smile to her face. "Ladies, this is serious. We have an emergency."

Esther leaned in close. "Greta, if you're having trouble getting to the ladies' room, they make these special panties that—"

"For Pete's sake, Esther, that's not what I'm talking about. And for your information, my bladder is just fine." She took a third sip. A fourth. Lord almighty, if she'd known it would be this tough to keep them on track, she'd have brought along a thermos of bourbon. "It's a romantic emergency."

"Speaking of romantic, Greta, is that Harold Twohig I see waving at you through the window?" Pauline said, gesturing toward the easterly wall. "Oh my. I think he just winked too."

Greta kept her gaze averted from that testosterone-loaded offense to humanity. "I am still trying to digest that cardboard they served for breakfast, Pauline. Do not mention that man or I might throw up in Esther's purse."

Esther nudged her pocketbook farther under her chair and shifted away from Greta.

"I'm talking about Luke and Olivia," Greta said. "Things are heading south, fast, between them."

"Maybe they aren't meant to be," Esther said. "I once dated a man for two years, only to realize that he wasn't the one. But if I hadn't dated Mr. Wrong, I never would have met my Mr. Right." She sighed. "I so miss my Gerald. He was a sweetheart."

"Well, I am sure that Luke and Olivia are right for each other. They just need some help to see that."

"I thought you said that they were talking and spending time together," Pauline said. "What happened?"

Life, Greta wanted to say, but no, that wasn't quite it. Something far more complex had come between her grandson and the pretty blond therapist. Luke, she suspected, kept putting up walls, and Olivia kept turning away instead of trying to climb them. Greta could hardly blame them, after all Luke had been through, and after Olivia had gone through that terrible divorce, but that didn't mean she wasn't about to give them a little push in the right direction.

"I'm not sure. Olivia was at Luke's house for a barbecue last night, it didn't go so well, and they haven't talked since. When I ask Luke, he won't tell me anything. When I ask Olivia, she brushes me off. So I think we need to intervene."

"Please don't say we're going to skip lunch to do it," Esther said. "Today is chicken and dumplings. You know how I look forward to chicken and dumplings."

"We don't even have to leave this building," Greta said. She leaned toward Pauline. "Doesn't your son work for Home Depot?"

"Yes, he got promoted to manager of the drill department the other day." Pauline beamed. "Anyone who needs a drill knows my son is the one to ask."

"Well, I need a favor, and it doesn't involve a drill." Greta looked around, didn't see Olivia anywhere, then told Pauline her plan.

Esther tsk-tsked, but Pauline sat with the idea for a while before she leaned forward in her chair. "Okay. I'll see what he can do—if you help me with this week's column."

Greta smiled. Thank God. Some sense in this group. "What's the question?"

Pauline rifled in her purse and came up with a typed letter. "This is the one I picked. I'm trying to jazz up the column, but it seems all I ever get are lonely-hearts letters. What I wouldn't give for a good meddlesome mother-in-law or prodigal son problem."

Greta waved that off. "Make up your own. Heck, with the amount of drama in this town, it'd be like writing for *The Young and the Restless*."

"We can't do that." Esther blanched. "It would be . . . lying."

"And your point is?" Greta asked.

"Well, it's wrong. Plain and simple."

"Lying is only wrong if it's done for nefarious purposes," Greta said. "There are lies that help people and lies that hurt people. Like, when I told you that dress you wore the other day was pretty. I was lying. I knew if I told you the truth, it would hurt your feelings and that would be mean."

Esther's face fell. Whoops. Damn Maker's Mark. Greta had just told the truth—by accident.

"You didn't like my dress?" Esther said.

Greta glanced at Pauline. The other woman nodded. "Go ahead and tell her. She might as well hear it from us."

"Hear what?"

Greta laid a hand on Esther's. "Neon isn't your color, dear. It washes you out and frankly makes you look like death warmed over. Not to mention, it hurts my eyes. I need a visor just to say hello in the morning."

"Oh." Esther pouted. "What about my patterns? The plaids? The florals?"

Greta grimaced. Pauline kneed her under the table.

"Because I have this fabulous new lilac plaid dress that I want to wear with my floral scarf. You know, the dark purple one? No neon in that." Esther smiled.

"Sounds wonderful. I can't wait to see it," Greta said. With a straight face.

"Me either." Pauline ruffled the letter. "Okay, back to the question at hand. I'll read it: Dear Common Sense Carla, I am a single man in his late fifties who likes long walks on the beach and margaritas by the pool. I think I have a lot to offer, but I have yet to find the right match. Should I try an online dating site? Or resign myself to being alone? Signed, Single Stud."

Greta waved her hand. "That's an easy one. Tell him to get a personality. That'll turn that dud into a stud."

"Greta! How do you know he has no personality? He could be a perfectly charming man."

"Esther, the man doesn't do anything but walk on the beach and sit by the pool. That is a dud in my book. Get him to take some salsa lessons or join a fishing club or something. My Lord, just his letter about put me to sleep."

"Me too," Pauline said, and gave Esther a somber nod. "Greta has a point, Esther. He does sound like a dud."

"My Gerald was the kind of man who would take long walks around the neighborhood every night, as soon as his plate was cleared. Why, sometimes he'd be gone two hours, and I'd fall asleep waiting for him. And I thought he was quite the stud."

"Sounds like he was that indeed," Greta said. She put on a nice smile. It never hurt to be polite, even to the dead. She glanced at Pauline. "So, our plan's a go?"

"Yes, indeedy," Pauline said. "I'll make the call right now."

"You mean you will after we finish our quilting today," Esther said. "We still have the morning room to ourselves for thirty minutes. Plenty of time to tack some squares or trim some edges."

Between Esther's insufferable passion for quilting and Harold Twohig's constant epileptic waving, Greta thought it was little wonder she needed some Maker's Mark to keep her from becoming homicidal in her old age. She hoisted her mug, thanked the stars in heaven she'd brought the big cup today, and took a long, long sip.

Eighteen

❦

Luke stood on Olivia's porch, with the dog plopped down beside him, and wondered what the hell he was doing. He didn't need to deliver this message in person. He could have just sent the driver over here and stayed out of the whole thing. So why had he offered to do it?

Because he'd told himself he could kill two birds with one stone and give her an update on how the dog was doing at the same time. Yeah, right. That was why he was here, knocking on her door. As if she couldn't see that answer for herself. The damned dog lived with him now, but still spent half his days in Olivia's yard, visiting with the puppies and Olivia.

He wasn't here to deliver a message or a canine update and he knew it. No, he was here because he regretted running her out of his house after the barbecue a few days ago like a door-to-door salesman trying to hawk overpriced cleaning products. Because that night they'd almost made love had stayed in his mind. Long after the sun went down and the heat of the day began to abate, he had thought about the taste of Olivia's lips, the way she had curved into him, how soft and silky and tempting she had been beneath him. The fire she had awakened in him, a fire he both welcomed and spurned.

He didn't need a woman in his life, or a relationship. Hell, yes, he wanted and needed sex, but sex often came with strings and Luke was not a strings kind of guy, not anymore. If there was one thing he'd figured out about Olivia Linscott, it was that she was the kind of woman who put down roots, planted herself, and made connections. She got involved—

And he didn't.

Well, he kind of had with the dog. And with the letter he'd mailed.

He shifted from foot to foot. Hell, this was a mistake. He didn't need to get any closer to Olivia, or anyone, for that matter. If he did, she'd want to know the truth about Luke. The story behind the scar.

And that was the one thing he never intended to share. He'd keep it buried deep inside and maybe someday the pain would ease enough and allow him to breathe again.

"Come on, Chance. Guess she's not home." Luke started to turn away when he heard the door open. He paused, then started forward, down the stairs, remembering to avoid the broken step.

"Hi, Chance," she said. "And Luke."

Greeting the dog before him stung a little, but he deserved it. He'd been an ass. He just hadn't found a way to change out of the jerk suit. Even Mike had been spending most of his days away from Luke's company. Finding reasons to be in town, or maybe just finding reasons to get close to Diana Tuttle, Luke wasn't sure. He was driving everyone away, and he just couldn't seem to stop.

He cleared his throat, turned back. "I just came by to tell you that there's a delivery guy in my driveway. He says he's got cabinets on the truck that you ordered. For some reason he had my address instead of yours."

"Hmm. Really?" She leaned against the jamb and ran a hand through her hair, displacing the blond waves. They resettled around her shoulders, enticing, pretty. "I thought

I canceled that order. And I definitely didn't have them delivered to your house."

At his feet, Chance and Miss Sadie greeted each other, tails wagging and dancing around and under each other. Clearly, two lost friends getting reacquainted, even if they saw each other every day. "Either way, there are cabinets in that truck for you." He thumbed toward his driveway, telling himself to get out of here, that he was just here to deliver a message, nothing more. "Since I'm not planning on redecorating, do you want me to send him over here?"

She sighed. "I think it would be a waste of time. I'll go tell him to take them back."

"Waste of time? Why? After all the work you've done?"

"Mike took a look at the house and called it a lost cause." Resignation laced her words together. "He thinks I should just sell it for the land and let it go."

Mike had the experience to back up his advice. He probably took one look at the house, then at Olivia, and figured one inexperienced woman on a limited budget should be smart and move on. Mike, however, didn't know Olivia the way Luke did. She had a hell of a lot of gumption and determination, and Luke had no doubt she could also pull off a miracle inside these walls.

"Do *you* want to do that?" he asked.

"It's not a question of want, Luke, it's a question of being practical."

He climbed the stairs and stopped in front of her. The scent of her perfume danced in the air. "Have you always been this practical?"

She let out a laugh. "Too practical. Until I up and decided to move here. New job, new place to live, new life. And so far, the only thing that's working out is the paycheck every two weeks, and even that has its challenges. So I'm not sure being impractical has had any upside."

"Don't forget the hunky guy next door."

"Oh, yes, Lois's husband, Doug, is quite the hottie." She laughed.

He shifted a little closer and tugged off his sunglasses so

he could see her smile better. "I like it much better when you're laughing, Olivia."

"Oh yeah? Why's that?"

Because it made him want to laugh, too. But he didn't say that. "Because it keeps you from yelling at me for being a jerk."

She chuckled. "It's all part of an evil ploy, is that it?"

"Of course." He coughed to cover the vulnerable crack in his shell. "Anyway, I think you should hang the cabinets."

"You just want to get that guy out of your driveway."

"No, that's not why." He slid the sunglasses back on his face and felt the distance build between them when he did. "Sometimes, Olivia, it's important not to give up on a lost cause."

He turned to go, calling Chance to his side as he moved down the stairs.

"Hey, Luke?"

He pivoted back. "Yeah?"

She leaned against the jamb, looking so pretty and perfect, he could have framed her as a picture. "Why don't I go talk to the cabinet guy and you stay here? It's hot out and I don't know about you but I could use some lemonade. I have some already made, chilling in the fridge."

The thought of icy lemonade, something he hadn't had in forever, made his mouth water. That and the thought of being with Olivia, kissing her, touching her. Just being with her, hearing that laugh, seeing that smile.

Damn. He should go home, stay there, mix his own lemonade. Instead, he gave her a smile and asked, "Freshly made or powdered mix?"

"Honey, I squeeze my own lemons." She laughed. "Okay, that sounded *really* bad."

He'd thought the word *honey* sounded nice. Especially coming from her, with that little throaty touch she gave the words. "I disagree. It sounded *really* good to me. I like a woman who squeezes her own."

She laughed again. "Well, come on in, then, and keep

me company this afternoon. I've had a heck of a day and after I deal with the cabinet guy, I'm thinking it'd be nice to sit on the lanai with a glass of lemonade and some cookies."

He thought of heading back to his hot, dim house. Of sitting alone in the dark again. Of eating leftover pizza for the thousandth time. Then he thought of Olivia's laugh, her lemonade, and her offer. "Lemonade and cookies sounds . . . perfect."

As he walked into her house and followed Olivia into the kitchen, he realized the real reason he was here. After sending that letter and opening a door he'd vowed to lock forever, Luke Winslow didn't want to be alone. Not with his thoughts and not with himself.

And definitely not when the response to that letter came. Aw, shit. What the hell had he done?

A few minutes later, Olivia sat beside Luke under the shady covering of the lanai while a warm, soft breeze whispered through the screened space. Ice cubes clinked as she poured them each some lemonade and put a plate of cookies from Tasty Tidbits Bakery on the end table. Luke thanked her for the lemonade, then sat back in the chair. Chance settled himself at Luke's feet.

"You've definitely made a friend," she said.

"He's probably hoping I drop my cookie."

Chance's ears perked up at the word *cookie*. Olivia smiled. Seemed someone was spoiling that dog.

"I think he's attached to you."

"Yeah, we're making friends." Luke rubbed Chance's ears. The dog let out a contented groan.

"Chance needs a friend," Olivia said. "Diana told me he wasn't microchipped, so she left messages at the other area shelters in case someone is looking for him or for the mother dog with the puppies, but there've been no calls for either of them. I'm going to put up some flyers tomorrow."

The dog leaned his body against Luke's leg, tail thumping

on the concrete floor. "He's a good dog. Someone's surely missing him."

"You would think, but sometimes people don't miss the things they're supposed to love."

An odd comment, and one that piqued his curiosity. Someone had hurt Olivia Linscott, and hurt her bad. But he didn't ask, because he didn't want to reciprocate with his life story. "So now you have the cabinets. What are you going to do with them?"

"I don't know. This house is a project that grows by the minute. It's like a weed. As soon as you turn your back, it's quadrupled in size."

He chuckled. "I think you can say that about every fixer-upper."

"They make it sound so easy on the TV shows. Just slap this up here, take that down there, add a little paint, and voilà, you're living in a magazine spread."

He rolled the cold glass between his palms. "The truth is rarely as easy as the fiction."

"You can say that again." She took a long sip of lemonade and thought about why she had come here, why she still kept shying away from probing for answers. Maybe she didn't want to know the truth, after all these years of writing her own fiction about who Bridget was and why she'd abandoned her newborn in the hospital. Olivia glanced down at Chance, who had shied away from her in the beginning, so scared of being hurt again. How she could relate.

She ran a finger along the rim of her glass. "You know, a part of me wants to admit Mike is right, and that I should just get out of this house before I get in too deep."

Did she mean too deep with the house, or with him, too? And why did he care? If he were smart, he'd be encouraging her to go, because that was far easier than dealing with the complications if she stayed. "But . . . ?"

"But the other part of me, the part that came here for a new start, and for answers, can't do that. If I let go of this house, I let go of what my biological mother left me. It's not much and yeah, it's an eyesore, but it's pretty much all I have from her. I can't . . . abandon it." The last two words scraped past her throat, raw, real.

True.

Olivia couldn't give up on the house. Walk away from it. Leave it to fend for itself or sell it to another. She had something to prove, to a woman who was no longer here, as illogical as that sounded, and maybe in the course of all this, prove something to herself, too.

"Like she abandoned you," Luke said.

Olivia nodded, her throat thick. She cursed the tears that came to her eyes because they said she was still hurt by that, even all these years later. She prayed Luke couldn't see the tears and that he wouldn't press her to talk, because right this second, she'd only blubber.

She glanced around the screened-in lanai. A blue indoor-outdoor carpet covered the concrete floor and made the ivy-patterned cushions stand out against the white furniture. Had her mother sat here, at the end of a long day, enjoying an iced drink and a last bit of warm air? Had she looked out over the green expanse of lawn and wondered where her firstborn was? If she was happy?

Olivia settled back against the cushioned seat and closed her eyes. Her fingers fluttered to the butterfly necklace and for a second, it seemed as if Bridget were here, in this room, sitting in the opposite chair. Asking Olivia what she was going to do with her legacy.

"I can't let go of the house," Olivia said. "Smart or not, I can't walk away."

"I didn't think you would," Luke said.

She opened her eyes. "Why not?"

"You are too damned determined to do that. You have been from the first day I met you, traipsing all over my yard, even when I told you to get out." He leaned forward. "You are the most determined woman I know. You don't quit, Olivia."

"Even when an ogre roars at me?" A smile curved up her face.

"Even then."

She took a sip of lemonade and faced the reality. She might want to keep the house and get it renovated, but she was only one person with a very small budget. "You have a point. But cabinet hanging requires two people, something I didn't think of when I ordered them."

Apparently getting distracted by all the shiny new knobs and faucets in Home Depot meant not thinking through the installation process. She couldn't have been more naïve if she'd hung a sign around her neck that read GULLIBLE.

"Yup, hanging cabinets is a two-person job," Luke said. "And unless Chance or Miss Sadie grows some opposable thumbs, there's only you."

She sat back against the chair and let out a sigh. "I know. I've been doing everything I can on my own, but right now, every muscle in my body is ready to stage a mutiny. I have pain in places I didn't even know I had nerves."

He chuckled. "You know, I could help you."

"You . . . what?" Had she heard him right?

"I used to work for a construction company in the summers during high school. It's not like I have a contractor's license or anything, but I can handle the basics. And if we need an expert, Mike knows how to do almost anything."

"Mike's expertise called this house a lost cause."

"Yeah, well, he called me one too, this morning." Luke took a long drink of lemonade, then changed the subject. "Anyway, Mike was probably just trying to save you a lot of hard work. He's a guy. He thinks with his head, not his heart."

"I guess that makes me the sentimental fool, huh?" she said. That would describe her, in a hundred ways. Holding on to a marriage that ended almost as soon as she said *I do*, moving to the other end of the country because she thought a house could bring her close to someone she'd never known, hanging on to a dream when others would have walked away.

"Nothing wrong with that. Nothing at all."

Her gaze held his for a long moment while birds chirped outside the screened walls of the lanai and a breeze rustled through the trees. She could lose herself in those blue eyes, become a sentimental fool again for a guy who wasn't interested in the same future she was. "Thanks."

Luke cleared his throat. "So if you want help, I'm here. With this . . . issue"—he waved at his eyes—"I doubt I'd be much good with the drill and those teeny-tiny screws, but I could be the brawn."

Oh, he was brawn all right. Just the thought of him flexing in front of her made her mouth go dry. "You're the brawn, so that must make me the brains?" she teased.

"And the beauty." A slight grin curved up one side of his face, and then just as quickly it disappeared, as if the flirting took him by surprise. Luke got to his feet, which made Chance scramble to all four paws. "How many cabinets do you have to hang?"

"Ten. And three base cabinets that I'm sure are too heavy for me to wriggle into place."

"Got a good cordless drill?"

"Um, is a DeWalt a good one? The guy at the store said it was the best one he had."

"Phew. Yeah, DeWalt is great. I was afraid you'd tell me all you had on hand was a Phillips screwdriver and we'd be doing all this by hand."

"Oh, I'm loaded up with all kinds of tools. Tools I have no idea how to use, I might add." She chuckled, then opened the door and led Luke back into the house. Chance brought up the rear, keeping his distance behind Luke, as if sensing the man's difficulty with seeing the path ahead. Chance kept glancing up at Luke, his love for the man showing in his brown eyes.

Luke might not realize it, but that dog already had a lifelong loyalty to his human caretaker. In a way, Olivia hoped she never found Chance's real owner, because the dog had clearly already found the owner he wanted.

Olivia flicked on the overhead light in the kitchen, bathing the room in a hundred and twenty watts of brightness. It had taken three tries and a lot of quality time on Google, but she had the ceiling fan and light kit installed. Every time she flicked that switch and was rewarded with light, it filled her with pride. Not exactly Harriet Homebuilder, but close enough to have light.

She grabbed the drill, then turned to Luke. He'd followed closer than she'd expected, and only a few inches separated her from him. She drew in a breath, told herself to stop staring at the planes of his chest, to stop fantasizing about the last time he'd kissed her. How close they'd come to making love. So, so close.

She swallowed hard. "Last chance to back out."

"Back out?" He shook his head, slow and easy. "Sorry, but I never back away from a challenge."

"And you think my kitchen is a challenge?" Damn, he smelled nice. Whatever cologne he wore, it curled around her with tempting fingers, urging her closer, closer. To touch him, to press her cheek to his, to do so much more than that.

"Everything about you is a challenge, Olivia."

God, she loved the way her name rolled off his tongue. How did he make it sound like a caress and a song at the same time? "I could say the same about you."

He reached up and swept her bangs off her forehead, then let his fingers trail down her face, along her jaw. Her lips parted at his touch, and her heart hammered in her chest. She wanted to back up, wanted to move closer, but most of all, she wanted him. Back on the lanai he had taken his sunglasses off and she stared up at those stunning blue eyes, so full of contradictions and mysteries.

"I'm not a challenge," he said. "What you see is what you get."

And what she saw was very, very nice indeed. Hot liquid pooled in her gut, and a rush of desire raced through her. If she closed her eyes, she'd picture taking him back to her bedroom, ripping back the fluffy white girly comforter, thrusting her onto the bed, and plunging into her in heated, almost savage need.

A bone-deep carnal need brewed inside her. Need for this man—still, essentially a stranger—and for him to fulfill the fantasies that filled her nights and left her in a tangled mess of sheets. But at the same time, a part of her shied away, remembering how very easy it was to get caught up in the fantasy—and end up hurt.

"What I see is a whole lot of cabinets that need to be hung," she said. The words shook as they came out of her throat, but they did what the commonsense side of her wanted—made Luke back up a step, his hand dropping away from her face. Disappointment curdled in her stomach, and her hormones cried foul. "So uh, let's get to work."

"Good idea." A shadow dropped over his features, and the sexy grin disappeared. "Show me where you want the first one to go."

The mood between them shifted from sexy banter to all business. She told herself she was glad.

It took them a few minutes to sort out the cabinets and their places on the wall, then draw a level line for the upper cabinets. Luke reached down and hoisted the first upper cabinet into place. She tried to reach past his arm to screw the cabinet to the wall, then realized her arms weren't long enough. "I, uh, need to get in front of you to do this."

He shifted his legs back, creating a triangle of space between the cabinet and his chest. She slipped into the space, hesitating for a second because she forgot why she was here. Her heart raced, every ounce of her aware of his body, so close.

She shook her head, refocused. Reached up and put the first screw into the wall. The drill whined, and the screw spun back and fell onto the countertop. "Whoops. I'm, uh, in reverse, I think."

"A little distracted?" Luke's deep voice tickled a warm path down her neck.

She flicked a glance at him. "I'm just not familiar with this . . . tool."

The minute she said the word, she heard the innuendo, and the flames rushed through her body and up to her cheeks. What was it about Luke Winslow that had her acting like an infatuated high school girl with her first crush?

"Need some help? Working the tool?"

God yes, she wanted to work a few tools with him. The kind you wouldn't find in Home Depot, that was for sure.

"No, I got it." She pressed the button above the trigger, switching the motor to forward, then leaned toward the cabinet back. This time, the screw bit into the wood, then the wall, and sank in place with a final screech. She scrabbled on the piece of plywood serving as a temporary countertop for a second screw, then the rest in quick succession. "All done."

Luke stepped back, and Olivia held her breath, half expecting the cabinet to peel off the wall and crash to the floor. But it held.

"Would you look at that? Miracles do happen," she said. Pride swelled again in her chest, along with hope that maybe Luke was right and she could pull this renovation off. His brawn and her brains made a decent team.

He chuckled. "Renovation work is like anything else. The more you do, the better you get."

"By the time I'm done with this house, I should have my own show on HGTV." She grabbed four more screws. "Ready for the next one?"

"Just point me in the right direction."

They repeated the pattern from before, with her guiding him into place with the cabinet, then slipping in front of his body to fasten it to the wall. The whole time they were hanging the cabinets, she kept up a constant chatter about the oak finish, the bronze handles she'd bought, the mental debate she'd had about laminate versus granite countertops. Talking kept her from thinking about the heat emanating from Luke's body, how her hips brushed his thighs several times, how it wouldn't take much more than a slight shift to press her butt against his cock. How only a few scraps of fabric separated her from him. A few snaps, a couple of zippers and he could be inside her, pressing her body against the wooden frame beneath her, sending her brain and her body into stratospheres she hadn't seen in a long, long time.

"You want this someplace special? Or do you just like seeing me holding the cabinet?"

"Oh. Sorry. Right there." She pointed to the next spot on the wall. They repeated the process, and her brain went south the second Luke shifted his hips behind hers.

The drill screeched, slipped off the screw, and dinged a gouge in the back of the cabinet. A *ping-ping-ping* announced the fleeing screw. "Uh, sorry. That one got away from me."

Luke leaned in and whispered across her neck, sending a warm gush of want into the southern half of her body. "You sure you got this under control?"

No. "Yes." She fished around for another screw and this time got it in place. But her hand shook and her heart fluttered and her concentration had deserted her.

My God, when had she turned into this horny, distracted person? Even with her ex, she'd never been this bad or felt this worked up and ready to rip off some clothes and get busy *right this second*. She needed some air-conditioning or a drink or therapy.

Or a really hot time in bed. With Luke.

"That's the last one," Olivia said, scrambling out from underneath Luke's reach before she caved to the temptation brewing inside her like a category five hurricane. "Thanks for your help."

"Don't you have some lower cabinets to do, too?"

"Yeah, but I can get those myself." She just wanted distance between them. Wanted him to leave, go home, give her a moment to breathe where she wouldn't inhale the tempting notes of his cologne and think about banging him on the tile floor.

God, she was a mess. She needed . . . something. Something that wasn't six feet tall and sexy as heck, and came with a chip on his shoulder the size of Detroit.

"Listen, you order some pizza, and I'll help you knock out the rest of these, and anything else you need lifted or moved."

She parked a fist on her hip. "Why are you so determined to help me? Last I checked, you wanted as little to do with other humans as possible." She knew she was barking at him, and not because she didn't want his help, but because being around him kept sending her hormones on a roller-coaster ride.

He glanced in the direction of his house. Shadows dusted his features, echoed in the set line of his mouth. "I just need to keep busy."

Just like that, the switch inside her went to *sympathy*. She had said those same words herself a dozen times and knew that ache that came with a vacant calendar, an empty house.

"I understand." She leaned against the counter and rested the cordless drill beside her. "In the first few weeks after my ex filed for divorce, I refinished a table, painted the walls in my town house twice, and signed up for not one, but two book clubs. I couldn't find enough to do, it seemed to fill . . . all those hours and keep me from dwelling on what went wrong and how I missed so many signs along the way."

"Yeah." He didn't elaborate. Didn't share. Didn't open up. "I like pepperoni."

She arched a brow. "You really want pizza again? I mean, that delivery guy is at your house so often, people are going to think he lives there."

He shrugged. "Pizza's easy and fast."

"And bad for you if you eat it three times a week." What was she, his mother? She shouldn't care what he ate. Yet a part of her did, the same part that took in stray dogs and held on to a marriage that had died a long time before the papers were signed. She shook her head. She needed to quit doing this. "What do you say to some steaks on the grill?"

That got his attention. "Steak?"

"And potatoes. I also picked up some corn on the way home from work yesterday." She bit her lip and felt a blush creep into her cheeks. "I've been craving some meat and potatoes, after one too many nights of reheated frozen dinners."

"So I'm not the only one making poor eating choices?"

"Well, when you live alone, it's easy to take the bad nutri-tion road."

"Then my pizza deliveries aren't so much of a mor-tal sin?"

She laughed, and pushed off from the counter. "Maybe only for your arteries." She took a deep breath, gave herself a quick mental lecture about not letting her hormones do the thinking, then stepped outside, started up the grill, and let it preheat while she and Luke got back to work, setting the base cabinets in place. Once again, she had to get between him and the cabinet, but with the deeper base cabinets, there was less touching, more distance between them. She couldn't decide if she was relieved or disappointed.

They wriggled the last one into place, a small cabinet that sat between the refrigerator and the wall. Olivia climbed partway inside the wooden box. She got one screw in place, but then the drill whined and skipped off the tip of the second one. She switched the DeWalt to reverse and tried to pull the screw out, but the drill whined and the screw stayed where it was. "Damn. I think I stripped it."

"Let me see." Luke lowered himself beside her, their two bodies crammed together in the small darkened space. He reached up, located the screw, then put out his hand for the drill. "I think I can back it out and get another one in there."

"Okay, good." She started to back out of the cabinet, but he touched her arm.

"Stay. Just in case I have trouble."

"But you won't have any room to work."

He turned to face her, his blue eyes smoldering. "I'll figure it out, Olivia."

She swallowed hard and stayed where she was, wedged against the side of the cabinet on one side, and wedged against Luke from shoulder to hip on the other. She inhaled the woodsy scent of his cologne. It teased along her senses, inviting her to lean over, draw in the scent on his jaw. She turned, just a few inches, as if she were watching him, and took in a long breath. His pulse ticked in his neck, and she watched that fast beat, wanting, oh, how she wanted to kiss that spot.

Have you always been this practical?

She kept retreating to that comfort zone, as if the water of adventure were too cold and she wanted to stay tucked in a blanket. Just a month ago she'd been so desperate for a change, a new life, and a little more spontaneity that she'd up and moved without a second thought.

That same longing for risk filled her when she looked at Luke Winslow. Desire for this brooding, dark man washed over her common sense, scared the hell out of her. It was stronger than her resolve, stronger than anything she'd ever felt before.

"I got it out," he said, holding up the damaged screw. "Now I can . . . put it in again."

His eyes met hers. Fire blazed in the blue now, and the beat in his throat hastened. Against her leg, she felt him harden, lengthen.

"I don't care about the damned screw," Olivia said, her voice husky. Then she leaned in and kissed that warm, intoxicating spot on his neck where his pulse beat a steady rhythm. He tasted like hot sunshine and dark chocolate, and before she knew what she was doing, Olivia was under Luke inside the cabinet, and her legs were wrapping around his and he was kissing her back.

The drill clattered to the floor. The screws spiraled away. Olivia didn't care. She returned Luke's kiss with a ferocity born out of need, out of a want that had been building since that first day in his yard.

His mouth tore at hers, hungry and harsh. She reached down and tugged at his shirt, nearly tearing the cotton in her eagerness to have it off. He reached back with one hand and yanked the tee over his head and tossed it somewhere behind them. She ran her hands down his back, sliding over the smooth contours, the rough pebbles of his spine. His broad chest pressed warmth against hers, and before she knew it, he was tugging her shirt up to expose her bra. She tried to slip out of her shirt, but the movement caused Luke's head to bang against the drawer above them. "I think we need to take this someplace more comfortable."

"Definitely."

They scrambled out of the cabinet, onto the kitchen floor, the fire between them burning too fast, too hot to pause to go upstairs or do anything other than fumble her shirt over her head. She threw the cotton tee to the side, then moved into a sitting position. She watched Luke's eyes widen as she flicked the hooks on her bra and caught the lace with one hand just before it slid down. The silky straps danced down her arms, and for the first time in forever, Olivia felt sexy, wanton, as Luke's gaze roved over her and a ghost of a smile toyed with his lips. "What's it going to take for you to move that hand?" he said.

She feigned deep thought, putting a finger to her lips. "A smile."

The half grin on his face spread into a full-out smile, a smile she glimpsed so rarely on him that every time she saw it, it made her quiver. Hot damn. She took in a deep breath, then removed her hand and let the lacy bra tumble to the floor. The cool air of the kitchen hit her chest, making her nipples pucker, or maybe they were reacting to the way that Luke looked at her, like she was the most amazing goddess he'd ever seen.

"You are . . . beautiful," he said. "And intoxicating. And desirable."

She beamed. "Thank you."

He leaned forward and covered her body with his again. "I want you to know that this time, I don't want to stop in the middle. And I"—he paused, grinned—"I came prepared."

She laughed. And laughed. And laughed.

"What?"

A hot blush filled her cheeks. "So did I."

Surprise lifted his brows. "You did?"

She nodded. "I couldn't bring myself to buy condoms in the Rescue Bay pharmacy, given how small this town is—"

"And how people talk."

"So I went to the next town and bought them."

"When did you do that?"

"The day after we almost . . ." The blush rushed to her face again.

"Really?" He seemed flattered.

She shrugged, looked away. "I'm nothing if not an optimist."

He tipped her chin until she was looking at him again. "And I like that about you. Very, very much." Then he closed the distance between them again and they stopped talking.

He tore off his jeans, and she did the same, then his boxers, her panties. She expected him to go straight for the condoms he'd tugged out of his wallet, but instead, Luke took his time with her. Sweet, hot time, kissing her from lips to breasts to belly. He lingered for a long time on her breasts, taking one nipple into his mouth and tasting it, swirling it with his tongue, before releasing it to perform the same exquisite torture on the other nipple. She arched against him, panting, wanting, needing. "Oh, Luke, please, just . . ."

"Patience, Olivia, is a virtue," he said, his voice dark and low. Then he slid down her body, kissing, tasting, nipping, before reaching under her legs to spread them apart. She held her breath, realizing what he was about to do. Shivers chased down her spine and anticipation fired in her veins.

He lowered his mouth and lifted her hips to meet his tongue. She gasped when his tongue slid along the folds at her entrance, warm, wet, delicious. He started slow and easy, then faster, pausing to suck her clit into his mouth and flick it with his tongue.

"God, Olivia, I love the way you taste." The words were almost a growl.

"Then please don't stop."

"You like this?" He ran his tongue between her legs once, twice, stopped.

"God, yes, please, Luke . . ."

He gave her a quick, hot smile, then dipped his head again.

Sensation built inside Olivia, storm-tossed waves crashing against a beach that had gone untended for so long. Luke tasted and teased her, and she fisted her hands in the pile of clothes, as the orgasm built and built and then exploded in a rush, rendering her breathless and blind for one long sweet second.

After a moment, she opened her eyes and exhaled. Her heart still hammered in her chest and little tingles reverberated deep inside her. "Oh my God. That was incredible. I've never . . . no one's ever . . ." She shook her head. What possessed her to tell him that now, of all times? "It was incredible."

He chuckled. "You said that already."

"Sorry. You just . . . surprised me."

He raised himself up to meet her face with his own, then reached out and trailed a finger along her jaw. "You deserve that, and more."

She smiled, then slid a hand between them to circle his erection. She stroked up and down, until Luke was groaning and pressing his hips to hers. "What was that about me deserving more?"

In answer, Luke reached for the foil packet beside him. He tore it open with his teeth, then slid the condom on. Olivia's hand chased after his and slid down his shaft, then up again, then down, until Luke put a hand over hers, shifted, and settled his body between her legs.

"Olivia." He exhaled her name in a long breath before catching her mouth with his. At the same time, he entwined their hands, brought their joined touch above her head, and in one long, smooth thrust, slid into her. She let out a gasp and bent upward, filled with such exquisite perfection that she wanted him to stay there forever.

"Okay?" he asked.

"Oh, yes. More than okay."

"Good." He lowered his head to kiss her mouth, her cheeks, her neck, while he moved with her, filling her almost to bursting, as liquid heat built inside her. Luke's gaze held hers, their hands clasped tight, and all Olivia could think was how right, how perfect this all felt.

Luke released her hands and slid his palms under her hips, lifting her just enough to deepen the stroke and send her tumbling over the edge, as fireworks exploded behind her eyes and inside her heart. His gaze never left hers, even as he cried out with her and their bodies came together for one amazing moment.

And as she came down again from a high she had never experienced before, Olivia realized that she hadn't just given her body to Luke in that moment. She'd given him her heart, too.

Nineteen

❧

By the time Luke and Olivia came up for air, the propane had burned away in the grill, and they ended up calling for pizza anyway. Luke tugged on his jeans and went to answer the door while Olivia hit the shower. The remains of their afternoon—discarded clothes, tools, and empty cabinet boxes—sat around the kitchen like a road map of afternoon debauchery. He chuckled, feeling lighter and yes, happier, than he had in . . .

Well, in a hell of a long time.

He fished his wallet out of his back pocket and peeled off a couple of twenties, then tugged open the recalcitrant front door. But instead of Martie from Pizza Plus, Greta stood on Olivia's porch, a familiar white box from the bakery in one hand and a surprised O on her face. "Grandma?"

"Luke. What a pleasant surprise to find you here."

"I was, uh, helping Olivia install some cabinets."

"Apparently, one doesn't need a shirt to do that." She grinned, then pushed the box into his hands. "I won't bother you while you're installing . . . whatever. I just wanted to bring Olivia some cookies."

He shook his head. "I know you, Grandma. Are you spying on us?"

She feigned shock. "Now why would I do that?"

"I can read what you're thinking, as clear as the newspaper. You were just a little obvious with the hip thing the other day."

"Wonders of modern medicine. Sometimes I'm better"—she snapped her fingers—"just like that."

He chuckled. Grandma was always trying to take care of him, to ensure his happiness. He loved that about her, even if he sometimes disagreed with her methods. "You should have been a politician, Grandma, because you can spin like nobody I know."

"I have no idea what you're talking about, Lucas." She patted the top of the box. "Just be sure to share those cookies with Olivia. Tell her I'll see her at Golden Years on Monday. So that means you two have all weekend to . . . install cabinets." Then she gave her grandson a smile, turned on her heel, and walked away.

At the same time, the pizza delivery guy pulled into Olivia's driveway. He bounded up the stairs two at a time. "Hey, don't you live next door?" Martie asked.

"Yeah. Long story."

"Whatever, dude. I don't ask questions, I just hand over pie." He exchanged the pizza for the money, thanked Luke for the generous tip, then drove away.

Luke took the pizza and cookies into the house. As he did, he passed an oval mirror hanging in the hall. He caught his reflection—bare-chested, carrying dinner, like a normal man in a normal relationship. Then his gaze shifted upward and he saw the scar that sliced a C along the side of his face, and he remembered.

He was a far cry from a normal man who could have a normal relationship. And the longer he kept playing this pretend game, the worse it was going to hurt when reality returned.

"Promise me, Luke. If anything happens to me—"

The happiness evaporated like rain on a hot summer

sidewalk. Luke laid the food on the kitchen table, gathered his clothes and the dog, then walked out of Olivia's house.

Before it got all too easy to stay.

If there was one key to handling teenagers, it was knowing the art of the deal. After they left the barbecue earlier that week, Diana promised to let Jackson keep one of the puppies if he went to school every day and stayed out of trouble. She threw in a *Keep your grades up*, sure that he would do two out of the three, but instead, as the days went on and Jackson spent his after-school hours at the shelter with the pups, his enthusiasm for school returned, and his Fs and Ds edged up into Cs and Bs. There'd been no reports home, no detentions, and no tardies or days skipped.

"Those puppies are going to need their first shots," Diana said to Jackson as they headed back home on Saturday morning. She'd treated him to lunch at Suzy's Family Dining after stopping in at the office for rounds and some supplies for the dogs. "I was planning on doing it today. Want to help me?"

"Is it going to hurt them?"

"A little pinch, like when you got your shots when you were little."

He scrunched up his face at the memory. "Little pinch? More like getting bit by a rattlesnake."

"Oh, it wasn't that bad."

He looked at her askance. "You weren't the one getting the arm tattoo."

"True, true. Sorry."

"Can we get them some dog treats for after, kind of like how the doctor would give to me?"

She smiled. "Sure. Whatever you want."

"Cool." Jackson glanced to the right, then quickly slumped lower in his seat and put a hand between his head and the window. "Shit."

She braked for the light, then flicked her directional for a left turn. "Jackson, don't curse."

"Then drive, Mom. Please."

Urgency peaked in his voice. "Why? What's the matter?"

"Just drive." He slumped lower. "I don't want to talk about it."

"I can't. It's a red light." She shifted her gaze to the right, to a trio of teenage boys standing on the corner, waiting for the light to change. They wore long dark jeans, dark T-shirts, and heavy boots, and stood like a wary pack of dogs, ready to lunge at any threat.

"Are those kids bothering you?"

"I. Don't. Want. To. Talk. About. It." He said the words through gritted teeth and kept his face averted from hers.

She sighed. Weighed the wisdom of pushing the subject or letting it go. In the end, the light changed, Diana made the turn, and as they left the intersection in the rearview mirror, Jackson's tense stance eased and he sat up straighter.

"Don't forget to stop at the store," he said, as if nothing had happened and the world had returned to normal.

"Right." But her mind was on her son and what he wasn't telling her, even as she pulled into the parking lot of the pet store and went inside with Jackson to pick out a bag of puppy treats. She wanted to ask but didn't want to disturb the fragile happiness in Jackson's voice when he talked about seeing the puppies. In the end, she let it go.

Some child psychologist would probably chide her for avoiding instead of confronting, but right now, the greatest thing in Diana's life was Jackson's smile, and she refused to dim it.

When Diana and Jackson entered the shelter, the puppies scrambled out of the kennel and over to Jackson, a tangle of awkward legs and eager noses. They yipped greetings, nudging each other out of the way to be the first to reach the boy. He laughed, bent down, and grabbed up one, then the next, then the third. The trio wriggled in his arms, like he was trying to wrestle a twelve-legged furry octopus. Jackson's smile brightened, his eyes softened, and he seemed to drop ten pounds of stress and angst off his shoulders.

Diana saw Olivia's car parked in the driveway of the house, but her sister didn't come out. Fine with Diana. She still wasn't sure how she felt about this whole sister-and-inheritance thing. Diana had talked to an attorney, who told her that she had a valid case if she wanted to fight the will in probate. Diana decided to sit with the information, let it digest before rushing to a decision. Maybe because she didn't relish a lengthy and expensive legal battle, or maybe because Diana's heart was softening toward this stranger who was trying so hard to make things right.

What would Mom want? That was the question Diana came back to again and again. She knew the answer.

She just didn't like it.

"Let's get their shots," Diana said, concentrating on the dogs, on doing her job. That was one thing she and Mom had in common. They both found solace in working with animals. Dogs didn't judge or question, they just loved. She thought of Miss Sadie and Chance, and realized her sister shared the same affinity for furry creatures.

Diana lowered herself to the ground and laid her supplies nearby. Jackson remained standing. Diana bit back a sigh.

For months, Jackson had maintained this invisible wall between himself and his mother, keeping his distance emotionally, physically. Hugs and bedtime kisses had been replaced with a sullen quiet. She didn't know if the aloofness stemmed from normal teenage divisors, or if he blamed Diana for his father's absence, or a combination of the two.

"You want to help?" she asked. "After all, these guys are partly yours, since you're the one who found them."

"Yeah, I guess they are." He shrugged.

"I don't think I told you this, but you did a good job taking care of them. They all look healthy and strong."

He shrugged, smiled a little. "Thanks."

Diana waited, but Jackson didn't move. She told herself not to feel disappointed, that there would come a day when Jackson would seek her out again, when they could build a bridge over all that stood between them. She fished in her bag for the rabies medication and some needles, while the puppies, unaware of what was coming, frolicked on the floor.

Jackson sat cross-legged on the kennel floor beside her, close enough to bump knees. Tears burned behind Diana's eyes. She turned away and dug in her medical bag for supplies she already had in her hand. "Okay, first puppy."

"This is Mary." Jackson picked up the brown-and-gold floppy-eared female. "She's the nicest of the three, but she keeps the boys in line, so if she gets her shots first, the other two should be more cooperative."

Diana raised a brow. "Mary?"

Jackson shrugged and handed the dog to his mother. "As in Peter, Paul, and Mary? The puppies are two boys and a girl, and when I was thinking about names, I thought about that group. Because, well, they have that song we both like."

Her eyes burned again, but Diana worked a smile to her face, and didn't care that it wobbled. "Blowin' in the Wind."

"Yeah."

"The answer, my friend," she began singing, low and slow, the words coming back like old friends. By the time Diana reached the close of the chorus, two voices were singing the sweet melody inside that kennel, one soprano, one a deep baritone. Diana grinned at her son and stopped singing because her throat had closed.

"I like that song."

"Me too," she said.

Jackson kept his gaze downcast, but she could see a smile toying with the edges of his mouth. "I thought, you know, 'cause we're taking care of these puppies together, that, well . . . it'd be nice to pick names that kind of go with you and me both."

"They're perfect names, Jackson. Absolutely perfect." Tears brimmed to the surface of Diana's eyes and blurred her vision. She reached, corralled her son around the shoulder, and drew him to her for a fierce, tight hug. He didn't squirm or pull away, and after a moment, his arm encircled her waist. He nestled his head in the crook of her shoulder, just as he had when he was a boy and she'd come into his room late at night, wipe away his tears, and reassure him that there were no monsters in the closet, no alligators under his bed. In the soft glow of a Curious George night-light, Diana would hug her son and make his world all right again.

A long time ago, he'd replaced that night-light with a neon lamp shaped like a guitar. He'd stopped calling out when he had nightmares and stopped asking about monsters in the closet. But in this hug on the cold, hard floor of a run-down animal shelter, the sweet connection between Diana and Jackson returned.

Some things, she realized, hadn't changed at all.

"I love you, Jackson," she whispered against his dark brown mop of hair.

"Love you too, Mom." His voice caught on the last syllable. Then he cleared his throat, drew back, and gave his head a shake, more to erase any evidence of emotion, she suspected, than to straighten his hair.

"Let's get these little boogers their shots. Okay?" Diana swiped away the tears with the back of her hand, then grabbed up Mary and gave her several shots in quick succession, while Jackson handed her dog treats and petted her head. They repeated the actions with Peter and Paul, working together in efficient, quiet moves. She admired the way her son handled the rambunctious pups, calming them and keeping them in line. He kept advising his mother on the best way to handle this one or that one. She smiled to herself because she could have been listening to herself in Jackson's words.

"You did great, Jackson," Diana said. "You know, if you ever want to come in and help at the practice—"

"I don't know. Maybe."

She nodded and decided not to push. She'd asked Jackson a hundred times to come to work with her. When he was little, he'd loved the office, the animals, the staff. But then around eleven or twelve, he'd stopped wanting to go to work with her, opting for a video game or TV show instead. The wall was being built, even back then, she realized, and she had just been too wrapped up in her job and the demise of her relationship with Sean to notice.

"Sounds like a puppy party in here."

Her pulse tripped and she turned at the sound of Mike's deep baritone. "Here to adopt a puppy?"

Mike put up his hands. "No way. Heck, I don't even have a permanent residence."

A reminder that anything she started with this man would be over before it began. He was married to the U.S. Coast Guard, and when his leave ended, he'd be gone. Charming smile and dancing blue eyes and all. A little fissure of temptation slid through her bones all the same. "We're just giving the pups their first shots," she said. "Getting them ready to find homes."

"I picked up some lumber and supplies." Mike thumbed behind him. "I figured the least I can do for dashing Olivia's hopes is to make myself useful around here and get this shelter fixed up and safe."

"Dashing her hopes?"

"I told her that house is a lost cause, but from what I see and hear, she's determined to keep trying. Luke was over there today, he said, helping her put in some cabinets," he said.

Diana admired Olivia for holding on to the house. For not giving up. She had to give her sister—oh, that word still sounded so odd—some credit. Olivia had determination and grit when it came to what mattered to her. A lot like their mother.

"I'm glad she's holding on to it," Diana said, and for the first time since she'd realized that her mother had left the house to someone else, Diana meant those words. "It'll be nice to see someone giving that house the love it deserves."

"Some people are eternal optimists," Mike said. "Even when the glass is empty." He gave the metal post a tap, as if adding a punctuation mark to the sentence. "I'll let you get back to work with the dogs. I've got some work to do, to make this place safe for the animals and the people. Hey, Jackson, want to help?"

Jackson looked at the puppies, then at his mother. Diana could tell her son liked Mike, and knew her dexterous son also liked doing anything that required power tools.

"Go ahead," she said. "I'll finish up with Peter, Paul, and Mary, then I'll come give you guys a hand, too."

Mike gave Diana a big grin. "You any good with a hammer?"

"As long as I have a big target."

"This big enough?" He put out his arms, gave her a wink, then walked off with Jackson, chuckling. The two voices, one deep, one still finding its range, carried down the hall, light with laughter. Diana sat back and held one of the puppies to her chest, and the tension she'd been carrying for so long slowly uncoiled its grip.

Twenty

Olivia was still singing—badly and off-key, but she didn't care—when she stepped out of the shower. The delicious warmth that had filled her after she and Luke had made love lingered long after she headed for the shower while he stayed in the kitchen to wait for the pizza guy.

She swiped a circle of steam off the mirror's face. Her reflection showed a happy woman, a woman who had taken a risk that she'd vowed to avoid. It exhilarated and terrified her all at once, but the song in her heart overrode everything.

She'd fallen for Luke Winslow, and fallen hard.

She kept on singing while she dried her hair, applied her makeup, and pulled on a pair of skinny capris and a V-necked butter-yellow T-shirt. A swipe of cherry-colored gloss on her lips, and then she was done and heading down the stairs, toward the scent of pepperoni and cheese. "Sorry I took so long. I hope the pizza isn't cold."

She stopped. The pizzas sat on the kitchen table, unopened, beside a white bakery box that hadn't been there earlier. Miss Sadie stood by the door, tail wagging. The new cabinets gleamed, blank oak faces waiting for hardware. Yet the silent room held an air of emptiness.

Olivia peeked in the other rooms, but Luke was gone. No note, no explanation.

"Did he go home to shower?" she asked Miss Sadie. The bichon yipped, wagged her tail, then sat down and put up her paws, already begging for pizza crust.

Olivia grabbed a pair of shoes, then headed next door, carrying the boxes of pizza and bakery goodies. She had no idea where those had come from but had one prime suspect. Greta. Another of her sweet but overt attempts to bring Olivia and Luke together. Either way, the cookies would make a perfect dessert for after the pizza and after more . . . well, *more*. When Olivia reached Luke's porch, she paused a second to straighten her hair, then knocked.

All the way over here, the song she'd been singing in the shower had resonated in her mind, pinging off the happy bubble in her chest. She smiled when Luke opened the door. "Hey, where'd you go?"

"I'm sorry. I probably should have said something before I left. I . . . I don't think this is a good idea," he said. "I was wrong for misleading you into thinking we could have something."

Just like that, the bubble burst and the song died. "*Mislead* me?"

He had gone back to the stone-faced man she had first met in the yard all those weeks ago. His blue eyes had gone icy, his jaw a block of granite. "I made you think there was a future with me. And there's not."

A half hour ago, they'd been on the floor, making love, sharing their bodies, their hearts. She had felt a connection between them, she was sure of it. Or had Luke just been a supremely good actor? "What the hell happened, Luke? A little while ago, everything was fine and now . . . I don't know what to think."

He let out a long breath and his gaze went to that far-off spot, the one she couldn't see, the place she couldn't reach. "If we'd met a year ago, six months ago, maybe things would be different. Back then, I was thinking about settling down after my commission ended. Maybe get a job at the airlines, or as a private pilot. But that's out of the question now, and always will be. I'm done flying."

"That doesn't mean you're done as a man."

He turned to her and now the ice in his eyes had given way to an angry fire. "I was done the day of the accident. I *killed* a man that day. I'm not some hero or the kind of man a woman like you deserves. You need someone you can depend on, who's there for you over the long haul. That's not me. Not anymore."

She started to speak, but he cut her off.

"You don't know the man I am, Olivia, and if you did, you wouldn't be standing on my porch." He let out an angry gust. "I never should have let things get out of hand between us."

"Get out of hand? You make it sound like making love with me was a mistake."

"It was."

The words stung like a slap. She stared at him for a long, cold second while the world went on and her heart stopped. "Yeah, I guess it was. I can't believe I was stupid enough to think you were different." Then she dropped the boxes to the porch and turned away, before Luke saw her cry.

As if things couldn't get worse—they did.

Olivia pasted a smile on her face and forced herself not to think about Luke. Or about how she'd fallen and gotten burned again. Or anything other than the job she was here to do. She signaled to Miss Sadie to come forward, and to sit.

Millie sat on the end of her bed, still wearing her pink flannel pajamas and blue house slippers. The sun streamed in the windows, bouncing off the windowpane quilt and the pale-beige carpet. The team had thought taking Millie's therapy to an area where she was comfortable—her apartment inside the Golden Years building—might encourage her to open up.

Kris stood in the back of the room, arms crossed, watching, ready to lend a helping hand if Millie decided to try any of the exercises. A quad cane sat to the right of Millie's hand, waiting for use. Millie could walk with the aid, she just had chosen not to touch the cane or get off the bed.

"Miss Sadie loves to go for walks," Olivia said. "She would be so excited if you took her for a walk." Olivia signaled to her dog. The bichon let out a happy yip. "Did you hear that? She's looking forward to going for a walk with you, Millie."

Millie glanced at the dog, then the cane, and then turned her gaze back to the wall.

Olivia laid the looped end of Miss Sadie's bright red leash beside Millie's hand. "Do you want to pick up the leash? Start there, Millie. Just pick it up."

Millie's gaze dropped to the leash. She shook her head.

Olivia glanced at Kris, who shrugged. The team had tried about everything they could think of, and nothing had worked. Millie was determined to stay in her dark world.

Olivia bent down in front of Millie. Miss Sadie hopped onto Olivia's knees and pressed her little body against her mistress's chest. Olivia kept her gaze on Millie's downturned head, her long white hair a shaggy mess, pale-blue eyes downcast.

How Olivia could relate. She remembered the days after her marriage imploded, when she'd realized the entire thing had been a sham, and she was the one who had fallen for her ex's forever act. "I know how you feel, Millie. I've been there. Not on the same road you're traveling, but on my own path. At the time it seemed so dark and lonely, like I was the only one who felt this way, and no one I knew could relate or understand. Then I met Miss Sadie, and I told myself I had nothing to give a dog, nothing to give to anyone, most especially myself. But she looked at me with that little face of hers, begging me not to give up on her, not to leave her in that shelter.

"I couldn't walk away from such raw . . . need and hope." Olivia ruffled the bichon's head. Miss Sadie pressed harder into Olivia's chest, a ten-pound doggie hug of gratitude and love. "So I took her home. She needed to be fed and walked and loved, whether I wanted to do any of those things or not. It didn't matter if I was depressed or mad, or feeling sorry for myself. I had to put all that aside and place Miss Sadie's needs first. This little dog saved me, and she wants to save you, too."

Millie raised her gaze to Olivia's. Her lower lip trembled, and her eyes shone with unshed tears, but she didn't speak.

Olivia gave Millie's hand a gentle squeeze. "I'm not going to give up on you, Millie, and neither is Miss Sadie."

No response.

"I'll be back, Millie. See you tomorrow." Olivia got to her feet, gathered her supplies, and left the room, with Kris following along.

"That was awesome," Kris said.

"Yeah, it would be if it had worked." Olivia sighed. Every time she thought she was making progress with Millie, she was wrong. Maybe she wasn't cut out for this job.

Kris draped an arm around Olivia's shoulders. "The Hollywood ending only happens in the movies, you know. You're making a difference with her, even if you don't see it."

Olivia thought of all the brave, good intentions she'd had when she'd moved to Rescue Bay. She fingered the letter tucked in the pocket of her skirt. She'd tried, tried her best; no one could fault her for that. But maybe the time had come to move on.

"Okay, Greta, spill. What are you hiding this morning?" Pauline narrowed her gaze and leaned in to study Greta across the small table. A jigsaw puzzle of the Eiffel Tower spread across the smooth oak surface. "Did you spike the nurses' coffee with Kahlua again?"

"No, and for the record, I never did that." Greta took a sip of tea, honest-to-goodness tea with no bourbon added, and fit a corner of the tower into place. "It was a rumored spiking."

Pauline laughed. "Whatever you want to call it."

Greta leaned back in her chair and grinned. Not admitting a thing. No one could blame her for something she never acknowledged as happening. "I'm just happy."

"Did you say happy?" Esther cupped a hand around her ear. "You? You're never happy."

"Well, I am today. It's a Monday, we're not quilting, and Luke is in *love*." Greta sighed. Finally, her grandson was living his life and moving forward. She couldn't think of a better partner for the future than the beautiful, spunky Olivia. Greta leaned forward and fit in two more pieces, *click, click*. They fit as perfectly as Luke and Olivia. "What more could I ask for?"

"A clean bill of health?" Esther said. "A bigger check from social security? World peace?"

Greta considered something sarcastic in response, then decided she wasn't going to spoil her mood. Even Esther couldn't irritate her today. "I'm so happy, I *almost* said good morning to Harold Twohig this morning when I saw him walking to breakfast."

"Almost?" Pauline turned a squiggly-shaped piece left, then right, and squinted at the already assembled pieces.

Greta grinned and reached over to pluck the piece from Pauline's inept hands, then press it into the right spot on the tower's spire. "It made me happier *not* to say it."

Pauline laughed. Always neighborly Esther tsk-tsked. Around them, the morning room filled with people, some sitting at the card tables for a game of rummy or a crossword. Greta sipped her tea and wondered how long it would be before she had great-grandchildren to spoil.

The door to the morning room opened and Miss Sadie trotted in first, wearing her little red THERAPY DIVA vest and eliciting delighted gasps from the residents. Olivia followed behind the dog, wearing a soft white short-sleeved shirt, a poufy pale-blue skirt, and red kitten heels. Her hair was back in a ponytail and, on the outside, she seemed like her usual chipper self.

Greta nudged Pauline. "Here she comes. Doesn't she look so . . ." Her voice trailed off as Olivia drew closer.

"Depressed?" Pauline supplied. "That's odd. I've never seen Olivia look like that. She's usually so sunny and sweet."

"Me either," Esther said. "Maybe she got some bad news today or her car wouldn't start or the power company raised her electric bill—"

"Hush, Esther. I'm going to go find out what happened." Greta got to her feet and crossed to Olivia. Miss Sadie came running up and nudged at Greta's hand. She petted the little dog for a second, her gaze never leaving Olivia's. The light didn't shine in Olivia's eyes, and even though she smiled, the gesture lacked its usual punch. "Why, hello, Olivia. How are you today?"

"Fine." A monotone syllable. "Sorry. No time to talk today. I need to get to the rest of my therapy appointments, Greta."

"It's only quarter till. You have a few minutes to visit, right?"

"I really should . . ." Her voice trailed off and she shrugged. Sadness emanated from her like perfume, and Greta wanted to just reach out and hug the poor girl.

What had gone wrong between the weekend and this morning?

"You seem off today," Greta said.

"A tough day at work, that's all."

"And personally, too?" When Olivia looked away, Greta knew Luke was behind that pain in Olivia's eyes. "Has my grandson forgotten his manners again?"

"I wouldn't know. I haven't seen him lately." Olivia raised her chin. "Maybe you can ask him yourself."

By God, she had not raised Luke to be this stupid. How could he break this poor girl's heart? Because that was what she saw in Olivia's face.

Heartbreak.

"I'm glad I saw you today, Greta. I wanted to thank you, for everything." Olivia took Greta's hand in hers. "And for being one of my first and last friends in Rescue Bay."

"What do you mean, last?"

"I just gave my notice to the center director. I'm going back to Massachusetts. I can't save the house, I can't get through to my patients. I can't . . . make anything work here."

"Oh, honey, don't do that. Rescue Bay needs you." And so did Luke, but clearly, her grandson was too big of a stubborn idiot to realize that. If he was here, she might have throttled him.

Greta waved toward the love seat that sat in a cozy nook near the French doors leading to the courtyard. Bright sunlight streamed through the doors and washed over the white cushions, which made the love seat a favorite reading place for many residents. Greta saw Colleen Morris shuffling toward the spot, a romance novel in one hand, and waved her off. "Come on, let's sit down for a little bit and talk," Greta said to Olivia. "You'll feel better if you do."

"Oh, I don't know if—"

"You have time. It's only quarter till, remember?"

"Okay. But just for a minute." Miss Sadie lay down at Olivia's feet, patient and quiet, her brown eyes on her mistress, her tail swishing softly against the tile floor.

Greta leaned over and whispered in Olivia's ear. That Esther had the hearing of a nuclear submarine, and the last thing she needed today was an Esther lecture. "Do you need a little something to get your day off on the right foot, dear? Because I'm more than happy to share my Maker's Mark with you."

Olivia laughed. "No, no. But thank you. It's a . . . sweet offer."

"Good." Greta patted Olivia's knee. "I'm glad you said that, because I think what you need, more than a sip of my bourbon, is to talk."

"Greta—"

"And talking is the kind of medicine that can't be found in a bottle," Greta went on, overriding Olivia's objection. Her daddy had always said that. He'd sit little Greta down at the kitchen table, a platter of cookies between them, and get her talking about the book she was reading in English or the boy she liked in math. He'd ease in with the easy subjects, and eventually the tough stuff would filter through. How Greta wished her daddy were here now, with his cookies and his odd bit of wisdom. He'd always had the right word at the right time. "I know my grandson has yet to realize that talking is good for the soul, but I'm hoping you're a lot less stubborn than that mule I helped raise."

"Maybe less stubborn, but I'm definitely more of an idiot." She shook her head. "I had this silly dream, and I thought if I came down here, I could make it come true."

"Nothing wrong with that. Dreams are what fuels us, dear."

"Yeah, well, mine just led me in the wrong direction, which is why I'm going back home."

Olivia's home was right here in Rescue Bay, with Greta, Pauline, Esther, and Luke. And yes, maybe even Harold Twohig.

"Maybe it was the wrong direction. Maybe it's not. I think right now, you're reacting with emotion instead of thinking this through." Greta patted Olivia's knee. "Now tell me what went so wrong. I promise, it will make you feel better."

"Okay." Then, like a waterfall held back too long by a big rock, the story spilled from Olivia. The abandonment in the hospital at birth, the loving adoptive mother and father in Boston, the lawyer on her doorstep, the house beyond repair, the sister who held her at arm's length. "I could probably work through all those things and stay here. And I was. But then this morning, the electricity at the house went out. I think I cut a line or blew something. I don't know. To me, it was a sign. I come in to work, and I think today's the day I'll get through to Millie, but no, it only got worse. There's another sign. And after Luke . . . well, let's just say I didn't need a billboard to give me *that* sign. I started to ask myself what I was doing here. I'm looking for answers from a mother who's never had any for me, and trying to build a life in a house that just wants to die."

Greta sat up straight. Looked Olivia dead in the eye. "You stop that right now, missy. You are *not* allowed to have a pity party. If you want answers, you go get them."

"Greta, Bridget is dead. I can't get answers from her anymore."

"Then go talk to her." Her face softened and she clasped Olivia's hand again. "After my husband, Edward, died, God rest his soul, I would go and talk to him at the cemetery. He never answered, of course, which was pretty much par for the course with him. Lord knows while we were married, I did enough talking for the both of us, but just being there and having it out with him made me feel better. I would stand in front of that headstone and yell at him for leaving me behind. Or tell him he was a selfish jerk for not showing me how to run the generator before he died. But most of all, I would tell him"—Greta lowered her voice, so no one would overhear her admit this out loud—"that I loved the old bastard and I missed him more every day."

Olivia smiled. "Why, Greta, I do think you're a romantic."

"Hush, now. You let something like that get around this place and I lose all sorts of credibility."

Olivia pressed a finger to her lips, but her green eyes danced with merriment. "Mum's the word."

"Good. Now I want you to think twice about leaving here, because there are people in this place and in this town who need you." Greta squeezed Olivia's fingers. "People like me."

Olivia nodded, swiping at the tears in her eyes. "Okay, I will. Thank you, Greta."

"It's nothing that I wouldn't do for my own grandchild, and I want you to know that to me, you are part of my family, dear."

Olivia pressed a tender kiss to Greta's cheek. "I appreciate it, and I appreciate you." She got to her feet, and Miss Sadie scrambled to join her. "Now I really have to go or I'm going to be late."

Oh, it softened Greta's heart to see Olivia happy again, she thought as Olivia headed down the hall, Miss Sadie trotting by her side. Maybe there was still a way to get this all to work out. Not just so Greta would have a happy ending for the Common Sense Carla column, but so she could give Olivia and Luke the happy ending they so deserved.

Because truth be told, Greta Winslow really *was* a romantic at heart.

Then she spied a familiar bane of her existence wearing a too-thin, too-tight tank top outside the window, waving at her. Exception—a romantic at heart when it came to everyone—

Except for Harold Twohig, the shirtless wonder.

Twenty-one

∞

Luke's dark mood had driven off Mike, who threw up his hands, read Luke the riot act about running a one-man pity party, then headed next door to take out some frustration on some two-by-fours. Luke could hear the hammering all the way from inside his house and figured Mike would be gone for a while. The two had been friends long enough that he didn't worry the blowup would damage that bond. Mike had been right and justified in calling Luke out for being an idiot. The problem was transforming from idiot back into human.

The idiot side of him had driven Olivia away— permanently. He couldn't blame her. He couldn't have been more brutal and cruel if he'd delivered his message with a sledgehammer.

He missed her. Damn, how he missed her. She'd become a part of his life, and without her, it was as if someone had ripped out a vital organ.

They had. His heart.

He glanced at the answering machine. It blinked red, over and over, reminding him of the message waiting for him. Emma, Joe's sister, had received the letter Luke sent her and wanted to talk.

Luke had ignored the message. Hadn't returned the call. What the hell was he supposed to say to her?

His doorbell rang, making him jump. He wanted to ignore it, but he'd done a lot of ignoring of things lately and it hadn't gotten him anywhere but alone again. He headed down the hall and pulled open the door. It took a moment for the incongruous sight standing on his porch to make sense. "Dad? What are you doing here?"

Edward Winslow hadn't changed a bit in the six months since Luke had last seen him. He had on the typical lawyer attire he wore every day—dark-blue power suit, crimson tie, crisp white shirt, and polished dress shoes. Not a hair out of place, not a speck of lint on his Brooks Brothers. "I came by to see my son."

Not *to see you* or *to visit with you*, but the impersonal *to see my son*. "Is it time already for your once-a-year lecture? I'm not in the mood for that." Luke started to shut the door, but his father stopped him.

"That's not why I'm here." Edward's face pinched. "Can I come in?"

Luke hesitated, then opened the door wider. "Fine."

Edward stepped into the bungalow, and if he had issues with Luke's décor, he didn't show it. He just strode down the hall toward the kitchen, as if he were striding up to the judge's bench to deliver an objection. Luke followed, already regretting opening the door.

Edward detoured for the table, while Luke took up a station against the counter. He reached for the coffee and realized he could see the pot this time. When had things stopped being all shadows and shapes and begun to shift into clear images? Had he been too caught up in his one-man pity party to notice the changes in his vision? His sight wasn't perfect, not by any stretch, but a whole lot better.

Luke filled the carafe, dumped some grounds into the

basket, then pressed the power button. He put his back to the counter and crossed his arms over his chest. And waited. He knew Edward well, and could see the windup to the lecture in the way his father tensed and knitted his brows in mock concern.

"I stopped by to make sure you were taking care of yourself," his father said. "Your grandmother said you have been having . . . difficulties since the accident."

"The accident that killed my best friend and left me partially blind? Yeah, Dad, it's been tough over the last couple of *months*. But nothing for you to worry about."

"I realize you may be angry at me for not visiting or coming by to take care of you when you got home. I had the National Bar Association conference in—"

"Frankly, Dad, I don't give a shit where you were. Thanks for the *Get Well Soon* card and the gift card for the supermarket. It really helped ease the pain." Luke didn't even try to keep the sarcasm from his voice.

"I . . ." Edward put up his hands. "You're right. I should have been here. I didn't know what to do. And your grandmother seemed to have it all under control. Like she always does."

"Dad, she's *eighty-three years old*. When are you going to stop dumping the parental role in her lap? It's about fucking time you started being a dad, don't you agree?" He snorted, then reined in years of anger. "Not that I need one now anyway."

For the first time that Luke could remember, Edward was speechless. He sat at the kitchen table, his mouth pursed like he'd eaten a lemon. "Is the coffee done?"

Of course. Change the subject, ignore the tough stuff. Why had Luke hoped for anything else? He glanced back at the pot. "Almost."

"Good."

Silence hung over the kitchen, a brick wall between two stubborn bulls. Luke willed the timer to beep the end of the brewing cycle so he could dispense with this whole charade of a friendly, paternal visit.

Then his mind went to Olivia. To their moonlit walk, and what she'd said when he'd told her he was afraid he'd fall on his face if he tried walking with her.

Yeah, you probably will. But then you'll get back up and try again because you have to. Besides, you can't stay on the damned porch all night.

She hadn't just been talking about the porch or the walk, and he knew it. She was telling him it was okay to take those steps forward in the dark, to try, and maybe fail, because it was time to get off the porch he'd built out of grief and regret.

Damn, that could almost be poetry. But it was true, and another way that Olivia had touched his life when he hadn't been looking.

She could read him, pretty damned well. From the minute she'd met him, Olivia had always seemed to say just what he needed to hear. Whether he listened was another story.

What better place to take those first steps, Luke decided, than here, with his father? Someone had to take the lead or they'd be stuck in this impasse forever.

Hell, he couldn't remember a time when they hadn't had this mountain between them. When Luke had been little, his father would come home at the end of the day, say hello to Greta, then head down the hall to his son's room. Luke would lie in his bed, the covers up to his nose, aware that his father was standing in the light of the hall. He would wait for his father to enter the room, but Edward never did. So Luke would pretend to be asleep and eventually Edward would walk away.

Now, as an adult, Luke realized he'd been lying there, desperate for his father to notice he was only pretending to sleep, while Edward was standing there, probably desperate for his son to notice he was home, and to run into his arms. Luke had been waiting for his distant father to thaw, and Edward had been at a loss as to how to connect with his daredevil son, so like the wife he had lost.

The impasse between them had started on those nights when they'd both so lonely, each needing the other to help them get through this new life devoid of the woman they had both loved, and yet both of them terrified to take those first steps toward the other.

"How was the conference?" As first steps went, that one was pretty damned small.

"Good. Same old boring people talking about the same old boring stuff. Lawyers can be pretty tough to be around all day."

Luke arched a brow. "You don't say."

Edward sighed. "I get it. I'm a terrible father."

"You *were* a terrible father. You don't have to keep being one." He could have recited a long list of Edward's faults, the times Edward had let him down or broken a promise, but he didn't. It was a new day and Luke was a new person, whether he liked that fact or not. Time to stop living in a past he couldn't change.

"So let's start over," he said to his father, and worked a smile to his face. "Hi, Dad. Nice to see you. You want some coffee?"

"I'd love some."

The coffeepot beeped. Luke filled two mugs, then brought them to the table. When he set the white mug in front of Edward, his father reached out and covered his son's hand with his own.

"Thank you, Luke," Edward said.

Luke held his father's gaze for a long moment. "You're welcome."

Then the two men sat and talked about sports and the weather and the rising price of gas, avoiding the big topics in the room, the ones they'd avoided for so long, it seemed easier to leave them to the side than tackle them. That was okay, Luke decided. He didn't need to change the entire world in one afternoon, just make a couple steps in the right direction.

Twenty-two

∞

A small half oval, simple, plain, seated on a grassy hill and flanked by two metal vases filled with fresh yellow roses. Etched in the dark-gray granite was an image of a butterfly, eternally flying above a few simple words.

BRIDGET TUTTLE
BELOVED MOTHER
1966–2013

Olivia stared at the gravestone, but felt . . . nothing. Even after all these miles, all this time in the house, she had no more connection to the woman who had given birth to her than she had the day Bridget had left her in the hospital. In those years, Olivia had had a thousand questions, but really, they all boiled down to one.

"Why?"

The word echoed in the still, quiet air of the Rescue Bay Cemetery. A bird squawked and flew off, and somewhere in the distance a siren sounded. No answer came back. No sense of peace. Nothing.

"Why?" Olivia asked again, louder this time.

The stone stared back at her, silent, cold.

BRIDGET TUTTLE
BELOVED MOTHER

Yeah, beloved by Diana, who had known her, who had all those years and all that time to say good-bye to Bridget. Beloved by the daughter she had kept. A total stranger to the one she had left.

"Why? Why didn't you want me?" Olivia asked, the words a pained whisper that tore at her throat. The stone didn't respond, nor were there any mystical whispers on the wind. There was nothing but the same thing Olivia had had all her life.

Silence.

She clawed at the butterfly necklace, tore the chain from her neck, and thrust it toward the stone. "You leave me this and that stupid, run-down house. Nothing else. Not so much as a *Hey, I'm sorry I left you* note on a Post-it. No explanation, just something that needs work and money and time. Why would you do that to me? Didn't you even think about how much that would hurt?"

"I know why she did it."

Olivia spun around. Diana stood behind her, her eyes shaded by sunglasses, her slim figure obscured by her lab coat. Olivia pressed a hand to her startled heart. Oh God, she hoped her sister hadn't heard that tirade. "Diana. I'm sorry. I didn't know you were behind me."

"I come here almost every day." Diana climbed the little hill and stood next to Olivia. Her gaze dropped to the gravestone. She bit her lip, clasped her hands. The two sisters shared the space on that silent hill for a long moment.

"I come here for the same reason as you did. I want answers." Diana sighed. "Answers I'll probably never have."

What questions could Diana have? Had Bridget been just as closed off with the daughter she had raised as she'd been with the one she'd given up? "I don't understand why she wouldn't at least want to say something to me, or tell me something, anything about why she left me behind. In the end, she left me . . . nothing. Nothing that was really *her*."

Diana shrugged. "Mom wasn't the kind of person who kept a lot of sentimental kind of things. She was . . . practical. She said she had the memories and that's all she needed."

"Well, she didn't even have those with me." Why had she even bothered to come to this place? There was nothing here that Olivia wanted. Olivia pivoted toward her sister and held out the necklace. "Here. I think this is more yours than mine."

Diana caught the butterfly charm in her palm. "Where did you get this?"

"The lawyer gave it to me when he came to tell me about inheriting the house. It was in an envelope, along with a picture of the house. My legacy." She scoffed. "Such as it was."

"This . . ." Diana's eyes misted, and she curled her hand around the necklace. "This never left her neck. I wondered what happened to it. One day it was on her neck, and the next, it was gone. I asked her about it, but she just said she gave it away. She told me that she gave it to someone who needed what was inside. She was so sick by then, I thought it was the morphine talking. She'd had all kinds of crazy requests those last few days. And I thought this was another one of them."

"Someone needed what was inside?" Olivia said. "But it's just a necklace. There's nothing inside."

"Oh, but there is. Watch." Diana ran her thumbnail along the edge of the butterfly. One wing sprang up, pivoting open on a miniature hinge hidden inside the thorax. Diana blinked, brows knitted together. "This isn't the picture I remember Mom having inside here. Of course, I haven't seen the inside of this necklace in years and years. But look, she changed the picture. It's . . . us." Diana turned the necklace toward Olivia.

And there, tucked inside the wing of the butterfly, sat two

tiny pictures. One of Diana and one of Olivia, both as older teens. It took Olivia a moment to place the photo, to wrap her head around how the image could be here in this necklace she had never seen, worn by a woman she had never met. "That's me. It's one of the photos in my high school yearbook. How did she get this?"

"I have no idea. She never told me about it."

Olivia traced over the miniature image of herself and realized this picture changed everything. It meant that somehow, Bridget had kept tabs on her firstborn daughter. Yet never made contact. Why?

"Is there anything else?" she asked.

"There should be." Diana turned the necklace around, and repeated the actions with the other wing. When the enamel side popped up, something small and gold tumbled to the ground. Olivia bent down and fished it out from between the blades of thick green grass.

"It's a key," Olivia said, placing it in Diana's hand.

Her sister flipped the key over in her palm a couple of times, confusion in her eyes that yielded to understanding. "Of course. It all makes sense now. I can't believe it took me this long to figure it out." She pressed a hand to her mouth. "Oh, Mom, I'm not surprised you'd do something like this, unique and clever and unexpected."

"Something like what?"

Diana lifted her gaze. Her green eyes mirrored Olivia's. Same color, same shape, both shining with hope and unshed tears.

"She gave you the key." Diana held it up, and the tiny key caught the sun with a twinkle. "And me the lock."

"I don't understand."

Diana closed the butterfly's wings, then handed the necklace and the key back to Olivia. "Come on. I have something to show you."

Olivia wasn't sure what she expected when she saw Diana's house. Certainly not the warm, cozy, inviting space that

Diana had created in the modest ranch. She'd decorated in soft earth tones, with thick beige sofas in the living room and a pale oak table and chairs in the kitchen, offset by cream-colored tiles and vanilla-painted trim. Pictures of Jackson filled one wall of the entry hall and the space above a dark-brown tufted leather bench that sat in the foyer, inviting you to sit down, tug off your shoes, and stay awhile.

Three dogs greeted them at the door, one an ancient chocolate lab, another a shepherd mix, and a tiny cairn terrier who danced in front of the bigger dogs. Diana apologized for the exuberant greeting and shooed the dogs outside. "Would you like a glass of water? Some coffee? I have lemonade, too, and some soda, if Jackson didn't drink it all."

"Ice water is fine." Olivia stepped into the kitchen and slid into a padded chair. Pale-yellow walls accented the distressed vanilla cabinets and light-amber countertop. Everything was neat and tidy: washed dishes drying in the strainer, clear canisters of flour, sugar, coffee, and tea marching along the far counter. A sunflower-shaped clock ticked the time away on the wall, while a calendar on the fridge held the only signs of clutter—dozens of notes and phone numbers paper-clipped to the pages of the calendar, along with a running grocery list hanging from a magnet. "You have a gorgeous house."

"Thanks. It helps that I have total control over the décor. For all the rooms except for Jackson's." She let out a little laugh while she filled two glasses with ice water and sat down in the opposite chair. She watched the dogs chase each other in the fenced yard for a little while, then let out a breath, turned back to the table, and steepled her fingers. "Sorry. You're not here for small talk, I'm sure."

"It's okay." Small talk might not tell Olivia anything about Bridget, but these little moments about decorating and dogs and kids gave her a peek into her sister's world.

Diana, however, had already shifted into serious gear. "About a week before Mom died, she asked me to go to her house and retrieve a few things, and keep them at my house.

I asked her why, and she said she just felt better knowing her things were in my possession. She was worried that while she was in the hospital, her house would be empty indefinitely. She was sick, really sick, and I didn't want to argue with her, so I did what she asked." Diana got to her feet, left the room, then returned a moment later. "One of the things she had me get was this box."

Diana laid a bread-box-sized container on the table. Constructed out of heavy cardboard and covered with pink-and-white-striped fabric, the box looked like an oversized version of those photo boxes people bought in hobby shops. The lid was secured with a hasp, and dangling from that was a small gold lock. It could have been picked or broken open easily. The lock mainly served as a pause rather than actual security.

"Why didn't you open it?" Olivia asked.

Diana sighed and retook her seat. "My relationship with Mom was complex. She and I loved the same things and dedicated our lives to the same things, but we couldn't seem to find a common middle ground. At the same time, she could be quirky and fun, and I remember days when I was little where she would keep me home from school and we'd spend the day exploring a creek or going to the beach and looking for horseshoe crabs. She would collect things from those journeys, little mementos that she said she was going to put in shadow boxes or make into crafts or something someday. But she never did, and when she had me grab this box, I figured that's what was in it. After she died, things with Jackson got more complicated, and I forgot about the box. Until I saw the key."

Olivia wondered about the things-getting-more-complicated-with-Jackson comment, but didn't ask. The connection with her sister was building a little at a time, and if Diana wanted to open up, Olivia suspected she would. Instead, Olivia turned her attention to the box. Anticipation filled her, as if it were Christmas morning and she had a mysterious package from Santa under the tree. "Let's open it. Together."

"It could be nothing, you know. A bunch of shells or some odd-shaped rocks."

"But we won't know if we don't look."

"You're right. Are you ready?" Diana looked at Olivia, and Olivia looked at Diana. Two women, joined by a common mother, and linked after her death by a key and a lock. Had Bridget purposely left Olivia the house and the necklace, as a way to force her to connect with Diana? Either way, here they were, in Diana's sunny, cozy kitchen, together.

"Yeah, I'm ready."

"Go ahead," Diana said. "You're the one with the key."

Olivia inserted the key into the lock and held her breath, worried for a second that it wouldn't work. She turned the key, heard a soft click, and then the lock dropped open. She slid it out of the hasp and laid it on the table. Diana leaned forward and lifted the lid.

The box bulged with a haphazard collection of pictures, newspaper clippings, and sheets of paper. On the top sat two white envelopes, inscribed in loose, loopy handwriting with *Olivia* on one, *Diana* on the other. Diana handed her an envelope. "This is yours."

For a second, Olivia just ran her finger over the letters. *Olivia.* Bridget had written this, had known her name, the name that Anna and Dan Linscott had baptized her with after they'd signed the adoption papers. What else had Bridget known about the daughter she'd given up?

The envelope's flap yielded with a slight tug, and a thick letter slid out. Olivia unfolded the sheets, but the words blurred in her vision. All she saw was the lines and lines of Bridget's handwriting, lines written to her, the communication she had waited so long to have, and now held in her palm.

Dear Olivia,

My sweet, darling daughter. Where do I begin? How can I possibly explain the last thirty-one years and

*why I did what I did? I am so sorry to give you this
letter instead of telling you these things to your face,
but to be honest, I was always afraid that you would
hate me for leaving you that day, and I couldn't bear
to see that in your eyes.*

*Please don't hate me, Olivia. I can take anything
but that.*

*I was seventeen when you were born. My home life
was terrible, and the first chance I got, I ran away,
following a guy I thought I loved to Boston. He was
gone as soon as the pregnancy test came back
positive. My boyfriend died a few months later from a
drug overdose. I've enclosed his name, but I don't
know much more about him than that.*

*I was scared, young, unemployed, and didn't
know what to do. After you were born, the nurse let
me hold you, and in that moment, I fell in love with
you. It was as if she had placed my heart in my arms.
You were so beautiful, so perfect, and so much more
everything than I ever imagined. More wonderful,
more amazing, more fascinating. I loved you, oh, how
I loved you.*

*Walking out of that hospital was the hardest thing
I've ever done in my life. I wanted so badly to keep
you and to raise you myself, but I realized how selfish
it would be. I had no money, no place to live, no
boyfriend, nothing at all. I knew there would be a
family who could love you and give you everything
you deserved. So I walked away and told myself I'd
never look back.*

*But as the years passed, I couldn't forget you. I
had Diana, and every moment I spent with her made
me wonder about you. I compared her milestones to
the ones I had missed with you. Did you walk at
eleven months? Did your hair come in blond or
brown? Did you like bananas and hate peas? But
most of all, were you happy? Were you loved?*

On the day of your fourth birthday, I hired a private detective to find you. For a while, I had thought maybe I could contact your adoptive parents, and have a relationship with you.

But then I received the first picture of you that the detective took. You and your parents were at the park. They were pushing you on a swing and you looked so happy, my sweet baby. I knew that my presence would only muddle things, so I let it go. I had my work, and I poured myself into that because I could tell the dogs about the day I walked away from my own baby and they didn't judge or curse or hate me. I know poor Diana suffered from my absences, and I pray that you and she will build a bond that helps fill those gaps I left behind.

Over the years, I had the detective keep tabs on you. Just a once-a-year update, to make sure you were okay. Then I got sick again, and as the clock of my life ticked away, I wanted to do something to make up for what I had done that day in the hospital. But how does a mother ever make walking away okay? How does a mother ever make up for leaving her child crying in a nursery?

So I gave you the only thing I had that was worth anything. The only thing that got me through those years of regret and recrimination. This house and the animal shelter. I know Diana was probably shocked and hurt that I didn't leave it to her, but please make her understand I never meant to hurt her. In my dreams, I imagined the two of you running this place together. Diana with her amazing veterinary skill and you with your intuitive touch with animals.

Please know that I always loved you. Every second of every minute of every day. I may have walked out of that hospital, but you never left my heart. Not for a single moment. I am proud, so, so proud, of the woman you have become, and will be eternally

*grateful to Anna and Dan for raising you and helping
you become someone who has surpassed every dream
I ever had for you. I love you, Olivia, and pray that
you forgive me someday.*

Love,
Mom

Tears clouded Olivia's sight. The letter slipped out of her trembling fingers and tumbled onto the table. "She . . . she said she always loved me. That's all I really ever wanted to know. That she loved me." The last came out in a choked sob, part grief, part joy.

Diana slid out of her chair and gathered her sister into a tight, true hug. Olivia's tears fell on Diana's shoulder, but Diana held on tight, and the two of them mourned the woman who had given them life, then given them a new future as a family.

"Let's see what else is in here, okay?" Diana said, drawing back, swiping at the tears in her eyes. "Hopefully nothing else in that box is going to make us cry. I don't know if I have enough tissues for an ugly cry."

The moment of lightness made them both laugh. The merry sound filled the kitchen as together, they started sifting through the box. They laughed over school pictures and newspaper articles about soccer goals. They oohed over prom pictures and first-day-of-school milestones. They compared their eyes, their heights, their style disasters. In this container, at least, the two sisters had grown up together.

The sun streamed in through the window, the dogs snoozed at their feet, and the clock on the wall ticked away the day. A little after four, Olivia's cell phone started ringing. She almost let it go to voice mail, then saw Kris's name bannered across the screen. "Hello?"

"Liv, you gotta come back. You have to see Millie."

"Why?" Olivia put a class picture of Diana in fifth grade back into the box, then turned her attention to the call. "What happened?"

"You have to see it for yourself. And bring Miss Sadie."

Olivia pressed Kris, but she wouldn't say anything else. After Olivia hung up the phone, she turned to Diana. "Sorry. I have to go. Something came up with a patient at work."

"Believe me, I understand. Kittens and puppies are usually born at the most inconvenient time." Diana fastened the lid on top of the box. "Why don't I put this in your car, and you can take your time to go through it?"

"If it's okay with you, I'd love to do that with you. Just in these past few hours, I've learned more about our mother than I ever realized."

Diana hesitated, then nodded. "I'd like that."

"Me too." Olivia drew Diana into a hug and thanked her again. The two words weren't enough for all that they had gone through in the past couple of hours, or how grateful she was that Diana had not opened just the box, but also her heart.

At the door, Olivia turned back. "You never told me what your letter said."

"She finally gave me the one answer I've wanted all my life, too."

"What's that?"

Diana bit her lip, then exhaled a long breath. "Who my father was."

After his father left, Luke cleaned out the coffeepot, then headed for the leather recliner in the living room. The rest of the day stretched before him, as empty as every one of the days since the accident. His gaze went to Olivia's house. Her car wasn't in the driveway, which meant she was probably at work. He missed her, more than he wanted to admit. A part of him wanted to go over there and apologize and make it all better.

But once he did, where would he be? Right back in the same spot, having to decide between taking what they had another step forward or telling her the truth about what happened that night in the cold Bering Sea. What woman would want a man who had done what he had done?

Yes, he'd made some strides in the conversation with his father. But that was a far cry from telling the woman he cared about that he had killed his best friend. When those words slipped out, Luke had seen the light dim in Olivia's eyes, the way she recoiled.

Like he was poison.

In a way, Luke supposed he was. He sure as shit wasn't the bona fide hero Lois had called him.

The phone rang and instinctively, Luke picked up the cordless extension on the table and answered it. The second he heard the first skittish syllables, Luke knew who was calling. Damn.

"I don't know if you remember me," the woman on the other end said, "but this is Emma, Joe's sister."

She sounded older than the last time he'd seen her. Sadder. Guilt rocketed through Luke, and he cursed himself for sending the letter. But more, cursed himself for not calling her back. He'd taken the coward's way out, and that wasn't the kind of man he'd been before. "I remember you."

"I . . . I got the letter and I wanted to talk to you about Joe. If this isn't a good time . . ."

There'd never be a good time to talk about Joe. Luke sank farther into the chair, pressed one hand to his temple, and let out a long breath. "This is a good time."

"I appreciate you sending me the letter. It was heartbreaking and wonderful, all at the same time, if that makes sense. Joe was so typical-Joe in the letter. Joking one minute, serious the next."

Luke could hear Emma's smile filling the distance between them. "That was him. He could make me laugh and get me back on track, all in one sentence."

"Yeah. I miss that about him."

"Me too." He swallowed the lump in his throat and willed himself to keep breathing, keep talking.

"You know, he came home on leave a couple months before the accident. Just before he left, he wanted a hug, and I gave him a quick one, because I was heading out to meet my friends. I mean, he was my big brother. To me, he was

always going to be there, you know? But if I had known . . ."
A breath whistled out of her. "If I had known that would be
the last time, I'd have given Joe a bigger hug."

He didn't know what to say to that. So he muttered something that sounded like "Yeah," then let silence hum across
the connection.

"Can you tell me about the day he died?" she asked. "The
Coast Guard gave us some information, but . . . it's never
enough, you know? And I keep thinking if I have more, then
maybe it'll make this easier."

It wouldn't, he wanted to say. He knew the whole story
and that had made it more painful, rather than less.

Promise me.

But it was a promise he couldn't keep. No matter how
much he wanted to. "I'm sorry, Emma. I . . . I can't." Then
he pressed the button, ended the call, and told himself he
had done the right thing.

He sat there for a long time in the recliner, the phone in
one hand, knowing he should call her back. His fingers
seemed frozen, unable to press a single button.

A wet nose, then a soft head bounced under his opposite
palm. Chance's tail thwapped against the chair's side, *tap-
tap-tap.* Luke turned, looked at the dog, and saw nothing
but compassion staring back at him from the golden's big
brown eyes. This dog, a dog he hadn't wanted or asked for,
but who had latched on to him all the same, and refused to
give up.

Luke rubbed Chance's ears. "I wish you could tell me
what happened to you, buddy."

Tap-tap-tap.

"Whatever it was, I bet it sucked, huh?"

Tap-tap-tap.

"Same here. You, at least, seem to have figured out where
you're going, even if you're crazy enough to make that place
here with me, you furry glutton for punishment." He chuckled, then sighed. "Got any ideas for me? Like what the hell
I am going to do with my life?" The dog didn't answer him.
And Luke didn't have any answers either. Mike had said

Luke could go back to the Coast Guard and work a desk job or do training—hell, vets from Iraq went back with missing limbs—but the appeal of the military had always been flying. Without that component, Luke didn't have the same passion as before.

It doesn't mean you stopped being a man, Olivia had said.

Luke's grandmother and Mike had been saying essentially the same thing. He needed to find a new normal, instead of mourning a past that was behind him. He'd spent too much damned time in the dark. Literally. Figuratively. Every way.

He clutched the phone and realized his darkness also shrouded others. Kept them from moving on, too. Emma had called him for answers, and instead of giving her what she wanted—no, *needed*—he'd taken the coward's way out.

He was a different man, and it was time he accepted that fact and made a different life, instead of cursing the hand he'd been dealt. He looked at the dog, still healing, though the bandage was gone and fur had begun to cover the wound, and realized Chance had done the same thing. Wherever the dog had lived before was gone, and whatever he did from here forward would be different.

The dog nudged at him again, then let out a bark. *Tap-tap-tap* went his tail.

Luke spied a coil of brown on the floor, reached over, and picked it up. Chance's leash. So that was why the dog had come over to Luke. He grinned. "Is that a hint?"

The dog barked again.

"You're smarter than you look. Probably smarter than me, too." Luke looked down at the dog, who just looked back at him, waiting, eager. Finally, Luke nodded. "Okay, but you have to promise to go easy on me, boy."

Chance barked some more, then plopped his butt on the floor and waited, patient as a monk, while Luke changed into running clothes, laced up his sneakers, and clipped the leash onto Chance's collar. He left the phone on the counter, then headed outside. When he hit the sidewalk, the sneakers felt odd, then perfect, molding more to his feet with each stride.

Luke and the dog started out walking, but then the familiar streets, the warmth of the sun, and the feel of the shoes worked their magic and before Luke knew it, he was jogging, then running. Chance kept pace at Luke's knee, never leaving Luke's side.

A quarter mile turned into a half, then a full mile. Another mile passed in a blur. The air rushed over his skin, and he drew in a deep breath, letting the sensation of speed fill him, ripple under his shirt, through his veins. As Luke closed in on the end of the third mile, his heart was hammering in his chest and Chance was starting to pant. Luke turned down his driveway and slowed to a walk.

At the door, Luke dropped to his knees, spent, grateful, overwhelmed. One simple event—a run with an animal as scarred by life as Luke was—and the raw, agonizing emotional wounds deep inside Luke had finally begun to scab over. He reached out and gathered the dog to him. "Thank you," he whispered.

Chance didn't bark or wag or make a sound. He just stayed there, his warm body pressed against the chest of the man who had found him and given him a second chance at happiness and life.

And now, finally, the dog had returned the favor.

Twenty-three

❧

Olivia and Miss Sadie headed for Millie's room. Kris was already there, waiting outside. "Glad you came in. I thought you'd want to see this yourself." She didn't say any more, just smiled and pressed the door open.

Inside the apartment, Millie was again sitting on the bed, but this time, she was dressed in pale-blue polyester slacks, a floral blouse, and a white cardigan. Slip-on sneakers covered her feet, and her hair had been brushed and fastened into a low bun. She had one hand on the quad cane, and in the other hand she was holding a thin cardboard five-by-seven photo frame, the kind that opened like a book.

The same one Olivia had left on Millie's bedside table a week ago. It was a little memento she gave to all the clients she and Miss Sadie worked with, an idea she'd gotten from another therapist. A portrait of Miss Sadie, with a little note on the opposite side, a way to cheer the patients between visits. Olivia had found that Miss Sadie often became a surrogate pet for her patients, and having a picture of the dog was a nice reminder of the bichon who brought so many smiles to their days.

"She's had that in her hands for the past hour," Kris whispered to Olivia. "Hasn't said a word, but she gave a pile of clothes to the nurse, who helped her get dressed. This is the most progress I've seen Millie make in months."

Miss Sadie beelined for the bed. She plopped onto the floor beside Millie's feet, her tail swish-swishing on the carpet. Millie stared down at the dog for a long time, then laid the picture on her bed and turned to Olivia. "Walk?"

"Sure," Olivia said, calm and casual, as if a breakthrough like this were an everyday occurrence instead of one that felt as rare as a comet sighting.

A single word, but that was all Miss Sadie needed. Her tail went into overdrive, and she darted back to Olivia's side, waiting for the leash to be clipped onto her collar. Olivia bent down, cupped the bichon's face, and stared into Miss Sadie's brown eyes. "Gentle, Miss Sadie, gentle. Okay?"

Kris helped Millie into a standing position. Olivia took up a station on one side of the elderly woman, Kris the opposite. Olivia held Sadie's leash in the space between herself and Millie. Miss Sadie trotted forward, staying far enough ahead to prevent too much slack. They headed out of the apartment and into the hall, an odd quartet of humans and canine.

At the end of the hall, Millie shrugged off Kris's touch. "Outside. I want to go outside."

Kris caught Olivia's gaze. She nodded.

"Okay, Millie," Kris said. "You got it." She pushed on the handle to open the door to the courtyard, holding it as Miss Sadie, Olivia, and Millie made their way outside. The waning sunshine dropped a golden hue over the lush gardens, cushioned seating, and charming bird feeders. Greta was sitting on one of the courtyard benches, talking to Pauline. She waved at Olivia, and then her mouth dropped into an O of surprise when she saw Millie.

Millie put the cane down, took a step, then did it again. Miss Sadie kept pace with her, turning her pixie face up to glance at Millie. As they rounded the corner, Millie paused, then caught her breath.

Olivia put a hand under Millie's elbow. "Do you want to go back in?"

Millie's blue eyes met Olivia's. She shook her head. "I want to walk Miss Sadie."

"Miss Sadie is loving this walk, and she'll go as far as you want to, Millie." Olivia smiled encouragement and trust for her patient. "I'm right here, if you need me." She handed the looped end of the leash to Millie. The older woman clutched it tight in her left hand, then lifted the cane with her right. Place, move. Place, move. Miss Sadie's tail wagged, and she continued along at that slow pace, as happy as ever.

When they reached the bench at the eastern corner of the courtyard, Millie stopped and settled on the plaid cushion. She patted the space beside her, and Miss Sadie obliged by hopping up and curving into the space beside her new friend.

Millie's arthritic hand came down, slow, tentative. She hesitated a moment more, then flattened her palm against Miss Sadie's soft fur. Miss Sadie settled deeper into the cushion, letting out a little doggie sigh of contentment. As Millie patted the dog, the sadness eased from Millie's features. Her eyes brightened, her cheeks pinked, and a smile curved across her face. "Thank you," she said.

Miss Sadie gave Millie's hand a doggie kiss, then laid her head on Millie's thigh. Millie's eyes misted and she reached out a hand to grasp Olivia's. "Thank you."

"Just doing my job, Millie," Olivia said, covering Millie's hand with her own, "just doing my job."

Olivia had worked with dozens of patients in the weeks she'd spent at Golden Years, patients who had become friends. But none of the smiles or praise she had received mattered a tenth as much as Millie's thank-you.

"That was wonderful," Greta said, after Millie had returned to her room. "You changed that woman's life."

"I didn't change it. She changed herself."

"Whichever way you want to butter your bread, it still comes out the same." Greta smiled. "Now tell me this means you've rethought giving your notice."

Olivia thought about the little salmon-colored bungalow at the end of Gull Lane. When she'd pulled into the driveway a few weeks ago, she'd been so full of enthusiasm and hope. But now the electricity was out, the plumbing leaking, the repairs expanding by the day.

In my dreams, I imagined the two of you running this place together. Diana with her amazing veterinary skill and you with your intuitive touch with animals.

If that was the case, then maybe Bridget should have left the girls a stack of gold, too, because fixing the place up enough to get it running was going to take some serious cash to pay for help and expertise. Olivia didn't have any of that. And even if she did, she'd be living next door to Luke. She wasn't going to lie and say that seeing his house every day— or worse, seeing him—wasn't going to hurt like hell. She'd fallen for him, fallen hard, and he didn't feel the same. Maybe never would.

And that, she knew, was at the core of her wanting to leave. Despite what her birth mother had asked of her, Olivia couldn't stay here and look at Luke's house, day after day, go on sharing the ownership of Chance, and pretend her heart didn't break a little every time she looked at him. Surely Diana could run the shelter alone, maybe even move her practice over here like she'd mentioned.

Maybe it was time Olivia faced facts instead of holding on to a dream that was far beyond her abilities.

She shook her head. "I got what I came here for. Answers. There really isn't any other reason for me to stay." Then she gave Greta a kiss before the other woman could voice an objection, and left.

Olivia pulled into the driveway and sat in the car. Diana's Honda was parked ahead of hers, which meant Jackson and Diana were probably at the shelter, tending to the puppies. Olivia let Miss Sadie out of the car, then leaned on the roof of her car and looked out into the distance, in the direction of the beach.

Rescue Bay. Such an apt name for the town.

The tippy-top of the lighthouse peeked above the trees, nothing more than a red spire atop a long white cone. A beacon for people who'd needed to be rescued for dozens and dozens of years.

Right now, swimming in the deep churning waters of emotions brought up by the last few days, with Luke and the box from her mother, Olivia certainly had that sensation of drowning. She didn't know which way to turn, which path to take. Whether to run or stay.

Diana strode down the worn grass path between the shelter and the house. She waved at Olivia. "Hey, Olivia, you should see the shelter. Mike's been working on it all day and it's really coming along. He made the kennel area safer, and he says we're only a few weeks from being up and running. I know this town desperately needs a shelter again. And as long as there are puppies involved, I think we can get Jackson to help without too much prodding."

A wave of panic threatened to engulf Olivia. She'd made this giant move, and now that she had what she wanted, the thought of staying, of settling down, of taking that risk on a permanent basis, terrified her. She needed time to think, time to breathe, time to figure out what she really wanted.

"I . . . I need to do something," Olivia said. "Can you take Miss Sadie into the house?"

"Sure. Where are you going?"

Her gaze went to the red-tipped building in the distance. It seemed to call to her, asking her to lay her problems at its feet. Okay, maybe that was a crazy thought, but Olivia didn't care. "The beach."

The Rescue Bay lighthouse cast a long shadow over the beach, like a finger reaching over the sand. Luke dropped his shoes into a pile and strode down the sloping hill. The sand was cool and soft, making his bare feet sink size-twelve impressions into the sand. Chance dashed forward to play in the surf.

Luke's gaze scanned the shore, and then he saw her, exactly where Diana had said. Twenty yards away stood Olivia, bundled in a thick gray sweatshirt, arms around her body, hair whipping in the wind coming off the ocean. Looking beautiful and sad all at the same time.

Regret urged him to let her be, but Luke had decided after his run that he was done with regrets. He had gone into the house, called Joe's sister, and finally had that long, difficult, painful conversation. In the end, Emma had cried, but thanked him for telling her the truth. It hadn't been easy, but it had been the right thing to do. Luke wasn't sure where to go from here, but he knew he sure as hell wasn't going backward. So he moved forward.

Toward the future. Olivia.

Chance reached Olivia first and jumped up to plant two wet paws on her chest. She shooed him down, laughing. As she petted the dog, Olivia lifted her gaze with a question, until she found Luke. The light dimmed in her features, and she turned away, walking down the shoreline. Away from him.

In that moment, he could see his future. Olivia gone, and his life back to being the empty dark nothing it had been for the last few weeks.

He broke into a light jog and caught up to her. Chance ran ahead, barking at seagulls he'd never catch, though the golden gave it his best effort. The temperature had dropped and the sunny day had turned dark and stormy. "Olivia, wait. I want to talk to you."

She kept going. "About what, Luke? You made it clear we don't have anything other than some sex between us."

Her words shot back at him like a swift, sharp backhand. "I didn't say that to hurt you. But to protect you."

"I'm a big girl, Luke. I don't need anyone to protect me."

She was right. And to be honest, maybe he was the wrong person to protect anyone, much less Olivia. But he couldn't let her go, not without saying what he had come here to say.

"My grandmother called me today and said you were leaving town." She'd also told him she hadn't raised him to be a total moron, and if he had even one decent brain cell, he would stop Olivia from leaving. Luke had hunted down Diana next door, who barely got out the word *beach* before Luke was gone.

He had known—maybe because he had good instincts or maybe because he and Olivia had a connection like none he'd ever known—exactly where Olivia had gone.

The lighthouse.

"So, you're running away?" he asked.

"I'm not running. I'm accepting reality. That house is a wreck. I'm going to take Mike's advice and sell it, and then I'm going back to Boston." She stopped walking and turned toward the ocean, wrapping her arms around her waist. "Besides, I got what I came here for. I moved to this town because I wanted to know my birth mother, and in the process I also found a sister I never knew I had. So"—she shrugged—"there's nothing else to hold me here."

"Nothing else? Really?"

She blew her bangs out of her face. "I just told you I met my sister and found out about my birth mother. That's really what this trip was about."

"Trip?" He came around to the front of her, not caring that the surf rushed over his bare feet, inched up his ankles. "Not a move?"

"It was a slip of the tongue. Nothing more. Trip, move, same thing."

"A trip implies an end date when you turn around and go back. A move is more permanent. You set down roots. You"—he came closer—"take risks, open your heart."

"I did that." But she glanced away when she said it. "And look where it got me. You were gone before the sheets even cooled. You talk to me about taking risks, Luke. When are *you* going to do it?"

He'd built a career on the word *risk*. Flying into storms, racing against time, battling Mother Nature on a daily basis. He'd been the cowboy, the one who leapt first and thought second, and in the end that same risky behavior that the government had lauded and rewarded with medals and commendations had cost the life of a good man.

"It's different for me, Olivia. When I take risks, people get hurt." He shook his head. Why had he gone after her? Why couldn't he just leave it alone? Why did he have to take this one more risk—

No matter how much the outcome might hurt?

"See, right there." She threw up her hands. "You put up a wall." She was the one to approach him now, her green eyes searching his. "Or is this all another way of saying you're not really interested in me?"

"Goddammit, Olivia, I am so interested in you, I can't think of anything else. Wanting you is not the problem. It never was. It's this." He waved at his face, at eyes that would never be perfect.

"You think I should stay away because of this?" She reached up, and touched his scar, light, gentle. "Because I don't care about what this did to your sight or your face, Luke."

He caught her hand and pulled it away. "It's not what this did to my vision. It's what getting this did to *me*."

"It didn't change who you are deep down inside," she said.

Did he know that for sure? Did he know, without a single doubt, that in the end, in a pinch, he could be the man others relied on again? Or would he someday let Olivia down, too, and break her heart—or worse? *That* was the war that waged inside Luke, even now, when what he wanted so badly was standing right before him, forcing him to confront those fears. "I killed my best friend, Olivia. That kind of thing changes someone in fundamental ways."

"Maybe it did, but in good ways, too."

He watched the sea wash in, wash out, erasing their footprints and turning the beach smooth and new again. The storm was carving new curves into the sand, then erasing and carving again. Maybe that was what the accident had done to him. Maybe it had erased part of him but replaced those parts with something in a different mold.

Olivia reached for his hands and clasped them tight, her fingers warm against the gusting wind. Every time she touched him, it was like medicine for his soul.

"Tell me, Luke," she said softly.

He hesitated, not wanting those tender feelings he read in her eyes to fade. But if he didn't tell her the whole story, he'd be doing exactly the same thing he'd done for the past few weeks—letting the past control his future.

Telling Emma had been the first step in the right direction out of the darkness, even though it had been the hardest damned thing Luke had ever done. *If I had known that would be the last time, I'd have given Joe a bigger hug.*

He couldn't give Emma back her brother and all the hugs she would miss, but he could give Joe the honor he deserved. His best friend had earned the right to be remembered, to be talked about, to have his spirit live on in jokes and war stories. Luke had tried to stuff all those things into the dark recesses of his mind, but it hadn't worked.

He watched the power of Mother Nature, pushing water in, out, and realized Joe wouldn't have wanted to be relegated to a corner of Luke's mind. He would have wanted to live on, still just as vivid and strong.

"Let's take a seat, and I'll tell you about Joe," Luke said. He waved to a rocky outcropping that anchored the base of the lighthouse. The storm brewing off the Gulf Coast ushered in a cold ocean wind and stirred the sea into an angry froth. It seemed an apt setting.

"When I was a kid, I used to come to this beach all the time, mostly with my grandmother," Luke began as they settled on the rocks and faced the ocean. "I'd swim and look for shells and get sunburned and generally have a great time. Every time we came to the lighthouse, I'd make Greta tell me about the pirates. My favorite story was about The Three Who Were Saved. That's always how she said it, with capital letters, like it was a fairy tale or something."

Olivia tucked her chin into her knees, wrapped her arms around her shins, and listened.

"I don't remember all the details, but way back in the late

seventeen hundreds, there was a hell of a hurricane up the coast. Every ship in the waters of the Gulf wrecked, except for three that made their way to Rescue Bay. The lighthouse guided them out of the storm and into the safety of the bay. Several of the crew opted to stay here and settle down. The town was just incorporating then, and that's when they voted to be called Rescue Bay."

"Because people who come here are rescued." She glanced out at the ocean, her voice filled with a faraway, almost melancholy tone.

"That's the legend anyway. When I met Joe, he told me he was descended from pirates, like ten generations back. He was probably pulling my leg, but if you'd met Joe, you'd have believed it. He was hell on wheels." Luke chuckled. "He had this charm about him that made almost anything forgivable, which is probably what saved him from being thrown in the brig a few times. Plus he was damned good at his job, and had great instincts for when to take a chance, when to pull back. When he found out I lived here, he vowed to visit someday and take a look for the rumored buried treasure. He said his pirate blood would point him in the right direction."

"Did he?"

Luke shook his head. "We never got a chance."

The surf crashed against the rocks, rising up to spray them with a saltwater kiss. Gulls patrolled the shore, looking for a meal, while terns danced in and out of the incoming tide on the beach. With the storm rolling in, no one was on the beach right now, and Chance took his time exploring the coast.

Luke propped his arms on his knees, then closed his eyes and finally opened the gate in his mind, releasing the tide of memories. The darkened cockpit, the radio chatter, the brewing storm lashing at the helo, tossing them in the air like a child's plaything.

"I should have turned around that night. We'd gotten called out to rescue some fishermen who had run aground in the storm. Their vessel was going down fast, and the water at that time of year is already so damned cold we knew we didn't have much time to get them out. We got to the ship with no problem, but as we were lowering the swimmer, I got that feeling in my gut that said things were on the verge of heading south fast, but I wanted to get one more rescue in, one more success on the charts." He let out a breath. "I joined the Coast Guard because I wanted to save people, not jump out of planes and shoot them. But then the saving became its own kind of drug. Joe and I would pluck a fisherman out of the water or get a man with a burst appendix to the hospital just in time, and we'd feel like heroes. We got to the point where we almost felt . . . invincible, smarter and stronger than anything Alaska could throw at us. I got cocky, and because of that, I let my confidence overpower my better judgment. I took a risk I shouldn't have. Stayed out in a storm when I should have turned back."

"But if you'd turned back, the people on the boat would have died."

"If I'd turned back, Joe would be alive today." He tossed a pebble into the water. It sank and disappeared into the frothy green ocean. Like the boat had that night. The helo. Joe. "That's what I told Joe's sister when I called her today. I expected her to hate me. To scream at me for being such an idiot."

"But instead she understood?"

He nodded. The forgiveness in Emma's voice had taken Luke by surprise. "She said Joe knew the risks when he got to AIRSTA Kodiak. He knew he could die. His attitude was that if he was going to go out, better to go out trying to do the right thing than with regrets." Luke watched an ocean growing angrier by the moment. They'd need to head in soon to avoid the storm, but he had to get this out now, or he might never say it. "We went down, but got out a Mayday in time, and another helo came in, saving the fishermen, me, my crew. Most of the crew anyway." Luke shook his head and cursed the memories, even as they filled his mind and lanced his heart. "It was already too late for Joe. The helo hit the edge of the boat on his side, and Joe was gone before he hit the water. I was powerless, completely powerless, to save someone who never should have died. I think that's been the hardest part for me to live with. I know Joe wouldn't blame me, and if he were here, he'd tell me he was doing his job, and he knew that job came with risks, and I needed to quit feeling bad about him dying."

Olivia's gaze assessed him. She laid a hand on his arm. "You're afraid if you let go of that feeling, you'll have to let another one take its place."

That made sense, and he could see it now. If he let go of the guilt, would the overwhelming pain of losing his best friend be the replacement? Or would he find peace? "Yeah. Exactly."

"I know the feeling." She retracted her touch, then huddled inside her sweatshirt, her knees tucked inside the fleece. "For years, I harbored this anger against Bridget. For leaving me, for not keeping in touch with me, but most of all, for not wanting me. It was easier to do that than to understand her and the difficult choices she had to make. And now that I know she loved me, that she was only doing what was best for me, I have to let go of that anger and replace it with compassion, understanding. And love."

He scoffed. "Look at the two of us, scared to do anything that takes us down a new path."

"We're both afraid of falling in the dark."

"Something I am very familiar with." He chuckled. "You know, I used to be the first one into the fray. The one who was never afraid of anything. And now I am afraid of loss, and that is what has kept me in that damned house day after day, instead of really living. I lost my best friend, I lost my sight, I lost my career." He shifted on the rock until he was facing her. "Until you came along, I didn't realize how much I'd lose if I stayed there, in that dark place."

She cocked her head, studied him. "What did I do?"

"You marched into my yard with your sassy smile and determined attitude, and you *demanded* that I get out of my little self-imposed prison and help you."

She grinned. "You refused, if I remember right."

"And you didn't listen. You came back, and so did the dog, and before I knew it, I was doing the very things I said I would never do again. Getting involved. Taking care. Then doing the one thing I thought I would never do at all."

"What's that?"

He met her gaze, those incredible green eyes, as dark as a forest at dusk. "I fell in love."

The words carried on the wind, which had increased in strength and was whirling around them like a dervish. Dark angry clouds filled the sky, blotted out the sun, and the sea began to churn and rise, splashing their bare feet.

She shook her head and rose, hands up, warding him off. "Don't do this, Luke. Don't tell me that now. I'm leaving. I'm going back—"

"You're running." He stood too, the wind buffeting their bodies like a jealous lover trying to push them apart.

"No, I'm just moving back to Boston and—"

"Olivia, I love you, and I want to be with you." As he said the words, the fear that had kept him from opening his heart loosened its grip. "Hell, I want to get married and fix that silly house of yours and take care of those dogs. I have no idea what I'll do for a job, but I don't care. All I want is you. The rest, we'll figure out."

"Luke . . . I can't." She backed up a step. "I'm leaving."

"You keep telling me I'm the one that's running. I've stopped, Olivia, and it's all because of you." He had stopped running, right here, in this storm, under the protective arm of the lighthouse, because he'd stopped letting his regrets control his future. When it was all on the line, Luke had made the riskiest move of all—he'd filleted his heart and given it to Olivia. "I want to be with you, to love you, more than I want to run."

She shook her head, backed up another step. Heavy rain began to fall, pelting the beach and the rocks with hard, wet drops. "I don't do settling down, Luke. I screwed up my first marriage. I screwed up my life here. If we get married—"

"What's the worst that can happen?" he said. "We have a fight? We disagree on who takes out the trash? We argue over what's for dinner on Saturday night?" He grinned. "If that's the case, I'll tell you that I don't care what we eat for dinner on Saturday or any other day, or whether we cook or we order out, as long as I'm with you."

She was shaking her head and backing up again and the rain was coming, the storm was seething. "No. That's not it."

"Then what is it?" He had to shout to be heard above the rage of the storm. She remained mute. "Olivia, what the hell is it?"

"I'm afraid . . ." She shook her head, shifted her weight to the right. The wind whipped her blond locks into her face, then away again, fast and hard. Chance barked at them from his place far below on the beach.

Luke closed the distance between them, not just so he could hear her answer, but so she knew he wasn't going anywhere. Not now, not ever. Finally telling her the truth had lifted a burden, pulled back a heavy curtain, and he refused to waste one more minute of his life when happiness was within his reach. "Afraid of what?" he said again, softer.

"I'm afraid you'll leave me!" The words exploded from her in a shout, and she moved again, another step, the wind blinding her with her own hair. "And I just can't—"

Then she was gone. Olivia disappeared over the side of the cliff.

Twenty-four

∞

Luke Winslow had long ago given up on miracles. He figured they were meant for other people than him. But the moment that Olivia slipped, time seemed to slow, and his vision seemed to clear. His hand whipped out—

And he caught her wrist just as she screamed.

"I've got you," he said, his voice calm and cool, the voice of a man who used to rescue people for a living. No rescue had ever mattered more than this one, and he knew he'd hold on for as long as it took to save her. "I've got you."

She scrambled for purchase against the wet rocks, but her feet were slippery and the sea was racing up the surface, licking at her knees, her thighs. She spun out, away, panicked. "I can't get up, I'm slipping. Oh God, Luke, please don't let go."

"I won't, Olivia." He lowered himself to the rock's surface, digging his toes into the crevices behind him. He reached out his opposite hand toward hers. "Grab my hand. Come on, Olivia, you can do it."

She spun toward him, her chest smacking against the rocky wall, and reached up. Her fingers slipped through his, but he jerked down, caught her by the wrist, then slid his grip up until their hands were joined.

He held her gaze and kept his tone even and low, even though his heart was running at breakneck speed. "Don't panic. It's going to be all right. I promise you. Now keep your feet on the rock. I'm going to pull you up. Okay?"

She nodded. Fear pooled in her eyes as the ocean rose and the storm shuddered in the air. Thunder boomed, lightning streaked across the sky, and the wind began to howl. He didn't focus on the palm trees bending to Mother Nature's will or on the constant slamming of a loose piece of siding on the lighthouse.

Luke pulled, and Olivia's feet slid, slipped off, and then she tried again, and this time she got it. Luke leaned back, and then she was there, up on the rock again, in his arms, wet and crying and scared.

And safe.

"I'm sorry, I didn't know it would be so slippery and I just—"

"I don't care," he said. He tipped her wet face to his and thought he'd never seen such a beautiful woman in his life. "You're okay, and that's all that matters."

She curved into him, and he shielded her from the storm with his body, then scooped her up and carried her off the rock and toward the nearest shelter, the lighthouse. The door was locked, but Luke kicked it in and brought Olivia inside the dim building. Chance followed them in, and after shaking off the water and spraying his humans with a saltwater shower, he dashed around the unexplored place to sniff at every corner.

Luke held Olivia close until her shivers stopped. "You okay?"

She nodded. "Just a little shaken up. But I'm fine."

"Good." Relief washed over him, now that the crisis had passed and he realized how close he'd come to losing her, or seeing her get seriously hurt. He bent down, making a quick assessment. "You sure nothing's broken? Hurt?"

She lifted one leg, then the other. "A few scratches,

nothing more. Thank you for saving me." Then she grinned. That smile, the one he loved, back on her face. "Though I distinctly remember someone telling me he didn't do rescue, not anymore."

"That was then," Luke said, tipping her chin to capture her deep emerald gaze with his own. "And this is now."

Then he leaned in and kissed her, tasting salt and sweet on her lips, her cool skin easing the fire inside him. His arms went around her and she pressed into him, curving like a puzzle piece finding its perfect fit.

The storm raged against the building. The lighthouse held firm. It had withstood worse storms and would survive this, too. The wind whistled under the siding, licked at the windows and the door, but the conical building held firm to its place on the shore.

Olivia clutched tighter to Luke. Her heart beat a wild staccato in her chest, then began to slow to its natural rhythm. His kiss deepened, becoming as familiar as her own name. She had never been with a man who knew her so intimately. It was as if he had memorized the guidebook to her body and her heart.

"Now that you can't get away," he said with a grin, "I want to try this again. I love you, Olivia Linscott. I fell in love with you the day you came over to my house, refusing to give up on that dog, and refusing to give up on me. If you don't feel the same way, I can live with that. But if this is just because you're scared of falling in love too, then I can't let you do that to yourself." He cupped her jaw and waited until her gaze met his. "I spent too many months scared of feeling again. Of caring for anyone. Of letting other people down. I'm not going to do that, not for one more second."

The same panic she'd felt on the rock returned. She was so tired of feeling this way, so exhausted by always running from the very thing she wanted. Luke had been right about her—she was a picket-fence, settle-down kind of girl.

"I'm trying, Luke. I really am." She let out a gust, then turned away and crossed to a bench. She dropped onto the wooden seat, propped her feet on the edge, and wrapped her arms around her knees. "I've spent my whole life telling myself I wasn't bothered by my biological mother leaving me in that hospital. After all, I had fabulous adoptive parents who loved me, and a great life in Boston. But I *was* bothered. There's something about being rejected and abandoned by the person who shares your DNA that doesn't go away. And then when my ex did the same thing, seeking out other women almost from the minute we said *I do*—"

"The man was a stupid jerk. Clearly had no idea what a gift you were."

A weak smile filled her face. "Thanks. You're right. Either way, that compounded those feelings. I didn't even put all that together until I came down here, thinking I wanted a change, but really, what I wanted was . . ."

"Love."

Hearing the word didn't terrify her as much as it had earlier. Warmth twined around her heart, easing the chill of her wet clothes, the stormy day. She *had* found love, with family, with friends, and now, with this man. She'd fallen for him that day in his house when he'd shown that wounded side of him, so raw and open. She sighed. "It's ironic."

He sat down beside her and wrapped an arm around her. "What is?"

"That you rescued me here, of all places, when I was running away. I guess we need to thank the lighthouse for one more save." She leaned into his warm, strong chest. "It's just so much easier to run than to be left behind when someone leaves you."

"I'm not going anywhere, Olivia," Luke whispered against her hair, his breath a warm caress. "You're stuck with this ogre."

"Oh, you're not so bad," she said, turning her face toward his and seeing honesty in his blue eyes, "for an ogre, that is."

The circular room echoed the merry sound of their laughter, as if the lighthouse were giving its stamp of approval. Chance came over and settled at their feet with a contented sigh. The golden had healed well and become a new dog: energetic, happy. Part of the family.

"You're the one who rescued me first. If you hadn't come along . . ." Luke shook his head. "Thank you."

"You're welcome." Simple words, but laden with meaning. She couldn't imagine the pain Luke had been in after such a tragedy. Like the dog, he was still healing, still finding his footing, but she had no doubt that he would be okay. He said she had rescued him, but Olivia suspected Luke had done all the work himself.

"Still want to move to Boston?" he asked.

"I was thinking I could live here. Right here." She wrapped her arms around his waist and held on tight. She could hear his heart beat a comforting rhythm. She liked that, a lot, and thought she could get used to that sound beside her in bed for the next fifty years.

"You have great timing. I have a vacancy right in that exact spot." Luke tapped at his chest.

"Does it need renovation work?"

"Oh yes, a lot. It's a real disaster in there, and you might even need to start from scratch." He grinned. "Still want to take on the challenge?"

"Honey, I only need one tool to fix you." A teasing smile played on her lips and joy bubbled inside her. "A roll of duct tape."

He laughed, the sound hearty and deep. How she loved his laugh, the way it made her want to laugh, too. "Oh, Olivia, I love you."

"I love you too, Luke," she said. They kissed again, a long, sweet kiss this time. The rain pattered a staccato song against the building. Chance lay at their feet, asleep and content.

After a while, Luke drew back and ran a finger along her lips, then down her chin. "Still afraid of taking that leap?"

She raised one shoulder, let it drop. After all, they had gone from zero to sixty in a short period of time. Now they were talking love and marriage, and forever. It felt right, but still a tiny bit crazy. "Maybe a little."

"Hell, you already leapt off a cliff. Falling in love and getting married should be a piece of cake after that."

He was right. How could anything that came next be any scarier? "And you were there to catch me when I fell."

"I intend to keep on doing that, Olivia." He brought her to him again, loving how her body seemed made for his. She was his perfect match, in a thousand different ways. "You did it for me, and the least I can do is return the favor. For the rest of our lives."

"That sounds like a plan, Luke. A very, very good plan." Olivia sat back with Luke on the bench, his arms creating a cozy cocoon around her, and watched the world outside the tiny window of the lighthouse. She had come here to Rescue Bay for answers, never knowing that the best gift was living right next door. Outside the storm subsided, the gray clouds parted, and the sun washed the world with hope.

Twenty-five

∞

"You were right," Pauline whispered to Greta.

Greta beamed. The Thursday Ladies' Quilting Club sat on the sidelines, beside the punch table, watching the bustling activity filling the morning room on Valentine's Day night. Pink-and-white lighting sparkled on the attendees, the furniture, the dance floor. Paper hearts hung from the ceiling and decorated the walls and the cloth-covered tables that had been moved to the side of the room. A local band played oldies, while couples filled the makeshift dance floor, waltzing their way through one melody after another. And in the midst of it all, the only couple Greta cared about.

Luke and Olivia, dancing, laughing, their attention on each other. Olivia's hand rested on Luke's shoulder, while the diamond on her finger glinted. Miss Sadie watched from the sidelines, perched on a chair beside Millie. Diana, Olivia's sister, had come too, and was chatting with Millie and showing her pictures of some puppies.

"It was worth everything we did," Greta said, feeling content for the first time in a long time. Luke was going to be fine, and maybe give her some great-grandchildren to spoil.

"It was worth everything *except* for missing our quilting time," Esther grumbled. "I'm never going to finish that wedding quilt before my niece gets married. And that one I was working on for my new grandbaby is only half done."

"Oh, Esther, there is more to life than attaching one square to another." Then she softened her frustration and gave Esther's hand a pat. Tonight of all nights, Greta refused to let anyone get her dander up. She'd even refrained from spiking the punch, though she had been sorely tempted to add the flask of Maker's Mark in her pocket when she'd heard Harold Twohig was planning on attending. Just this morning Greta had vowed to be more Christian and nice to her neighbors, as a thank-you to the Big Guy for his help with Luke and Olivia. Might as well start with Esther. "Maybe we could add an extra quilting day to the week, at least until—"

"Really? Oh, Greta, I would love that!" Esther's face exploded into a smile and she looked like she wanted to hug Greta. "I'd love to quilt every day—"

Greta put up her hands. "Whoa, whoa. *Every day?* Let's not go crazy."

"That's right," Pauline added, giving Greta a nod of support. "Because we still need time to work on our Common Sense Carla column at least a couple days a week."

"Oooh, do we have a new letter to answer?" Esther asked. "Because it was such fun to see this one come true."

Greta hadn't told the girls that the letter that had started all of this hadn't been written by Olivia after all. Greta had asked her about it last week when Olivia came in to Golden Years, with a rock on her finger and a smile on her lips. Either way, the letter had been sweet serendipity. Maybe even a little gift from her daddy up in heaven or the Big Guy himself.

"I've got a new letter right here." Pauline dug in the pocket of her sweater and unfolded a white sheet of paper.

She got out her reading glasses and put them on her nose to see better in the dim light. "Dear Common Sense Carla, I'm a single dad with two kids who needs to—"

"May I have this dance?"

Greta whirled toward the interruption. Harold Twohig stood in front of Greta's chair, one hand out, like a beggar needing a quarter. Her six-foot-two nemesis, though he didn't look much like a nemesis tonight. Especially fully clothed. She blinked, sure she was seeing a mirage. "You own a *suit*?"

Harold tugged at his cranberry tie, then smoothed a hand down his dark-gray jacket. Some women might have said he looked handsome, dapper even. Though Greta wouldn't admit that to a single soul.

"I thought I'd dress up for the Sweetheart Dance. Because I might like to ask a sweetheart to dance." He gave her a wink.

Pauline nudged Greta. "He means you," she whispered.

"He's drunk," Greta whispered back. "Or senile. Or both."

"I'm sober as a judge, Greta Winslow, and though I have my moments when I forget where I put my keys, I've also got all my marbles." He knocked on his thick head of white hair, then put out his hand again. "So, may I have this dance?"

She hesitated, then glanced at Luke and Olivia, who were watching her with approving grins on their faces. They waved encouragement and pointed to a vacant spot on the dance floor near them. Only for her grandson would she subject herself to this torture.

Greta let out a long-suffering sigh, took Harold's hand—surprisingly, it wasn't sweaty or covered in eczema—and headed for the dance floor. As Harold put one hand on the small of her back and took her other in his hearty palm, she heard a gasp go through the crowd. "It's just a dance," Greta said to the nosy old biddies already talking about her and Harold, "not a truce."

"Why do you hate me so?" Harold asked.

She refused to answer the question, instead sidestepping

them closer to her grandson and his wife-to-be. "What on earth made you ask me to dance?"

If he was put off by her sharp tone, Harold didn't show it. He just gave her that patient-as-a-loony-monk smile of his. "I'm just following the advice I read in Common Sense Carla last week. She advised grabbing the bull by the horns and going after the woman you love. She said not to let anything stand in your way. Not even a little revulsion."

Greta shot a glance over her shoulder at Pauline and Esther, who were sitting on the opposite side of the room, thick as thieves and laughing like hyenas.

Luke leaned in toward Greta. "I hear you're not the only one with a little matchmaking ability, Grandma," he said.

"Oh, I'm not, he's not—" Greta cursed. She hated being flustered. And with Harold Twohig, of all people. "I have no interest in this man. At all."

"That's what I said," Olivia said with a smile, then flashed her left hand. "And look where I am now."

"You never know where or when your happy ending is going to find you, Greta," Harold said, leaning in close enough to kiss. Or clobber. "So you might as well let it—"

"Drag me away, kicking and screaming?"

Harold winked. "If that's what it takes, Greta Winslow, I'm your man."

Lord, have mercy, Greta thought. Or maybe the Lord was having a little laugh at her expense. She never should have stolen Esther's thread. She'd put an extra dollar in the collection plate this week. Maybe two.

She whirled out of Harold Twohig's arms before the man got the idea that she did anything other than despise him. Luke and Olivia chuckled and kept on dancing.

That was the kind of happy ending Greta liked best. One that left Harold Twohig sputtering and alone, and her free as a bird and heading for the cookies.

With a little detour first to the punch bowl.

Turn the page for a preview of the next book
in Shirley Jump's Sweetheart Sisters series

The Sweetheart Rules

Coming in February 2014
from Berkley Sensation

One toddler meltdown in the center of Walmart and Lieutenant Mike Stark, who had battled raging winter storms in the violent, mercurial Bering Sea to pluck stranded boaters from the ocean's grip, had to admit he was in over his head. Mike stood between a display of As-Seen-on-TV fruit dehydrators and a cardboard mock-up of a NASCAR driver hawking shaving lather and watched his own child dissolve into a screaming, sobbing, fist-pounding puddle of tantrum.

"I want it now!" Ellie punched the scuffed tile floor and added a couple of kicks for good measure. "Now, Daddy. Now, now, now!"

Mike looked over at Jenny and gave her a help-me smile. "Do something. Please."

Jenny shrugged and turned toward the shaving cream. "This is your department, dude."

When did his oldest daughter get so cold and distant? For God's sake, she was eight, not eighteen. On the outside she was all kid, wearing a lime-green cartoon character tank top and ragged tan shorts, her dark brown hair in a long ponytail secured with a thick pink elastic. Ellie had opted for denim shorts and a *Sesame Street* T-shirt that made her look cute and endearing.

Except when she was pitching a fit.

A mother at the other end of the aisle, whose toddler son sat prim and polite in the child seat of her cart, shot him a look of disapproval. Then she whipped the cart around the corner. Fast. As if tantrums were contagious.

"Give it *to me*!" Ellie's voice became a high-pitched siren, spiraling upward in range and earsplitting. "Now!"

"No, Ellie," he said, aiming for patient, stern, confident. The kinds of tones the parenting books recommended. Not that he'd read a parenting book. His education about how to be a father was mostly the drive-by kind—meaning once in a while he skimmed the forty-point headlines on *Parenting* magazine. "I told you—"

"I don't care! I want it! I want it! Buy it, Daddy. *Please!*"

Across from him, Jenny shot a look of disdain over her shoulder, then went back to mulling over men's shaving lather. Clearly she wasn't going to be any help.

Not that Mike could blame her. On a good day, Ellie was a category five hurricane. When she was tired and hungry and in desperate need of the third new stuffed animal of the week, she was a three-foot-tall nuclear explosion in Keds. One most people ran from, but Mike, being the dad, was supposed to step in to *deal with*.

The trouble? He had no idea how to handle his daughter. He could count on one hand the number of times he'd seen his kids since they started walking and talking. It wasn't something he was proud of, and on the long list of regrets Mike Stark had for the way he had lived his life up till now, being a sucky father topped the list.

Now he had thirty days to change that, and if he was smart, he'd start by laying down the law, being the stern parental figure who didn't put up with this temper tantrum crap. Yeah, take a stand, be a man, set an exam—

"Daddy! Please!" Ellie's raging fit ramped up another level, more fist-pounding, more kicking, and then the shriek that could be heard 'round the world. Several shoppers turned around and stared. "I neeeeeeeeeeeeeeeeeed—"

"Here," Mike said, yanking the stuffed animal off the endcap display and thrusting it at Ellie's flying fists. *Take it, please, and just stop that screaming before my head explodes.* "But that's the *last* time."

Uh-huh. Just like the toy he bought this morning and the two he bought yesterday had been the last time, too. Not to mention the cookies before dinner and the pizza for breakfast he'd caved on. No more. He was going to have to take a stand before Ellie became a spoiled brat.

In an instant, Ellie turned off the screaming fit and scrambled to her feet, grinning and clutching the cream-colored bear to her chest like a prize. A toothy grin filled her face and brightened her big blue eyes. "Thank you, Daddy. Thank you, thank you, thank you."

When her little voice came out with the extra lilt on the end of *Daddy*, it was all Mike could do to keep from scooping Ellie up and handing her the world on a plate. "You're welcome, Ellie."

Jenny shot him a look of disgust and shook her head, then marched over to the cart and plopped her hands on the bar. "Come on. We need peanut butter."

She sounded so grown-up that, for a second, Mike had to remind himself he was the one in charge, the adult. Then he glanced at his triumphant preschooler, who had just re-inforced her belief that tantrums brought results. Okay, the adult figurehead, at least.

Why was it that he could take apart a Sikorsky MH-60 helicopter, work his way through the complexities of the engines, rotary, and hydraulic systems, figure out the prob-lem, and put it all back together again, but he couldn't man-age a three-year-old child?

"If you give her what she wants all the time, she's just going to be a brat," Jenny said as they rounded the corner and headed toward the market side of the store. "You do know that, don't you?"

"Of course I do. Who do you think is the parent here?"

Her arched brow answered the question. "Peanut butter's this way." She shifted the cart to the left, one of its wheels flopping back and forth like a lazy seal.

He bit back a sigh. What did he expect? He'd come home on leave to see the kids only to have his ex, Jasmine, dump the girls in his lap and tell him she was going on an extended vacation and they were his problem now. The welcome mat to Jasmine's place didn't include him and he wasn't about to leave his kids in the dump she owned, so he'd packed up the girls and taken them to his friend Luke's old house, vacant since Luke had moved in with his fiancée, Olivia, next door.

The kids hadn't wanted to leave their house, or their neighborhood, or their rooms, but Mike had taken one look at Jasmine's house and decided there was no way his girls were spending another night in that run-down trailer masquerading as a home. Last time he'd been here—heck, six months ago—Jasmine had been living in a rental house on the south side of Atlanta, a rental house Mike was still sending her a monthly check to finance. At some point, she'd moved into this hellhole, and when he'd asked, she'd refused to say why.

No way was he going to leave his kids in that hurricane bait for one more second. But he'd underestimated what he needed to feed, clothe, and entertain two young girls, which had brought him here, to the fifth level of hell, also known as grocery shopping on senior citizen discount day. In Rescue Bay, Florida, with two kids who barely knew him and barely liked him, when he'd expected to pop in and visit Ellie and Jenny for a few days, then head for a secluded beach on St. Kitts with a buxom stewardess who had promised to "forget" her bikini top. The only thing that could make this worse was—

"Mike?"

That.

Diana Tuttle's surprise raised her voice a couple octaves. He turned around, and when he did, his body reacted with the same flare of desire as it had every time he'd seen Diana, ignoring the memo from his brain that Diana was the exact opposite of the kind of woman he wanted.

He hadn't seen, talked to, or emailed the veterinarian in months. Not since the night he'd left her sleeping in her bed and taken the coward's way out of ending things between them. Other than a scribbled note he'd left on her kitchen table, he'd had no other contact with her.

From the minute he met Diana, it had become too easy, too quick to pretend he was a stay-in-place, dinners-at-the-family-table kind of guy. She had a way of wrapping him in that world, like the proverbial lotuses that captured Odysseus's crew, and he'd forget reality for a little while.

The reality was that he was a crappy father who lacked staying power and was in no shape to be someone's depend-on-anything. Especially right now.

"Daddy?" Ellie said. "I'm hungry."

"Okay," he answered, but his attention stayed on Diana's wide green eyes, and the combination of surprise and anger lighting them.

He'd known, of course, that he would see her if he came back to Rescue Bay. In such a small town, they were bound to run into each other. Mike had convinced himself that he'd see her and move on. Forget.

Yeah, not so much.

Diana still looked as beautiful as he'd remembered. No, even more so. Her shoulder-length blond hair, so often in a ponytail, hung loose around her shoulders, longer than he remembered, dancing above the bare skin with a tease that said *I can touch this and you can't*. The blue floral dress she wore scooped in an enticing V in the front, then hugged tight at her waist before spinning out in a bell that swirled around her knees and drew his attention to long, creamy legs accented by strappy black sandals and cardinal-red polish on her toes. In the few weeks he'd known her, he'd never seen Diana in a dress. Jeans, yes; shorts, yes; but never anything like this, and a flare of jealousy burst in his chest for whoever the lucky guy was who'd get to see her like this: sweet, sexy, and feminine.

Then he reminded himself that this sweet, sexy, feminine woman also had a sharp side that could level a man in seconds.

"What are you doing here?" Diana asked.

He started to stutter out an answer, but Jenny beat him to it. "We're *bonding*," Jenny said with a touch of sarcasm most kids didn't master till puberty kicked in.

"Bonding?" Diana asked with a little scoff of disbelief. "You."

It wasn't a question, and the word made him wince a little. Maybe because the truth stung.

"We're just grocery shopping. I'm staying out at Luke's for a few weeks, with my daughters." He gestured toward Jenny, who gave him another of her scowls, this one saying, *Please don't think I'm with him*, and then toward Ellie, who still wore her look of tantrum triumph. His youngest daughter danced a circle in the aisle with her teddy partner.

Mike scowled before he blurted out another word. Diana had put him on the defensive. What was it about that woman that made him feel compelled to explain himself?

"Oh. Well. Nice to see you again." She gave him a little smile, the kind people gave to relatives they tolerated only because of the DNA connection, then turned away. The little basket on her arm was filled with a single package of chicken, a single loaf of bread, and four of those frozen dinner things. It screamed "alone on a Sunday night."

Something caught in his chest. The same thing that had caught inside him the first time he saw her, six months ago, when Olivia had brought her sister over to Luke's for a barbecue. The same thing he'd ignored when he'd walked out of her house a few weeks later. He ignored it now, because if there was one thing Mike sucked at, it was the whole settling-down, being-responsible thing.

Case in point: Thing One and Thing Two.

Ellie marched up to Diana and raised her chin. "Are you a friend of my daddy's?"

Diana gave Ellie a smile and bent at the knees to match Ellie's eye level. Diana's skirt danced against the tile floor, like a garden bursting from the dingy gray tile. "Sort of a friend."

Four words that didn't even begin to encapsulate the hot fling they'd had a few months ago. But he wasn't going to explain *that* to his preschool daughter.

"Do you fly big he-wa-coppers, too?" Ellie asked.

Diana laughed. "No, I'm a veterinarian. Do you know what that is?"

Ellie nodded, a proud wide smile on her face. "A puppy doctor."

"Exactly. Do you have a puppy or a kitty?"

"Nuh-uh." Ellie shook her head and thrust a thumb into her mouth. She was still doing that? Mike thought Jasmine had said Ellie quit sucking her thumb a year ago. "I wanna see one. Can we go now?"

"Well . . . " Diana shifted her weight, and shot Mike a glance.

"Ellie—"

"I wanna see one now." Ellie crossed her arms over her chest, strangling her bear.

"Ellie, I don't think that's a good idea," Mike said.

She ignored him and lifted her chin toward Diana. "How's come I can't go? Aren't you Daddy's friend?" She popped her thumb back in her mouth.

The question hung in the air for a moment. The Muzak shifted from a jazz version of a Beatles song to a peppy instrumental.

Diana flashed Mike a look he couldn't read, then gave Ellie a patient smile. "Well, maybe someday you can visit the place where I work. We have a cat in the office who just had kittens. And they love to play and cuddle."

The thumb popped out. "Can my daddy come?"

The smile on Diana's face became a grimace. "Sure." Though she said the word with all the enthusiasm of someone volunteering for a colonoscopy.

"If I come ova there, can I have a kitty?"

Diana glanced at Mike, then back at Ellie. "Well, your mommy or daddy has to say yes first."

"Neva mind. I don't wanna see any stupid kitties." Ellie's face fell, and the thumb went back in her mouth.

Mike glanced at Jenny, but his eldest daughter had turned away. What was that about?

"It was nice to meet you, Ellie," Diana said. "I—"

"I don't wanna talk to you anymore." Ellie spun toward her sister, and clutched the teddy bear tighter.

Mike cringed. "Sorry," he said to Diana. "She's . . . temperamental."

A wry grin crossed Diana's face and she straightened. "I have a fifteen-year-old, remember? He makes being temperamental a sport." She let out a little laugh and, for a second, the tension between them eased.

Mike remembered Diana's son. Good kid, overall. "How is Jackson?"

"Fine. Thanks for asking."

Just like that, the ice wall returned. He should be glad. He should get the hell out of here, and put Diana out of his mind. He should do a lot of things, but didn't do any of them. Because he couldn't stop staring at Diana's legs and wondering why she was so dressed up. "You, uh, headed to work?"

Lame, lame, lame. But there didn't seem to be a good way to say, *Hey, I know I have no right to know, but you going out on a date?*

"Daddy? I's hungry," Ellie said.

"I better let you get back to your shopping," Diana said. A polite but firm *stay out of my business.*

Why the hell did her dismissal bother him so much? He had more than enough on his plate right now. An ex-wife who had run out of town, leaving him with kids that were more like strangers. A career that was hanging by a thread. And then there was his father—

A topic Mike didn't even want to think about, never mind deal with. The last thing he needed to add to that mix was a stubborn veterinarian who made his head spin and wanted things from him that he had no business giving. Diana Tuttle was a settle-down, make-a-family, live-in-traditional-lines woman. Mike was . . . not. At all.

"Daddy! I want ice cream! Now!" Ellie stomped her feet and made her mad face. "I's hungry and you *promised*!"

Case in point.

"We have to finish shopping first, El, then we can get—"

"Now!" The word exploded in one over-the-top Mount Vesuvius demand. Thirty days, he told himself, thirty days, and then Jasmine would be back and he'd be free to return to Alaska.

Yeah, that's what he should be looking forward to. The problem was, he didn't want his kids to go back to living with Jasmine. Mike might rank up there close to number one crappiest dad on the planet, but when he'd picked up the girls, he'd finally seen what he'd been blind to for so long. The dancer he'd married in Vegas was a distant, hands-off mother who had blown his monthly child support checks on parties and shoes. While his daughters went around in too-tight, too-short hand-me-downs and ate store-brand cereal three meals a day. That had pissed him off, and when he'd gone through the house to help the girls pack, it had taken every ounce of his strength to stop himself from exploding at Jasmine.

Because truth be told, it was his damned fault they lived this way, and if he'd been the kind of man and father he should have been from day one, then none of this would have happened. Yet another chalk mark in the failure column.

"Ice cream!" Ellie screamed. Several people turned around in the aisle, giving Mike the glare of disapproval.

Diana backed up a half step. "I'll let you go. Have a good vacation with your daughters."

He swore he heard a bit of sarcasm in the last few words. Mike told himself he should let her leave but a part of him wondered about that dress. And wondered if she'd thought about him in the last six months. Plus, she seemed to have a way with Ellie, a calming presence that he could sure as hell use right now. At least until he figured out what the heck he was doing. "Do you want to get some ice cream with us?"

"Ice cream! Ice cream!" Ellie jumped up and down, the teddy bear flopping his head in agreement.

"Just what she needs, sugar," Jenny muttered.

Diana began to back away. "Uh, it seems you have—"

"Come on, it's ice cream," Mike said. "Everyone deserves ice cream at the end of the day." He nodded toward the basket in her hands. "Unless you have somewhere you need to go."

Could he be more pathetic or obvious? Somewhere she needed to go?

"Please?" Ellie said. "Please go with us? I like you and Teddy likes you and Daddy is grumpy."

Diana laughed, and seemed to consider for a moment. In the end, she was won over by Ellie's pixie face. "Well, who can resist an invitation like that?"

Ellie jumped up and down again, then ran back and forth in the aisle, nearly colliding with other shoppers, singing, "We're getting ice cream, we're getting ice cream."

"Ellie, quit," Mike said.

Ellie kept going. Jenny studied a hangnail.

"Ice cream, ice cream, ice cream." Ellie spun in a circle, almost crashing into an elderly woman in a wheelchair. "Teddy loves ice cream, Jenny loves ice cream, Ellie loves ice cream."

"Ellie, quit it!" Mike said again, louder this time.

Ellie kept going, like a spinning top on steroids. Her song rose in volume, her dancing feet sped up. She dashed to Mike, then over to Diana. "Ice cream, ice cream!"

Diana bent down and put a light touch on Ellie's arm. "If you want ice cream, you have to be good for a little while, and help your daddy finish the shopping."

"I wanna sing my ice cream song!"

Diana gave her a patient smile. "I'm sure everyone wants to hear your ice cream song"—an exaggeration, Mike was sure—"*after* the shopping is done. Because if we stop to listen now, it's going to be a long time till anyone gets ice cream." Diana picked up the teddy bear's floppy paw. "And that might make Teddy sad."

Ellie stopped spinning and whirring and singing, and stood still and obedient. "Okay," she said.

Mike stared at his Tasmanian devil child, who had morphed into an angel. She slipped into place beside Jenny, standing on her tiptoes to place the teddy bear in the child seat, and turned back to Mike. "Daddy, we need to do shopping. Jenny says we need peanut butter."

Mike turned to Diana. His gaze connected with her deep green eyes and something dark and hot stirred in his gut. He remembered her looking at him with those eyes as the sun set and the last rays of the day lit her naked body like a halo. She'd slid down his body, taken him into his mouth—

Mike cleared his throat. "Thanks."

Diana shrugged. "No problem."

"Are we shopping or what?" Jenny said, with a sigh of frustration.

"One sec, Jen." He turned back to Diana. "I only need a few more things. Do you want to meet over at the Rescue Bay Ice Cream Shop in, say, fifteen minutes?"

"And then what?" she asked.

"Then nothing," Mike said. "It's just ice cream, not a date. No expectations."

Diana glanced at Ellie and Jenny, then back at Mike. "You know, I'm going to take a rain check after all. Ellie, I'm sorry."

"Diana—"

She met his gaze and the warmth he had seen there six months ago had been replaced by an icy cold. "No expectations, remember?"

Then she was gone. Ellie started to cry. Jenny marched off with the cart. And a part of Mike wondered if it was too late to make his flight to St. Kitts.

Once passion ignites, you can't stop the flames...

From *New York Times* Bestselling Author

JACI BURTON

Hope Flames

Emma Burnett once gave up her dreams for a man who did nothing but hurt her. Now thirty-two and setting up her veterinary practice in the town she once called home, she won't let anything derail her career goals. But when Luke McCormack brings in his injured police dog, Emma can hardly ignore him. Despite her best efforts to keep things strictly professional, Luke's an attractive distraction she doesn't need.

Luke knows the only faithful creature in his life is his dog. After an ugly divorce that left him damn near broke, the last thing he needs is a woman in his life. Fun and games are great and, as a divorced man, the single women in town make sure he never lacks for company. But there's something about Emma that gets to him, and despite his determination to go it alone, he's drawn to her feisty spirit and the vulnerability she tries so hard to hide.

PRAISE FOR JACI BURTON AND HER NOVELS

"Jaci Burton's stories are full of heat and heart."
—Maya Banks, *New York Times* bestselling author

"Passionate, inventive...Burton offers
plenty of emotion and conflict."
—*USA Today* Happy Ever After blog

jaciburton.com
facebook.com/AuthorJaciBurton
facebook.com/LoveAlwaysBooks
penguin.com

M1260T0213

A KISS TO KILL

"Suspense just got a whole lot hotter!"
—Allison Brennan, *New York Times* bestselling author

Eight months ago, Dr. Gina Cappozi and CIA black-ops commando Captain Gregg van Halen were lovers . . . until he committed the ultimate betrayal. She knows that Gregg lives in a shadowy world of violence and darkness—and that he is watching her every move.

But Gregg is not the only one following her . . .

With the threat of enemies at every turn, the passionate pair will be forced to realize that the power of betrayal and revenge is nothing compared to the power of love.

penguin.com

M532T0312